Burning Rose

Kirsty Archer

For you, for starting this journey with me.

"No man chooses evil because it is evil; he only mistakes it for happiness, the good he seeks." Mary Wollstonecraft

MAP OF DOMAIN

FOR A LARGER VERSION OF THIS
MAP, PLEASE GO TO:
KIRSTYARCHER.COM

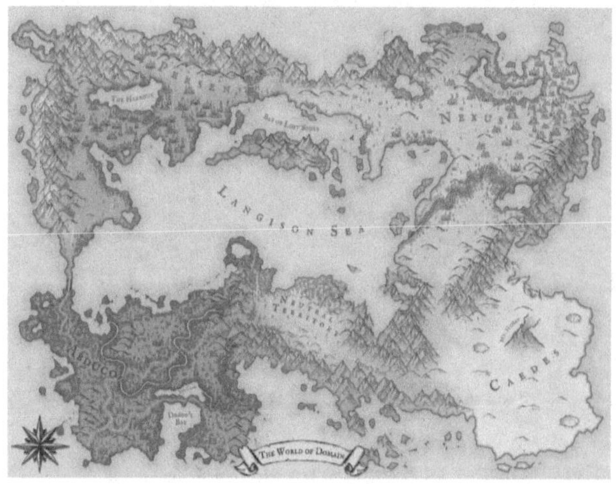

Contents

Content Warning

Welcome to Domain, it's a brutal world out here. Burning Rose is a new adult fantasy romance novel that contains some mature scenes with descriptive spice. It also contains occasional instances of PTSD, death, panic attacks, assault, violence, language, and substance abuse including alcohol and drugs.

Please remember to look after your mental health.

1

CHARITY

I spat blood onto the pavement, the vibrant red lost to the downpour of relentless rain hitting the tarmac. How appropriate for Halloween. At least I didn't have to worry about standing out.

Another red smear greeted me across my palm as I wiped my mouth; brilliant. I tapped the tender skin around my lip, summoning the courage to check all my teeth were still in place. They were. I swore and continued to run down the street, wanting to put as much distance between me and my so-called home as possible. Few trick-or-treaters came to this part of Drabshire; the weather didn't have to keep them away; the neighbourhood did that all on its own. It was the one time of year I was glad I didn't have any siblings, fewer people to watch out for.

As if to spite me and prove me wrong, a group of three small girls rounded the corner dressed as a cat, witch, and a ghost. Fortunately, they were before the stage of embracing the more adult Halloween costumes that flooded the market these days. Not that I was judging. If I could have afforded one when I was several years younger, I would have wanted to show off. After all, I was twenty-three now. Apparently, I should know better. But these girls were different. They were innocent, and this meant they were absolutely in the wrong place.

One girl was unfortunate enough to be carrying a damp paper bag crammed with sweets, which promptly fell apart in the rain, sending the candy scattering everywhere.

My foot smacked the ground as I brought myself to a stop, sending pain shooting up my left leg. I had to resist the urge to swear in front of them, especially as I tasted the metallic tang of blood in my mouth again. I forced myself to swallow it. If these girls were from around here, they'd have seen enough and didn't need another horror show to add to their night.

The three figures stood frozen, most likely looking at the state of my mouth. I hadn't had time to check a mirror before I ran, so I could only imagine what I looked like. I hoped they assumed I was going for a beat-up-girl-on-the-run-from-her-psycho-stepdad as my costume tonight. I shifted my foot to the side where it met a giant gobstopper encased in plastic. I picked it up and held it out to the girl, who was still assessing me with wild eyes.

"Take it," I huffed, not wanting to be held up any longer. "Then get your things and go to another street. The ones here won't have anything for you."

The small ghost next to her whimpered, "Can you tell us how to get back to Pine Avenue? We were supposed to stay by the houses there, but we got lost."

I mentally rolled my eyes. *Of course.* Pine Avenue was in a much more upmarket part of town that lay surprisingly close to Northwood, where we now were.

The cat, the witch, and the ghost were all still staring at me. If they were already asking for help from a worse-for-wear woman with wild dark hair and makeup down her face, then they really shouldn't be left alone out here.

I sucked in the air through my teeth as I realised I couldn't leave them here like sitting ducks. "It's not safe to be out here on your own. You'll get lost again if I just tell you. I can show you the way, but you have to keep up with me. Do you have someone looking for you there?" The girls nodded, and I motioned for them to follow me back in the direction they'd come. My petite frame wouldn't be much of a match if we encountered anyone sinister, but at least I'd be able to stop them from approaching anyone they shouldn't. People were assholes. I knew that just fine. I tried to black out the harshness of my evening and concentrated my efforts on helping them instead. After all, who knew what I would go back to?

It took us fifteen brief minutes to reach Pine Avenue, at which point we were all drenched. It said enough that we hadn't passed a single trick-or-treater when in Northwood, but as we reached the more amicable part of town, the streets became busier with children and adults of all ages, knocking on doors and gathering up sweets.

"That's an awesome costume, by the way," the bravest of the girls ventured. "The blood looks so real."

"Yeah, I'm gonna go as a zombie next year," another chipped in.

Wow. "Um . . . thanks?" I said. It was better that they didn't know just how real it all was. Wyatt, my mother's current boyfriend, had proved that he could hit me and my mother wouldn't say anything, so here I was, hiding out in the street for safety. The irony of it all.

We settled into silence, though I caught whispers from the girls asking about how I'd made my lip swell, which was no doubt still inflating by the second.

The street we turned into was empty of cars, save a single vehicle, which started. It flooded the street with lights as it drove towards us. The window descended to reveal a panicked woman at the steering wheel who gasped as she took in the sight of the four of us.

"Where did you go?" she asked the girls. She reached behind her and opened the car door before motioning them in. "I have been out of my mind with worry."

The girls seemed too ashamed to reply from the back of the car, so I figured I'd do it for them and make sure they never ended up back there. I cleared my throat and once again ignored the urge to spit.

My voice came out thick and croaky. "They were in Northwood. They claimed to be lost."

"Northwood! My goodness girls, you must NEVER . . ." The woman paused as she registered my appearance and the penny dropped as she realised that was where I was from. At the same moment, she took in my face. "What's happened to you? You poor thing. You need to go to a hospital."

She started offering to drop me off on the way home, but I was already backing away from her solid and dependable family car. I didn't have a family like that to look out for me, and I sure as hell wouldn't survive in my neck of the woods by trusting anyone.

In a last moment of desperation, she called out, "Please, tell me who I can thank for bringing back my girls."

I'm not sure why I gave into her request. I guess a part of me just wanted to get away, so I turned and gave her a swollen smile before answering, "Charity."

The rain had eased off by the time I was back in the familiar streets of my neighbourhood. As I trudged past a flickering street lamp, I pondered what to do. Granted, my evening had not turned out as planned. Then again, things rarely did. If my mother had seen my actions tonight before Wyatt had hit me, she might have realised I wasn't always the one to push back and cause arguments. However, Riley didn't seem to see anything beyond her latest boyfriend. This had been my reality growing up.

I didn't know my dad; he'd taken off earlier than I remembered. As a result, my mother had dedicated the rest of her years on this planet trying to replace him, only to be let down each time.

My legs were sore from all the running. I hadn't concentrated on my form tonight and I was feeling all the worse for it. When Wyatt's fist had connected with my mouth, I'd taken one look at my mother's blank face and fled. Running was a means of freedom for me, and I was grateful for it. The adrenaline coursed through me as I'd run out of our dingy flat and pounded down the dark street. Curtains twitched as I charged past the terraced houses, the torrent of abuse from Wyatt fading to blissful silence.

I'd been the fastest in my year at school and my reactions were even faster. Mother's boyfriends, while strong, were too slow to catch me. Unfortunately, tonight, I was completely caught off guard.

I felt relieved for the three girls who had been safely delivered back and decided to return home. Wyatt would be away, out drinking. My mother would be fine as she'd sided with him, so for now, I had a few hours' respite.

I slowed down and put in my earbuds, sighing. At least my old phone had enough room for a few songs.

I bent my head down to block out my surroundings as I walked, losing myself in thoughts of a better life as I grew closer to the flat. Imagining what I'd do if I had the money to get away from this life took me away from the reality I was returning to. Perhaps I'd find a roommate where I could have a functioning friendship, spending our days drinking coffee and watching Saturday morning TV, or whatever normal people did. I had a plan to get out.

I repeated the phrase inscribed in my only book at home, one that had been with me since childhood.

Your only limit is your imagination.

While my life sucked, it couldn't hurt to dream. In fact, it was necessary. I had a bar job that was going nowhere. Any friends I made always seemed to move on. But there was no limit to what I could imagine. Hopefully, if all went according to plan, it wouldn't have to be a dream for much longer. Without the constant threat of my money being stolen by my mother, I'd be able to afford my rent, and then might even think about things like college. I'd never paid as much attention in school as I should have, but I enjoyed learning, and given the chance, might even be considered academic.

I was so intent on planning my ideal future, I didn't see the stranger standing in the middle of the pavement.

And I marched straight into him.

Technically, I collided straight into the stranger's chest, as he was a good foot taller than me. I instinctively sized him up: he was massive height-wise, with broad shoulders and strong, well-defined arms that were visible even through his clothing. I took a step back. If he turned out to be a threat, he'd be difficult to outrun.

The impact caused one of my wireless earphones to stop playing, and one fell out of my ear. My reactions were quick from growing up here, but he still got there first, his hand deftly catching it before it dropped to the ground.

I put out my hand to receive it back and did a double take when instead he put the earbud into his ear, causing the song to blare back into life. Fast-paced rap lyrics blasted for an abrupt few seconds until I had the sense to yank the earbud out of my ear and take a step back.

"Interesting, I didn't expect that," he said in a deep voice as he tilted the corner of his mouth up.

The audacity! To comment on my music taste, with a smirk, as if something was funny. It didn't matter if his voice was deep and velvety. It *didn't.*

"Right. Thanks," was all I could say as he handed it back to me and our hands brushed.

A frown flickered across his face, emphasising his angular cheekbones and dark features. Though it disappeared so quickly, I might have imagined it.

Clutching my earphones, I took him in. He was tall, with jet black hair and a sharp jawline that unfortunately sat several inches above my line of sight. This meant as I looked up, it was impossible to miss. What a bastard.

"I'm Anton." He interrupted my thoughts. To my horror, my cheeks flushed, and I hoped he wouldn't notice in the dim light. I wasn't used to making conversation with anyone I met around here. The corner of his mouth lifted again in the smallest hint of a smile, which dropped as he cast his eyes over me, leaving me all too aware of my messy hair, damp clothes, and cut mouth. He frowned as his eyes passed over my lip, but he said nothing.

"I'm Serrk," I said, still distracted by the idea of conversing with a complete stranger and weighing up whether I was in serious trouble here. *Wait what?!* "I mean, Serrk is my second name. I'm Charity. Sorry for running into you." *Wow, I sound like I'm sixteen again. Did I really just introduce myself as my surname?* I gripped my arm to bring myself back to reality.

"Not a problem." He ignored my embarrassment. "I'm sure it won't be the only time, as I'm here on business." He held out a card to me that had *Anton Abduco* written in fancy letters the shade of green lightning, as if there was such a thing. *Who is this guy?*

A twig snapped at the other end of the street and both of our heads shot up, instantly finding the source of the sound. But it was just a black cat. Happy Halloween and all.

Despite the false alarm, it was enough to put my guard back up. I handed the card back to him and raised a brow as I shot back, "I doubt I'll see you. Most people here on *business* don't hang around for long." Dressed the way he was, the only business he could carry out here was drug-related or something else illegal.

"I suppose we'll have to see, won't we, Serrk?" He didn't seem taken aback or even offended at my response as he pocketed his card. He smirked yet again, as if there was some private joke I hadn't yet been included in.

My pulse quickened and my stomach did an annoying little flip that it hadn't done since I was a teenager whenever I saw someone I liked. His hair caught my attention and I couldn't help but stare. I hadn't noticed anything out of the ordinary at first with his head turned and him so much taller than me. But now I could see, while one side was indeed so dark it appeared dyed, it was now apparent the other side was a brilliant platinum blond. Despite being soaking wet from the rain, the colour was split perfectly, with not a hair out of place. I wondered how long he'd been standing here to get so wet, even if he still looked good.

His eyes were a dark pine green. They were unnatural–maybe contacts? His whole demeanour was something else. He carried himself with an air of confidence that was somewhere between self-assured and arrogant. His posture was strong, his head tilted up high, unapproachable. While that attitude might fit in around here, his clothes didn't. He was clearly from somewhere much more well-off.

I realised I'd let myself become distracted again. "It's Charity, not

Serrk. See you around, or not." My remark might have been more effective if I didn't look like a drowned rat.

"Pleasure, Serrk," he responded as I struggled to step around him, feeling as though the pavement had been replaced with tar. Annoyingly, the rain didn't seem to cling to him the same way it did with me.

My hairs stood on end as I turned my back to him and my lip throbbed as if to warn me to get going. While a part of me wanted to keep talking, I'd been in enough danger already today. Sure, he was gorgeous, but I didn't know if I was more attracted to him or scared of him. I set off as quickly as I could without breaking into a run, keeping my ears open for any sign he was following me.

Resisting the urge to look back, I continued down the street, my feet slapping the wet pavement as I imagined his stare burning into my back. Perhaps I was worried about what I would do if I turned and saw him following me. Maybe a small part of me wanted him to.

The door to the flat was already unlocked. All was quiet except the faint snores from Mother, fast asleep on the sofa. She liked to wait up and check that Wyatt didn't come home and trash the place while drunk. However, she often fell asleep, so it happened anyway. I reached out to pull up the thin blanket that had fallen off and brushed my lip by accident; the movement sending a twang of pain through my lip like an electric current. The blanket fell out my hands, and I let it crumple on the floor. I'd stuck up for my mother a lot over the years, and as a result, I'd learned to live without a lot of love. And apart from that one time, I hadn't had to worry about my physical safety until tonight. I'd told myself if it ever happened again, I'd be out. It confirmed I was doing the right thing by leaving. I had a plan in place to get myself a loan to get me on my feet and was waiting on hearing from the bank to confirm I could put things in motion.

I made my way to the small room at the back and collapsed on my mattress. While thin and jagged with springs, it was like a cloud to my aching muscles and I drifted off to sleep within minutes, my last thoughts of a tall stranger with two-tone hair and green eyes.

2

CHARITY

I had never visited this city, not even anywhere close. This one was unlike any other. I walked through the street, flanked by buildings Parisian in their aesthetic: elongated architecture in understated colours, the brickwork in light sand with pale grey roofs. A soft palette for a romantic city. I descended steps made of polished marble. Gold tones shone through the smooth white beneath my feet, as bold as lightning illuminated in the night sky.

The warm hue of the sunset coated the sky in wonderful golden and pink tones. Birds flew overhead, a calmness in their agile movements. The entire atmosphere worked in perfect harmony. Colours complimented the evening summer breeze that passed through the empty street. The perfect temperature. Not too warm or too cold. With the breeze came the floral scent from the garden below. Like everything else here, it was subtle.

The cityscape stretched out in every direction before me. My focus was lost in the sea of buildings, with their Parisian roofs and windows offering a slice of insight into the activity within. I thought of the individual lives led in each of those many streets that lay before me like veins running through a leaf. I was aware of the lack of lights within the *buildings. It was evening, and the city was at peace.*

The dream changed, and I was back in the street I'd been in last night. I felt . . . shorter. A movement beside me told me I wasn't alone. A cool hand wound its way into mine and I met the dark green eyes of Anton. He tilted the corner of his mouth up into that smile. "This isn't even the half of it."

A door slammed, snapping me out of what was about to be an all too pleasant dream about the stranger I'd met yesterday; Adam, or Aaron, or something. We had been in some foreign place but as I tried to hold on to the details; they slipped into somewhere inaccessible, the endless abyss where forgotten dreams live. The tension in my muscles from last night brought me back into my bedroom. I needed to get myself some boy action if I was fantasising about some guy I'd just met, who I *definitely* remembered was called Anton, as much as I tried to convince myself otherwise. I'd dated guys here and there; most recently there had been Kieran until I tired of competing with his phone for his attention. Granted, I'd maybe given up too easily, but I was quick to let people go. I hadn't been able to let my guard down with anyone since Greg had . . . Actually, I didn't want to even think about that right now, or ever.

As the dream slipped further away, the ache in my head grew. I wasn't hungover, so why did it hurt so much? It wasn't unbearable; it was more as if I had tried hard to concentrate on something and had pushed myself too far. Strange.

The noise in the kitchen and a quick check of my phone told me that Wyatt had returned home at the respectable hour of seven in the morning. As always, he thought nothing of waking up the entire house with his arrival. I dragged myself out of bed, hoping that by this time he might have sobered up somewhat.

I tied my hair up in case this encounter had me running again. My hair was long: partly because I liked it that way and because it meant I didn't need to worry about whether I made it to the hairdresser every year or not.

The food in our dingy kitchen emitted an acrid stench and should have been thrown out days ago. We didn't like to waste meals, especial-ly when money was scarce, but Mother made a habit of always making sure Wyatt had something waiting for him when he came home from drinking. He only ate it half the time, and I had learned the hard way to not touch it under any circumstances even when he left it sitting out on the counter, claiming he would come back for it, but often forgetting and leaving it to spoil.

Wyatt sat at the kitchen table looking at me with bloodshot eyes. His voice was something between a snarl and a bark. "Decided to get up then?"

"That's what most people do in the morning after they've slept," I said as Mother appeared in the kitchen, shooting me a warning look. It was clear she had slept little; her mousy hair was unkempt and hung around her face, which had a greyish tinge. I did pity her. My father had clearly impressed on her. So much so that she felt she wasn't capable of functioning without a man by her side. It hadn't stopped her from helping herself to anything I brought into the house in order to keep any partners happy. I'd be lying if I said I wasn't fucking resentful. But she was my mother, even if she didn't act like it.

"You watch your mouth, you little ungrateful bitch! Especially after what you've been up to!" Wyatt slammed his hand on the kitchen table, causing Mother and me to jump. I should have known by now not to push people like him, but my smart mouth refused to shut up at the best of times. How could my mother fall for someone like him? My hand shook against the table and I had to force myself not to grind my teeth. She would always be family, but I couldn't help but rage over her poor judgement. I gripped my knuckles until they cracked from the pressure. Adrenaline flared in my chest, but a stab of fear interrupted it. The envelope in his hand could only mean one thing: the bank had written to me.

I concentrated on keeping my feet flat on the ground in case another blow to my face came like the one last night. Instead, he stepped towards me and held out the letter that was addressed in my name. My blood turned to ice as I scanned the page.

Dear Miss Serrk,

Further to your request, we are unable to grant you a further loan of £2000 because of outstanding debts on your accounts with us. Our records show you have several accounts in arrears, and we have sourced information from your credit score to imply this is the case with other lenders. If you need financial help, please contact . . .

I stopped reading. A knot was growing in my stomach. This wasn't supposed to happen. Unknown to Mother and Wyatt, I'd applied for a loan last week. It was my account, after all, not that it had stopped my mother from emptying it and various others over the years. Money was freedom and all I'd wanted was enough to allow me to get away and set up on my own. I hadn't expected letters addressed to me to be opened. *Stupid.* I should have been more careful.

Wyatt's eyes were coal black. "After everything we've done for you, putting a roof over your head, giving you the food on our table, you try to pull something like this? You ungrateful cow."

I seethed in front of him. He'd been in our life for a little over a year, and contributed far less than I did. I wanted to scream that any food on the table came from us.

My plan unravelled further before me, causing the air to be punched out of my lungs. Wyatt turned to my mother. "I want her gone by the time I'm back, otherwise you'll be sorry." He then slumped out towards the front door, slamming it behind him.

The realisation in my mother's eyes gouged a hole in my chest. *She isn't actually contemplating his request?* When I realised they'd even applied for credit on my behalf, I knew I had to go, but I'd wanted to ensure I had somewhere first. I'd wanted to offer my mother to come with me, but I'd voiced the thought before when I was younger and she'd been outraged at the idea. It had taken weeks before she'd spoken to me again. Our relationship was very one-sided as far as caring went. It hurt, but I had learned to accept that a long time ago. It hadn't been a simple decision. But I'd decided I had to go, even if it meant leaving her behind.

A thought hit me like a truck. I barely scraped by enough from my odd coffee shop shifts and my work at the nightclub to contribute to our shared rent, let alone my own. Yes, I'd wanted the freedom, but without the loan, where would I go?

The resignation on Mother's face told me she had already decided. "It's probably for the best, dear," she said as she turned her back on me and poured herself a coffee. "You are the only thing he and I argue about."

"That's only because you're willing to let him behave the way he does," I said back, trying to ignore the hurt growing in my chest.

Mother turned towards me and placed the coffee cup on the counter with shaky hands. "You'd better get your things together. I don't want you here when he gets back."

I held back my sob at the fact I was being made to leave my home. "He's a monster."

She met my eyes and held my stare for the first time as she said with conviction, "I need to get to work." I snorted at that. My mother was a con artist. That's how she was able to fund his drinking. "I don't expect you here when I'm back, and certainly not when Wyatt gets home. If you want to help, leaving is what you need to do. It's not that you're not enough, I just need more, I need a life too. I'm sorry."

She stepped towards me and wrapped her arms around me in a weak hug. The realisation hit me I didn't know when I would see her again, but despite this, it didn't hurt as much as I had expected. Without another word, she released me and headed out the front door. I watched her leave, the numbness preventing me from saying anything.

I sank into the chair in disbelief. Our dingy flat had never been anywhere I'd particularly liked, or any of the places we had stayed for that matter, but it was home and a place to come back to each night. Now I had nowhere. I ran my nails down my skull, just to feel something other than the stab of rejection that she had chosen another boyfriend and money over me. It all became too much, and I put my head into my arms and allowed myself to sob.

It could have been minutes, or closer to an hour, before I moved from that table. Perhaps the best thing I could do today was get out in the fresh air to clear my head before my shift tonight. For now, I had to think about where I was going to stay and take things one day at a time.

It took almost no time at all to grab all of my things into my black duffle bag, which I slung over my shoulder. I only cared about the book I had been given as a young child, far too young to remember. It was a fairy-tale book, much too babyish for me now. Yet still I opened the well-thumbed pages to reveal the ink at the front.

Your only limit is your imagination.

I looked again at the sentence that was now a mantra for me, despite not knowing who'd written it. I tucked the book into my bag, ensuring it was safe, and I took one last look around our flat—now Mother and Wyatt's flat. Then, holding back tears, I held my head up high as I walked out the front door. I went to lock it behind me and then realised they would want my keys, too. They clinked as they hit the floor on the other side of the letterbox, and I winced as the back of my hand gained a splinter or two along the way. I pulled them out, imagining they represented Mother and Wyatt, then let them fall to the ground as I turned and headed into the street.

Too many hours and only one sandwich and a can of juice later, I was sitting on the bench at my local park wondering what the hell I was going to do about finding somewhere to stay. I'd visited The Coffee Shoppe where I worked my second job to ask if I could do any extra hours, but they'd been unable to offer me anything other than a free lunch, which I'd still gratefully accepted.

I'd walked all over my neighbourhood, moving as if I had a purpose, while ignoring the growing panic that for the first time in my life I had none. My contacts list didn't offer any hope; it was full of likely old numbers and various ex-boyfriends of my mother. Living at home at twenty-three when my house wasn't the friendliest place didn't do me any favours in making friends. There had been people from school I'd been close with, but they had moved to different towns, started careers, moved to study, had families, lived life.

I couldn't help but begrudge the fact I'd stayed at home living with my mother, but I'd had to. The jobs I had when I was younger hadn't paid enough for me to move out with such a chunk going towards rent and food. Because of her own financial situation, I'd always been required to pay. Unable to save anything, it was a relentless cycle of trying to make ends meet, all the while knowing I'd be better off on my own. My mother didn't have any contact with the rest of her family because of her doing the same with their funds as she had with mine. School had offered grants, but Mother had insisted we didn't need any charity once they'd started asking too many questions. My mother hated questions, and when people started asking too many, we moved. Again.

It got worse when I turned eighteen and had more bank account options. They'd found one of my bank account cards in the post and had used it. I contacted the bank about my missing card, and they informed me it had been *well* used. And this was why I had trust issues. If only I knew how much more complicated everything was going to become.

3

CHARITY

The drinks on the bar reverberated in time with the music as I raced to keep up with an endless sea of customers at the bar. The club where I worked–*Core*–was at full capacity with their sell-out Phonk music night, *Get Phonked*. It was all the rage at the moment.

I pulled down my black crop top where it had ridden up, hiding my exposed skin from prying eyes both behind and in front of the bar. I didn't even recognise anyone working with me. Staff came and went–people a few years younger than me who moved on to other jobs with more sociable hours.

I watched the *payment processing* message flash across the screen as I served yet another customer, daring to dream about what else I might have done were I able to make something of myself. Perhaps excavating lost ruins in a desert or a job where I could help people, like a psychiatrist, if I put my mind to it and used my academic side. It felt stupid to exist without a dream. I had just come to accept that it wouldn't be an option for me.

"Hello?! I need my card," spat the customer whose card I was holding. I held back a shiver as the many spirits on his breath washed over me.

I looked down at the machine and read out the message that flashed in red. I sighed. I'd dream another day. "Payment declined, mate. You need another card."

The man was appalled. "I don't have another card. That one is fucking fine."

Great, I thought. *One more charming customer who's had one too many and doesn't enjoy being told no.* Core wasn't famous for great customer service, and I wasn't about to start. A loud beat thumped from the DJ booth, giving me confidence and I stood with my hand on my hip, moving the card still in the reader out of his reach as he swiped for it.

"You mistake me for someone who gives a shit." It was so loud in the club, I had to shout over the music, admittedly enjoying his embarrassment as his friends fell about laughing around him. Had he not been so rude in the first place, I would have likely let it slip, but I wasn't about to entertain this arsehole.

The man had gone very red and looked like he was about to hit someone. Just as the music paused between songs, he leaned over the bar, his face a picture. "You can't speak to me like that, you dumb bitch."

"She can speak to you however she likes." A voice cut across the busy room and I turned to see the person I was least expecting who seemed to have materialised from nowhere.

Of course, it has to be him.

Anton stood at the bar, wearing a dark suit that made him look ridiculously overdressed for this establishment, but it didn't stop him from catching the eye of every girl and a few guys, too. This time, he had swept back his hair, making the two opposing sides immaculate.

The man turned to direct his anger at Anton, but sized him up and seemed to think better of it.

"Excellent decision. Leave your drinks and go." Anton must be used to getting what he wanted, as he didn't show a hint of surprise when the man did just that.

I sucked in a breath as I turned to Anton. "Thanks for that. What can I get you?"

The music started up again. His dark eyes scanned the bar, and he ran his thumb along his lip in mock thought. Then he leaned in so I could hear him over the heavy bass. "There's nothing tempting here. At least to drink anyway."

I was glad there was a bar between us that felt like a barrier to my racing heart, which hammered with each syllable. *Had I heard him correctly?* But to my frustration, he was already walking away.

The rest of the night passed in a sea of impatient customers and in the chaos, I forgot I was no closer to working out where I was going to be staying that night.

All too soon, I had to face that reality again when my shift ended. I swung my bag over my shoulder and collected my envelope with my cash from the evening. I'd asked anywhere I'd worked to pay me in cash once I'd realised my mother and one of her previous partners had learned they could use my name to apply for credit. With everything done online these days, it was easy for them to apply on my behalf. Once they had the accounts, they had pushed them to the limits and then some. The minute the money had fallen into their hands, the men always found some excuse for the relationship to end. Sometimes they didn't even bother with the courtesy of an excuse; they took off with the cash, leaving my mother devastated and on the rebound to fill the hole of betrayal they left behind.

I'd always had to contribute towards the rent and bills, often higher amounts than she did after her partners drank away her money. Throw in poor credit, and the prospect of living independently became difficult. At one point, I wasn't allowed a bank account, ironically because of the fraud I'd reported, which cut off ninety-five per cent of the jobs I could apply for, leaving me stuck working odd jobs just to keep afloat–hardly a budding CV. And so the cycle had continued. I cursed as it hit me once again how close I'd been to breaking it, or so I thought.

I walked out of the club and saw a woman younger than me attempting to walk to a taxi but falling over. A group of guys were laughing and pointing at her while one recorded on his phone, charming. I went over to her and grabbed her under the arms to pull her to her feet. She smiled down at me through bleary eyes, then burst into tears, telling me she'd lost all her money. I sighed but helped her into the taxi, giving the driver some of my precious funds and checking he knew the exact location of the address that she mumbled. As I did, her phone clattered to the floor. I picked it up and sent a message to the people in her contacts under "Mum", "Dad", "Rob" (followed by a stream of hearts) and "Sarah Bestie," letting them all know she was on her way back home in a taxi from Core. I wasn't usually the good Samaritan that I'd been the past few days, however I knew first-hand what could happen around these streets.

I had shifted my bag to my other shoulder and set off down the pavement, away from the thinning crowd, when there was a shout behind me.

"It's that girl that was giving you cheek."

"Not so tough without a bar between us, are we?"

It was the group of men who had had the misfortune with the card. I kept walking, itching to look back but refusing them the satisfaction. I didn't back down for anyone, even if it landed me in more trouble. I knew it was an irresponsible side of me, but it wasn't something I could control. I didn't submit, not anymore.

"I think we should introduce ourselves properly to her," said the largest of them. He was tall and chunky, with brown hair combed to the side. He looked like he'd grown up on a diet of quality home-cooked meals, something I'd never experienced.

Sensing the threat, I turned at his words and scanned the street, looking for any of the staff heading towards the car park behind the boys, but no such luck. The last remaining people seemed to have evaporated, leaving the street empty, save for me and this group of four amateur, but large, thugs.

I grabbed the keys to the club in my pocket and arranged them between my fingers. I wasn't supposed to have a set, but they'd been lying around and I figured I could head back there and sneak in once the place was empty as a last resort if I couldn't find anywhere to stay.

"Maybe she wants some company." This time one of his friends spoke, his hair black and his eyes blacker as he scanned me up and down.

"Maybe you should go fuck yourselves," I shot back. It was a poor retaliation. The smug look on their faces told me I had shown I was rattled.

The one with the brown hair stepped forward. "Calm down, we're only having a bit of fun, aren't we? No one's going to get you out here, especially when there's four of us, and only one of you."

There were two voices in my head, one told me: *run*. The other practically snarled: *stand your ground*.

They all took a step towards me. Then another. I inhaled at the small dark alleyway they were boxing me into and saw red. Adrenaline coursed through my veins, giving me courage, but also something else. A strange sense of power. *Let them come.* I could practically see their lurid thoughts dancing in front of me. The darkness shrouding their mind. If anyone deserved to be hurt, it was these guys.

I sized up the men in front of me. I wasn't strong, but I was fast. Whatever they were planning, they wouldn't get to me without a fight, and I wouldn't feel guilty for any damage I did on the way. My anger flared as my heart skipped a beat. I felt at one with the tarmac below me, like I could do anything. My fear left me as I wrapped myself in all the anger that had built up over the course of my life and I channelled it into the figures in front of me.

"GET IT OUT!" The brown-haired boy fell to his knees, screaming and clutching his head.

What the fuck? I wondered if he was reacting to drugs.

"Get what out?" asked one man with short blond hair.

"I CAN'T SEE! The shadows . . ." The man was mumbling and whining to himself. His friends danced around him frantically, unsure what to do as he writhed on the ground as if in pain. I was confused too, but that man wasn't my problem, not after I'd seen his intentions. Whatever was happening, I was grateful for the distraction, so I focused on getting out instead as I crept around them.

"What the hell did she do?" One of them was stuttering now, his voice panicked.

Did I fucking cause this? No. That was absurd. I was about to turn and run without dignifying that question with an answer when a voice that didn't match the four mouths in front of me boomed from the entrance to the alleyway. "There you are. I've been looking everywhere for you." It was Anton.

Relief spread through me, like sinking into a warm bath. I had never felt so grateful to see him standing in that clearing, even though he was arrogant, but he displayed no trace of smugness as he stared down at the scene in the alleyway. The men were tall, but he was much taller and something about him spoke he was a threat, even when outnumbered. I didn't think twice before closing the distance between us. The man stopped whimpering and appeared to recover.

Anton put an arm round my shoulders and addressed me, but his bitter tone told me the words were for their benefit. "They won't follow us. They know how much they would regret it if they did."

The group shrugged to each other and slunk away in the opposite direction, the three men questioning what had happened to their friend, but he didn't seem to have answers for them.

My heart was hammering for multiple reasons: I should think about what had just happened, but all I could concentrate on was Anton's comforting embrace and wondering why he hadn't removed his arm yet. Just as this crossed my mind, there was a rush of emptiness, as he apparently had the same thought. I tried not to shiver as I missed the contact.

"Are you okay?" Anton said, his velvety words slowing my racing pulse.

"Yes. Well, not really, but people around here are assholes and I'm just lucky that guy had some strange freakout that distracted everyone."

"If that's what you want to call it." He frowned, his face coated in the shadows from the streetlamps. I didn't know what he meant by that, and allowed myself a second to study who I was walking next to. His pale skin was such a stark contrast to the jet black hair that was swept back. As he ran a hand through it, his rings caught on some of the platinum side, sweeping it into view.

"Thank you for helping back there." I buried my hands in my hoodie pocket, twisting the material between my fingers. "I keep seeming to run into you."

There was a glint in Anton's eye. "I told you I'd see you around didn't I?" He must have registered the fact I'd stiffened next to him as he said, "Plus, it looked like you had it covered."

"If by that, you mean someone couldn't handle their drink and I took advantage and tried to run."

"You know that's not what I'm talking about." His eyes darkened as they scanned me.

I thought back to the surge of power that I'd had. It couldn't have been me. Maybe someone had slipped me something in the club? Impossible, I always poured my drink, downed it, and then flushed any extra down the sink to avoid any risk. So then, why was Anton looking at me as if I'd caused whatever it was to stop that man?

I realised I was shaking. My chest threatened to cave in with every breath. The walls of the street closed in on me. Everything felt too small. Since I was a teenager, small, dark spaces terrified me, but I only had panic attacks when I was confined. This was different.

"It's shock," Anton said. "You're not crazy. You're reacting to what you just did." Despite the absurdity of his statement, Anton was deadly serious, his shoulders back as he eyed me intently.

"I didn't cause it," I gritted out, my head spinning as I focused on taking deep breaths and grounding myself. He was obviously crazy, but I couldn't get away until I knew I wouldn't pass out.

Anton exuded calm, the opposite of the panic that was rising in my chest at the thought that I could do such a thing. Or that I was even entertaining the option.

"You could, and you did," he summarised, nodding in the direction the men had left. "They won't bother you now. But we have little time. I need you to come with me."

"Tempting, but no thanks. I wasn't born yesterday," I said, steeling myself to put some serious distance between us.

"So you're just going to go back and continue like that didn't happen?" His footsteps followed me. Given he only needed one step for each of my two, he caught up easily.

"Yup," I said, continuing straight ahead, my eyes focused on the hanging baskets outside the grocery shop ahead of me. People weren't able to just cause others to drop to the ground in pain, or whatever the hell that was. No, it had been a stroke of luck. That's what had happened.

"Not an option. I was sent to come and get you." His voice came from right behind me, not even out of breath. "I need you to come with me, because after what just happened, you're in danger if you don't."

"Sent to come and get me. By who? You're not with the police, are you?" My chest was tightening. I didn't know whether to run or to question him further. None of this was making any sense.

"Not the police. I understand none of this makes sense," said Anton, as if reading my mind. "If you walk with me, I'll explain more and you can decide what you'd like to do."

"So I have a choice?" I asked, fidgeting with my bag strap. A flock of birds sounded overhead, their silhouettes caught in the moonlight. I think it was geese.

"If you mean do you have a choice between returning to danger, or choosing your best shot at a better life, then, yes, you have a choice. But I'll be hoping you chose the latter." The dim streetlamps outlined the contours of his face. As much as I didn't want to trust him, I didn't see the malice that I had in the four faces in the alleyway. I cast my eyes over his flawless outfit and fidgeted inside my hoodie self-consciously before I remembered that this was my turf and that he was the one out of place.

I made my decision. "Okay, after helping me, I trust you enough to hear you out. But that doesn't mean I'm coming with you."

Anton gave the smallest of smirks. "Lucky me. You can take your hand out of your pocket, though. I won't let anyone near you."

He spoke in his drawl, but his words made my stomach do another traitorous flip. I was confused; it was possessive and everything the streetwise part of me went against, but I couldn't help being drawn to him. Plus, given what had just happened, he was a safer bet than walking around the streets alone. Though that didn't mean my guard was down yet. Despite his words, I kept my keys close, just in case.

My free arm swung limply at my sides. Suddenly, I was overly conscious of everything my body was doing. *Could I trust him?*

To answer that, I asked the one question that had been on my mind since he showed up. It couldn't have been by chance. "How did you know where I was, in the alleyway?"

Something flashed across his eyes, green a few shades brighter than his pine hues. I looked over my shoulder, expecting to see a car or whatever had caused the reflection, but found nothing. Maybe I'd imagined it.

"We have our ways."

He certainly was cryptic, so I figured I'd get straight to the point. "I'm willing to hear what you're offering. But nothing sexual." I had to make my boundaries clear, just in case he had the wrong idea. It wasn't unusual to see prostitutes around the area. People did what they had to in order to get by, but that wasn't what I was offering here.

"I didn't plan on it," Anton said. I tried to swallow the rejection at how disgusted he sounded at having anything to do with me in that way, even though that was the attitude he should have in the context I was speaking about. Plus, why would he be interested in some girl from a rough part of town? He probably had some posh lady back home where they sat playing chess and drinking vintage wine out of crystal glasses or something.

I got back on track with what I was trying to accomplish here. "You said you were here on business. I was wondering if there was anything

I could help with to give me some cash to get by? I know the area well. In fact, I think I know it much better than you. I blend in a lot more, which could be useful."

There went my big mouth running off on me again, but Anton smiled, albeit not a warm smile, more as if something I said had genuinely amused him. When he met my eye, I could see I hadn't imagined the change in them. They were definitely lighter. "The thing is, Charity," he drawled, "*you* are my business here. And although I said you had a choice, that's the thing about us Shifters, we lie."

Shifters?

I was so confused over the word, it took me a second to react to the latter part of his statement. He was lying. This had all been a big mistake. I knew I shouldn't have trusted him. I should have used my instincts.

He studied me for a split second, and the look in his eyes was almost apologetic. I caught a flash of silver as his fingers grasped my wrist and the heat from his touch licked at my skin. Before I could react, my bag fell to the ground with a thud, and I was filled with a swooping sensation as if the floor had given way. I didn't know what he meant by *Shifters,* if I'd even heard him correctly. I supposed the last strand of my sanity evaporated when the world as I knew it vanished around us, and I plunged into darkness.

4

CHARITY

My feet hit the floor almost as quickly as they had left it. We weren't standing in the park now. We were in a stone courtyard outside a large, imposing building that was decorated for Halloween. Retro lanterns hung from the stonework, flickering in the limited evening light, and cobwebs encased the streetlamps in a way that had me questioning if they were fake. Music echoed from inside the building as I glanced through the murky windows at the party within.

Anton pretended to brush an imaginary speck of dust from his shoulder. From the corner of my eye, I could see him watching me. I scrambled backwards as if he were some kind of wild animal, putting as much distance between us as possible as I looked around, trying to place where we were. I recognised nothing. It was like he expected me to doubt my senses as I took in my surroundings, which I was. I had so many questions about what had just happened. But, when I came to speak, all I could manage was, "Where *in the absolute fuck* are we?"

"It's a lot to take in, I understand," was Anton's only response. He gave me his full attention and I couldn't help but notice his eyes were darker again, his stare making my breath hitch.

Terror seeped through me. Just seconds ago, I was in my local park. Now, I was in a part of town I'd never even seen before. Was I drugged? Knocked out? Perhaps this was some elaborate coping mechanism my brain was using to deal with the trauma of the past twenty-four hours. I imagined it was not unheard of for the brain to fabricate new versions of life because of such events.

I couldn't process the fascinating yet unfamiliar scenes that danced in front of me as I turned a full three hundred and sixty degrees once more, taking everything in from the ongoing party inside to the people hurrying through the courtyard. They all seemed to come from or go into the building. A small voice told me if Anton had sinister intentions, we wouldn't be somewhere so public.

Anton cut across my internal battle. "This is Domain. It's a different world to the one you live in."

"A different world?" I blinked at him, confused by his statement. "Right mate, thanks for everything, but I'll be going now."

Without giving him a chance to react to the fact I'd just called him *mate*, I bolted down the cobbles, darting through an archway in a high stone wall that led into a courtyard covered in greenery. I didn't have a clue where I was going, but at least it was an excellent place to hide. Anton might be well built, but he probably hadn't grown up with my lifestyle, the kind where you had to run to survive.

His deep voice reverberated through the foliage, telling me I'd been wrong to assume he wouldn't find me. "I don't expect you to understand immediately. You humans are taught to believe certain things as you grow up to avoid the detection of places like this."

I knew it was too good to be true. He might be gorgeous, but he was bat shit crazy. He must have drugged me to get me to go with him. I kept silent to avoid giving my location away and slipped out back into the cobbled street, losing him in the foliage.

I ran, waiting for the familiar adrenaline to kick in, to fuel my strides and make me feel alive. In a few seconds, I was in the zone, invincible, unbeaten, *free*. This was where I was at my happiest, the world a blur around me, always moving. Though the pleasure was short-lived, as I realised the street was wobbling, then spinning. I was used to panic attacks from my claustrophobia. I'd suffered from it ever since that . . . incident . . . when I was younger, but we were outdoors. This shouldn't be happening. It must have been the shock of everything like before. My vision clouded at the sides and I realised if I didn't stop, I was going to faint.

I stopped and bent forward to put my head towards my legs as the world spun around me on a new axis. I was acutely aware of the fact the street was busy and I must have looked ridiculous, but I couldn't have cared less. Desperate to clear the disorientation, I didn't even startle at the dark shape who caught up with me. "If you concentrate on something else, that might help."

I didn't have the energy to argue and did as he asked, focusing on the people passing.

A woman with a streak of blonde hair similar to Anton's nodded curtly in his direction as she slipped past, her outfit also immaculate. Another wave of dizziness hit me and I focused on someone else, anything to feel better. A man with hair the colour of rust and dressed in a three-piece suit that seemed to belong to a different era frowned as he passed us. He seemed to rethink his actions as his eyes met Anton's, and he hurried on his way. I straightened up just as another woman with magenta hair wearing a white catsuit flashed us both a grin in greeting, the boldness of colours complimenting her dark skin beautifully. These people wouldn't have fitted into anywhere I could think of. They stood out in the same way Anton did. Eventually, the lightheaded daze left me, and my cognizance returned.

As I came round, the realisation of what he had done hit me. I turned to the nearest woman. "Excuse me, I've arrived here by accident. I need to get back to Drabshire." The woman dressed in purple gave a small gasp at my words and hurried on her way. I noticed that far too many people were staring at me, yet were doing nothing to help. *Why are they staring?*

"They're used to this response from humans," came Anton's voice.

I stepped back from the Shifters choosing to ignore me and addressed Anton again. "I thought you were going to help me, not take me somewhere against my will."

Unease trickled through me as I grew aware that I shouldn't be speaking to him like this without knowing what he was capable of. Something told me it was a lot.

Anton's face was awash with guilt and the same apology written across his features as I had glanced before we travelled here. "Trust me, now you've shown the promise of Shifter abilities, it won't be safe for you in your world until you've harnessed them. I meant it when I said you don't have a choice but to be here."

He held out his hand to help me up, but I didn't take it, drawing myself back up to my full, if minuscule, height when I stood next to him. "Who are you? *What* even are you? How am I supposed to trust you?" I was furious and full of questions. I'd been let down by too many people and fire coursed through my veins, ready to explode.

"You can't trust me," he said. He answered my last question only. "But that doesn't mean I don't want to help you." His shoulders sagged, and his impeccable posture appeared defeated. I hadn't seen this side of him during our brief encounters so far.

The honesty of his statement caught me off guard, and the fire in me simmered.

"Let me explain things."

Torn, I didn't trust him. But I was out of options back home. I cringed, thinking back to the response from the bank about my loan given the credit history my mother and her partners had racked up. This could be my chance to start over. It was a risk, and an enormous risk at that, but a small voice told me perhaps this was exactly what I needed. I decided to hear him out, and would take it from there.

"Fine," I said.

The tension between us evaporated, and Anton motioned for us to continue down the street back in the direction we had come.

"So, you're not human then?" The statement sounded crazy coming from my mouth and had the past hour not happened, I wouldn't have believed him. If I couldn't smell the freshness of the rain on the pavement and the crispness of the evening air, I would have assumed I was hallucinating.

Anton said, "I'm not from the same world as you. I live here, in Domain. I'm what they call a Mind Shifter, though here, we just refer to ourselves as Shifters. We are a civilisation engineered to keep the increasing complexities of the human mind under control."

Muscles or not, he had to be joking. "You *what*?"

"It's quite simple. Our world, Domain, exists parallel to yours and our function is to keep the minds of the human world in order. There are limitations to what we can do, of course, but that is essentially it."

I swallowed. "Well, at least I know I'm dreaming now."

Anton smirked to himself before he spoke. "No. This is real. Dreams are something that comes from our world to yours in order to direct your thinking. It's one of our functions. Or, sometimes we leave thoughts and memories behind when we're inside your head, which causes them to appear to you as a dream."

I focused on the surrounding people again to stop my mind from spiralling. This was too complex to be a hoax. Although everyone looked so different, there was a synchronisation to their movements. People didn't walk–they glided. Their steps were so smooth, they almost blended into the street itself. Everyone I saw held themselves with an air of confidence, though from their reactions to Anton, there was a hierarchy here. In fact, everyone who passed us seemed to acknowledge Anton.

I drew my gaze along his jaw, feeling more like myself again. "Do you know *everyone* here?"

"I know a lot of them." Anton's mouth flicked up at the corner in a knowing smirk. "How are you feeling now?"

I considered his question and gave an honest response. "I'm pretty pissed off that you brought me here without my say so."

"You didn't have a choice. You are here because you're exceptional." His face remained deadpan.

"Thanks, but I'm not in the mood for compliments."

"Don't flatter yourself," he shot back, but there was a hint of a smirk there. "All human females who show promise come here, to Domain. Some abilities manifest as babies, whereas some arrive at adulthood, like yours have. We have a longstanding prophecy that a woman of exceptional power will change the way Domain runs. It's uncommon for people from your world to show potential, but when they do, they come here and prove their worth through their Actuation."

I swallowed the information overload, wishing it was food, as my stomach grumbled. It would be easier to concentrate on the crazy things he was saying once I'd eaten. I swayed on the spot. "Right."

He nodded, and I could see the tension in his jaw. "Perhaps something to eat will help. I need to head into this party. I will explain more there." It wasn't a question, though this time, I hesitated. He was clever. I still didn't know why I was here, who I was with, and where I was. He read my unease. "If you don't like what you see in there, this is a door. We have many of them in Domain and you're welcome to use them whenever you please."

I rolled my eyes at his joke. I had questions, plenty of them, and was still wary, but my stomach was rumbling from the lack of food and I had no money and nowhere to stay. This was my only option for now. The giant doors that were at least twice my height. Not sure what I was walking into, I said, "Lead the way."

5

Charity

Anton pushed open the doors with an air of confidence and I followed him into the room. We stepped into a large atrium where over one hundred well-dressed people stood, taking up every inch of floor space, sipping champagne or something expensive looking. The walls were dark with panelled mahogany detail and green curtains framed long elegant windows. Shiny tiles with shimmering sparkles glittered through the gaps in the crowd. I'd seen nowhere quite like it.

There was an instant hush in the conversation as everyone turned to look at Anton and raised their glasses before looking me up and down. I tugged at my hoodie, frowning. I wasn't interested in fancy things. My lifestyle had revolved around essentials, not luxury. However, I didn't like to be in places that reminded me of this either, as deep down, I knew I wanted to know what it would feel like, just for a day, to not feel limited by money, to have just enough to feel free. *Is that how these people feel?* My thoughts spiralled out of control as a wave of self-consciousness hit me and reminded me I didn't belong here.

Your only limit is your imagination.

I wasn't about to let the stares of others get to me. Even when my hair stood up on end, I held the eye of one woman in an emerald green dress until she dropped her gaze down into her glass; her face hidden by a curtain of blonde hair. Next to her, a man with mahogany skin dressed in a violet suit grinned and raised his glass at me rather than Anton. I returned his smile. At least someone here was friendly.

Despite the stares from around the room, no one said anything, and once they had finished their acknowledgement of Anton, the bustle resumed as quickly as it had stopped.

Not wanting to look as ignorant as I felt, I held off questioning him on his role here just yet.

"Follow me," he instructed as he wove through the crowd, who parted to let us through.

I stayed close to his back and focused on the colours of his two-tone hair as I tried to match his pace. He glided the same way everyone else did, and I found I had to walk faster than usual to keep up with his smooth strides. Other than the man in the suit, no one took any more notice of me. Maybe it was better that way.

We reached stairs leading to a mezzanine floor that was considerably emptier than the rest of the atrium. Anton cleared the area of people with the subtlest flick of his hand and gestured towards two wingback chairs separated by a table that looked out over the entire room.

"Take a seat." He signalled for someone to bring drinks. I'd hoped they were going to bring some food, too. I was grateful for the noise downstairs that hid my rumbling stomach.

Still reeling from the absurdity of everything he had told me so far, I sank into the comfortable chair. I nearly groaned out loud from the relief it gave my aching muscles, but gripped the arms to steady myself as I remembered who was in front of me. Whether I could trust him, that was still very much up for debate. We sat there for several long moments, looking out across the party scene. When I couldn't keep my curiosity to myself any longer, I said, "Can you tell me more about this prophecy?"

Anton quirked a brow. "It would be better if you knew a bit more about our world first while we wait for our food to arrive."

I breathed a sigh of relief at the promise of food and did my best to ignore the swell of Anton's biceps as he removed his jacket and folded it over the back of the chair. Realising I was staring, I forced a question out. "Well, for starters, this mind control thing, how does it work?"

Anton flicked his mouth up at my comment. "It's not mind control, it's directing the mind for humanity's own good. Totally different."

I realised I was twisting a strand of hair around my finger as I was listening and dropped it like it was on fire. Anton's eyes didn't miss the movement. I saw a flash of lighter green in their darkness. This guy wasn't human. *Why is that exciting?*

A so-called *Shifter* with jet black and blonde hair in a side parting placed two glasses down on the table in between Anton and me without so much as a sound, instead giving Anton a curt nod as she took his jacket to hang up. *What is it with everyone paying so much attention to him? Can no one pass by him without nodding?* My mind was in overdrive. Against my better judgement, I lifted the glass to my lips without hesitating. It had been too long since my meal in the park, and right now I could do with a drink. The bubbles fizzed in my mouth before I swallowed, leaving a perfume-y aftertaste. It was some kind of champagne, but with a hint of rose petals. I knew little about these things, but like the grand room I was in, I could tell it was expensive. As I continued to sip, the need to eat dampened.

Feeling flustered and out of my comfort zone in this environment, I avoided Anton's gaze. Instead, I focused on the Shifter who had set our drinks down. She produced a receipt, and Anton tapped two fingers on his temple without even looking at it. The Shifter made a nod of acknowledgement as she checked a device at her hip and left.

"What was that?" I asked as she glided away.

Anton took out his phone, and I prepared myself to have to wait for his reply. People could become so obsessed with phones. But he pocketed it. "In your world, minds are limited to thinking. Here we use the mind for everything: paying for things, travel, even our sport, chasm."

I had so many questions that arose from that, but I had to stick with the most immediate ones about his world. "Why does everyone here look like you? Are you all related?"

Anton sat back in his chair and laced his fingers together. "You *are* observant. Shifter biology differs from human biology. You could find people of different skin tones within the same family. Stylistically, we all share the same traits, though. Those with my hair colours are from the House of Abduco. Shifters from the House of Nexus have darker hair. Those from the House of Caedes have red or auburn hair, and the House of Persen are more forward-thinking in their style—expressing themselves through colour—so they can present themselves in any form they choose."

I gazed at the stark contrast between the two sides of Anton's hair, still coloured into two halves even when his hair was tousled. The interaction between him and the woman with similar hair now made sense. "Is it just hair colour that links Shifters belonging to each House?"

"No, it's more of a personality than anything else. It all links back to our function. We have certain traits that relate to our purpose here." I raised a brow at him, but continued to listen. "Just like the Shifters, the territories where we live are different in style. Nexus is quite a modern city, having undergone several imports; Abduco favours the classics and the forest; Persen is our newest House and is an urban steampunk jungle; and Caedes is an unpredictable and fiery desert. These stylistic differences are the reason for the variety that you'll see around Domain."

I scanned the sea of black and platinum hair on the level below. "So it's nearly all people from the House of Abduco here, then. Are we in Abduco now?"

"You catch on quickly, Serrk."

I frowned at what was becoming his nickname for me, yet didn't object. Instead, I repeated what he'd said, as if to make it seem more real in my mind. "So we are in another world from the one I live in, called Domain, and in here there are four different Houses, each belonging to a different group of Shifters who monitor the human mind?"

"Precisely." Anton looked bored, as if this was all incredibly obvious.

I ignored his expression, taking another taste of my champagne, which had loosened my tongue. "How many of you are there?"

Anton took a sip from his own glass, running his tongue across his bottom lip. "Many. It's hard to say an exact number. People come and go so often, and sometimes there are . . . disagreements. These disagreements result in being sent to Langison, which is like dying."

Now I was curious. I shifted in my seat and leaned even closer. "What do you mean 'like dying'? Can Shifters not die?"

But Anton frowned and waved off my question, staring into the distance. Something had distracted him. His eyes flashed their lighter green, and he looked deep in thought, as though he hadn't even heard me.

A second passed and his eyes darkened, and that malevolent smirk returned. My fingers gripped the glass a little tighter. I'd only ever known fear from the shouts and now fists of my mother's previous boyfriends, so Anton's calm but commanding nature had me off guard.

I set my glass down to hide the slight shake of my hand and tried another question. "Why would Shifters disagree with each other?"

"Sometimes we clash because of our function. Each House exists to perform a different function within the human mind. As I'm from Abduco, we lead people away from negative thoughts and actions. Persen Shifters inspire people, like influencers in your world. Nexus helps people heal and accept. Then Caedes," he paused and his jaw ticked, the grin faltering on his face. "Their role is to destroy minds, should they prove a threat." Anton seemed to take my silence as a sign to go on. "Some people have also disagreed about the way things are run here. The Apex families run things in their House, with the Cerebral Council in charge of Domain. A bit like your government."

I frowned, confused by more terms I hadn't heard before. "Apex families?"

As two plates of food arrived, my question remained unanswered. I sent a silent prayer of thanks to whoever was listening as I realised Anton had ordered me a giant burger and chips along with something fancy for himself. Maybe he had heard my stomach rumbling after all.

I hesitated, saliva pooling in my mouth at the smell alone. Could I trust him? *What if he'd put something in the food?*

Anton picked up his fork. "It won't kill you. It would have been much easier to poison your drink. But I'll swap with you if you don't believe me."

I was being too trusting, but a final pang from my stomach reminded me I was too hungry to care. The first chip melted on my tongue and I decided that there were worse ways to die. I was kidding. Sort of.

Anton ate his meal with more grace, forcing me to slow down every few bites so that I could digest both my meal and what he was saying. He placed his fork down at the side of his plate. "Yes, each House has an original family of Apex Shifters who manage their House and the rest of the Meso Shifters within who follow orders. Besides that, we have Demi-Shifters, i.e., humans, who take up a permanent residence here."

"Let me guess, you're an Apex Shifter." I rolled my eyes, putting another salty chip on my tongue.

"Naturally," Anton said, though I didn't see the smug look on his face that I expected to.

I took another swig of my champagne. It didn't go so well with the burger. I set it down again. It was better to be alert, anyway. "How can you tell the difference?"

Anton's eyes were lost in the crowd again. "More on that later; I'm getting bored with your questions."

"Well, you told me to ask them." The words were out my mouth before I could stop them, but I was confused. His sudden abruptness threw me, especially since he had been quite happy to explain the nature of Domain to me until that moment.

The bubbles were sending my thoughts into overdrive. I couldn't help myself when yet another thought crossed my mind. "If Abduco Shifters lead people away from bad thoughts, why don't you stop people like Wyatt?"

Anton turned back towards me and his eyes flashed with the lightning green I was coming to recognise. "Perhaps we decide who is worth bothering with and who isn't. We had bigger things to deal with than your petty family troubles."

What the fuck? I looked back at him. "Excuse me?"

"Shifters are busy, and we have much more pressing things to attend to than a mother that makes bad choices and her hot-head daughter."

Where the hell did that come from? Anton's charm had evaporated, and anger swirled in my stomach as I lost a grip on my emotions and the glass crunched in my fist. "Looks like whether or not you have a lot of power, you can still be an asshole." My blood thrummed in my ears, dulling the pain in my hand. Not caring that I was personifying the hot-head he had described, I swept the shards off my palm onto the ground and made to leave. "You're no better than the likes of people like Wyatt. You and your prophecy can get fucked."

Laughter rang out across the room and I turned back, surprised to see the noise coming from Anton. He drained his glass. "Oh, you didn't even tell her why she's here. This is too good."

I frowned, unsure who he was talking to. His face contorted, his mouth pulled back into a sneer. I knew Anton as smug, but I'd never seen him like this.

He continued, now looking at me but addressing himself. "I suppose he didn't tell you who I am, either."

I was getting fed up with his confusing antics. My burger was three quarters finished. That would have to do. It wasn't worth sticking around for this. "Thanks for the burger, but I'll be off now."

In one fluid motion, he stood and crossed in front of me, blocking my path to the stairs. He towered over me and my insides froze as I realised how serious a mistake I'd made in keeping company with someone I knew so little about.

"You are speaking to Allium, not Anton," he bit out, his voice different from the velvet timbre he'd used.

Confusion replaced my fear. "Allium?"

"Anton's Other. You understand nothing about our kind, do you? You can't be who we are looking for."

I stood rooted to the spot. "How am I supposed to understand anything about your kind? I just found out you existed." It was all too much to take in. *Who they were looking for? And what did he mean by Other?*

It seemed Allium didn't care about these cold, hard facts. "For Hymev's sake, You *Nihils* are so ignorant. All Shifters are born with an Other–a second consciousness, or personality, if you will. I am Anton's Other, Allium."

I didn't know what he'd just called me, but it didn't sound good. "How long have I been speaking to Allium for?"

"The past few minutes."

My eyebrows must have reached my hairline as I gaped at him. That explained why Anton had turned sour. I'd heard about people with multiple personalities before, but had never met anyone in that position. Where Anton was confident and inviting, Allium was cold and cruel.

"Well, I'd like to speak to Anton again."

"Not possible. And you would do well to not confuse us again." Allium's mouth was drawn back in a snarl. Anton always stood tall, but there was something different in the way Allium held himself. He held his chin higher, like he thought he was better than everyone around him. I couldn't mistake the look of disgust as his lip curled when he met my stare.

I was used to Mother's boyfriends looking at me like I was nothing, but I hadn't seen quite this level of disdain since Sophia Walker had made a comment about my old ripped clothes at school and had caused the whole lunch table to fall about laughing. I'd taken one look at the tuna sandwich hanging from the corner of her mouth and internally vomited. Then I smacked her headfirst into the table in front of her. No one laughed after that. No one called me poor either. And this dickhead would not be the one to start. I returned his glare as the words dripped from me like acid. "How could I not confuse you?

You're the same person."

Anton, or rather, *Allium*, ran a hand through his hair. "It's like dealing with a baby speaking to you." He rolled his eyes. "There are many differences between us, more than I care to explain to the likes of you. My eyes are lighter, his are darker, they change according to who is present."

Had I not studied Anton's features, the change would have been subtle. However, to me, the difference was stark. His eyes were the most obvious, now lighter with the flashes of green I'd seen earlier. But it went deeper than that. While I didn't regard Anton as a cheerful character, all traces of joy vanished as his expression had changed to one of hatred. He was still startlingly handsome, but he was harder to admire when he looked at me in such a brutal way. I couldn't decide whether to confront him or create as much distance between us as possible.

His attitude was even more insufferable than Anton's. Where Anton was smug, Allium eyed me as if I was something unpleasant under his nose. Had I not been so curious about Anton's words to do with a prophecy, I would have skirted around him and taken my chances around Abduco, if that's even where I was. After all, the sensible side of my brain was still trying to convince me that this was some elaborate prank.

I knew the buzz downstairs had died down, so lowered my voice. "If I'm so ignorant, maybe you can explain why I'm here instead."

What I now knew as Anton's eyes were dark as he tried to speak. "Let me tell her." Then they changed to their lighter hues and Allium returned with an evil smile. "Oh no, this is too fun. Allow me, Anton."

His apparent conversation with himself transfixed me too much to refuse his gesture as he ushered me back towards our vacated seats, though I had now lost my appetite.

Allium chuckled, lacing his fingers together. "Why do you think you're here?"

I bit my lip, unsure where he was going with this. "Anton mentioned there's a prophecy that might relate to me. Something about people that show promise?"

Allium's lip curled in a sinister smile. "And that's something that's said to you often, is it? That you show promise? In that slum of a town you call home."

The words cut into my skin and I swallowed, unsure what hurt more: his dismissive tone of the place I had grown up, or the fact even I had noted how out-of-place someone well-dressed like Anton seemed around there. Not to mention, no one, not once, had ever mentioned I'd shown any kind of promise. That was, until today.

"I don't want to be here." I began to rise from my seat again.

"It's a privilege to be here, talking to me." Allium's tone forced me to take my seat again. "You know how many Shifters would give to be sat where you are? How many humans, if they knew about our existence? You might not be here by accident, but neither Anton nor I believe there's anything exceptional about you. You're here because we have a prophecy about a girl from both worlds and we need to clarify that it isn't you. Nothing more, nothing less."

I digested each icy word. "Well, here's some clarification for you. It looks like you both made a mistake as I hadn't heard of this world until today, so I can't be of both worlds. You both have the wrong person. Sorry to have taken up so much of your precious time."

This time, I rose fully and turned away from Allium, who was laughing again as I fled down the stairs, furious at myself for having such blind trust in a stranger for help.

I was grateful the crowd had thinned out as I slipped between the remaining bodies. No one paid me any attention when I was without

Anton. I saw a small doorway ajar on the far wall of the room that offered me an escape, and I took it without hesitation.

I slipped through and clicked it shut behind me, cutting off the sound of any music. I leaned back against the cold smooth stone and reached for my duffle bag to check my phone. *Maybe I could see if a taxi driver has ever heard of Domain?* But my bag had gone. I used it so often, the phantom sensation of the shoulder strap had allowed me to think I'd had it all along. I thought back and remembered the thud of my bag on the ground before Anton had taken my wrist. I realised it hadn't made it to Domain with me. The last connection to my home had been severed along with the one physical thing I cared about: that book. It was the only thing that had given me hope that there was someone out there who'd cared about me. I was now trapped in an unfamiliar place, with no one to turn to for help.

Registering I was alone, I smashed my knuckles into the wall, thinking it would give me a much-needed release. Instead, a sharp pain rose above all other sensations in my body as I hit the same hand that had crushed the glass. Agony flared through me as my bones shuddered with the impact. *Damn me and my knee-jerk reactions sometimes. Why do I have to be so impulsive?* I winced, cradling my hand as I curled up against the wall and waited for the throbbing to pass.

What the fuck am I going to do?

6

CHARITY

I was hollow. Not to mention kicking myself for having even looked at Anton and his overly-chiselled jaw. I had been stupid enough to think the fact he had helped me out had meant something, but of course he wasn't interested in me beyond a means to an end. So why had Allium's words hurt so much?

I stared at the door I had just come through. Fortunately, it didn't look like Allium was following me. I continued on down the corridor to find another way out of the building that didn't involve going back out into the crowd.

A loud cackle of laughter exploded up ahead as a group of women came round the corner laughing hysterically. It wasn't a pleasant sound, more like a joke made at someone's expense. As they drew closer, their cloud of mixed perfumes hit me before they did.

The leader of the group was beautiful in a deadly sort of way. She had pale skin, auburn hair, and was dressed for the party in a way I was not. We were complete opposites: while I was often regarded as short, this Shifter towered over me, her flashy smile even more prominent because of the scarlet lipstick framing bright white teeth. I had a relatively small frame courtesy of not enough food on the table coupled with my running, whereas the woman's red dress fitted around her hourglass figure, emphasising every curve. I would have been jealous had I been my younger self, though I had learned to accept the pros and cons of my stature over the years.

The laughter stopped as the group regarded me, the rest of the members looking at the woman in front for confirmation of how to react.

She fixed me with a quizzical look as she took in my clothes, my hand, and my likely still-bruised lip from yesterday. Her tone wasn't sympathetic. "What on earth happened to you? And why are you dressed like that?"

I didn't have the energy to explain, so I summarised. "It's been a long day. Who are you, sorry?"

Her eyes narrowed. This was the wrong thing to say. "Who am *I*? I'm Scarlett Brunelli from the House of Caedes. You have confirmed who *you* are with your ignorance. You're another prophecy plaything. Your name doesn't matter to me. I can already tell you're not worthy. All I know is you have come from your simple human world to challenge us, and the sooner you go home, the better."

Her friends roared with laughter at her statement. *More obnoxious Shifters. Just what I need.*

I didn't rise to her taunt and congratulated myself. After all, as it wasn't like me not to talk back. Maybe I was just too exhausted. "That's me all right. I'm just looking for a way to get home."

Her friends laughed harder, as if I'd just said the funniest joke in the world. She turned towards me. "You're so clueless it's hilarious. You need Shifter abilities to do anything here, something you evidently don't have. Otherwise you wouldn't walk about dressed like that." Her gang laughed once more.

I was tiring of this woman. I pushed past her and made to walk away when a thought occurred to me, waking my big mouth up. "Caedes destroy minds, right?"

Scarlett turned to her friends with her eyebrows raised in confusion.

I might as well dig my own grave. "You really went to town. Leave yourself a few brain cells next time."

Scarlett's eyes bulged out of her head, and one of her lackeys spluttered a laugh. As quick as a flash, Scarlett was in front of her friend and slapped her hard across the face, the sound echoing down the hall. The other woman drew back in shock, holding her cheek, but said nothing. Before I could even react to that, Scarlett was in front of me and grasped my jaw, her long manicured nails biting into my skin. "The prophecy might protect you now, but it won't forever."

My reaction was instant. I summoned all the hate I could inside of me and pushed her as hard as I could. The action caught her off guard and sent her rocketing across the room.

"Yeah? You'd better hope there's one to watch out for you." A voice in the back of my head wondered where this hate was coming from and whether this was the right thing to do, before more anger blinded me, obscuring rational thought.

I'd only just met this woman, but I was shaking with fury. I wanted to hurt her and make her pay for her disgusting attitude. The small voice in my head was louder now, reminding me that Shifters had powers, something I didn't understand yet, and warned me to be sensible here. However, my wild side knew if it came to a fist fight, I was sure to have the upper hand and I was ready to try with what I had.

But it never came to that, as Scarlett's face cleared of all disdain and drew her attention elsewhere down the corridor. "Honestly, Rivers, use your mundane abilities elsewhere. I'm just helping our newest pathetic little *Nihil* understand how things are here."

I stood confused, wondering what on earth she was speaking about. Then a kind voice emerged from the direction Scarlett was looking toward.

"We don't use that word for Demi-Shifters. Leave her alone."

I followed her gaze: the voice belonged to a woman smaller than me and that was saying something. She had brunette hair to her shoulders and wore an expression that was warm and inviting, despite her fierce words.

The woman held her ground and appeared to be concentrating on something. I stood motionless, unsure what was happening.

After a few seconds, Scarlett turned to her friends. "Let's not waste any more time here. I want to join the last of the party." She eyed me. "You'd better hope I don't see you around." Knocking my shoulder as she passed, her gang followed her out of sight through the door I'd just entered from.

Part of me wanted to shout after her I hoped she would, though I was also glad to have been relieved of a fight now that I could think again. I had to learn more about what powers Shifters had before trying to take on any.

"Are you okay?" The kind voice interrupted my thoughts.

I met with a pair of clear blue eyes. "Yeah, what is her problem?"

The woman giggled. "That's Scarlett. She likes to live up to the Caedes stereotype of being nasty. She takes it seriously. I feel sorry for her boyfriend."

I couldn't help but laugh along with her. Laughing was infectious, especially when it was so genuine.

"I'm Perrine Rivers from the House of Nexus," she said, holding out her hand. "My Other is Ordette. You're Charity Serrk, of course. I've heard all about you."

I shook her hand, confused. "Heard of me?"

"Everyone has, of course! We've been searching for Demi-Shifters in relation to this prophecy for years, so it's always exciting when someone comes from your world."

I gulped. Having been anonymous most of my life, this was unfamiliar territory for me. But judging by my recent encounter with Scarlett, I wasn't sure if being notorious was a good thing, either.

I then realised the significance of Perrine being from Nexus. She could help people heal and forget their hate. "When Scarlett spoke to you there, were you using your powers on her?" I wondered how long the effects lasted.

She smiled. "I was getting her to forgive and forget, yes. Nexus helps people to heal and accept what they cannot change. Of course, some people are beyond our help, but that doesn't mean we don't try."

Her warmth was refreshing. I grinned back at her. "I should thank you for sticking up for me, then."

"Anytime." She slipped her hand into mine before reaching for my face. "Sorry, old habits. We can heal things physically too, do you mind?"

"Sure," I said, fascinated, as the tension lifted from my lip and the pain evaporated. I touched it to make sure it was fine, as was my hand. "Thank you." I gasped at her work as I inspected myself. "You're a useful person to have around."

"It's what we're here for." She smiled back at me.

At that moment, the door opened and Anton strode in, his eyes dark and his voice velvety once more. "Thanks, Rivers, I'll take it from here."

I raised my eyebrows at her before turning to him, pleased to see he'd returned, though that didn't mean I forgave him. "Maybe I don't want her to go."

Perrine cut in, "It's okay, Charity. I need to head back to Nexus anyway. There's no shortage in your world of people needing to heal, so I'd better get back to work. I'll see you soon, though." She looked at Anton before giving me a small nod as she disappeared in the direction she'd come.

I glared at Anton as we stood awkwardly in the deserted hallway together. His dark eyes met mine and threatened to pull me under his spell, but I wasn't having any of it. "You should have explained about Others at the beginning."

"I was trying not to overwhelm you. If I'd told you that right away, would you have believed me?" The briefest shard of vulnerability flashed across his face before his composure returned. "As for Allium, I'll admit he's something."

"I'm having trouble knowing what to believe as it is right now, and don't even get me started on Allium."

"How about we walk and I'll fill in the rest?" Anton suggested.

I took a deep breath to allow myself to think. Unsure where else I could go, I nodded. "If Allium reemerges–"

"He won't," Anton cut me off. "I'll make sure of it."

We walked down the corridor which was lined with paintings of various Shifters, all with the same black or platinum blonde hair. I assumed these were all important members of the House of Abduco, given their similar looks and stern expressions. Their resemblance to Anton was clear. If he was a so-called Apex Shifter, maybe these were some distant family members. I would have asked him, but that would seem like I was interested. Perhaps I still was. Not in Allium. He was vile. But Anton was . . . different.

We came to a door at the end of the hallway and he held it open for me to pass through. I brushed past him; he smelled powerful, but clean. Like scorched earth on a warm day, with a hint of mint. I wasn't even sure if it was cologne and I had to concentrate on continuing through the door without stopping in my tracks.

The crisp autumnal air cleared my head, and I took a moment to marvel at where we were as we walked down the tree-lined street. It was hard to know where to look. Although it was dark, I couldn't help but notice the sheer amount of greenery lit by the old-fashioned street lamps. We walked up a road that ran through a giant forest. Large mansions shrouded in woodland peeped out from the foliage, visible only from the lights within. Anton didn't seem to mind my silence as I took everything in.

He allowed me time to examine our surroundings before he started speaking. "We have had a prophecy here for some time and it talks about a girl from both worlds shaking up everything in Domain."

"But I'm not from both worlds. I'd never even heard of your world until today."

"I understand, Serrk. It's likely it's not you."

"Then why did you bring me here?"

Anton hesitated. "I was under instructions, and I wanted to help."

"What instructions? From who?" I pressed him. His version seemed different to Allium's. I saw the way his eyes lingered on my now healed lip. He wasn't cruel, like Allium had implied.

"It doesn't matter who, but I've been watching you for some time," Anton said, averting his gaze and fixing his eyes on the cobbles beneath us. My pulse quickened at the idea he'd been watching me, even if ordered to. Something about that didn't sit right with me. He didn't seem like the person to follow orders, but I didn't want to provoke him right now, not when I was getting some answers.

As we continued down the road, I turned over Anton's words in my mind. "So what do I need to do to see if the prophecy is about me? Is there some kind of test?"

"Well, you'll need to hear the prophecy, and see if anything of it means anything to you. Then, there is a test of sorts. We call it a Shifter's Actuation. Your Actuation happens when you're around eighteen, but as you're a Demi-Shifter, it just depends when your abilities emerge."

"What about my bag?" I asked. "I have nothing to wear." That wasn't my actual issue, but I wasn't about to tell him I was missing a book.

"You'll have everything you need at your accommodation," explained Anton.

I was full of questions now. "What does my Actuation involve? Is it a written test?" I was busy thinking back to school. I could have done much better. I just couldn't handle being told what to do, which led to trouble more often than not. Hopefully, the skills I had wouldn't leave me embarrassed.

"Not written, no. There's a mental part and a physical part. You can work with people I trust and hone your skills to prepare. It'll all make sense once you start."

I hoped so. Because not much was making sense now. "And what if I don't pass this test?" I couldn't even comprehend I might possess any kind of magical powers.

"If you don't, you either remain in Domain as a Demi-Shifter, or you can return to your world with enough to start afresh."

I had to admit; it seemed like a win-win: either find out I was legendary in another world, an unlikely but potentially pleasant option, or return home though far from empty-handed.

I nodded. "I'll do it. But I'm certain I'm not who you're looking for."

Anton winked. "Allium tells me you nearly broke a glass on him, so there's maybe a hint of Caedes in you yet."

"He'd better be prepared for what I have to say when I see him next."

Anton's face darkened. "Go easy on him. Allium is more complicated than you think."

I rolled my eyes. "And meanwhile, you're the charming one."

"Your words, Serrk, not mine." Anton's expression remained deadpan, causing me to blush.

We stopped at the top of a street lined with mansions hidden in the foliage.

"You're expected at Abduco Manor where you'll begin your training to prepare for your Actuation," Anton said, as he stared at the large buildings ahead peeking out from the trees.

"Training?"

"Yes. The biggest threat to a Shifter in our world is through their mind. If they come for you, they will try to break you. More likely mentally than physically. We'll need to practise."

"Who are 'they'?"

He hesitated before he replied, "Well, anyone." Something told me that wasn't the answer he'd intended to give me. But now wasn't the time to delve deeper. Perhaps I'd imagined his reaction.

"And I'll be staying in one of these houses?" I was keen to know more.

"Yes, my family home. It's tradition as the ruling Apexes in the House of Abduco."

I looked up the street at what I could see of the vast houses. They were larger than the schools I'd been to over the years, full of dark corridors and hidden places to get locked away in if I failed. I couldn't go back to that place in my mind, couldn't get lost under the floorboards, trapped for over two days . . .

Fear and panic clawed at my resolve. I was out of my depth. *I can't do this. Not here.*

"I'm not going. I don't want more stares from everyone," I garbled, trying to find a plausible excuse to avoid giving away my real reason.

"Not going?" There was that flash of light green again and his fists curled, although he shook it off.

"Is there somewhere more off the beaten track I can go instead?" I then added for good measure, "You owe me for not being upfront about Allium."

Anton considered this and appeared to be in silent dialogue with Allium. Danger rolled off him in waves. Then, surprisingly, his shoulders dropped, and he relaxed as he said, "As a matter of fact, I know just the place."

He was an enigma.

We walked down a much narrower path and headed away from the mansions where the trees thinned, and the buildings wouldn't have looked out of place in Drabshire. It differed from anywhere else I had seen in Abduco. I couldn't imagine why Anton would come here when he lived among such beautiful mansions.

I wondered how Allium would fit into all of this, despite barely knowing him. I hated him, as well as Scarlett too, but, not wanting further pity or embarrassment, I didn't tell Anton about my encounter with her.

Anton interrupted my thoughts. "What's on your mind?"

In fact, I was wondering if Allium had said anything sincere at all or if he had just wanted to spite me. "Why do Shifters allow people like Wyatt to exist? Why don't people like you help?"

Anton's eyes searched mine. "You heard what Allium told you?"

"Yeah."

"But you don't believe it?"

"No, I don't."

He furrowed his brow. "Why not?"

"I don't believe an entire race exists to perform one function that they then ignore."

Anton's mouth flicked up at the corner. "You're interesting, Serrk. I'll give you that. You're right, Allium gets carried away sometimes."

I bristled at his comment. "That's an understatement."

Anton ignored my retort. "You're correct in our purpose as Shifters, though the reason people like Wyatt exist is that while as a race we perform well, not everyone is perfect, and some enjoy the chaos of allowing such events to play out. Just like in your world."

"Let me guess, Caedes Shifters enjoy the chaos." I was aware we were leaving all signs of civilisation and into a more deserted area of Abduco. *Where on earth are we going?*

Anton strode just ahead of me as I hurried to keep up, adding over his shoulder, "You're catching on. I can lead people like Wyatt away from bad choices, and there are many like me that do. However, Caedes are the ones responsible for destroying the most dangerous minds. They have a lot of power, but Caedes Shifters have a certain temperament for risk taking and enjoy the destruction that occurs when such minds live. Things slip past us and bad things happen. Again, just like in your world."

"So you saw what Wyatt did then? What he's been doing."

"I have seen what happened. He won't be troubling you any more."

I stiffened. I hated Wyatt, hated him. But I didn't want him dead. *Did he mean–*

Anton cut in, "Before you ask, he's not dead. But like I said, he won't bother you again. I was hoping to intervene before . . ." He trailed off as he pointed to my now-healed lip. "As you saw, I didn't make it in time."

I scoffed. "I wonder how many other acts of misfortune could be prevented if Shifters made their appointments on time."

Anton stopped and turned to face me, and his eyes darkened as I stared him down. "Not everything is black and white, Serrk."

"Clearly." I eyed him with venom. "Things here are much more morally grey." Then, remembering that he was finding me somewhere to stay, I added to his retreating back. "Thank you for taking care of it, though. The ones in charge here, that Council, don't they do anything about it?"

I caught up with him just as he paused in front of a large building. He was rummaging in his pocket for something. "It's complicated. Good doesn't exist without evil as a benchmark. We have that in common, your world and mine. That's enough questions for tonight. Your human brain might explode if you try to take on any more."

I was out of time to ask anything else as we reached our destination. The dark building stood several floors high, containing flats. By the derelict appearance of the place, no one had lived there for some time.

"Welcome to my home." Anton smirked as he pulled a key from his pocket and slid it into the lock.

"Your home?" I raised a brow as I stepped towards a door that was falling off its hinges. The key seemed redundant, as someone could have kicked the door down with ease had they any need to get into the building.

I couldn't quite believe that Anton lived somewhere like this. He must have another place that was more permanent, where he spent his time.

We stepped into a hallway. Wooden panels hugged the walls and crooked stairs spiralled upwards out of sight. The hallway was more well-lit than expected by sconces that flickered with a soft glow. I frowned, sure that the building had been darker from the outside.

Following Anton up the stairs, I took care not to let him see I was out of breath from keeping up with his pace. I would have thought my running had served me better, yet here I was puffing away like an engine.

As we reached the top floor, we met a dark green door with ornate gold panels. This looked more like Anton's style, even though it was out of place in the decrepit hallway.

Anton used his key again, swung open the door, and gestured for me to step in.

I walked into a smart flat that resembled nothing of the hallway or the building outside. A coat stand and a neat row of shoes lined the wall near the door I had walked through. I removed my shoes as a courtesy to the spotless space as I continued into the open plan living room and kitchen.

The area was small, but it was Anton in its taste. A dark green sofa sat opposite a real fireplace. It was flanked by a drinks cabinet and an enormous bookcase that held many titles. The kitchen behind the living room area had a fancy marble island and cupboards that matched the emerald curtains that hung from the ceiling height windows.

The green hues complemented both the light carpet and tiles beneath my feet. I rolled my eyes. Naturally, Anton would live somewhere stylish. It looked like something out of a magazine, despite its inconspicuous location. The dark mahogany doors added a masculine aesthetic to the flat, and I could tell that this was somewhere where he was at ease.

"It's not like the mansions of the other Apexes. I can find you somewhere more suitable, if you prefer."

"Are you kidding?" I cut him off, realising this is what he meant by somewhere off the beaten track. I walked to the bookshelf and ran a finger along the spines that were lined up. "This place is perfect."

I looked over my shoulder just in time to see his grin before it vanished again. I couldn't believe he also housed a total monster in such a perfect exterior. At least it would stop me from getting carried away during my time here.

Anton showed me through the rest of the rooms as I continued to compliment various aspects of the decor. Eventually, we came to the spare room. It was simple, but elegant. He placed a hand on the wall. "I should mention: the outside is a glamour to keep people away. You could say I like my privacy."

I couldn't help my fascination as I stared up at him. "How did you do that? Is it some kind of mind trick?"

"Essentially. I own the whole place. Anyone apart from the owner of the property sees an old building that is not worth restoring and, thus, I can have my peace."

"Of course you would own a building. That is so Anton of you," I replied, feigning being impressed, and I glimpsed the ghost of a smile before his mask was back in place.

"I'll leave you to sort your things. You will find clothes in the wardrobe that should be in your size and style. I'll put things in place to meet with Viktor tomorrow and we can look at the prophecy then, too."

"Things in my size?" I was half speaking out loud. How could there be clothes for me? We'd only just arrived here.

"And style, Serrk. I had everything transferred over on our way here. Welcome to Domain. It's amazing what is possible here." His brow lifted a fraction as he spoke.

I wished there was a quicker way for me to solve this complicated riddle, though there were worse places I could spend my time than in this flat. Anton had said we'd be meeting someone called Viktor tomorrow. So once he'd left, I'd have the evening to myself to digest everything.

"How do I know if I have these powers?" I said, making my way to my door and resting my hand on the handle.

Anton rolled his eyes. "It's Shifter *abilities*, Serrk, not mind powers. We'll start with the prophecy tomorrow." He made to step out of the room and turned back to me. "Oh, and Charity? I'm glad you stayed."

My breath hitched at the use of my name, and that he was glad I was staying, however much or little that was related to the prophecy. Then he spoiled it. "And I'm sorry to have brought you here. Allium and I are sure we'll have this sorted before you know it and you can get on with your life."

I wanted to trust him, and explore my potential place here, but as long as there was Allium, I could never let my guard down around Anton, and he had to know that. I took a step closer to his large frame in the doorway and tilted my chin up in his direction. "Thanks for giving me somewhere to stay, Anton, but for what it's worth, if the prophecy is about me, the first person I'll be directing my *Shifter abilities* at is Allium."

Anton's composure faltered for a second before recovering. "I'd expect nothing less." He turned to leave before calling back over his shoulder. "Oh, and, Serrk?"

"Yes?" My heart pounded. *So much for me not getting attached.*

He gestured at the only door we hadn't been through. "You're free to go wherever you like, except the room across the hall. That's where I'll be."

My eyes did a double take at his large form lingering in the doorway. "You're staying here too?"

Anton raised a brow. "I said this was my home. Where did you think I'd be?"

Shit. I hadn't realised he was going to be staying here, too. This was about to get very complicated.

7

CHARITY

The suns blazed, rising one hundred and eighty degrees apart in perfect synchronisation. Between them, they illuminated the circular core of the city: a vast expanse of sand surrounded by structures, which gave the centre a ring-like appearance.

Here was the epicentre of the district and where the wealthiest lived above ground. Perpendicular to the cracks were deep caverns housing buildings tens of stories high built into the vertical plains underneath. Sand-coloured buildings cut into the rocks with crisp precision. Multi-story works of art with balconies and windows jutted out beyond the realm of possibility, even for this world. This architecture was only possible by harnessing the available solar energy that their district favoured, using it to burn the architectural features into the brickwork itself. Laser cutting had nothing on the technology used here.

Outside of the principal centre, the city might have looked like nothing more than a desert from above, stretching out for an unfathomable distance, the ground marked with thick cracks from the dry climate. Nothing of interest other than the odd pools of water and trees as far as the eye could see.

They were clever that way.

The cracks in the sand led to the more clandestine buildings in the district. These were the most familiar. There lived the vast population, as well as an underground network of bars, markets, and emporiums, where only the rarest items existed. Two suns provided more than enough sunlight below ground for anything to thrive. Fire burned more readily here than anywhere else, and that was how they liked it.

If only he could have her, but he couldn't. It was not his place to decide who belonged, only to remove who didn't. There was too much of a risk. If they discovered him, he would lose everything.

He knew what he had to do.

The pain in my head was enough to wake me. Panic set in as I looked at the unfamiliar ceiling and imagined footsteps above me. Even years later, I still couldn't bear the sound. It reminded me of that day that I still refused to revisit in my head.

I brushed my horrors aside. They would not help me today. Instead, I thought back to my dream, trying to sift through what I'd been imagining and what had happened since I'd arrived here. I think I'd been watching the dream from Anton's perspective, but it was hard to tell, as I hadn't seen him directly in the dream. I glanced at the door. It was hard to believe I was in his flat right now with him just a few feet away in bed.

I tore myself away from my thoughts as I remembered my words to him last night, ensuring he was off limits. It was difficult to get my head around the fact that Anton and Allium were parts of the same person. I made a note to ask him more about how Others worked so

I could avoid Allium at all costs. That side of him was evil. It dripped from him.

My mind drifted to my mother. Despite getting away, I wondered how she was getting on and how she was reacting to whatever Anton had done to Wyatt. I made a point of asking him.

A soft knock told me Anton was outside. I smoothed my hair, raced to make my bed, then opened the door.

I inhaled as I took in his casual clothes. His black t-shirt clung to every inch of his broad back, which tapered down into a sculpted waist. He even had those muscles above his ribs that were too close to my eye level to not stare at. As for his sweatpants, somehow they contoured everything more than his suit trousers; it wasn't fair, there were too many outlines.

Mortified, I looked up and found him smirking. "Tea, Serrk, or did you have something else in mind?"

Whoa. There was forward, and then there was Anton. I knew he was only flirting to get a rise out of me. It was infuriating how much he could get under my skin.

I couldn't ask him about Wyatt after he'd come out with something like that. It was just as well, as my mouth had turned to cotton, so I rolled my eyes and moved past him to the kitchen. Anton shrugged in satisfaction and set about making us breakfast and a pot of tea.

As he poured, I took a breath at the fact it was green tea. My favourite. My caffeine withdrawals were kicking in and my last cup at The Coffee Shoppe had seemed a lifetime ago. As he poured the water, a single leaf floated at the top.

"That is not actual ivy, is it?" I exhaled. I had heard of extracts being used before, but I was sure that didn't extend to whole leaves and couldn't tell if it was safe to drink.

"It most certainly is. Your world still uses the most primitive ingredients for your brews. I know how much you think you enjoy yours, Serrk, but the flavours here would shock you."

The scent floated into my nostrils. The aroma was a cross between a plant and a flower. There was a bitterness, but a softness to it at the same time. It was intoxicating, the company and the tea.

Get a grip. He just insulted you and the whole of humankind, you idiot.

I arranged my face into my mask. Ready to play the part and build a better life for myself. I'd always worked alone. This time was no different.

Focus on the task. "When can I hear the prophecy?"

I watched his movements as he pondered my question. His large hands removed the filter containing the mixture of ivy leaves from the teapot with an unexpected grace. He lifted the cup to his lips, sipped, then set his it down with impeccable precision. I tried not to pay too much attention to his mouth.

Get a grip, Charity.

"Let's finish breakfast and I'll explain how it works."

We ate in silence. This was down to the fact I'd never had such an array of food to choose from. I helped myself to croissants, toast, a yoghurt, and had just moved the fruit bowl towards me when I noticed Anton watching.

I quirked a brow at him. He understood my challenge. "Go ahead. It's refreshing to see someone who goes after what they want."

You've got to be kidding me. If only he didn't have any connection to Allium.

But he was right. When it came to some things, I did always go after what I wanted. Because why the fuck not? Given my life was pretty depressing, I hadn't deprived myself of things within my control, whether that was food, running, or men. I remembered one guy had scoffed on a first date when I'd told him I rated myself a solid ten out of ten.

You think someone like you could be a ten? Tens are Victoria's Secret models, he'd said, laughing. We didn't have a second date. I didn't want to be with someone who didn't think I was anything less than perfect. I'd rather be alone. Of course, I wasn't perfect. But I had this idea that I could be somebody's idea of the word. I shook myself as I realised I was staring into space. I locked onto Anton's gaze, which was hovering near my thumb that was wiping crumbs off my lip. Scolding my lack of manners, no doubt.

Once we had finished breakfast, I made to stand and was shocked to find Anton behind my chair, pulling it out for me. He looked as stunned as I did, before muttering something about "old habits" and making quick work of the dishes until his marble kitchen was once again immaculate. He motioned us through towards the sofa and I sat down, feeling too close to him already.

"In our world, everything through the mind. Prophecies are no different and are heard mentally in order to get a genuine feeling for them. It's written somewhere, but this way is much easier."

I pulled a face. This world just got stranger. "Do you mean I'll be able to hear it in my head?"

"That's exactly what I'm saying," Anton said, his scorched earth smell washing all over me from our proximity. He was so close, I could feel the heat that radiated from his body. "Whenever you're ready."

"I am." Even though I was uncertain what to expect.

It was like putting on headphones. A cool female voice spoke in my head somewhere between my ears.

Woman of both worlds,
A revolution on the horizon,

Four halves can be whole.
Unlikely allies hold answers to the past;
Only the burning rose connects it all.

The voice went silent, and Anton gave me one of his pointed stares, waiting for my response.

"That was quite something." I was left bewildered at how things worked here.

"Did any of it mean anything to you?" He'd moved forward, so he was closer to the edge of the sofa, his body angled towards me on tenterhooks.

I tried to ignore the fact that there was now less than a foot between us. "No, I'm afraid not. I know nothing about your world, so most of those things make no sense to me." His heady scent was interfering with my rational thinking. *No, fix this.* "Plus, there's not a chance in hell Allium will ever be an ally of mine. I'm afraid you've got the wrong person."

Anton drew back. Hurt flashed across his face. I glimpsed the lighter green across his dark hues and I wondered if Allium had heard my response. I hoped he had.

Ever the gentleman, Anton recovered. "Understood, Serrk. You've still got your Actuation of course, just so we can be absolutely sure."

"Of course," I nodded, grateful that he'd moved further away. A chilling thought caused my heart to skip a beat. "Anton?"

"Yes?"

"Can you–can Shifters read minds?"

The seconds before he answered were agonising. "Yes and no; most of your thoughts are your own, but there are ways your mind is accessible. I've arranged for my brother, Viktor, to bring you up to speed for anything you'll need for your Actuation. Perrine will also be there, so you'll have a familiar face." I nodded even though he hadn't answered my question. It seemed like he knew as he said, "No, I can't tell what you're thinking, Serrk. You should work on hiding your expression, though. That is easy to read."

Oh.

"I'd rather you didn't." I flushed with embarrassment and stared at my feet to hide as much of my face as I could.

"Don't worry, Serrk, we all have our vices," Anton said, delighted at my discomfort once again. His mouth pulled back to reveal those immaculate teeth and his hand raked through his hair in an act of nonchalance. "Even though we're meant to blend in, Allium likes to stand out, so here we are. He is more acquainted with our old ways, yet is also something of a rebel. He has the platinum blond hair, by the way. I'm the dark side, just so you know which part you prefer."

Scrambling to cover my tracks, I changed the subject to hide my embarrassment. "I wasn't thinking about that. I was thinking you keep your home and this building so well disguised."

"Even I have to admit, the glamour here is flawless." Anton accepted my subject change. "My home is invisible to anyone other than those I want. Everyone else sees a scrambled image, complete with sensations to match."

"It's amazing," I admitted, not realising I was speaking out loud. I was too busy turning over his words *those I want* in my mind.

"What can I say, Serrk? I'm a man of many talents. Well, I should say, Allium is, it's he who designed this. He has more of a mind for it than me. But I still helped. I have a lot of time on my hands when I'm not playing my role."

"What do you mean, playing your role?" I ignored his mention of Allium.

Anton looked surprised, as if he'd revealed too much. But then added, "There are certain expectations of me as an Apex, about how we treat Mesos, and Demis, for example."

"Mesos? Demis?"

"Meso Shifters and Demi-Shifters. Any Shifter who is not an Apex. All Shifters understand we need a hierarchy in order to function. However, some Shifters take it further in how they deal with anyone who's not an Apex, treating other Shifters as lesser beings. It's become somewhat expected of us."

Stupid rich arseholes. But it was interesting to see this side of him. "And you don't agree?"

"It's not something I want to be a part of more than I have to." Another interesting statement.

"So what do they expect you to do as an almighty Apex?" I dropped my smile when I saw Anton was not in the mood for lighthearted banter.

"This is a conversation for another time." His eyes were on the table, and he looked grave. "When I want to get away, I come here. It's hardly admirable, but–"

"I can see you're trying to be better," I finished for him. He sounded so much older than his years, even though I didn't know how old he even was.

"You're too kind, Serrk." He ran his hand up his arm. "But ask me about something else instead."

I thought about it before raising my question. "What's a Nihil?"

"Where did you hear that?" He set his cup down on the table harder than I imagined he'd meant to, the sound echoing across the silence that followed his question.

"Allium." His name souring my tongue. I decided not to tell him about Scarlett yet.

"It's a derogatory term for Demi-Shifters. It's not one I approve of, but Allium feels differently."

"I see." I dropped the hair I realised I was playing with once again.

He studied me. "Tell me what you're thinking, seeing as I can't read your mind."

"Well, Allium is an arse, but you already knew I thought that. But I was wondering, just how old are you?"

Anton laughed. "That's fair, on both counts. And how old do you think I am?"

I had no clue how age worked in Domain and voiced my fear: "Oh no, you're eight hundred or something, aren't you?"

Anton smirked at the table. "Your imagination is something else, Serrk. Don't worry, I'm not too old for you. I'm only twenty-seven."

"That's not what I meant," I said, unable to add anything else, as I didn't want to rise to his challenge and become flustered once again. *Why did I sometimes get so silent around him?*

Without warning, his eyes lightened, and I could tell Allium was now present. "I need some space," he said before heading out of the room sharply and closing the door before I could sneak a look inside. Well, that was that.

Hoping Anton would return soon, I set about enjoying a warmer than usual shower, making use of all the fancy products provided. By the time I stepped out, I felt like a new woman. I found that the drawer under the mirror in my room housed makeup—including eyeliner. What a bonus. I spent as much time outdoors as I could to allow the sun to tan my skin and avoid the need for makeup. That said, even with my limited funds, I found it difficult to forgo eyeliner and mascara. They framed my hazel eyes with the perfect amount of, "hey you" or, "stay the fuck back", depending on my mood. It was still early, so I painted a natural look and selected a pair of sports leggings and a red fitted racer-back top from the wardrobe. I'd been moping about yesterday in my scruffy hoodie, however, if I was going to be here for a while, even a short while, I was going to make the most of some well-fitted outfits. Trainers finished the look nicely. I hoped I'd be able to find somewhere to run once my meeting with Anton's brother had finished. The thought pushed my nerves to one side. I'd barely even finished school, let alone college or university, but I imagined it would be something like that. It was surreal being here, but I couldn't help but feel that my luck had changed and that this was my second chance to live the life I wanted.

Fortunately, it was Anton and not Allium waiting by the time I returned. I didn't miss the clench in his jaw as he glanced over what I was wearing. He'd changed into a smarter outfit than my running gear and was now dressed in suit trousers of the darkest green and a crisp white shirt.

"I have some things to attend to this afternoon." He gestured to his clothes. "However, you'll be in excellent hands while I'm away."

"Okay. Where are we going to meet your brother?"

"The Bureau. It's Abduco headquarters. We do all our research there. We can leave whenever you are ready."

"What's he like?" I wondered if Viktor had an Other too, and if he was as obnoxious as Allium. I supposed he'd be good-looking like just about everyone else I met around here. These Shifters had a lot going for them. Bastards.

"Not like me. At all. You two will get on famously." I wondered what he meant by that and what he thought about how he and I got along. I brushed the thought aside as we left the flat and stepped out into the misty morning air.

It turned out there were various means of travel around Domain, including cars. However, given the ease of disappearing in one place and reappearing in another, travel Shifting was the most popular means. Anton had explained that Shifters required idols to travel this way. As long as they had the idol, they could travel between Domain and even into my world in the blink of an eye. An idol could be any object, though each Domain used similar things.

"Abduco Shifters use rings, passed down through the families for generations," said Anton as we landed on our feet outside a large, imposing building. "Caedes uses weapons. Persen have more freedom over what they choose, but it's always something small and easy to conceal, and Nexus uses their bees."

"Bees?"

"Yes, Serrk, I believe they have them in your world, too. Six legs, two sets of wings, makes honey."

"I know what a bee is. It's a little random that they're used for travel."

"I imagine someone from Nexus would tell you it wasn't random at all."

"I'll try to remember that," I said, unable to picture what that must look like and already feeling like I'd learned enough for one day, and I hadn't even started yet.

Anton was light on his feet for someone of his size, perfectly toned, as though being agile was part of his daily routine. I wondered how one moved through minds, and if that was in any way responsible for his developed physique.

As we entered the building, a grand staircase as wide as a road spread in front of me. The marble steps led to a platform which then split into two further staircases that reached their own landing, and the process continued so that each staircase halved in size with every new level. They continued right up to the ceiling, where the smallest were wide enough for only one person at a time to pass. Each led to a doorway that was illuminated by the same candles that dotted about the giant hall in clusters.

I'd been walking closer than I'd realised to Anton as he turned to me, the start contrast of both tones of his hair unmistakable. He sucked in through his teeth, as if bracing himself. There was about two feet between us, but we could have been touching by the tension that lingered in the air. It had been there all morning. *How could I be somewhere so fantastical yet all I wanted to look at was him?*

He peered at me through the strands of hair that hung down over his forehead, giving him a more carefree and boyish look.

"Prepare yourself. I'd like you to meet my brother, Viktor."

8

CHARITY

Shifter 101: To avoid confusion and unnecessary repetition, when addressing Shifters, use the name of their dominant personality only, unless expressly referring to their Other.

"**B**rother, and somehow best friend, is what you mean, Anton," a shout came from my left. I glanced and remembered that Shifter biology in Domain was different as Viktor bounded towards us. I recognised his tall stature and grin as the man who had saluted me when I'd arrived at the party with Anton. His rich brown skin made the blond stripe that ran through his hair even more striking. He was both taller and broader than Anton, and his short sleeves meant I could make out tattoos that ran around his massive biceps.

Viktor smiled to reveal perfect white teeth as he stepped towards me, and any residual tension in the air evaporated. "Charity, it is so good to meet you. I'm Viktor!" His voice carried the same honeyed tones as Anton, but with much more warmth. He was instantly likeable.

I returned his smile. "It's good to meet you too Viktor–oh!"

I had extended my hand to Viktor, but he lifted me with both arms as if I was a bag of sugar.

He set me down. "Sorry, girl, I prefer hugs over handshakes. Plus, how else can I remind everyone that not all Abducos have to be moody bastards all the time?"

I couldn't help but burst out laughing at his words. "Touché, and if you call that a hug, I'll take it."

He punched me in the shoulder as a reply, but in a brotherly way. He bore a family resemblance to Anton: the style, the grace, the hair, but in terms of personality, they were polar opposites.

Anton shifted his weight next to us, as if he had come to the same realisation, and the carefree look that he had been wearing vanished. I watched the muscle in his jaw twitch, and my stomach fluttered as it hit me. It was a sign of jealousy. He hated not being the centre of attention. Good.

Viktor looked between the two of us and read his brother's expression well. "Anton, calm down. I'm not here to steal anyone. As you know, half of me doesn't swing that way, anyway. So, I guess you're only half safe." It seemed the forwardness ran in the family. He winked at me while Anton rolled his eyes and whispered something in his ear.

The whisper sounded a lot like, "You know we're not like that," though I could have misheard, so, for my pride, I ignored it and instead looked up at Viktor, who stood well over head and shoulders taller than me.

I had to crane my neck to address him. "When you say half of you . . ."

Viktor laughed. "Yes, like Anton, I have an Other. He's Forrest and the better half of me. You'll meet him soon. We switch all the time, we're pretty similar. The only thing we don't switch is partners."

I laughed again.

Anton's expression was sour. "She doesn't need your life story in the first five minutes, mate."

This time, it was Viktor who punched Anton in the arm, much harder though still with love, earning himself a scowl from the latter. "But my life is so much more exciting than yours, brother dearest—who wouldn't want to hear about it?"

His laughter was infectious, and I couldn't help but giggle along, too. As Viktor joined in, my laughter rose to a cackle, and before long, we were helpless, our giggles echoing off the tall ceiling. Anyone passing seemed to think nothing of this and continued on their way. If Viktor was as notorious as his brother, his antics were too.

"I'll see if there's a room ready for you," said Anton. I'd never seen him like this. When he wasn't flirty, he was the epitome of Abduco, moody and grumpy.

"Sorry, Charity, I bring out the worst in him." Viktor gestured at his retreating back as we followed him across the vaulted room.

"Only because you're the happiest bloody Abduco around here." Anton groaned from ahead, massaging his temples.

"I've got no reason to be sad, mate," Viktor called to Anton. "Forrest is in a steady relationship with Julian, and I'm happy with my dating life."

"So you're bisexual?" I realised that was forward. But Viktor seemed like a forward guy.

"Depends on how you look at it. Forrest is gay, I'm straight. Call that what you will." He winked at me again. I didn't need to call it anything—good for him. "It's not without complications, but I couldn't be happier. Plus, it's a new year. What is not to like about life?"

"A new year?" I was confused. It was only November.

"Yeah, Abduco's season is autumn, so for us it's the new year. See, you're learning already!"

I grinned, wishing I could share his positive outlook. It must be nice to walk through life so carefree. Though, as we continued walking, I had to admit that my own worries had lifted, and even Anton eased up. By the time we had climbed the first flight of stairs, they had settled into friendly sibling banter that involved each winding the other up as much as possible.

We came to a halt outside a wooden door that led into a crescent-shaped room. It looked like a small lecture theatre, with rows of seats rising to the end. At the front, there was a large board and a desk, where someone would stand to speak. A large stained-glass window filled the curved wall at the back, sending soft light across the room.

The room was empty, apart from one person on the bottom row who appeared to be rolling a die. It was unclear what he was playing, though he appeared to glean something from the number he'd rolled as he cracked a smile, then stood up and walked towards us.

"Anton, Viktor, always a pleasure, and a new friend too. My dice roll told me it was going to be a good day." He extended a hand to me.

I shook it, unsure what to make of his introduction. I didn't know if it was a prerequisite in Domain that the guys here worked out, for I could see muscles even through his baggy clothes. He was just shorter than Anton, and had blond hair with pink dyed tips. His entire attire was comprised of black grungy style clothes. His tattooed skin was visible, all coloured with ink except for his face.

"Spyder, I forgot you were coming along too." Viktor interrupted my thoughts as he pulled him into a fierce hug. Spyder appeared to know Anton well too, as he slapped him on the shoulder.

Anton turned to me and bent down to murmur in my ear, sending a shiver through me. "You'll have fun today—guaranteed. Spyder has never had a boring day in his life." He then turned to his friend. "This is Charity."

Spyder looked ecstatic. "*The* Charity?

"Nice to meet you," I said. With his jigsaw piece hanging round his neck, Spyder looked like he didn't fit any mould. I knew little about Domain yet, but if I had to guess, he fitted Persen.

"I'm delighted you're here." He grinned, highlighting the snakebites pierced on his lower lip. "Do you ever wonder how many snails you've stepped on in your life without knowing about it? I do. It keeps me up at night just thinking about it."

I looked at him, bemused, before turning to Anton who gave me one of his smirks. "I need to go away and deal with some business. As I said, I'm leaving you in excellent hands. Oh, and take these." He passed me a notebook for all my *Shifter 101* as he called it, as well as a flashy phone, something much more high-tech than I'd ever owned.

I tucked the notebook under my arm and looked down at the screen of my new phone. To my surprise, a stream of letters flew out of the device and rearranged themselves in front of Anton. My stomach dropped as they spelled out:

Damn, you're gorgeous.

Anton smirked again. "It's a Shiftsung. It sends your thoughts, saves typing things out. Though you can turn it off if you like. It's Allium's technology. He developed the whole thing."

"Turn it off, NOW!" I demanded, mortified, as Viktor and Spyder fell about laughing.

Anton pressed some buttons and returned the phone to me, un-bothered. "I'll see you later. Just message if you need anything."

Without waiting for a reply, he turned and walked out the room with the exactness of an athlete. What an asshole.

Viktor leaned in. "Don't worry about it, Cee. Anton winds us all up." He eyed Spyder who was now twirling his jigsaw piece necklace. "Also, if you're going to be spending the day with us, you should know–Spyder, he's insane. It's one of the many reasons he's brilliant."

Spyder looked up and shrugged as if to confirm this.

"Do you have an Other?" I directed at Spyder, noticing he hadn't mentioned one.

He stuck out his tongue, which was pierced too, and made a face. "I did, Bradley, but he was far too beige for me. So I removed him. Now it's just me."

"Removed your Other?"

"Yeah, most Shifters choose to do this to make life easier for themselves once they get into relationships and things. Anton and I are the only two Apexes in our family who exist with their Others," Viktor explained. "It's a way of showing your true love, blah blah blah, and making sacrifices. So many people do it in marriage."

"Does it hurt?" It sounded a lot. Removing an entire part of yourself, like destroying part of your soul. I didn't know how I felt about it, but chose not to voice that, given I'd just met Viktor and Spyder.

"Meh, I've had worse," Spyder said, then winked. "I prefer life just me. It's easier to ground myself if I get too carried away."

I nodded as I took all this in, though the faint scent of gunpowder that lingered around him meant I could only imagine what he meant by getting 'carried away'. "How do they decide who removes who? Aren't all Others just as much as part of you?" I had to ask at least that much.

"It depends on who we consider as the Other. Bradley was my Other, so he went. Forrest is Viktor's Other, but they get on like a house on fire. Allium is Anton's Other. He's always under pressure to remove him."

I tried not to linger on that fact. As much as I hated Allium. I could see why Anton wouldn't want to remove an entire part of himself.

I realised Spyder was analysing me, holding the jigsaw piece up in front of my face as if it held answers. I questioned my theory out loud. "You're Persen, right?"

"Damn Charity, why do you even need to be here? You've got us all sussed already!" Viktor said just as Perrine entered the room in an aqua one piece. She glided with the same grace of the Shifters I'd seen and had her brown hair scrunched up on top of her head.

She approached the three of us and grinned at me. "Hi, everyone. Charity, it is good to see you again and I'll endeavour to bring you up to speed as soon as possible with everything. Spyder, I understand you already have ample knowledge of Domain, but you're here to refresh your knowledge following your adoption." Her voice softened when addressing Spyder, but he didn't seem affected by her words. "And finally–" she paused, looking confused at Viktor's presence.

"Anton wants me to watch Charity," Viktor said.

Perrine nodded. "Excellent. Then we'll get started. Today, we'll cover the fundamental elements of Shifter history."

Spyder moaned, "Are you really going to play the teacher's role with us? I already know all about that."

He received a harsh look from Perrine who said in a fierce voice, "Not from this perspective. From what I've been told, your presence here is as mandatory as Charity's, so I suggest you do not interrupt again."

Wow. This is not someone to mess with. Go Perrine. I added her name to the growing list of Shifters in Domain that fell into this category.

"Crikey, Ordette," said Viktor.

"Ordette?" I was confused again.

"Perrine's Other, she's badass," he replied.

I remembered Perrine had mentioned her Other when we'd met.

She sounded like a force to be reckoned with.

We took seats, and I found myself sandwiched between Viktor and Spyder. Perrine pulled down a screen that showed a projected image of a timeline. She explained Shifters had originated at the same time as humans, out of necessity, and had kept their existence a secret from the beginning.

"Write any of this down if you like," she added enthusiastically over Spyder's loud yawn.

I opened the notepad in front of me and figured it couldn't hurt to make a note about anything useful I learned about Domain.

Several hours flew by. I learned that there were originally four main Shifter families that operated out of Domain in order to coordinate and control the human mind. After many years of wars over territory, the four families divided everything up according to each House: the desert belonged to Caedes who destroy minds, the forests to Abduco who lead away from bad thoughts, the mountains to Persen who inspire, and the rose gardens to Nexus who heal. In order to keep things fair, they established a ruling body, known as the Cerebral Council, who would have the final say in all matters relating to Domain. The four Apex families passed down traditions through the centuries, with the same descendants of those families running their Houses today. "Everyone thinks Nexus has it easy, and healing is the soft option, but it's actually a troublesome thing to master," Perrine concluded.

I realised that somewhere during Perrine's explanation, Spyder had put two feet on the table in front of him. He leaned towards me. "What anyone from Nexus won't tell you is that Caedes are the ones that started the trouble and continue to cause it today."

This was new information to me. "Causing trouble in what way?"

It was Viktor's turn to lean in. He frowned, then added, "The Caedes gang, the Reapers, are famous for their development and use of

Mindchill. It's a drug that allows them to control Shifters by detaching mind and soul. It's dangerous and illegal but seeing as Shifters don't play by the rules anyway, it's difficult to enforce. Recently, it's been getting even worse press than usual, as Shifters have disappeared."

Perrine had heard us talking but didn't seem annoyed that we had gone off topic. Instead, she sat down and joined us. "So, what is being done about it?"

Viktor explained, "Well, we keep busy in Abduco trying to stop it entering our territory. Unfortunately, the only way we can do so is by adopting similar gang-like tactics ourselves. If you didn't already know, Anton and Allium run the Dragos."

I wasn't as shocked as I should have been. I suppose I hadn't been wrong about my early assumptions about Anton when he'd shown up in Drabshire.

Spyder chimed in, "And I manage the Hydras, though as some Persen Shifters are anti-politics, our numbers are nothing like Abduco and Caedes."

My first lesson was proving fruitful. "And what about Nexus?"

Perrine answered. "We used to have the Archangels, though they retired because of low numbers, with Nexus being a pacifist House and all."

"And how does the prophecy link in with all this?" I still couldn't work out how it all tied together.

I was stunned when they all recited what I'd heard earlier that morning:

Woman of both worlds,
A revolution on the horizon,
Four halves can be whole.
Unlikely allies hold answers to the past;

Only the burning rose can connect it all.

"That's only slightly creepy," I said, laughing.

Perrine continued, "Sorry, force of habit. All Shifters learn the great prophecies at school. Prophecy lore is just one of the subjects we study. We hear them so often, it's impossible not to know them off by heart. All of them have been fulfilled over history, except for the one that concerns someone from both worlds. It's the most anticipated and researched out of all the prophecies as it speaks of a huge forthcoming war. There are many who believe that it causes some of the unrest that Viktor and Spyder speak of, as different Shifters disagree about what should be done when such a being is discovered. Given they're going to be the reason for the war."

I stiffened in my seat. *Well, that doesn't sound good, Anton forgot to mention that part.* Viktor slid towards me as if he sensed my discomfort. Spyder was back to twirling his puzzle piece.

"But of course, you're most likely fine here. Especially if you have an Apex watching you." Her eyes lingered with hidden meaning, glittering.

"For Hymev's sake, be more obvious you two," said Spyder.

"Hymev?" I was unsure who he was speaking about.

"Just an old Shifter saying." Perrine's eyes were still focused on Viktor. "It comes from an old story about a Shifter called Hymev who had the rare ability to control the sky and fancied himself as a god."

"And he wasn't a god?" The words sounded incredible from my mouth. But given everything Shifters could do, if controlling the sky was on top of that, I could hardly blame the guy.

"We don't have gods here," Perrine said with conviction. "But he must have done some work to get others to see him as such, because the saying 'for Hymev's sake' remained."

By the time the lesson finished, my mind was buzzing with details of Apex families, Meso Shifters, Demi-Shifter humans, and the apparent hierarchy in place in Domain. Viktor and Spyder seemed like decent people, as well as Perrine of course. It was strange feeling like I had potential friendships here, something I had experienced for little of my life.

After once again clarifying I didn't want to blow things up with Spyder for the rest of the afternoon, I received my first assignment to look into the burning rose aspect of the strange riddle that was the prophecy. Perrine had helpfully supplied that Nexus was famous for roses and would be a good place to start. My next training session wasn't for a few days; in the meantime, Viktor and Perrine had instructed me to take everything in, read up on Domain customs and work on my assignment before then. There would be plenty of time for practising mind control and Shifter travelling, apparently. It was just as well, as the two concepts were alien.

Perrine left early as she had more duties to attend to in Nexus. As the rest of us exited the Bureau and back into the streets of Abduco, I enjoyed the smell of fresh rain for mere seconds before I was enveloped in the downpour that seemed constant here. Viktor offered me his jacket. "I can take you back to Anton's the same way you travelled here, if you're comfortable with that."

"That's fine." I was keen to see more Shifter abilities in use, even though it wasn't my favourite way to travel.

Spyder tipped us a salute kind turned away before remembering something and shouting back at us. "Oi, Charity?"

"Yeah?"

"We're partying a week on Saturday. You'd better be there. It's your arrival celebration after all and is being held in honour of you. We always have one when a Demi shows up. We'll show you how much better Persen is at partying than Abduco."

Viktor gave him a mock scowl, and I waved just as we turned on the spot and vanished, before appearing outside Anton's flat again.

This time Viktor said goodbye and assured me that Abduco held the better parties, voicing his astonishment that Anton hadn't told me about it already. I'd had little time to party back home, so I figured it might be fun to experience this new life I had, at least while I could, anyway.

As I climbed the wooden staircases, I realised just how mentally exhausted I was after today. I was accustomed to always keeping my guard up, but this was different. This was taking on new information at every opportunity. As much as I had so many questions for Anton, a part of me just wanted to sleep in my comfy bed and let everything wash over me.

I reached the flat and let myself in, using the key Anton had somehow put into my leggings pocket. My phone buzzed as I stepped through the door.

Anton: I need to go away for a few days on business. Viktor informs me you already know about the arrival celebrations taking place on Saturday. The flat should have everything you need, and Viktor's number is on your phone. Don't leave unless he knows about it - AA.

That was quick, though things moved that way here. He must have just left as the flat still smelled like him; that, and the kettle was warm. I wondered if he'd signed his message from Anton Abduco or Anton and Allium. A part of me scoffed that there was another order in there, but seeing as he wasn't here to argue with, I guessed that bed was my next option. The minute my head hit the pillow, I slipped into the soundest sleep I'd had in years.

The days passed in a sea of leafy walks, attempts at finding references to burning roses in the books Anton had in his flat, and looking into Shiftstory, a term I'd learned was for Shifter history. By the end of the week, I'd got a handle on the basics and would recognise which House a Shifter belonged to if I saw them in the street, though was no closer to any connection to the burning rose.

Perrine had been in touch, and we'd set aside tomorrow in order to go shopping for the party later that day. It would also give us time to explore Nexus in relation to the burning rose.

Meanwhile, I had barely seen Anton since I'd agreed to stay at his flat. I wondered if that was intentional. Any time I had seen him, I was relieved Allium had the sense not to show himself. While the initial anger of our first meeting had rubbed off, I was in no mood to entertain him. However, I also didn't want to be rude to Anton, given I had somewhere to stay after all.

In some ways, it was everything I'd dreamed of back in my world: having my own place. Not having to look over my shoulder, at least not within the four walls of my so-called home, anyway. Yet, it still wasn't enough. I felt selfish for feeling that way; this life was already so much more than I'd experienced back in my world. I wondered how my mother was getting on. Despite not wanting to see her, I hoped she could find the strength to be happy on her own and get herself back on the straight and narrow. *A tall order, I know.*

I guiltily remembered that I still hadn't asked Anton about my mother's reaction to Wyatt and took the phone Anton had given me out of my pocket. I rarely used it, and always kept it out of sight, just in case it was watching me or listening in.

Before I could second guess myself, I typed a message out and sent it into the unknown.

Charity: I have a question for you.

Anton: Go ahead - AA.

Charity: What happened to Wyatt? And how is my mother doing?

I paced the room for almost an hour as I waited for a reply. Finally, once I'd assumed I'd have to ask him when he was back, my phone chimed with a message.

Anton: She is learning to live alone and enjoy it. Wyatt has taken up beekeeping in the woods near Drabshire. He now prefers their company to humans, though cannot work out why he gets stung so often, despite taking good care of them - AA.

Charity: Wow, you really put thought into these scenarios don't you?

Anton: I aim to please - AA.

I was still chuckling over Wyatt's fate—it was more than he deserved—when Anton's last message came through, sending butterflies straight to my stomach with their double meaning. It seemed my mother hadn't taken long to forget Wyatt at least. I put the phone down, feeling lighter than I had in days. Despite my feelings towards her, I didn't want to see her come to any harm, so I was pleased to see she was learning to cope on her own, even if she'd had some Shifter persuasion without her knowing. I brushed away my thoughts of feeling unfulfilled aside. There was plenty of time to work out what I wanted to do with my life. I could enjoy a few home comforts for a few days and worry about that later.

It turned out clothes weren't all Anton had provided. Although he was out for most of the week, the fridge was always full of the freshest foods and all the clothes I left hanging on the chair in my room seemed to find their way back into my wardrobe clean and pressed again. I assumed he must have had some sort of housemaid who came when I was out exploring. The luxuries some people had when they were that rich.

Friday rolled around, and I drew the curtains to another rainy and misty morning in Abduco. *I know this weather would be perfect for some, but give me a burning sun or a crisp breeze any day.* That said, it made good running weather, so I wasn't one to complain. After only investigating the immediate vicinity of Anton's flat, the rebellious side of me was itching to ignore his request. I hadn't been on a run since I'd left my flat, my old home, on Monday. What a different life that felt like. I guess it was.

Fuck it. My wardrobe was full of trainers and gym gear. He'd told me to let Viktor know if I was leaving, but I'd snuck out several times already with no repercussions, so I guessed today was no different. I showered and changed into black leggings, a burgundy sports bra, and trainers of a similar colour. I swept my long hair up so that my face was free of any distractions and again cursed for not having my original bag here with my earphones.

The cool air dusted my face as I closed the door to the glamoured building. I turned and headed up the deserted street towards a leafy trail that led into a thicker part of the forest. I breathed in the smell of earthy rain that seemed to linger here, grateful for the canopy above that provided cover from the worst of it. Although it was still early, it could have been evening under those trees. It was mysterious, though not scary. More entrancing, like a place where I could escape.

Left

Right

Left

Right

I increased my pace and kept my wits about me to avoid tripping on any large roots that made up my bumpy trail. It was incredible to get out of the flat and to feel *free* again. No walls, no doors, just space to move. I pounded the ground, working my way up to a sprint, but something was missing, something that would allow me to feel that euphoria I could only find when I was running as fast as my lungs would allow. My music. Without it I was only eighty per cent there; good, but still not enough. I ran faster still, chasing the high I knew I couldn't catch, wanting that escape, craving it. Eventually I tired, just as my foot collided with an angled root and my heart leapt in the moment both feet left the ground.

Shit.

I landed in a heap, clutching my ankle as if that would somehow take the pain away. I sat there for what felt like an eternity, avoiding the knowledge of how injured I was. When the damp had worked its way into my leggings, I gingerly rose to my feet and tried to put weight on it. It wasn't comfortable, but I could manage. Running would be off the cards for a few days, and I swore in frustration. Being here was incredible and a damn sight better than what I'd come from, but I still felt so restricted, so limited. Just because you set a hamster free in the jungle, doesn't mean it will thrive.

It took me much longer to retrace my steps, and I imagined it must have been late afternoon by the time I'd returned to Anton's flat. I'd been so used to walking into the empty space, I wasn't expecting him to shoot up from the sofa the second I walked in the door, his face awash with concern and annoyance.

"Where have you been?" he demanded.

"Out, running." At least I sounded braver than I felt.

"You didn't notify Viktor."

Feigning concern, I answered, "I didn't realise I had to."

I began taking my shoes off and winced as I struggled to remove the trainer on my sore foot.

Anton's anger evaporated as he narrowed his eyes. "What happened?"

"Like I said, I was out running, and then I fell."

"Sit down, leg up, now." His voice was a growl and while I internally screamed that I didn't take orders, another part of me melted. The two sides of me battled it out, and finally I obliged before I knew what I was doing.

Anton removed my shoe with surprising care and examined my ankle. The coolness of his rings was such a contrast to the heat of his skin. I studied one as he worked. It was silver and had a dragon etched into the onyx stone. I couldn't work out which I preferred, the heat or the coolness. They were both comforting in their own way. Several seconds felt like hours as he gently pressed each part of my swollen ankle with a feather-light delicacy I didn't expect him to have. All I could think was that I didn't want the contact to go.

"Does this hurt?"

"No."

"Here?"

"Ow! Yes."

His hands passed over the tender part of my ankle, sending a delicious tingle up my spine. "As you know healing is more of a Nexus thing, but given it's not serious, I can fix this if you'd like."

I nodded. I did that a lot these days. Since meeting him, I was running my mouth or resembling one of those nodding dog ornaments people used to put in their cars. Not that I'd had one, or even a car, for that matter. But they were funny.

I flinched, but it wasn't from the contact. I thought I'd seen a flicker of movement up his arm, disappearing behind his sleeve. Then I realised his arm, *his tattoo* was moving. The scales of the dragon were shimmering and smoke curled around his arm, looking incredibly realistic.

"Did I hurt you?" His rough voice jerked me from my thoughts.

"No, I was just looking at your tatt–" I stopped short. "Is that *moving*?"

Anton glanced down at his arm and the corner of his mouth tipped up in a smile. "I should have mentioned tattoos in Domain do that. They are still when we're in your world, so as not to attract suspicion."

That was pretty awesome, but I didn't tell him that. "Nice," I summarised.

Anton continued working on my ankle before he spoke barely louder than a breath. "Lean into me."

"Sorry?" My mind tried to catch up with his words.

Anton raised his brows to suggest he knew exactly how I'd reacted to his words. "I need to channel the healing into you directly so you can heal yourself. It's how our abilities work."

Hesitating, and knowing this was a bad idea, I shuffled closer and leaned in. I could smell woody smoke, like someone was burning the most delicious fire. *Why am I so attracted to trouble? And where has he been all this time? He looks tired.*

"Serrk?"

"Yes, sorry?"

"How's that now?"

I looked down. The swelling had subsided, and my ankle tingled rather than throbbed. "Better. Thanks."

The smirk returned with a hint of warmth. "Anytime."

I took advantage of this rare moment of calm. "Where were you? You were gone for days."

The warmth left his gaze. "Like I said, on business."

That was that then. I was about to question him on what he meant when I noticed my foot still in his hand. I didn't know what had happened to the time in the room, but we both seemed frozen there. He didn't remove his hand. I didn't remove my foot. *Had he got closer?* It was difficult to form coherent thoughts when I was sitting next to him like this. We were so lost in the moment, neither of us registered the shuffling at the front door, which was still open.

"What the *fuck* is going on?"

My head snapped round. I knew that voice.

It was Scarlett, and she was furious. She looked like she was going to explode as her gaze focused on my foot still in Anton's lap.

Then the penny dropped. Perrine saying she felt sorry for Scarlett's boyfriend.

Surely not.

Anton's brow furrowed as he kept his hand on my ankle. His touch burning into my leg. "Scarlett, I thought I told you we wouldn't meet here."

What kind of response is that?

"I'm pretty sure I can meet my boyfriend where and when I like," she snapped, her words punching me in the gut as I removed my foot like it had been touching flame. She couldn't be his. She was *vile*. Still, a part of me couldn't help but feel a stab of guilt. I would have felt the same were the roles reversed. It didn't help the hurt that was spreading across my chest. I'd been so stupid. Anton watched my reaction, the tension in his jaw visible.

Scarlett kept talking. "What does Allium think? I know you two are a package deal, but I'm sure he'd have a thing or two to say about *her* being here."

I stayed silent, not trusting myself to speak to either of them. All I could think about was how I'd got myself involved in something very wrong.

Anton's tone was stern. "She's here for the prophecy and you know that. Go to Abduco Manor. Mother is expecting you for dinner as we had planned for tonight. I'll meet you there in five."

Was I imagining his tone with her?

"Fine, babe." Then she turned to me a final pointed look, which I returned, before she sashayed out the door, slamming it behind her.

He looked up at me guiltily. "In case it wasn't obvious. That was Scarlett. My girlfriend."

That bastard.

9

ΛNTON

Shifter 101: An Apex may not enter into a relationship with a Meso Shifter or Demi-Shifter without prior approval from both sets of parents. The exception to this is when the pair are recognised as Covalents.

S *hit.*

That hadn't gone the way I'd thought. The minute Scarlett entered the room, I sensed the tension in Charity's leg still resting on mine. In some ways, it was a good thing that she'd had come in–I'd been seconds away from leaning into Charity and making a mess of everything. Everyone knew I was a flirt, and we'd entered into some strange game of flirting with Charity to prompt a reaction and irk her. But I imagined she had little idea just how much she affected me. I couldn't let her in, let her know just how much she fascinated me from the second I'd watched her put three others before herself moments after being on the receiving end of some of the shittiest acts of humankind. Wyatt had got lucky that Nexus had been involved in the decision-making process over what to do with him. I would have planned far worse for him.

The door to Charity's room slammed, jolting me back into the realisation that I'd fucked my chances with her. She now considered me some kind of cheating bastard. If we were talking about mentally, then she was right. I was grateful I'd switched my Shiftsung to private mode, so that I wasn't giving her a blow-by-blow account of some scenes that danced through my head whenever I was around her. Yes, I technically was a taken man, but if she knew the circumstances of that, she might see things differently. Might see me differently.

After all, she wasn't only selfless; she was outspoken and not afraid to stand up for what she wanted, and for the love of Hymev, *the way her hips moved when* . . .

Her very absence in the room told me this was not what I should think about right now. But despite that, there were times I'd caught her looking. Wondered if she felt something, too. Not for Allium, of course. His apathy towards her was similar as far as I knew. He shut off most of what he felt around her, but I knew him well enough to guess. Allium liked to see something already broken and pulverise it. Granted, I wasn't perfect, sometimes even cruel, but he was on a whole other level.

The second she'd understood about Scarlett, Charity couldn't have moved from me quickly enough. I wished I could tell her that anything between Scarlett and I is all a fabrication, set up between two fathers more interested in power than their children's happiness. But then I'd have to tell her everything about me. And if she hadn't already run, she would then.

I massaged my temples as I stared at her bedroom door. It stayed closed. I thought about knocking and giving her some kind of explanation, but something told me she needed the space. Plus, I had work to do for the Dragos tonight. Not that I wanted to. It had all seemed so simple in the beginning, maintaining the territories and keeping order. But I'd soon seen the much darker side of gang life in Domain. Yet, provided I kept up the facade that this was my life and I loved it, everyone was safe. As safe as one could be in a world that was heading towards a war. These disappearances linked to Mindchill were getting more common, and I reminded myself with a shiver that we wouldn't keep it out of Abduco forever.

But I'd deal with the catastrophes closer to home first; and I was going to do some serious damage control. Act like the ever-faithful boyfriend to Scarlett. She was a Meso Shifter but an ambitious one, keen to work her way up to Apex status through marriage. I couldn't tell if she liked me. She was possessive, but she didn't know the first thing about me. I didn't care. If I wasn't an Apex, she wouldn't look at me twice, and, in all honesty, it would be fucking easier that way for a lot of things.

I groaned, realising I'd told Scarlett there had been an ongoing glitch with the glamour for my apartment when I'd first shown her the derelict building I'd be living in instead of the mansion next to my mother and father's. I'd laid it on thick, telling her it wasn't safe for her here. I'd hoped it would deter her, but she seemed to think I'd change my mind about living in somewhere so atrocious. She, of course, hadn't seen what this place looked like. She must have broken through the glamour when it allowed Charity through. She must have been following her, and I had Allium to thank for that.

A growl rose in my throat at that until I realised I had no right to be possessive over Charity. She wasn't mine, and Allium could allow who he wanted into our apartment.

Fuck fuck fuck. I couldn't be thinking like this. This was why I needed Allium. Ruthless. Cunning. Cold. Perfect. If it weren't for him, I'd have crumbled ages ago.

My responsibilities with The Dragos had eaten into my time, and tonight was no exception. It turns out justice didn't care what was going on in your personal life. Who would have fucking thought?

When I realised Charity would not come out of her room anytime soon, I summoned my bodyguard, Bronx, and we headed to deal with two Reapers from Caedes caught trying to distribute lethal doses of Mindchill. These were small pawns in the scheme of things. But they'd been trying to deal outside a school and that was enough for them to be placed on my hit list. I'd done so many unsavoury things during my lifetime. This was my way of giving something back.

It was midnight, and the hostages had revealed nothing. My father had warned me to stay away from what he called 'petty crime', but Viktor and I had several side projects within the Dragos that he didn't know about, and planned to interrogate them, *interrogate* being the polite word. We were in an abandoned warehouse on the border of Abduco. Unknown to anyone else, Allium had glamoured the building to look more decrepit than it was. In an area with so much wealth, people left broken things alone. And that's how I liked it.

Bronx had been my bodyguard for three years now. He'd been following from a distance all week. I'd told him to keep away, not wanting to unnerve Charity. He cut quite an image: seven feet tall, buzz cut, built like a tank, and always dressed in leather. Bronx had links to the Ivanov dynasty in Eastern Domain. While not an Apex family, they had connections to all aspects of the crime underworld and were more than capable of handling their own. In short, he was a handy man to have around, even if he always smelled of leather and blood.

"You want something to drink, boss? Last time, you stay all night," he said with a slight accent.

I rubbed my bloody knuckles, willing Allium to come back and take over; this was where he excelled. Something to take the edge off would help. "Whiskey. Straight."

Bronx rubbed his shaved head and disappeared behind the bar.

The low light of the room offered little to no description of where we were or who we were with. I preferred it that way. Preferred to see as little as possible.

They're Shifters of the lowest rank, Allium reminded me. *Get on with it.* It gave me the strength I needed to carry on.

I channelled my anger into my fist and had to admit it wasn't awful when it connected with one of the men's noses, breaking it on impact. I might not have enjoyed all aspects of gang life, but I was still an Apex. We were Alphas, top of the food chain. The man strained at the ropes tethering his hands and spat in a rage, but he was powerless to do anything. They always were. He was lucky Allium was taking a step back tonight and letting me work out my demons, otherwise he would have brought his toolbox out and gone to town on these fuckers. We saved the real offenders for Spyder. Man, was that kid fucked up. But he had a one hundred per cent success ratio with interrogations, so he was also useful to have around.

I snarled at the fucker in front of me who thought that he could ignore my line of questioning. "I'll ask you again, who supplied you with Mindchill? Who are you working for?"

"I already told you," the Shifter spat at my feet, "you're wasting your time."

Viktor's eyes were sombre. Apart from Allium, Viktor was the only one who knew how much I hated this part of my life. Not that I hated gang life–I *wanted* to punish anyone who distributed the Mindchill that was wreaking havoc throughout the House of Abduco. I just hated having to act like I thrived on the gore and violence when I didn't. I just wanted to make things right again and didn't know any other way how. Having to act and behave in a certain way in order to keep everyone happy. Having to make sure I calculated every move, so that I didn't upset or endanger anyone.

I could tell Viktor wanted to be elsewhere as much as me, but we had a job to do. Seeking justice for those who couldn't speak up for themselves didn't let you take a weekend off just because you fancied a break. I forced myself to think about what these men had done as I rolled my sleeves up theatrically. "We've been pretty lenient with you so far, but you haven't met my Other yet. He might not be so kind."

The man gained a sense of confidence despite his precarious situation. "Give me a break. You Abducos can't scare us. What are you going to do? Lead me away from my next poor decisions? In Caedes, we destroy minds; we cause *actual* damage. It's you that should feel threatened."

My Apex instincts kicked into overdrive, and my fists curled. Maybe a part of me thrived on this after all. Allium came further forward into my mind, not taking over, but urging me on.

He's asking for it. He's insulting your entire family. Our entire family.

Allium wasn't lying.

"Oh, looks like I've struck a nerve with our chief Apex. Not so tough–"

Another punch to the face broke his sentence.

And again.

And again.

And again.

Viktor had the sense not to flinch. This part of gang life he was used to. Blood sprayed back, covering my suit, and Allium basked in it, wanting more. He always wanted more.

The Mesos we'd brought with us, new Dragos recruits, were looking up at me in awe like I was something.

You are something, Anton. You're the leader they need.

I let Allium flicker at the edges of my consciousness, letting him take the reins as I swallowed my guilt. On the twelfth punch, the other hostage crumbled, and revealed the rest of the supply was at an abandoned mansion about a mile from Abduco headquarters. We'd despatch a team there and have it recovered within the evening.

Bronx returned with my whiskey and removed the men, one now unconscious, to have their memories modified before returning them to Caedes. We could have killed them, but we saved that for the ones that deserved it. Better to send them back and monitor their movements in order to reach the supplier. Memory changing was illegal in Domain. The Cerebral Council had banned it decades ago when it became apparent the Reapers had been planning a coup. Nearly everyone involved was sentenced to a lifetime in Langison. Their souls still floated through the great river into the sea today. I shivered. It was a prospect worse than death. Existing endlessly. Unable to die, unable to heal, unable to do anything but float, barely conscious for all eternity.

But as long as we were thorough, it was worth the risk. Given pretty much everything we did was illegal anyway, there was little difference.

I sipped my drink, the praise from the new recruits falling flat at my feet. Allium took it all in. He was my silent hero. He gave them what they needed and played the parts I couldn't.

I wiped a hand on my suit jacket, frowning at the fact it was yet another jacket ruined with the smell of blood. There was something else however, a faint scent of charred petals, rose.

Her.

It seemed seconds ago we'd been in my flat and she had leaned into me as I took longer than I needed to examine her ankle. The brief contact was all she'd needed to mark my clothes with her scent. Well, if *that* wasn't a fucking metaphor for the way she'd bulldozed into my life and taken over. I couldn't blame her. It was my task to bring her here. I'd allowed her to stay at mine. Granted, she'd only agreed because she thought I wasn't living there. I had been so sure she'd say no when I'd offered, and then I'd seen her face when she'd seen my home. No one had ever looked at it that way before, like they'd understood. Hymev, I barely even knew her. But I couldn't help but admit she fascinated me.

Allium frayed at my thoughts, annoyed. He was right. We were losing focus. I returned to the task at hand and let him take over as Bronx led in the next band of hostages to be interrogated.

Later that night, I sat swirling more whiskey in front of the fire at my family home. I needed a fuck ton of whiskey to get through nights like tonight. My father paced up and down the room, drinking from his own glass.

My father's boss, Draven, completed our unhappy social gathering. "I said monitor her, not bring her to your house." He slammed his glass down on the walnut table. He was broad-shouldered and had the signature Caedes red hair that fell in thick waves past his shoulders. But the most unnerving thing about him was his eyes. They were amber tinged with red. He hadn't had an Other in the time I'd known him, so I didn't know what the eye colour was about. I didn't know anyone else with eyes like that, but it was unnerving, even to me. You did not want to get on his wrong side.

My father was a powerful man, but then, so was Draven, and being from Caedes, he was much less predictable. They had worked together for over two decades, though their relationship had changed. What had started off as a close friendship had turned into a steady case of blackmail from Draven to my father. I was tangled up in it along the way through my work with the Dragos. It was another reason I chose the line of undercover work I did. To show them that no one fucking controls me.

I chose my words carefully, not wanting them to draw any conclusions. Not that there was any to draw after tonight, anyway. "She wasn't willing to study at Abduco Manor. It was that or return to her world without completing her Actuation."

Draven turned to me. "Do you realise how that looks? A De–*Nihil* living with you?"

I ignored his question. It looked bad. "You asked me to bring her here and train her for her Actuation. I did what I had to do to ensure I carried out your instructions. I was expecting more of a thank you."

My father narrowed his eyes at me in warning. I was pushing it, and I knew it. I didn't tell them I'd outright offered her to stay with me because I was just as cautious about the things that went on in this house as she was. My father spent a lot of time cooped up here. It was reflected in his sallow skin. He gave me one of his looks. "We ask you to do a lot of things. That doesn't mean you twist them to suit you."

I laid it on thick. I had to appeal to his better nature, not that he had one. "Trust me. I'd much rather someone like her wasn't living under the same roof as me." How could I have been so stupid? I'd risked everything by bringing her to mine. By acting on impulse. I'd seen the fear cross her face when I'd mentioned staying at Abduco Manor. There was a story there for sure, but it was unlikely she'd ever share it with me. Despite that, I knew about the things that went on here and couldn't bring her to suffer more.

"Perhaps she could stay in Caedes instead. There are plenty of options in our stronghold for her," said Draven.

If there was one place that was more dangerous than here, it was fucking Caedes. The whole place was a ticking time bomb. Fortunately, my father jumped in before my heart jumped right out my chest. "Won't it look in poor taste? We've already planned the arrival celebrations here at Abduco Manor for her."

Thank fuck for my family and their social climbing tenancies.

Although I could hear Allium screaming in protest, I leaned on my father's point. "Plus, it might look suspicious."

"Fine. Keep her here. I trust everything is in order for the arrival celebrations?" said Draven.

"Yes," my father replied. "They will take place before her training begins for her Actuation. We'll be able to monitor everything."

Draven made a tutting sound. "It will be a waste of time, anyway. She's unremarkable and will be back in her world before she knows it." He then paused and turned his attention back to me. "What did you think of her?"

My heart skipped a beat. "What?"

"What was she like?" Draven was eyeing me. He then mistook my silence for something else, or, if I was being honest, he mistook nothing at all. "Don't tell me you're getting attached?"

My father narrowed his eyes at me. "Anton, you know you can't. We can't. It's not our way unless–"

"Unless it's an Apex I know, or the adopted daughter of an Apex too, of course," I said, gesturing to Draven. "And believe me when I say there is no attachment there. Allium enjoys taunting her. She's a simple girl from a simple world." At least there was one accurate statement in there.

"Good. Make her feel it." The low light illuminated the scars that lined Draven's arms and neck as he spoke.

His statement didn't surprise me. Caedes were the least tolerant Domain of humans. They didn't even refer to the ones that came here as Demis, instead using the derogatory term *Nihils* instead. They all but detested them, despite our purpose for being here being so interconnected. It was a train of thought that was spreading to Abduco. Trust my luck to have my father and him scheming to bring our families together at mine and Scarlett's expense. If she'd been decent, I might have even felt bad for her having a man like Draven for an adopted father.

My father tried to refill my whiskey, but I covered the glass. "I'm fine thanks, there're some things more whiskey can't solve."

My father pursed his lips. I'd hear about that one later.

Draven's voice dropped. "You let him away with too much, Verde. If that were my son—"

My father found his feet. "But he's my son, not yours."

Draven stood with his chest thrust out, his muscles flexed in the deadliest stance. "You think it wise to test me? If it weren't for me, you'd be in Langison, rotting away. Slowly."

The conversation continued back and forth for some time. It should have been soul destroying, hearing such things, such threats and atrocities, but I was used to it, and instead cursed my family's poor decisions for the millionth time as I drank up.

It was time to leave, and we rose from our seats in the dark room. I knocked the last of my whiskey back in one bitter go. As Draven left, my father turned to me. "I mean it, Anton, you do not get attached."

Even if I didn't want to understand, Allium did. He purred with satisfaction at the request.

10

CHARITY

Shifter 101: Humans may only enter Domain in order to test the prophecy.

"**I** know they say it's Nexus Shifters that specialise in healing, but I have to admit Anton did a great job." Perrine grinned as she examined my ankle. "There's nothing more I can do here."

We met outside Anton's and Perrine spoke to something in her hand; the next thing I knew, we were standing in a tree-lined street. We sat under a large cherry blossom so Perrine could heal my foot before we walked anywhere, though that was unnecessary now. In contrast to Abduco, the weather in Nexus suggested it was spring or summer. A breeze warmed my cool skin, and I inhaled the aroma of the sweet blossom that fell from the trees. There were many benefits to Abduco, but I had to admit, it was nice to feel the sun on my face instead of the constant drizzle. I felt like I was the only person who ever got wet there, too. I reminded myself to ask Anton how that worked.

"Anyway, your ankle is fine. You'll be able to walk on it normally. He's completely fixed it," she concluded.

"Of course he did," I said, rolling my eyes. Perrine's eyes widened as I explained last night's revelation about Scarlett.

"I'm so sorry; I assumed Anton had told you," she apologised.

"It's okay. How could you have known I'd put my foot in it?"

"Literally," Perrine admitted, and we couldn't help but giggle at that. "But that's not to suggest you don't still have a chance. Anyone who sees them together can see how awkward they are. It's a strange choice, that's for sure."

I tried not to read too much into her words. As far as I was concerned, Anton was a flirt, but that was it. And a spoken for flirt was still off-limits. I couldn't deny that there was some chemistry, though for all I knew, he had that with everyone.

"Maybe you'll meet someone at the party," Perrine said with a wink.

"I think I'd better worry about other things, like this prophecy, and what I'm doing with my life," I shrugged, the absurdity of that statement sending a chill through me.

"I disagree. From what you've told me about where you came from, you've earned this. Enjoy it."

We stood and walked up the street. As we turned the corner, I froze. I recognised this.

"Everything okay?" Perrine asked.

"I think I've been here before." I explained about the dream that I'd had.

"Ooooh, that sounds like Nexus. What did it look like?"

"I was up high, in some sort of garden, looking over the city."

Perrine was jumping up and down with excitement. "I know where! Dress shopping can wait!"

We stood in the rose garden from my dream. The outlook was the same: the same Parisian landscape with the waterfall around where the Eiffel Tower should have been.

Standing somewhere that I had only dreamed of should have scared me. But I guess that was how Domain worked. The mind related to everything. It almost made sense. "It's just beautiful." I turned around, taking it all in. "Just like Paris. Or what I imagine Paris would be like." After all, I had never visited.

Perrine laughed. "Where do you think the Parisians got their ideas from? Believe it or not, this was here first."

A large bee landed on one of the rose bushes. It was much bigger than normal, about the length of my finger. Like in my dream, I knew they wouldn't hurt me. Bees weren't hostile creatures, and despite its size, I had no reason to think any differently. It was incredible; its wings glistened iridescent in the sunlight and its rose gold and black body matched the tones here. If each House in Domain had its own colour palette, Abduco was green, but Nexus was a pale rose gold.

"They're our idols. We can communicate with them, though only Nexus Shifters can. Did Anton explain about idols?"

"He mentioned Shifters need them to travel. When you do that thing where you instantly vanish and reappear somewhere else."

"Yes, Abduco has their rings. We use bees." Of course. Now I knew what she'd been speaking to in her hand when we'd travelled here.

Unsure whether it was from processing the sensory overload before me or something else, an ache was forming in my head, similar to the one I had after my dreams.

We split up and looked around the entire garden. I found more bees as I felt my way around the rose bushes, looking for any that stood out from the rest. Despite feeling eerily familiar, there was nothing in particular that called to me.

After about twenty minutes of searching, we met back up in the middle of the grounds.

"Any luck?"

"Nope. No burning roses here." I sighed to myself. I had been sure we would find something.

"Damn." Perrine threw her hair over her shoulder as she shook her head. "I really thought we were onto something with your dream."

"Don't tell anyone about my dreams please," I said, knowing I could trust Perrine. "I'm maybe confused. Maybe it's a dream I had since I was here. Or maybe someone planted it there. Anton said Shifters can do that."

"Rubbish. I could tell you were something from the start. You'll have no problem with your Actuation, I know it."

I wasn't so sure. Apart from that encounter in the alleyway with the men which I still hadn't come to terms with, I just couldn't see how I could now access a bunch of untapped power inside of me.

A small voice told me I couldn't be that great. *In case it wasn't obvious,* he'd said, *my girlfriend.* He was an Apex Shifter, so it made complete sense he'd have someone like her.

I brushed the thought aside. "Let's go shopping. Anton said he's given you the money," then frowned as I realised what this meant. "He must not trust me."

Perrine looked embarrassed but said nothing. I gaped at her as we made our way down the hill towards the shops, and she remained silent. "He *doesn't* trust me?" My heart hammered against my ribs. I'd been half joking when I said it, but did Anton think I was going to run off at the first sign of money? Although he'd lied, he'd also given me more comfort and security in the past few days than I'd had in my life. I wasn't going anywhere.

"No, it's not that." Perrine kept her eyes at her feet.

"Well, what is it then?"

"It doesn't matter. The amount isn't the issue at all." Perrine was stumbling over her words now, and her cheeks had gained a faint rosy tint.

She was behaving oddly, twisting her hands as I studied her. "Just how much did Anton give you?" I put my hand on her arm to stop us. "What is it, Perrine? You can tell me."

She kept her eyes on the ground. "Well, he didn't give me an amount. In Domain, we use Neurocurrency."

"Yes, I remember. I saw Anton. Neuro as in . . ." I trailed off. It sounded too bizarre to finish my sentence out loud.

Luckily, Perrine finished for me. "Yes, as in our minds. We process everything to do with currency using Shiftcoins. Just like you have cryptocurrency in your world. It's all in our minds. It's not been around for that long and is very useful, saves us carrying purses and crime rates have even dropped too."

I grinned as I realised something. "So, you're telling me Anton has asked us to get something for tonight and he hasn't given us a spending limit?"

She gave me a small smile. "Something like that."

She was still acting oddly. Though I could hardly talk, this was the first time I'd been able to shop without looking at the price tags before. We spent the afternoon walking into the type of shops that I'd only seen in magazines. It was surreal trying on velvet ball gowns simply because we could. Next came extravagant ostrich feather dresses and finally, a gold silk one that Perrine said would be perfect for the arrival party.

"You are the reason the party is happening, after all!" She giggled. Her mood had improved since I'd told her to think about the dresses and not the prices. Together, we were pretending the tags didn't exist.

"Don't remind me. Everyone is making this big deal and is just going to be disappointed. I'd rather just blend in and enjoy myself."

That wasn't true. A part of me didn't mind being the centre of attention. It was a delightful change to be noticed for the right reasons. However, Perrine wasn't one to brag, and I mirrored her. She was someone I could trust and might be a good friend. I didn't want my big mouth impeding that.

"Aren't you getting anything?" I became aware that she'd stopped trying on dresses.

Perrine tucked her hair behind her ear and muttered something about already having a dress, without looking at me.

I straightened the strap on a silver metallic dress. There was something different about the material of Shifter clothes. This one looked like liquid metal and I could see tiny movements in the fabric as I looked in the mirror, as if the metal was flowing. It skimmed my hips, and I knew that this was the one.

"It's beautiful," said Perrine. "You should get that one."

"I have to admit, it feels great. Your turn now."

"I already said I've got–"

"Perrine, I'm only here because of Anton's money. I don't have any of my own, so I'm not judging. If he didn't have so much, I wouldn't even be here spending his, but he does, and I believe you deserve it just as much as I do, if not more."

Perrine's eyes watered. "It's not just that. Charity, I don't come from the same background as the likes of Anton. My family would be disgusted if I came home wearing something that cost as much as the dresses in these shops. I only came here because I know Anton will expect you to wear something like this. He gave me a list of establishments to go to."

"He gave you a *what?*" The anger in me flared, and then I processed the important part of what she'd just said. "I'm sorry, I didn't realise. I know what it's like to feel you have nothing. My family wasn't the nicest, so I'm grateful for this second chance."

Perrine's eyes widened. "Oh no, I didn't mean my family was horrible. My family is *lovely*. But it wouldn't be fair to them to wear something that cost more than what we earn in a month."

"I understand," I said. I took a last look at the stunning gown in the mirror. Dresses were nice, but friends were more important. I'd never had these things in my old life. I could manage just fine without them here, too.

"Thank you." She stood sheepishly outside the changing room, wringing her hands. "I'm sorry. I find it difficult to talk about. It shouldn't be something I'm ashamed of, but in a place like Domain, it's difficult. It's easier with Ordette. She just punches anyone who says anything against me."

"Good for her." I remembered Perrine's fiery Other and stifled a laugh. "But you should never be ashamed of where you come from." It was typical that a place like Domain had plenty of wealthy Shifters with questionable morals, yet someone like Perrine worried about having less. Then I had an idea. I changed out of the dress and handed it back to the shop assistant.

"Would you like this gift wrapped?" The assistant held out her hand to take the dress back.

I handed it back to her. "Oh, no, thank you. It's a beautiful dress, but we're going to go elsewhere." I beamed as I linked my arm through Perrine's and we walked out of the shop.

"Charity, what–" Perrine cut in.

"Anton doesn't get to determine where we shop. Even if he is paying. You wear gorgeous clothes. Where do you get them?"

"You're something else, you know that?"

It wasn't the first time I'd heard it.

We made our way down a few streets where the fancy shops thinned and became market stalls. Perrine and I bought dresses in a similar style to the one I'd tried on in the shop. They were both full length with thin straps and flowing material. Despite not trying them on, I knew they would look brilliant. The fabric stayed still, just like any material would in my world, but that didn't bother me in the slightest. Perrine chose mauve, and I had silver.

As I handed them over to pay for them, Perrine chipped in, "It would be irresponsible to abuse Anton's money."

I grinned back at her. "Well, it's a good thing I'm that irresponsible person, then. Anton has more than enough money, and I'm certain he was expecting a much bigger dent in his Shiftcoins than he is going to have. And, frankly, he has some making up to do."

Perrine linked her arm back through mine. "Thank you. I'm glad you don't let this all get to you. It's just as well too, as I think we're in for a hell of a night tomorrow."

I couldn't believe we'd spent the entire day here. It was easy to be around Perrine and not feel judged. As we made our way back, the sun set; tinting the sky a rosy pink that bled into everything around us. It was beautiful here.

The arrival party was being held at Abduco Manor, Anton's family home. I hadn't spoken to him since that night Scarlett had found us on his sofa. Mortified, I had needed some time alone in my room, and by the time I came out, he'd left, presumably to join Scarlett for dinner at Abduco Manor as he'd mentioned. It was fine. If they wanted to play happy families, so be it. I wouldn't let it spoil the fact that I had a party to attend with three new friends. Something told me a night with Viktor, Spyder, and Perrine would be a hell of a night indeed.

I swallowed, thinking about the rest of the attendees. Not only would Anton be there; his entire family, plus the various Shifters from the three other Domains, would gather in order to celebrate another human capable of solving the prophecy–me, apparently. It still hadn't sunk in. Still, if it meant Perrine and I could spend an evening drinking fancy champagne, then I could oblige. I'd show them just what people from my world were capable of.

11

CHARITY

Shifter 101: All Shifters must undergo an Actuation in order to establish their House within Domain.

The arrival party was unlike anything I'd seen before. Abduco Manor was an enormous Gothic mansion. From certain angles, it looked more like a cathedral than a house. It stood five stories high and had tall arched windows with actual gargoyles above them. Its location in the middle of the forest made it look like something out of a fairy tale, albeit a very extravagant and luxurious fairy tale. Although the Halloween decorations were now down, not much had changed. I was glad I'd chosen not to do my training here; the place was intimidating.

Perrine collected me from Anton's flat. He was required to attend here beforehand and had left her instructions to travel here with me. I'd been able to see her speaking to the bee this time. She spoke too quietly for me to hear, but the next thing I knew, we'd vanished from the flat and appeared on the doorstep of Abduco Manor. I wouldn't get used to that aspect of Domain.

The November chill nipped at me as we walked up the steps,

through the giant mahogany doors, and into a large reception room. The manor must have had a lot of staff, as someone had been responsible for stringing fairy lights across the high ceiling in a crisscross pattern, making the atmosphere more welcoming than the exterior suggested. Speakers hidden around the room emitted tasteful background music, barely audible above the lively chatter.

There must have been one hundred people in the room already, but I glanced across and saw Anton just in time to catch a foxlike smirk as he noticed me too. He headed straight in my direction.

"I'm off to get drinks." Perrine disappeared into the crowd just as Anton reached me.

"Evening, Serrk. Didn't they tell you we were to dress up?" His voice taunted me with its velvety warmth. He reached over me for a glass of champagne from a tray passing, causing the hairs on my arms to stand on end.

So he wants to pretend to insult me like nothing happened. Well, two can play that game.

"They did. I'm sorry the memo didn't reach you, though."

Anton gave a rare laugh, then frowned as he took in my outfit. It looked like he wanted to say something, but stumbled between being well-mannered and being honest. "Did Perrine take you to the shops I suggested?"

I took a drink off another tray that had materialised right next to me, snaffling the last glass that had my name written all over it. "Oh yes, we got your *list* just fine."

"And this is from one of the named boutiques?" He raised an eyebrow at my dress.

I didn't know what Shifters put in their drinks here, or if I'd just had access to terrible drinks back home, but this was delicious. "If it was, would you approve of it more?"

"Grey isn't your colour," he said. "It makes you look ordinary."

Who does he think he is? I cocked my head. "I thought Abduco Shifters were supposed to be charming."

He leaned down, so he was a fraction closer to my ear. "You deserve something that shows you for who you are. The next time you go shopping for a party, I'll get you something you deserve."

My mask snapped into place. *Show him you're off limits if he is.* I stepped back. "I can pick a dress for myself, thanks." I avoided his gaze as I examined the fingerprints I'd already left all over my glass. "Oh, and I got Perrine a dress, too."

But he just smirked instead. "I would have expected nothing less."

"Then you shouldn't have expected me to be told what to do and where to shop." I took a larger gulp than I should have, given the company I was in. Old habits and all, the quicker I got rid of a drink, the less chance anyone could slip anything into it.

That first drink had given me confidence, but Anton seemed to enjoy it, and genuinely chuckled at my remark, the warmth in that sound unnatural based on what I knew of him so far. I tried not to notice how well-fitted his suit was. It was another one of the darkest green, with a subtle pattern of checks detailed across it. From a distance, it looked black.

There was a lull in the conversation that seemed to say more than our words might.

"Enjoying yourself?" I decided to extend an olive branch, keen not to draw attention to whatever this was between us, and instead nodded towards the room. I had to focus.

"You could say that." He took another sip, considering the flavour before swallowing. "When I find something that I like, I try to make the most of it."

I could feel the flush creeping up my neck. *I'm in trouble.* He was a taken man after all, and despite his flirting, he was off-limits, for many reasons.

"Well, don't let me stand in the way of you enjoying your night. I'm sure you've plenty of people to see, like Scarlett." I had to distance myself from him, from his voice, his smell, everything.

Anton chuckled into his drink, unfazed by the reminder of his girlfriend. "Oh, I hate these things, but I couldn't be happier where I am."

I raised my eyebrows at him, trying not to read too much into his words. *Is he drunk?* "You realise what you said is a complete oxymoron, don't you?"

"I suppose that's the perfect way to describe me." He gave me a wry smile and his dark eyes glinted as they ran over my dress. I got the impression that he didn't hate it as much as he let on. Maybe it was the drink, but the tension radiated in that short distance between us.

A Shifter with rainbow hair interrupted us to wish me luck for my upcoming Actuation. She snapped a photo of us together on her Shiftsung, gushing, "I have to show my friends I'm not lying, so good to meet you!" She then disappeared into the crowd, leaving me dumbfounded. I scanned the room looking for Perrine, wishing she'd hurry with the drinks that she'd disappeared to get. She must be chatting with someone, she was so friendly. I met various eyes around the room, all analysing me. I could tell I was some source of interest. It wasn't a common occurrence for humans to be brought into Domain.

"Why do you hate these parties normally?" I asked Anton, trying to block out the prying eyes around me. I wasn't used to this kind of attention, despite knowing the party was being thrown for me. Once again, his hair sat in two immaculate halves, one jet black and the other platinum blond. Tonight, he had slicked both sides back, ensuring that the divide remained even.

"Does it matter?" His mouth drew up at the corner. The question hung in the air between us. Something told me we weren't talking about the party anymore.

Nerves curled in my stomach and settled there.

He dropped his mouth down to my ear. "I didn't think so."

My eyes widened, and my heart gave a single thump, jerking my consciousness back to reality. The pulse somewhere in my lower abdomen reacted to the hum of his voice.

I couldn't keep lying to myself. The effect he had on me was staggering. Of course, he had to be taken, the good ones always were. The drink must have been getting to me if I just considered Anton a *good one.*

Though I couldn't deny that he was.

Anton swaggered off, full of confidence and none the wiser at the crushing effect his mind games had on me. He was such a bastard. In the best way possible. Exactly the sort I found attractive.

"And now, the moment you've all been waiting for." A voice addressing the room caught my attention and my head swivelled towards the staircases. "This party wouldn't be happening if it weren't for us celebrating Charity Serrk as she prepares for her Actuation."

The room burst into applause. I looked around, taking in everyone, yet seeing no one at the same time. I turned my attention to the landing where the two staircases met. It seemed to be used as the stage for the large room and I could see both Anton and Viktor standing there, along with two other Shifters who I could only assume were their parents.

It was Anton's father who had spoken. He was tall, with long dark hair that had a white stripe through it. Their mother must have been shorter than me, with almost completely platinum blonde hair that had dark panels underneath.

Anton's father continued talking about the trials I would face; *I did need to find out more about that.* Anton had assured me they weren't dangerous, though I wasn't sure how much I could count on that. Domain wasn't the place where everything came up roses by the sound of things.

I realised everyone in the room was raising their glass to me and I returned the gesture, feeling out of place but determined not to show it. There was another round of applause, and Anton's mother signalled for everyone to return to their conversations around the room.

Several more Shifters came up to me to congratulate me and ask me questions about my place in the 'real world'. Of course, this was the real world for them and my world was fantasy, so it was even more exciting for them. I smiled and answered questions as I sipped at my drink, but my attention was only half there. The other half was following Anton as he spoke with several other Shifters who I could only assume were Apexes, given their clothing and command of the room. I was watching the way his eyes kept flitting up towards me every few seconds, a look I couldn't place casting over his face whenever our eyes met.

Just when I thought I'd lost him in a sea of platinum blonde and jet black, I turned around and there he was, along with Viktor and his mother and father. I gulped my champagne, wishing I'd taken that third glass slower than the first two. The room already looked a little fuzzy.

"Charity, I'm Sage. It's wonderful to meet you. I must say, that is a beautiful dress, one from *Venelles and Vêtements,* yes?" It was clear Anton got his manners from his mother, as his father was currently scowling at me.

I took her outstretched arm and breathed in her crisp perfume.

"Thank you, Sage. It's good to meet you too. As for my dress, it wasn't from a shop."

"Oh, your own collection, then? You have wonderful taste."

This time I looked Anton's father right in the eye before turning back to her and replying. "It was from one of the market stalls in Nexus."

Viktor snorted into his glass while Anton's mouth pressed into a hard line. His mother replied, "Oh," as if she wasn't sure what else to say.

"Are you sure someone of your *apparent* status should be shopping somewhere like that?" Anton's father lingered over the word.

I wouldn't let him shake me. "Well, it's a lot better than what I'm used to. Sorry, I didn't catch your name?"

Anton's father looked taken aback at being addressed by someone who wasn't going to be rattled by him. I saw the faintest of smirks at the corner of Anton's mouth, but he hid it well.

"Verde," he said, holding out his hand to shake mine just a touch too forcefully. "You'd better learn that there are customs we have here. It would be disrespectful not to adhere to them."

"I'll make sure I'm on my best behaviour." I didn't mean for it to sound sarcastic, but my mouth had a mind of its own at the best of times, and today was no exception. Anton's mother seemed lovely, however, so I made sure I flashed her a genuine smile, which she returned.

"We'll leave you to it. You'll have lots of people who want to see you." Verde jerked his head in the direction of the room, his fury shining through his stare.

I gave him a curt nod and another smile to Sage as they left. Viktor also made his excuses, leaving Anton and me alone.

"Well, that went well," I summarised.

"I'm impressed you held your own. Believe it or not, they'll respect that." Anton set his drink on a passing tray, along with my empty glass. He brushed my hand, and it took everything in me not to jump at the small contact.

"Neither of them mentioned their Other," I said, keeping my eyes to the floor to avoid getting flustered again. I wondered where Scarlett was and why Anton wasn't with her.

"My mother and father choose to live without their Other. It is quite common here. While all Shifters are born with an Other, we can choose to allow one to take over until the Other disappears."

I remembered Spyder talking about this the day I'd met him. I wondered how common it was in Domain. "Do they ever have the same expectation of you?"

Anton's face changed to a hard mask, his mouth in a tight line. "You heard my father, Serrk. Lots of people want to see you tonight. If I were you, I'd give them what they want. They'll be interested to see what company you keep."

Keep your guard up, Charity, said a small voice in my head. "Point taken. You've made it clear I'm beneath you, and you don't want to be associated with someone like me."

This time, his jaw ticked. "I didn't say that."

Spyder stumbled into the room, cutting our moment short. He was clutching a half-finished bottle and singing loudly. It seemed to be some kind of Shifter song.

Apexes are this and that. I just find them lame.
Demis, Apexes, Mesos, we're all the one and same.

Perrine emerged from behind Spyder, following his trail and trying to rectify the destruction he left in his wake. His song was getting a few remarks and eye rolls around the room, including Scarlett, who I'd located. She looked me up and down in disgust. I held her stare, and fought the urge to bare my teeth at her. My rage was palpable. I had a lot of reasons to hate people, but I'd experienced nothing like this since arriving in Domain. My hatred for her, and especially for Allium, caused me to feel things I'd never felt before. I'd hated people like Wyatt, like Greg, but they were acting out because they had a shitty hand in life and felt like it was acceptable to do the same to others. They'd never believed they were entitled and better than everyone else. It awoke something deep in my chest just thinking about Allium's smug face as he walked around, believing he was better than those around him.

"Charity! Our prophecy girl! Let's do shots!" Spyder threw his arms up in the air as he reached us and curled one around Perrine's shoulder. I decided I liked him even more. He was an outcast who didn't give a fuck. Just like me.

"I hope you can hold your drink, then." I said, as he led the way to the bar.

"Game on!"

12

CHARITY

Shifter 101: All family members belong to the same House. All Shifters must still undergo an Actuation Ceremony, even if their House is determined by family.

It turned out Shifter shots differed from what I was used to. A group of us broke off from the large entrance hall into a smaller room with a separate bar. By number three, the room was spinning, and I had to tap out. Spyder managed eight before he said the same. He'd also finished the bottle in his hand. I didn't have to understand much about the drinks here to know he'd drunk a staggering amount.

Viktor joined us for the last round with a girl on his arm. She had violet hair that matched his suit and hung on to his every word.

There was a crash as Spyder fell off the stools we'd been sitting on at the bar. I burst out laughing, unable to stop myself. I put my hand over my mouth, hoping I hadn't offended him, but found him laughing, along with Viktor and his date. Spyder must have held some impressive standing in Domain, as this was a posh party, yet no one batted an eye at this behaviour. Either he was powerful, or this was a frequent occurrence. Or both.

Viktor removed his arm from his date and extended it to Spyder. "Easy, Spy. I think you've had enough."

Spyder swayed, flailing his arms around him as he tried to stand. "The fuck did that come from?"

"Where did what come from, mate?" Viktor had to bend down to help him up.

"The train?" Spyder rubbed his head in confusion.

Viktor pulled him to his feet and slapped him on the back. "Hymev, Spyder, just how much have you had?"

"Not enough! The night is young and I want to PARTY! Let's play a game!"

A velvety voice interrupted the conversation. "A game? I'm interested."

I turned and locked eyes with Anton's dark ones. There was just the briefest flash of green, showing that Allium wasn't far away. Now that the few of us were in a separate bar off the main party, it was harder to ignore him. *Pity,* said the drunk voice in my head. My room was much blurrier than it should be after three drinks and a couple of shots, but then my tolerance for Shifter alcohol was likely to be low anyway.

Viktor's date looked interested. "Oooh a game, what kind?"

"A drinking game, obviously!" Spyder responded as he wobbled again and had to be steadied by Anton.

Viktor chuckled. "Well, we guessed that. How about, Never Have I Ever?"

A few other Shifters heard him and joined us in a circle so there were twelve of us sitting facing each other: Anton, Viktor, Spyder, Perrine, Scarlett, and six others that I didn't know, including Viktor's date. I wondered if Scarlett would say anything about the other night with Anton. If the look she was giving me right now was any sign, she hadn't forgotten. Super.

"I'm-not-gonna-tell-you-the-rules-because-you-know-the-rules, if-you've-done-it-then-drink. I'll start," slurred Spyder. "Never have I ever cheated in a relationship."

Anton drank.

That's fucking interesting.

Viktor and two others also drank. The rest of us watched. Scarlett noted Anton's drinking and scoffed. "Obviously not when with me."

"Course not," said Anton. Though there wasn't much warmth in his words.

Viktor addressed the circle. "Me next. Never have I ever made out with a girl." He then immediately took a sip. Along with Viktor, the rest of the boys drank as well as one girl I didn't recognise. He spoke again. "That was from Forrest! Okay, my actual turn. Apart from when I'm Forrest, never have I ever made out with a guy."

This time, I took a drink from my glass, as did all the girls and Spyder. "What?" He shrugged. "I don't let something as trivial as gender determine who I like."

"Scarlett, you next!" said one girl who had been standing with her.

She wrinkled her nose in my direction. "Never have I ever grown up in the human world, ignorant of Shifter life and unable to afford proper clothes."

There was a muffled intake of shock around the circle. Anton took a sharp breath before putting his hand on her wrist. "Scar–"

I didn't want his pity. I could hold my own. Narrowing my eyes at her smug face, I finished my glass–of course I was the only one–but I refused to be riled by her.

"Excellent sport, Cee!" said Viktor under his breath.

"Yes! Prophecy girl can play the game!" shouted Spyder, forgetting the rules and drinking, too. "You next!"

It was too easy. "Okay then." I stared Scarlett down. "Never have I ever been an insecure bitch."

This time, the intake of breath was audible. Spyder sniggered and spat out his drink, coating us all in a fine spray. I could have sworn I saw the corner of Anton's mouth flick up. I hope she noticed.

"Perhaps we should do something else." Perrine's eyes flitted between us, sensing danger.

"Whatever, it's a stupid game, anyway." Scarlett rose from her seat and her friends followed. "Anton, are you coming or not?"

Anton met my eye almost apologetically and followed her out. I took another shot from Spyder to hide the ache that watching him leave left in my stomach.

"Anyone want to blow something up?" Spyder looked around the silent room. "Just me then. Suit yourselves." There was another crash as he knocked over an actual suit of armour on his way out. Without warning, a skinhead thug dressed from head to toe in black emerged from the shadows from behind where the suit of armour had been. He dusted himself off and followed Spyder. Apparently, everyone expected this behaviour, as no one batted an eye.

Viktor and his girl were getting cosy next to me, his face buried in her neck as his hand moved further and further up her leg. Another Shifter came up to him and bent down to his level, whispering something. He shook his head and motioned for him to get out. It was the first time I'd seen anything resembling annoyance cross his face.

"What was that about?" I asked as the other Shifter retreated, knowing it was none of my business, but I was feeling the effects of the shots too much to care about niceties.

"Mindchill. He was asking if I wanted any to silence Forrest for the night so I can enjoy myself with Raven here." He gestured to the female Shifter next to him.

"Silence Forrest?"

"It's one of the more social uses of the drug. People like me who have different sexual preferences depending on my Other use it so they don't have to be present, or some people just want a break from their Other. Either way, it does more harm than good and we're against it in Abduco. Anton would be furious if he found out someone was trying to sell it here. Don't tell him, will you? He's got enough on his plate."

I wondered what he meant by that, but knew I didn't have the subtlety in my current state to form the right questions to ask, so instead I nodded.

"Anyway, I'm going to get on. Keep an eye on Spyder if you see him, don't mind him and his drunken state. He gets upset about his parents, his actual parents, sometimes and uses drink as a coping mechanism."

I remembered Spyder talking about his adoption when I'd met him. "I'm sorry to hear that. What happened to his parents?" The thought that he was hurting sobered me. Despite his craziness, he seemed like a good person.

Viktor leaned forward and lowered his voice. "They died during a game of chasm, our sport." I remembered Anton mentioning that. "They were both famous players here. Though, many, Spyder included, think there's more to it than that. He's had a rough time of it; believe it or not, he used to be quite shy. But he never was the same after their accident. He doesn't like to talk about it." He pulled me into a quick hug, leaving my heart breaking for Spyder and his family. "Anyway, I'd better get on. Bronx will look after you when he's back, plus I can see Perrine is here. Stay close to her. She'll look after you."

"Bronx?" I looking around for who he was talking about.

Viktor's eyes widened a fraction. "Forget I said anything, just enjoy your night, Charity, and stay in company!"

He left me confused over his words as he left with his date. However, before I could dwell on everything I'd just learned, Perrine came running over, whispering. "I cannot believe you said that to Scarlett! It's about time someone took her down a peg or two. But you need to be careful."

I grinned at her, Viktor's words already distant in my head. "I know, I know. Did you see the look on her face, though?" We both laughed. It was good to have a friend.

I spent the rest of the night meeting some of Perrine's friends and speaking to so many people I started forgetting names. Everyone wanted to hear about my thoughts on the prophecy and whether I could shed any light on it, only to be disappointed when I told them I couldn't find anything that linked us. I had kept my task of researching the burning rose private to our small group and Perrine had agreed that this was best for now.

Something vibrated in my bag, making me jump out of my thoughts. I'd almost forgotten about my phone. I opened it and my heart fluttered when I saw it was from Anton.

Anton: Meet me in the North Corridor. Perrine will tell you how to find it.

I showed Perrine the message, and her eyes glittered. "I wonder what he wants. The North Corridor is the easiest one to find. Just keep climbing the stairs until there are no more staircases. I think it's about five floors up."

"Do you think it's a good idea to meet him?" I said.

She raised her eyebrows at me. "Would my answer stop you?"

"No." I bit my lip. "It wouldn't."

"I don't know what's going on between the two of you, but I suggest you find out. Message me if you need anything. I've got a

Shiftsung too, a gift from Anton for the work I'm doing with you. So, if that doesn't tell you something, I don't know what does." She took my phone and keyed her number in.

"Thanks, Perrine." I smiled at her and left the room with my heart in my mouth.

I was breathless by the time I reached the top floor. Running had to move up my list of priorities while I was here. *Why is the alcohol hitting me this way?* I hadn't had enough to cause the room to spin in the way it was.

"You thought you'd try your luck with Anton, didn't you?" A voice sneered from behind me.

Great, just what I needed, Scarlett catching me up here, trying to meet the very person she was with. I wondered what excuse he would give when he arrived. I went on the defensive. "No, I–"

She didn't give me a second before she launched herself at me. Suddenly, the room changed.

We were standing in a room filled with doors, different to the one I'd been in, though I hadn't had the familiar swirling sensation like when I travelled. The doors stretched down as far as the eye could see. Scarlett walked towards the first one and kicked it open. Something told me I didn't want her doing that. She went in, and, powerless; I followed her. Together, we watched a memory play out from when I was eight years old of one of my mother's boyfriends hiding his stash of weed in my birthday cake because it was "funny". The joke had been on him as I put the "magic seeds" back in the patch of mud we called a garden, not realising what they were. I had thought I was going to grow some flowers, when all I ended up with was no dinner.

Shit. Shit. Shit. Fear clawed its way to the forefront of my thoughts. These doors housed memories. We were in my mind. If she could get behind these, she was seeing into every element of my existence.

Scarlett was ruthless. She tried another door, kicking hard. Then another. My head hurt from the impact. Then she came to a red door. A shiver went down my spine as I realised what must be behind it. She couldn't see this one.

She kicked and kicked, but I prayed the door would stay closed.

"Who knew your sad little mind had something of interest in it, after all?" she sneered.

A flash of anger from me was all it took for the door to swing off its hinges. She'd taunted me and it had worked. She was in.

A kitchen table. A chair thrown across the room. I knew the scene she was watching so well. But it didn't stop the pain of seeing it play out before my eyes as if I was some bystander.

Sixteen-year-old me being dragged by the hair into the basement. Calling it a basement was generous. Designed for storage, it was hardly bigger than a chest freezer. The screech of the fridge being moved over the hatch. Shouting. Banging. Scratching. Anything to get out. A heartbeat. Breathing faster and faster. A flash forward to the next day as I grew desperate, scratching my nails down to my fingertips trying to gouge a hole in the wood. The bloodstains on the underside of the door, only visible when I was finally let out. I wasn't capable of measuring how much time had passed by then.

I was back in the hall at the top of the stairs again with Scarlett in front of me looking triumphant.

My breathing hadn't slowed. I couldn't think. My vision was closing in on the sides. I was having a panic attack. I couldn't think. Couldn't see. Couldn't think. Couldn't breathe.

Everything else was fuzzy. All I could think about was trying not to suffocate.

I felt hands on my chest. Not hands. Claws. Bruising strength. Stronger than I expected from her. The pain only a momentary distraction.

Another step back.

Then another.

Where were we going?

Before I knew it, she'd backed me into the end of the hallway. There was only one door.

All I could choke out was, "I'm not your enemy, Scarlett."

Her face twisted in disgust. "Don't give yourself credit. You're nothing to me."

The pain in my chest had reached a point where I was left with no choice but to turn and grab the door, not knowing where it would lead.

It was pitch black. A cupboard.

A massive push. I fell in headfirst. The lights cut out.

No. Not this. Anything but this.

She'd shut me in. The light went out in the hall outside, and I heard quick soft footsteps leaving me. Too light to be human.

It felt like dying. It did every time.

You're not dying. This will pass. You're not dying. This will pass. Your only limit is your imagination. This was all in my head. It had to be. Hugging my knees, I waited for the worst of it to end.

It wasn't passing. Seeing the scene play out as if I'd been there was too much. I'd thought I was going to die that day. Had come to terms with it. Had realised I'd done everything that I could and accepted that water would not arrive. Once I was out, I'd pushed the memory to the darkest depths of my mind, never wanting to think about death that way again. My breaths came shorter and shallower.

Heavier footsteps. The door opened. The hallway was only dimly lit. Or maybe that was just my compromised vision.

Him.

I could smell him. Could hear his deep voice. "Serrk, Perrine said you–what's wrong? Why are you on the floor?"

"Help me." I was getting pulled to my feet.

"What?"

"Distract me."

Of all the things I expected would happen, I didn't expect to feel hands in my hair, the resistance of his rings as they ran through my waves.

Then, smoke, earth, and mint. Very close. Too close.

Without warning, his lips met mine. I tensed in surprise, then melted into him. The tension rose out my chest and I inhaled before pressing my mouth to his once more. One half of me was telling me this was utterly wrong and that he shouldn't be doing this. *But is it?* Because the other half of me was saying this was euphoric. And I wasn't pushing him away.

I could only moan in response as he dragged my lip between his teeth. "Helping?"

Our kiss grew more intense as a response and he moved a hand to round my waist, the other pressed against the wall beside us. He used his hips to back me into the wall, but it wasn't aggressive. It was just *right*.

After an eternity, we broke apart, and I could breathe again.

He leaned in again. "Was that an okay distraction?"

I grinned into his kiss, pushing away the feeling that we'd done something wrong. Or that the timing was terrible. I blocked the thoughts out, still riding the high of what had just happened and forgetting my encounter with Scarlett. "You could say that. Is this why you wanted to meet?"

"Wanted to meet?" his voice was barely audible as he grazed my neck.

I snapped my head forward. "You messaged me."

"I didn't send you anything." He drew back and pulled out his phone, his eyes on his screen as he scrolled through his messages. "That wasn't me. Someone sent you a message off my phone." He scanned the dark room. "How did you end up here?"

The penny dropped. I saw red when I realised what she had done. If I had any guilt about kissing a taken man, it had vanished. "It doesn't matter. I'll see you back at yours, okay? Oh, thanks for helping me." I gave him a small smile, but his attention was elsewhere, preoccupied with his phone. I was too furious at Scarlett to process what had just happened between us. Perhaps he didn't know how to deal with it, either. A part of me wanted to revel in it. But a larger part of me was aching for a fight with her. I was going to train to get the best handle on my Shifter abilities. At the very least, I'd take her down in a fistfight. This time, I would prepare myself.

I'd told her I wasn't her enemy. I guess I'd lied.

13

CHARITY

Shifter 101: All illegal gang activity within Domain is punishable within the realm of Langison.

My clash with Scarlett gave me the motivation I needed to throw myself into my studies to prepare me for my Actuation. I'd finally been told what to expect, though sometimes I still felt clueless about what I had to do.

Perrine had taken me through the various stages we would prepare for. She'd explained that all Shifters practised four different Shifting types: Mind Shifting, which I already knew about; Travel Shifting, which involved travelling from one location to another; Object Shifting, where one pulled an object from somewhere else into existence; and finally, Form Shifting, where Shifters would take the form of something else.

"Don't worry about breaking into anyone's mind accidentally again," she reassured me. "That happens as a result of humans suppressing their power. That's why you didn't have a choice but to go with Anton. Terrible things happen when humans refuse to leave their world."

I thought back to the times when Wyatt had exploded for no reason. Like when he'd hit me out of the blue. I wondered if I'd done the same thing then. Perhaps I was safer here after all. I hated it when Anton was right.

His departure 'on business' spared us from any awkwardness, though it would have been nice to see him just once, so I could have gauged his reaction to what had happened between us. This way, I didn't know if he was genuinely away or if he was just avoiding me.

I hadn't told him that Scarlett was the one responsible for my panic attack. I didn't want him in the way when I got my own back. Jealousy unfurled in my stomach as I thought of them together. I couldn't work out why he would choose someone like that. But then a part of him had chosen me in the cupboard too. I didn't tell Perrine; even with Ordette, I could tell what a good person she was. Better than me. And in all honesty, I felt guilty, and taken advantage of.

I swallowed my anger as I spread avocado onto my toast. A new thing for me. I'd never had access to anything like this back where I was from. It didn't bother me I was having breakfast on my own more times than in company these days. I had built my little routine of singing whatever was stuck in my head. I'd then scan the pages of *The Notion*, the newspaper that circulated around Domain, in order to keep up to date with what was happening. Watching the pages flicker before me was fascinating, updating like a live feed–the newspapers here differed from the ones in my world. After I'd finished with that, I'd take my tea onto the balcony to watch the mist clear over Abduco.

Perrine came to collect me just as I was draining my mug and scanning the missing Shifters section. Anton said it was barbaric to drink tea out of a mug instead of a cup, but I loved winding him up. A quick mutter into her hand and we were back outside the Bureau again. She led us back to the curved room we had been in previously. This time, it looked different. It had a hint of Perrine about it. Translucent curtains swayed in the breeze, and soft notes of rose floated through the air, along with the sweetness of honey. It was both calming and pleasant. No wonder Shifters used both in their tea.

Perrine turned to me. "We might as well start with Mind Shifting straight away. I'm going to enter yours now." She reached out to rest her fingers on my arm.

Just like with Scarlett, we transported and were standing in my mind. I watched helplessly as Perrine walked to the nearest door, the one with the memories of Anton and me in the cupboard, and pulled it open.

No, no, no. Please no.

I didn't want her to see this, but I didn't know how to stop it. I tried to close the door, but it wouldn't move under my grip. Heat rose to my cheeks as I watched the scene unfold before us. She had the decency not to react. She shut the door and shook her head.

I was back in the breezy room. I flushed with embarrassment at what Perrine had seen.

I tried to explain myself. "Listen, I–"

"You don't have to be embarrassed. I'm not judging."

"Am I an awful person?" I knew the answer already. I'd thought about that kiss a lot. Something about Anton's reaction had surprised me. I hadn't expected it. He was apparently such a gentleman. Not that I'd minded of course. I'd asked him to distract me and I hadn't pushed him away. Quite the opposite. The more I thought about it, the more confused I became.

"We have different definitions of what defines awful here. Have you spoken with him about it?"

"No," I said, feeling like a petulant child.

"Perhaps you should. I've seen the way he looks at you. How did this happen?"

I ignored the part of her statement that set my heart fluttering. I explained about my encounter with Scarlett at the top of the stairs, though left out about my claustrophobia. It still felt too raw to return to.

Her arm remained on mine. "I'm sorry I wasn't there. It's even more important we help you gain control over your mind, so you can protect yourself in the future. Now, I'm going to try again. I want you to focus on your doors, particularly the lock. Think about the type of key, the type of lock, the mechanism. It can be modern or old. Whatever is clearer for you to visualise in the moment. Your lock could even be a code or a more traditional turn key. The choice is yours."

A gold lock with a dainty key sprung into my mind. I concentrated on adding this detail to my doors as I stood back in my hallway. Perrine reappeared again and approached the same door. This time, I could feel the lock resist as she turned the handle and entered the same room with the scene in front of her.

The breeze touched my face again as I found myself back at the Bureau once more.

"That was better!" Perrine jumped up and down, clapping her hands together. "Let's continue."

"You still got in." I felt defeated. Defeated and furious that out of all the people in the world, Scarlett was the one that understood my biggest weakness. Had seen the moment I'd been physically and mentally crushed. My skin crawled just thinking about it. I was glad I was doing this with Perrine. I couldn't imagine what it would be like to have my mind so open to anyone else here, along with half of the thoughts I was harbouring. "Maybe I'm not cut out for this mind business. How do you even know I can learn this all?"

"It's possible to train any mind, Charity. We came from the human mind, born out of the need to keep such a thing under control. Domain might be a sister world to yours, but underneath, you're no different from us. You just have to harness what you already have," she breathed.

With renewed motivation, I let her continue and concentrated every effort on mastering locking my doors. It was hours before Perrine let me rest. Each time, I returned to the breezy room, dusted myself off, and braced myself for another round.

Perrine entered my mind again and again, each time trying the same door. Even with her gentle approach, it was draining. I knew she was holding back, well aware that when Scarlett had reached my mind, she had been twice as forceful and anyone else trying would be the same.

With lots of practice, I built up a level of resistance to Perrine's attacks. If I concentrated on keeping the key in the lock, refusing to let it turn, I could delay her entering the room. I was glad, too, as part of me wanted to die from embarrassment at the number of times Perrine had now seen Anton and me together in compromising positions. Each time, she said nothing.

As she worked on reaching a room involving Anton and me on his kitchen island—a daydream rather than a memory—I decided enough was *enough*. I couldn't let her see another private thought. I gritted my teeth and while the lock vibrated; it did not turn. Then we were back in the room in the Bureau.

Perrine's heart-shaped face lit up as she sang, "You've done it!"

Combat training with Viktor had its own challenges, too. In order to perform well in the more physical elements of my Actuation, I had to ensure my base fitness was at peak level before attempting things I had barely even dreamed of before. He'd asked me to meet him in the ring at a place close to Anton's called the Hideout. All I'd been told was that it was somewhere near Drago's Bay. It lived up to its name as it took me some time to find it, given it was accessible by entering through the roots of an enormous tree. It didn't get more Abduco than that.

Viktor handed me a pair of boxing gloves. "This will cushion any blows that land. I won't be going easy on you, as no other Shifter will. Anton told me you like running, so I know you'll already be starting from a good foundation."

I stored that detail about Anton behind another poorly guarded door. "I understand."

Viktor circled me, transferring his weight back and forth. "No time like the present. Shifters are fast, you understand, so when I come at you like this–"

I ducked out the way. Call it instinct, most likely growing up where I did, but I knew how to avoid a punch. Viktor's mouth hung open in surprise, and I gave him a smirk of my own. He recovered and said, "Fair play, girl. You've got an excellent set of reactions on you too. Let's see if you can outsmart me when I–"

Another punch came from the hand I wasn't expecting, and I only just moved aside as it narrowly missed my cheek.

"Not bad! I see you and Anton's constant keeping out of each other's way has helped your dodging skills."

This time, he hit me right in the mouth. I fell backwards, and the ropes sagged under my weight. But Viktor had been right: the glove softened the blow, and it was more the shock that caught me off guard.

He held out a hand to help me back up. "And that, my dear, is your weakness. You bring your emotion into everything that you do." He grinned at me. "If someone can wind you up, they win."

Mortified, I had to agree. It had been the same with Scarlett. I'd always been an emotional person; I wore my heart on my sleeve and let my anger guide my actions. It might count for something that I'd brought my fitness and quick reactions from my old life, but learning to use them without emotion would be a much bigger challenge for me.

We circled each other again. This time I made a jab at Viktor; he dodged it. "What can I do to help myself?"

"You need to use that emotion and channel it into something that can help you. Rather than distracting yourself with other thoughts, use what you're thinking about as motivation to do well."

"So you think Anton should be my motivation to succeed in my Actuation?" I tried to hit him, but he was too fast.

"Well, imagine wiping the smug look off his face when he sees how well you do." Viktor appeared at my back, and I had to shoot out of the way to avoid him.

"Now that's something to aim for!" I fended off another hook that he'd slyly tried to land.

Over the next few weeks, visualising my mind and strengthening my mental shields became easier after my sessions with Perrine, and I noticed my fitness and strength building after bouts in the ring with Viktor. Between that and my running, I felt more unstoppable than ever. Before long, I could enter my mind and had made enough progress in my combat training to satisfy Viktor. I couldn't help enjoying the warm feeling of achievement when Perrine and Viktor said I was ready for more advanced training. I'd never accomplished much in my life so far, and it finally felt like I was doing something right.

While I might have been progressing in my training, what I hadn't mastered was talking to Anton. We just existed together. We were both so busy, I hardly saw him. When I did see him, the moments were fleeting. Our time together was so limited, it was easy to learn his habits. When he was in a good mood, he would make some conversation, eat a pastry for breakfast, and make us both tea. If things were going badly with the Dragos, Allium flickered at the edges of his consciousness and he said next to nothing. It was as if he was concentrating all of his efforts on keeping Allium out so that he didn't cause a scene. I was glad for it, as the more I learned about the potential I had, the harder it would be not to fight Allium, even if he were in Anton's body. So we continued, living in a strange harmony balanced with the suffocating tension between us.

I threw myself into my training and tried to put my situation with him out of my mind—literally, so that Perrine did not find it. She was right; it was possible to train any mind. Through sheer willpower and lots of training, I was progressing. Perrine always joined me and had showed me how to add the features of the doors, the handles, and the floor to make it personal. Behind each door held accessible memories or thoughts. I'd locked most of my doors now, and Perrine understood that there were some that had to stay locked for privacy. Like the memory Scarlett had seen. I still hadn't confronted her; I wanted to be ready.

I came back from training one wet Abduco evening, freezing as I kicked off my shoes at the front door. Anton was in the kitchen making dinner. Over the past few weeks, we'd never been in the flat at the same time in the evenings. He'd always been out and come back once I was in bed. Even though he was quiet, I always stirred at him returning home. I had considered getting out of bed to see him, but I thought it might make it look like I was waiting for him. I'd also thought about messaging him but cringed at the thought of them materialising in front of him and whoever he was with.

Hey, so we kissed. What was that?

Any messages we sent were very factual such as *Fridge has been restocked - AA*. I was aware how strange it was that I was even still living here while he had a girlfriend. It surprised me no one had asked about it, though my daily routine had kept me out of most people's way.

Until today. Here he was. For the first time in weeks, he looked almost cheerful. I could only assume things with the Dragos were going better than of late.

Then, the traitorous little flutter in my chest disappeared like a burst balloon as his eyes lightened and I faced Allium instead.

"Do you like beef bourguignon, Serrk?" His mouth was curled back as he stared down at the pot in front of him.

"In English, thanks. Is that a fancy word for a beef burger or something?" I shot back. He probably wanted me to walk straight out the door. But I wouldn't play into his game. If he saw he couldn't rattle me, maybe he'd leave Anton and me alone. And then I finally could ask him what the fuck that kiss was all about . . .

Allium put his thumb and forefinger on the bridge of his nose as he shook his head. "No, not even close. You are so uneducated."

I laughed bitterly at his reaction. "So are your opinions." I wouldn't let him get to me. Anton had made us a lovely meal. It would be unfair to him for me to leave. I folded my arms and shrugged. "I'm not fussy, I'll have it."

Allium placed a steaming pot onto the kitchen island and began plating up, smirking as if the uncomfortableness of the situation was enjoyable for him. Sick bastard. Why did Anton's perfect exterior have to house someone so evil? He frowned as he saw the disgust written across my face, realising I was directing none of it at the food.

But *the food*. I hadn't realised Anton was such an excellent cook. It smelled like home. A home I'd never had. I'd had no opportunity to experience much home cooking, but as I inhaled the rich aromas, I appreciated it was yet another thing I'd missed out on. I could already tell this was going to be delicious.

We sat at the kitchen island on high bar stools as Anton sliced a French baguette.

"Pretty fancy meal just to put in a sandwich," I stated, grinning.

"Hymev, you're dense. The bread is for dipping, Serrk. You don't put your dinner in a sandwich."

"Oh, I see," I replied, feeling foolish for the first time in front of him. Then, back on the offensive, I put my walls up. "Listen, as nice as this heart to heart is, I think Anton was planning on making this dinner and I'd much rather have his company than yours."

His tone was cruel as he eyed me sinfully. "Oh, how *sweet*. You think things have changed after that kiss?"

Whatever was left of the hope in my chest fizzled out. "I don't want to talk about it with you." I concentrated on blocking him out, but it was useless. Like trying to keep liquid from falling through a sieve.

He chuckled. "Why? Did you enjoy it too much?" His eyes were flashing, and that fucker was licking his lips. If he hadn't shared a body with Anton, I would have been tempted to take my fork and stab it through the back of his hand. I shuddered at having had such a thought. This man brought out the worst in me.

"Hymev, Allium, get *fucked*," Anton's voice broke through. His eyes darkened to signal that he had returned. He tipped his head back in frustration and ran his hands through his hair. "Sorry about that. My mental shields are shot after my time away. Do you think there's any chance we can get a normal evening back again?"

I nodded. Too numb from Allium's words to respond in the moment. It wasn't fair that Anton had to deal with that side of him. They were so different; how could anyone see them as the same person?

"I'm not judging how you eat, by the way. I'd give anything to not have to follow every manner and rule that's put in place for me," said Anton as he started eating his own meal.

It wasn't fair to be rude to him. It wasn't his fault he shared his mind with a monster. And he had made a delicious dinner, so I picked up my fork and took a taste. It was sublime. I made a mental note to find the recipe so I could try to recreate it later. Turning over his words, I enjoyed another mouthful. "I didn't have you down as someone who followed the rules. Being a top Apex and all."

"That's why I have to," said Anton. I got the feeling he was speaking more to himself than me. His eyes flashed, and he seemed to retreat into himself. We finished the rest of our meal in silence.

After Anton had cleared our plates, he fixed himself a drink and held up an empty glass in offering for me. I nodded and watched him pour a spirit into the second glass before adding a dash of powdered ivy–a specialty in Abduco, I'd learned–and tonic. He tilted his head to the balcony door, signalling us to go outside. We sat down and I took a sip. As always, everything tasted better here. Anton sat back in one of the chairs under the partially covered area and lit a cigarette as we looked out into the pouring rain as it thrashed down, muffling all other noises from the surrounding trees.

"Tough day?" I could see it all over his face after all.

"You have no idea." He took a long drag of his cigarette as we stared out at the dim lights among the trees. He then held the packet out to me. "Care for one?"

"I don't smoke."

"I didn't know that," he frowned, quirking a brow.

Unsure why that detail seemed to bother him, I added, "I've just never found they helped me feel any better."

"Well, they sure do help me." He put the cigarette to his mouth again and closed his eyes.

"Suit yourself. But there are other things that are more effective. What about Scarlett? She seems such a pleasant and caring person." My sarcasm was out before I could stop it.

His tone changed, and he retreated into himself again. "Don't involve her."

"I know it's not my place, but I don't understand why you would be with–"

Anton threw the rest of his cigarette away and sat up. "You're right, you *don't* understand. Being an Apex doesn't mean we're free; we're puppets, we don't get a say in who we're with."

That hadn't been the response I'd been expecting. I held my ground, choosing my next words carefully. "What do you mean by that?"

Anton was gripping his glass with such force it was amazing it held. I could see the veins on his arms standing out and snaking their way up his arms to his tattoo-covered biceps. "Never mind."

Well, it was like that then. I huffed louder than I'd intended, tying my hair up when Anton's arm shot out to stop me. "You suit it down," he summarised.

The nerve. That just made me want to tie it up more. "You can't tell me how to wear my hair."

His grin grew wider. "True, but you'll struggle to put it up without this." He held out the bobble that he must have somehow swiped from my wrist without me noticing. These damn Shifters and their speed. I made a grab for it, but he was ready for me and slipped it on his own wrist like a bracelet. "Now, whenever you see it, you'll remember how nice it looks down."

What the actual fuck? The man was an enigma. Was he going to keep it on his wrist? I'm pretty sure Scarlett would have a thing or two to say about that. I couldn't keep track of his hot and cold ways.

"So you can tell me that, but you don't want to talk about that night?" I asked, glaring at him. If he wanted to be forward, so could I.

He stared straight ahead, understanding I meant the kiss, and I knew I'd shattered whatever moment we'd just had. "No. I don't," he said.

His words burned a hole in my chest. I pushed my emotions behind my closed doors like Perrine and I had been practising and ensured my guard was up. "Stay out of my way, then."

He rolled his eyes in frustration and ducked back into the living room, leaving me in the pouring rain. The veranda wasn't doing as good a job now the wind had picked up, and I realised I was getting soaked. I hadn't noticed how cold it was until I didn't have the warmth of him next to me. Before I'd decided what I was going to do, he stuck his head back out.

"Come back inside. You're getting soaked out there."

I wasn't going to allow him to confuse me further, so instead brought my knees up to my chest and hugged them. "I like it out here, and unlike you, I can't avoid the rain." That wasn't totally honest. The scenery was beautiful, though I absolutely hated getting wet. But fuck him and his riddles. I could endure some rain.

Anton stepped back outside, his t-shirt clinging to every inch of his sculpted torso. "Aren't you meant to be practising this with Viktor?"

"We haven't got there yet. You'd know this if we spoke to each other from time to time." I knew I was pushing him too far, but a month of walking on eggshells had me wound up to the point it felt good to say some of how I felt.

Anton sighed. "Come here, then." He sat down next to me and

used his hands to part the rain above my head. If I wasn't seeing it with my own eyes, I wouldn't have believed it possible. He moved the rain like a curtain and the new drops followed the new curve, leaving a dry window around me like an invisible umbrella.

We sat there, frozen in time for only a few seconds, but it felt like forever.

"When you walk, you can avoid the drops, but this is useful for when you're sitting here."

"Thank you." I watched the rain now falling around my invisible umbrella. He was so close. *Why did he have to sit so close?* His smoky smell wasn't from the cigarette, it was more like burning wood. It complimented the smell of the mint beautifully.

"Charity–"

I didn't realise I'd leaned into him and I straightened up immediately. "I keep thinking about that night," I blurted out, unable to help myself. Although I'd been busy over the past few weeks, this had been on my mind a *lot*, and I had to say something.

But Anton was already looking away. "Don't do this. Please."

I drew back. "Are you just going to ignore the fact we kissed? I'm assuming that's why you've been distant and refuse to have any form of proper conversation."

Anton's face was grave as he turned back. "Charity, we didn't kiss that night."

That backtracking bastard. I eyed him as I stood. "Wow. Don't bother denying it. I was drunk, but I wasn't that drunk. I only asked you to distract–"

"No, Cee." My heart fluttered at the change of nickname. "I mean it wasn't us that kissed. It was you and Allium."

14

Viktor and Forrest

Shifter 101: Shiftcoins are to be used for purchase of goods only and cannot fund any activity, including but not limited to: extortion, laundering, funding gang activity, supplying or purchasing Mindchill, engaging in illicit services, or any other illegal means.

I paced around the ring as I waited for Charity. She was pissed. Seriously pissed. It was a miracle she'd come to training at all. But I knew the Hideout fascinated her. After all, it wasn't every day you got to train among the roots underneath one of the largest trees in Abduco. Few people knew what we'd built here, so, Shifter or not, it was pretty interesting.

A tap on my shoulder signalled she'd arrived. I removed my headphones and changed the music so it echoed around the room. We said nothing: I could see the determination in her eyes. She matched me beat for beat as she anticipated and dodged every move I could throw at her.

"Careful, Viktor, you'll need to try harder if you want to impress your date with your stories tonight."

Did I have a date tonight?

Forrest was quick to interrupt. *No, idiot, it's a tactic! Look out! Your jaw–*

That sly little minx had used my game against me and distracted me just enough to land a left hook right across my jaw. She was quite frightening when she was angry. The power behind her fist sent me staggering back, tripping over my own feet. She flashed me a triumphant grin as she held out a hand to help me back up.

I ran through the routine Charity would follow tonight. She was performing extremely well in her mental tests: she could lock her own doors well and was now working on breaking into Perrine's mind. The last element of the mental Actuation would involve being presented with a mind and her decision would determine her Domain if she succeeded. That was the only part of the test she couldn't prepare for.

I pressed play on my playlist and heavy metal guitar flooded my ears, sending a spike of adrenaline round my body. *Technically, also my body,* said Forrest. We differed from most Shifters: so in tune; we flitted between each other without most people noticing. There were no physical features that distinguished us; only our approach to relationships and our sexual orientation. I was straight, and enjoyed casual dating, whereas Forrest liked men and had only ever entertained long-term relationships.

One relationship, he corrected me, as I performed a series of jabs, hooks, and uppercuts to finish warming up.

"Not bad, girl, I'll give you that one," I said, watching Charity complete the routine as I reset my jaw into place. At least, that's what it felt like.

"Well, you told me to get to know my enemy," she replied, grinning. I sighed. Despite the work we had to do, I couldn't help but feel proud of how far she'd come in the few weeks that she'd been here.

Although we'd become friends and spent a lot of our free time together, she wouldn't tell me what was bothering her and I wished she would, as it was having a serious effect on the progress she was making in some of the other areas of her training.

She'd excelled in our early lessons thanks to her quick reactions and love of running. But something had happened, most likely involving Anton, as he also looked cagey whenever I asked him if he knew anything.

Perrine had just given me a *don't go there* look and said no more. Whatever was up with Charity, I hoped it resolved itself soon. Her Actuation would occur just before Christmas, which meant we had a limited amount of time to make a shitload of progress.

No time like the present, Vik, Forrest chimed in. I supposed we couldn't leave it any later and announced, "Right, Shifting next."

The triumphant grin on her face changed to worry as she dragged off her gloves and threw them to the side of the ring.

As far as her physical preparation went, she was over-achieving in combat. During my bouts with her, I hadn't expected to be on my toes so much. She'd have no trouble there. She'd also astonished herself by grasping the basics of object Shifting quickly, and could summon minor items. However, our work on Shifting to another physical space had been stagnant for some time now. I understood it was a complicated process to master, though I knew she had the potential to do it. It wasn't the difficulty of the task that was hindering her; it was something internal, something she hadn't told me, and until she came to terms with whatever it was, we couldn't begin work on the final physical test: Shifting to another form. Truthfully, I was getting worried. The test was fast approaching, with a little over two weeks to go, and she was only ready for two out of the four elements. Granted, she had only been here a short time, but the examiners wouldn't care about that. She needed to pass three out of the four in order to succeed, including the mind trial, which was non-negotiable.

We stood on opposite sides. "Remember, try to clear your mind of everything and visualise where you want to be, over here next to me."

"I've got that bit." Her voice was flat and quiet. The determination that she'd brought into the room had evaporated.

I remained positive. "Great. Next, imagine squeezing your mind into something the size of a grain. Your body will then follow and before you know it, you'll be here."

"Yup . . . trying . . ." Her face contorted in concentration, or from whatever was on her mind. She almost looked like she was in pain. Shifting shouldn't be painful. It was a technique for sure, but once you had the hang of it, it was as second nature as breathing.

We had tried for another two hours with no progress when I finally called it a day. I saw from the relief coupled with disappointment in her eyes that she was doing everything she could to make this work. Several times, I'd asked if there was anything I could do to help, but she'd just given me the same flat look she was giving me now.

I took her back to the flat, twisting my ring and keeping her next to me so that she could Shift alongside.

Forrest's boyfriend, Julian, was waiting outside the derelict building belonging to my brother. It was technically brothers *plural,* but in Domain it was a common custom to refer to the main consciousness of the Shifter unless you were specifically addressing their Other.

Warmth spread through me on seeing Julian. I knew that had come from Forrest and let him take over so they could spend time together.

The words came from my mouth. "Hi, Charity, it's Forrest now. This is my partner, Julian."

Julian was tall, dark, and handsome. He had long, jet-black hair swept up into a man bun that Forrest was just a sucker for. It accented his Asian features perfectly.

Julian held a hand out to Charity who introduced herself. He then put an arm around me, and we made our way up the stairs to Anton's.

As we walked in, Charity bristled next to me. I came forward and relieved Forrest of the obvious awkwardness between her and Anton. He didn't handle these situations as well as I did.

"Look at the two of you. It's like looking in a mirror." I wasn't one for subtlety as I pointed at their echoing body language. Anton flashed me a look as if to say, *you're dead*, as he closed his book and stood up from the sofa. I'd been hearing that for years. His threats were empty–at least for me–I couldn't say the same for the rest of Domain.

My eyes flitted between Anton and Charity. She gave him a look and then promptly tied her hair up. Whatever that was about. The two of them were so tense around each other. Could this be what was throwing Charity off her studies so much? I think I already knew the answer to that one. And I had just the plan to fix it.

"That's it, we're going out," I declared, firing a message off to Spyder on my Shiftsung.

"I'm game," said Julian with a smile. He then recognised it wasn't Forrest and turned it into a grin instead.

"I've got plans tonight," said Anton, looking at the floor. He was such an Abduco. No wonder he was the main Apex heir of the Domain. My father sat me down when I was younger and told me that Anton stood to inherit everything. I couldn't have cared less. He deserved some compensation for everything he did. Anton had said he would split everything with me anyway, but to be honest, as long as I had a place by his side, that's all I needed.

"What plans?" Spyder stepped in from the hallway. "Persen is calling. The stars told me so."

"Give me a few minutes. I'll change," Charity said, surprising us with her enthusiasm as she excused herself.

We helped ourselves to some drinks while we waited. Meanwhile, Anton returned to his book.

"Aren't you coming?" I asked.

"I have plans with Scarlett," he replied, looking miserable about it. He didn't miss Charity flinching at the name as she walked back in.

"Bring her! Four's a party!" said Spyder.

I raised my eyebrows at him. "There's six of us, mate, seven if Bronx is coming, even if he's in the shadows. That's not even including Others."

Spyder remained undeterred. "Well, even more reason to get going! I'll start up the helicopter while we're waiting."

Charity seemed surprised as she adjusted her top. I didn't miss Anton's eyes following her. She asked, "We aren't Shifting there?"

"Persen is somewhere you should see from the road the first time you visit. It's quite something." It was Anton who addressed her, stopping for a second as he took in her high-waisted black jeans, combat boots, and halter top. Everything hugged her slight frame. Did these two realise how obvious they were? If they knew we were all still in the room, they didn't show it. They looked at each other like they were the only two people in the world. I felt for Anton. Not only was I well aware how Allium felt about Charity being here, but I also knew he was only with Scarlett out of a sense of obligation. I didn't know the ins and outs; he shut me out from all of that, mirroring Charity's reaction any time I'd tried to talk to him about it. It didn't take a genius to realise they were both caught up in each other.

"Oh, I didn't realise we had company tonight," a voice sneered from the doorway. This time it was Scarlett, dressed in her usual Caedes garb–a fitted red dress suitable for clubbing and not much else.

"We're going out," said Anton, setting his book down again, this time with enough force to show he was annoyed. "All of us."

Scarlett froze as she spotted Charity. "What's she still doing here?!"

Anton's face remained void of all emotion as he massaged his neck with one hand. I had to hand it to him. He had balls. Letting another girl stay with him when someone like Scarlett was his girlfriend. "Complications with arrangements at the manor. As Charity is our guest of honour in Domain, we offered her a suitable alternative."

"I'll be on my best behaviour if you are, Scarface." Charity stood with her shoulders back, her smaller frame every bit as threatening.

Anton suppressed a smirk. It was so subtle I knew I was the only one who would have noticed. Julian snorted and buried his face in my shoulder. *Damn, Charity.* Scarlett might have had flawless skin, but I could tell the nickname bothered her. She said something under her breath that sounded a lot like, "whatever bitch" as she grabbed Anton's arm and marched them out the door. It was going to be an interesting night.

We made our way downstairs towards the increasing thrum of helicopter blades where Spyder was waiting with Bronx in the pilot's seat. "Bronx brought his entire stuffed cow collection, so there isn't room for everyone." He rolled his eyes in the bodyguard's direction.

Scarlett piped up, "Oh, I love cows! I want to go, but I brought my car already."

Julian surprised me by linking her arm and pulling her towards the parked flashy car on the street. "Is that the new Maybach with the bounce mode? How perfect for the Caedes terrain! I just *have* to see how well it performs on the climb up."

Scarlett looked annoyed, but didn't deny him, and they headed off. Julian shot me a wink over his shoulder, and I did the maths as I looked at the rest of us.

That sly dog, said Forrest in my head, as he pulled my mouth into the ghost of a smile.

"We still won't all fit," Anton said, our antics lost on him. "Viktor takes up enough room for at least two people. I'll take the Jeep and see you all there."

"You take Charity," I said, enjoying her eyes widening at my statement. She'd missed nothing. "Like you said, you should see it from the road for the first time."

15

CHARITY

Shifter 101: Shifters can only use their own idols to travel and cannot use the idol of another. The exception is when Demi-Shifters are required to travel with a Shifter using side-along Shifting.

We set off in Anton's flashy black Jeep. The vehicle was a monster in itself, but I supposed if we were going to be driving up mountains, it made sense. And very few things made sense around here, so I accepted rational thinking where I found it.

I let my hair down again and pretended I didn't notice the hair bobble still on Anton's wrist. I also pretended I didn't notice the corner of his mouth flick up the way it did when he was happy about something.

After a while, we left the trees behind as we crossed a large bridge, and the road opened up into a mountainous landscape ahead. Anton put on a Phonk playlist which thumped through the car speakers. I'd never had time for such luxuries as driving, but now that it was here, I was obsessed. It was like running, but faster, and with more adrenaline. With everyone's reactions here, speed limits weren't a thing. As accidents were minimal, we could weave through the cars, lost in our own world.

I sat back in my warm seat and took in every second of this. I felt free. The music was loud, so I didn't have to worry about what I was going to say or getting flustered. I simply sat back and enjoyed the view. The view from the window, of course, not Anton's arm on the steering wheel or the other dangerously close to my lap. His car was an automatic. Why did he have to rest it on the gear stick, anyway? It would be too easy for him to hook his hand round my leg . . .

I wanted more than anything to reach out and take it, knowing that his cool skin would be an antidote to the fire that raged through mine. I was still furious about Allium kissing me, *furious*. But that hadn't been Anton. I still didn't even know how he felt about it.

He caught me looking and turned the music down. Suddenly, his giant car felt small, but not in a claustrophobic way that would send me into a panic. The glass sunroof saw to that as I gazed up at the stars twinkling in the purple sky above us.

"Don't do that, Serrk." Anton sounded strained, but his eyes stayed on the road ahead. It was the first time he'd spoken in a while.

"Why not?" I read his conflicted expression, confused. "I'm only looking at the stars."

"Because although our reactions are fast, even Shifters can get distracted, and seeing your neck arched back like that is driving me insane."

I jerked my head down. I hadn't expected him to say that. "You're joking."

"I'm an Abduco. We don't joke." His face was serious. My confusion had reached additional levels. *What the hell did his words mean?* Allium had kissed me, but hated me. Anton was flirting with me though he was very much with Scarlett. The bastard even carried on speaking as if he hadn't just flipped my world on its head with one comment. "Care for a drink?"

"Ummm, sure?" My heart twisted inside. There was so much I wanted to ask, but I was enjoying the moment too much and didn't want to bring everything crashing down with the cruel reminder of reality. I fiddled with the air conditioning as it had become boiling in the car, despite us nearing the mountains.

Keeping one hand on the wheel, Anton reached into the back and pulled open a small door that revealed a whole mini bar. "What's your poison?"

"Just water for now, thanks." My mouth was dry and getting tipsy would not help me make sensible decisions here.

He's with Scarlett. He's just a flirt. I reminded myself as I drank the icy cold water to steady my senses and looked out of the window to distract myself.

In fairness, the view was spectacular. We gradually climbed higher and higher until the road out my window sloped into a deep valley. Dots of light littered the sides of the mountains, people choosing the remote life over the apparent buzz of the city. I'd heard about it from others. Persen was a digital metropolis in the mountains. I didn't know what to expect, but the faint glow I could see up ahead outlined the tall, looming mountain in front of us, and I knew it was going to be impressive.

As we approached the mountain, Anton's driving slowed. He took his eyes off the road for a second and his look blazed into mine. I stared at his mouth, wondering if Shifters could kiss and drive at the same time.

He was also my lips; I wondered if he was thinking the same.

Without warning, pitch black enveloped us as we entered a tunnel under the mountain. I'd been so distracted by his damn mouth,

I hadn't realised we would have to drive through it. My breathing constricted, and the car was too hot, the walls closing in, the music too quiet, the tunnel too dark.

"How do you turn your music up?" I reached for it in the dark, looking for something, anything, to stop me spiralling.

His cool hand met mine and took it, causing my breath to hitch.

"Stay with me. You've got this." The tunnel was a fraction brighter now, but still not enough.

"What?" Panic was rising in my chest for several reasons now.

"Your claustrophobia. I assumed from your reaction when I used side-along Shifting to bring you to Domain that the first time. Focus on me. Find something that you can channel your thoughts into."

His hand in mine. I clung to it like my life depended on it, aware that I was going to break into a cold sweat soon. "Your rings."

"Okay. Focus on those."

I ran my fingers over them, stopping at one. "What is this one?"

"The dragon is my family crest." *Was his thumb stroking my hand?* "Abduco's are famous for their connection to dragons. Didn't you learn this from Viktor or Perrine?"

"They might have mentioned it." I was distracted by the patterns being traced on my arm. I didn't want to let go. Ever.

We stayed like that for what felt like an eternity. Me grounding myself by focusing on the coolness of his rings and him keeping me at his mercy, but calm, just from the trace of his touch.

"Do you trust me, Cee?" he asked.

"Yes." I did.

The music matched the pace of his driving perfectly. The dim tunnel lights blurred beside us, and he drove with one hand on the wheel, the other still clasped in mine. I let it drop to my lap and when he kept it there, my life didn't exist beyond this car anymore. My heart thumped to the bass and threatened to rock my ribs from the thrill of it all. I never thought I'd find myself in darkness feeling like this.

Your only limit is your imagination.

Before I knew it, the darkness lifted, and we were outside again. I wasn't sure what to take in first, the fact we'd made it, or the view that stretched in front of me.

Now I saw why we'd driven.

The city in front of me was like nothing I'd ever seen before. It was like someone had taken the lights of Tokyo, the peace of the mountains, and had fused the two into one giant metropolis. The roads came off the ground and wound their way through the air and down into the city below. Giant billboard advertisements clung to the sides of the buildings and some even floated of their own accord. While Abduco could pass for some leafy part of the world I was from, this was something unique. I *loved* it.

The car pulled into a small spot separate from the road and slowed to a stop at the edge of the cliff. It was a beauty spot designed for people to take in the view, and what a sight it was. I was speechless as I gazed out over the sea of lights that danced in front of my eyes.

Anton took his hand off the wheel, but didn't remove his other from mine. "I know it's why you're stuck on making progress."

"Sorry?"

"With Viktor. He told me you're having trouble Shifting from one location to the next."

"Oh." *That.* He was right. My fear of being pushed into the tiniest of spaces, even for a split second, was stopping my body from even trying. I hadn't wanted to tell Viktor. I couldn't see a way past my weakness. It was a part of me, after all. If I admitted that, I was worried he'd give up and not train me anymore. He'd never given me any reason to think so, but minds worked overtime here, especially when it came to overthinking.

"Maybe it's just because I'm human after all," I ventured.

Anton squeezed my hand. "I think we both know that's not the case. You wouldn't have managed half the things you have since you've arrived here."

I had thought about this a lot, but had denied myself the opportunity to become excited about the prospect of staying here. I had done extraordinary things, but Perrine had said it was possible to train any mind. Only the Actuation would tell for sure where I belonged.

"Who did this to you? Made you afraid like this." His voice dropped an octave as he gripped the wheel again, but he kept his eyes ahead.

"I don't want to talk about it," I said, refusing to fall for his overprotective charm.

He considered this, but relented, and his expression softened again. "Then next time you're stuck, I want you to remember here. Remember that you got through this tunnel and look at what was waiting for you on the other side. Amazing things can happen when you learn to control what's on your mind. You've got this. I've got you."

His words sent my heart fluttering. "Thank you. If you'd told me a while ago that I'd manage something like that, I would have called you crazy. But why are you doing this?"

"Why am I doing what, Serrk?"

"Being nice."

He clutched his chest in mock pain. I missed the contact from him and it took everything in me not to grab his hand back. "I'm wounded. But if you must ask, I think we were long overdue some time with no complications. Allium has agreed to give us tonight. Well, not the entire night. But here, now. No arguments, no one else. Just you and me. Then I go back to being distant. It's just the way it has to be here."

Part of me wanted to say, *that's one convenient way to describe meet-*

ing up behind your girlfriend's back, but something told me there was more to it than that.

"Why does it have to be that way, though?" My mouth was speaking for itself again. I always had to ask the tough questions, but better that than to struggle in silence.

"If it wasn't obvious, I have to be with Scarlett. It's a prior arrangement between our fathers. It's not something we chose for ourselves."

Oh. *Oh.* The implications of what he was saying hit me like a brick. Granted, I hadn't been free in life because of my financial limits, but never had I stepped into a cage built for me by my status. Which is what he had laid out for him.

"That wasn't obvious," I said. "So that means you'll need to–" It seemed ridiculous to use the word 'marry' in front of him.

He saved me the trouble. "Yes, that is their plan for us. Arranged marriages are common in Domain. There are many here who accept a life of convenience for the greater good; plus, it's the only way Apex Shifters and Mesos may be together, unless of course they're Covalents, in which case, pretty much anything goes."

"Covalents?"

"Your perfect match. They're extremely rare, but can you imagine what it would be like to find someone who understands and admires every aspect of you and you them?"

Honestly, I couldn't.

If the city wasn't such a buzz before us, I would have thought time stood still. We seemed to have been here for seconds, yet also hours.

"Well, she likes you a lot." I summarised, unable to add anything else positive about Scarlett.

"She likes what I stand for, for the power and the security I could give her." *Why did I have to feel the stab of jealousy over him even talking about this?* "But other than that, I don't think there's much interest there. And as far as that's concerned, the feeling is mutual."

I was stunned at this revelation, though his actions and comments were making much more sense now. Not that I could get too excited. He was still off-limits. I concentrated on the scene in front of me once again as the car walls closed in on us and threatened me to do something stupid like kiss him.

A car overtook us at high speed and drove onto the floating road into the city. It was a view I'd never get used to. The lights twinkled and flashed like a thousand cameras. An iridescent array of colours splashed across the horizon.

"It's so beautiful." My voice was almost a whisper.

"Very much so." He wasn't looking at the city. His voice had dropped lower again, though this time it wasn't out of anger.

I swallowed, trying not to react to his compliment. "Thank you for bringing me here."

Anton took my hand and squeezed it again, leaving me giddy with nerves. "There are a lot of beautiful things in the world, Cee. You deserve to see them for what they are."

Were we still talking about the city stretched in front of us? I couldn't deny it anymore. Despite how unavailable he was, he *did* like me. It was out in the open. Well, between us anyway. Those last words had been his confession. Even if we couldn't go there, I knew I hadn't been imagining everything.

I hoped the look I gave him would say everything I couldn't. "Thank you."

Anton went on in his velvety voice, making my heart spiral. "In another life, Cee, this might have worked well."

I ran my thumb over his hand. It was such a simple gesture the way he kept holding on, yet so much more intimate. "It's a shame it can't." I'd never been one for rules, but I couldn't ignore my thoughts about

Allium. "Why does Allium have such a problem with me?"

"You represent everything he doesn't stand for. I imagine it's that."

"You imagine? Aren't you in each other's heads all the time?"

Anton's brows furrowed. "Not with you."

"So why did he kiss me?"

Anton's face darkened. "He's kept his reasons from me, too. But I imagine to keep us apart."

I filed that away for later. It must be because he didn't want Anton seeing all the ways he'd love to humiliate me, or kill me, or whatever it was he did with people he didn't like.

Anton ran a hand through his hair. "Allium is complicated. Do you know what it's like to feel that you exist your whole life, but never live?"

I did. I'd had an entire lifetime of it, but even I still had limits. "It doesn't give him the right to be an asshole, or to kiss me because he feels like it."

"From what I saw, you didn't hate it." *Was that jealousy I could see?* His mouth pressed into a hard line, and his mask snapped back into place as he continued. "But no, it doesn't give him the right to act like that, and he feels guilty. That's why he's giving us a reprieve tonight. He feels he owes that at least. He's used to being the bad guy. That's how everyone sees him, regardless of how he acts. He wasn't always quite like this, but over time, he moulded himself to their expectations. He's my Other, not my equal, in their eyes. I feel differently about him of course. I know he's much more than that. If anything, *he's* the strong one, the one who should be next in line to lead Abduco. If only they knew how much I need him. I've tried telling people, but they aren't interested. They just see evil. But not the kind we accept."

"What do you mean you need him?" I was hanging on to his every word. I was still angry at Allium, but this was the first time Anton had opened up to me and things were falling into place.

"Not all aspects of being an Apex are parties and champagne. There's a much darker side," Anton said, looking ahead.

"Like what?"

"I don't want to go into it. Not right now."

"I understand." And while I understood his need for privacy, it looked like, despite making progress, there were some things he still needed to keep to himself. I suppose that was fair. I couldn't expect him to open up to me about his entire life when I'd only been in his for a few weeks. Time had flown since I'd arrived in Domain, but in the grand scheme of things, I hadn't even been here for two months yet. I congratulated myself for being reasonable and not rising to his challenge.

Anton looked at war with himself before he continued. "There are just aspects of my job that I can't do, that Allium can, that he enjoys. It's not that I'm not ruthless. You just need to be more than that in order to survive the more sinister side of life here. You need to be more than morally grey, you need to be–"

"Allium?"

"Allium," he confirmed. "Without him, I wouldn't be where I am. I owe him everything."

"Well, it's a shame that him and I don't get on. You exalt him. And I think the same of you," I said.

"Serrk, you're making me blush," he brought a hand to his cheek, even though there was no sign of redness there.

I playfully shoved him, curling my arm round his bicep. *Damn, that felt good.* I was a sucker for punishment tonight by reminding myself of what I couldn't have. He was a decent person. Not perfect, other than his looks, of course, but he was trying.

I sat back. "Thank you for this. For the clothes, for paying for everything. You've given me access to a life I never thought I'd have. It's not that I expect any of it. Or need it. I just realised that I never thanked you."

He gave me a genuine smile that warmed me from the inside out. "Like I said, it's me that should thank you. It turned out to be a pleasant drive here in the end. Much better than I'd expected for my night."

"A lucky twist of fate we drove here, I guess," I said

His dark eyes sparkled with promise. "Oh, it wasn't fate."

I raised a brow at him. "But you weren't going to bring me here? It was only because Julian went with Scarlett that you and I ended up in your Jeep at all."

He gave me a knowing look. "Wasn't I?" When I still looked bewildered, he added, "I may have used a bit of mental persuasion with Julian, and might have pointed him towards taking Scarlett's spare seat instead."

My eyes widened. "You can't manipulate other people into doing what you want!"

"Yes, I can. It's literally what I do. I'm an Apex." He smirked.

I turned away from his perfect features and stared straight ahead, grinning. "You're abhorrent."

"Remember I'm an Abduco Shifter, so that's almost a compliment."

For someone who said he didn't joke, he was surprisingly funny.

Anton looked at his watch. "We'd better go. We've been away for ages."

"How long is ages?" I was aware that I'd lost all concept of time, responsibility, and just about everything since stepping into his car.

"I think just over five hours."

Five hours?! I thought it had been a couple at the most. I hadn't realised we were so far away. "Does time work the same in Domain as in my world?" It felt weird calling it that. I felt more at home in a brief space of time here than I ever did there.

"Your imagination is something else, Serrk. Time is the same here as in your world. We took the scenic route as it's the best. And you deserve the best."

God, this man. I was becoming a master of self-control. I sighed louder than I meant to. "It's a shame your truce has to end."

"My truce with Allium might be over, but I'll be thinking about this for a long time," Anton admitted. "We had better show up for our night out, though. I can sense he's becoming impatient."

I looked over the city, etching it into my mind for later, and vowing to revisit again when things were simpler. But for now, Persen was calling.

"It's been quite the night already." It had been nice while it lasted to see beneath the mask that was Anton. I would take what I could.

"Oh, Serrk," Anton gave me the smirk that made my heart skitter as he pulled the car back into the road and headed for the city lights. "We're only just getting started."

16

VIKTOR AND FORREST

Shifter 101: Mindchill is a drug that detaches the soul from the mind. Its use throughout any House in Domain is illegal.

I didn't know what happened on that drive, but I would have loved to have been a fly on the wall. The view alone was always best from the road, and the look on Charity's face when they rounded the corner would be a picture. They'd taken their time, arriving later than everyone else, and when they did, I sensed the tension between them had evaporated.

Scarlett must have sensed it too, as she was quick to wrap herself round Anton's arm as we gathered outside the busy casino. But Anton just leaned down to Charity's level and gestured at the door. "Hydra Headquarters. It's the same as the Bureau for the Dragos in Abduco."

Charity eyed the door, frowning. "Will we be okay here?" She knew of the gang feuds between the houses, but was less familiar with the understanding between Abduco and Persen, what with Anton and Spyder being in charge of their respective gangs.

"Oh, yes." Anton winked, earning himself a tighter grip from Scarlett as she scowled at him. "Remember when Spyder said he was the head of the Hydras? I'd say we'll be just fine."

At the sight of Spyder and his pink-tipped hair, the doormen parted to let us through. I spotted Bronx already at a machine in the corner. He was trying to win another stuffed cow for his collection. Despite being built like a house, the man was like a ninja. Though that was part of his job: to follow Anton around unseen as their bodyguard. He'd upped his game recently. I hadn't seen him about as much and made a note to follow this up with Anton. Normally, the two were inseparable. Or maybe I'd just been too busy with everything going on with Charity.

Spyder wasted no time in loading his Shiftcoins into the nearest poker table. I joined him. Anton sat down, and I heard the notification chime of a generous sum of money entering my account. By the looks of the faces around the table, Spyder, Scarlett, and Julian all had too. He then said, "I'm fronting everyone's buy-in."

Now it made sense. He'd done it so Charity could play. She didn't have any neurocurrency, and couldn't earn any yet. This would be another benefit of her passing her Shifter Actuation. In Domain, the Apex Shifters only worked with human minds as their full-time career. Meso and Demi-Shifters still worked with minds, but on a much less frequent basis. For jobs, they did all the things required to make Domain run: working in shops, teaching in schools, even joining the ranks of the Nebulari–our police force.

Charity didn't seem like the person who enjoyed getting things paid for her, but she'd have no problem landing a job in Domain. I'd seen how hard she could work. I noted her small nod of thanks in Anton's direction as the Shiftcoin stack materialised in front of her. She was independent, and I could see how difficult she found it to trust people.

The dealer dealt the cards and Anton made a big raise pre-flop.

With Charity's apparent lack of knowledge of poker, she played along just because one of her cards was a Queen. I only knew she was holding a Queen as she hadn't understood how to hold her cards so that the others couldn't see them. Everyone else was observing her cards, too. I'd seen it before. People who were unfamiliar with the game got excited every time they had a Jack, Queen, or King, making rash decisions based on that alone.

Charity sat with wide eyes. "I've got a Queen and a two, is that good?"

"It's Queen deuce, and you're not meant to say it out loud, Serrk," Anton said under his breath, frowning.

The rounds progressed, and Charity's pile of Shiftcoins diminished. Just when her pile had reached three figures instead of five, when she had squandered enough for everyone to lose faith in her as a threat, she started to play. She had a cunning side; I'd give her that.

By the final round, Spyder had exhausted his Shiftcoins and had gone off to the bar. Scarlett was sitting over Anton's shoulder, looking furious at having lost to Charity. I'd been speaking to a blonde who seemed interested and was accepting of my situation with Forrest and Julian, so we were bound to have an interesting night ahead. I always explained to the woman that I met that I'd need to leave afterwards to allow Forrest and Julian time together, too. If they were on board, it was a win-win for everyone. No awkward sleepovers for me, no nasty surprises when the bed was empty in the morning for them. She joined me at the table. Her company seemed a more interesting option than poker, anyway. Still, I sat watching where only Anton and Charity were left playing.

"If you think I'm falling for your 'don't know what I'm doing' act, think again, Serrk." Anton frowned, looking at his own cards.

"What act?" Charity gave him innocent doe eyes as she looked down at her cards and bit her lip. Scarlett's hand tightened on Anton's shoulder and my better-than-usual Shifter hearing heard the grinding of teeth coming from her direction.

Despite the drinks, I could see what she was doing. Between biting her lip, and glancing at Anton's rings, she was leading him into a false string of tells. By the look on his face too, he was falling for it. Anton was often razor sharp at this sort of thing, but he was too busy following her features to have noticed. He had appeared to have forgotten Scarlett was still at his shoulder. Had his back not been to her, I was sure she would have had more to say about the expression that crossed his face as he watched Charity, mesmerised.

The dealer dealt the flop: Ace, Ace, Queen.

Charity jumped all in. Anton called without hesitation. They both must have had excellent hands as they looked pleased as the last cards turned.

Charity's smile lit up the room as she showed her hand. "Queens full house," she said, her face shining with pride. Damn, Queens full of Aces. Hymev, if Anton had a hand that beat that . . .

But he didn't. He eyed her cards and said with surprising modesty, "Nice hand." He folded his own cards, gesturing to the chips in front of him. "They're yours now. I was bluffing to see if you'd take the bait, but I only had seven deuce. You knew better."

"Always got to keep them guessing," Charity said. "Never let them know who you are, right, Viktor?" She flashed me a smug grin, and I gave one right back. She'd played us all, so she deserved this.

We all rose from the table and fanned out across the casino. As the dealer collected Anton's cards, one hit his hand and flipped, the Ace of Spades flashing upright for a second and betraying that he couldn't have had the hand he'd said. He'd had Aces full of Queens, and he'd let her win, anyway. I glanced round. Other than Anton, I was the only one who'd seen.

He shot me a look as if to say, *speak, and you're dead*. Of course, the venom was there, but there wasn't any truth in it, I think.

I wasn't even angry about handing over my money. As Anton and I joined everyone at the bar, Charity looked overcome with emotion as she made her first purchase of a bottle of champagne with her winnings. Her transaction went through, earning her a slap on the back from Spyder.

I knew enough about where she'd come from to know that it was unlikely she'd ever had an amount like it in her account before. I could see why Anton had allowed her to win, and why she could never find out he had done so. He wouldn't miss it, yet it would mean the world to her. While it wasn't life changing, it meant she could now buy things and enjoy herself a little. Something she'd had to deny herself until now.

I saw how he'd looked at her across the table. I'd only seen it once before. It was how Julian looked at Forrest and vice versa.

"I can't believe Charity beat you, Anton. You're supposed to be our calculating poker prince. She even beat me! Gambling is my middle name." Spyder was none the wiser about what had played out at the table.

"I suppose I used a small bit of creative licence with my tells," Charity admitted. "It may have led a few of you astray."

Scarlett looked outraged at this revelation.

"It was fair game, Cee-erk," Anton started, then took a drink to hide his near slip up of the name. I didn't miss it. Scarlett didn't either, judging by her face.

I jumped in. "*Experientias determinare nos non actiones*. It's my actions that will determine who I am. It's our Abduco motto. If you won by outsmarting everyone else, that says more about them than you."

She gave me a small grin as she took the bottle and poured herself a glass of champagne.

"Yeah well, do you know what the Caedes motto is?" Scarlett had a faint blush creeping up her neck. "It's how we move forward that matters. So, let's move forward from this not-very-dramatic event that everyone is making a big deal of, and get on with our night."

"Oh, are we doing mottos? You know what mine is?" Spyder paused for effect, chewing his lip and making his snakebites appear lopsided. He kept us all in suspense as he took a long swig from Charity's bottle. "It's . . . 'fuck it!'"

We all fell about at the sheer ridiculousness that was Spyder.

Julian took that moment to growl in my ear. "Yours could be *fucking it later.*"

"Still Viktor here, mate." I slapped him on the shoulder, well used to the mix-up.

"Oops, my bad!" He didn't even look embarrassed. Such was life in situations like ours.

"Just because you and Forrest are monogamous until the day you die doesn't mean I have to hear all the juicy details." I nudged him in the ribs.

Just because you have more dates than I have cups of tea in a day, doesn't mean we both need to, Forrest retorted.

The transition between Forrest and I was so smooth. It was almost as if we were the same person with humour and morals, but opposite in our approach to dating or settling down.

After things wrapped up at the casino, we headed to a bar. It was getting late and the only bars that were open were the ones that had a dance floor. Forrest kept flickering to the front of my mind, eager to get back home with Julian. I was also keen to get back to my new friend. . . *Shit, what is her name again?* People knew enough about me to know that I wasn't a relationship man. It wasn't because of any trauma or terrible thing that had happened when I was younger or anything like that. I was just happy being by myself. Well, with my dating life, I was rarely by myself, anyway. It didn't stop me treating everyone with courtesy and respect, well most of the time, as sometimes that didn't extend to learning all the names when each encounter was so fleeting.

Julian's arm curled round me and I shrank back, leaving them to enjoy the moment for a while. By the time I came back forward to use my moves on the dance floor, Scarlett was dancing with her back up against Anton. The girl had some moves, but unknown to her, his eyes were on Charity, who was dancing with Spyder.

Charity and Spyder had grown close from all our hanging out, but I could tell there wasn't meaning in it like that. Plus, while dancing with Spyder, she was staring right back at Anton over his shoulder, her eyes alight. If only there weren't a thousand traditions and rules keeping them apart, they'd make a good couple.

Anton's shoulders tensed with the type of fury I only saw during our business with the Dragos. There was jealousy written all over his face. I bet he wanted nothing more than to go over there and . . .

I finished that thought with Forrest, laughing to myself. Damn rules keeping them apart. A sexually frustrated life was not a fun one. For anyone.

Scarlett caught Charity looking and "accidentally" elbowed her, sending her rocketing into Spyder and taking the pair of them down. It was like a move that we would have used back during our time at Moonglade Academy. But the hilarity that followed reminded me of one of our post-exam nights out.

A couple who had been dancing nearby helped Spyder and Charity to their feet again. Both Shifters seemed interested in Spyder, and the three of them paired off into a more suggestive dance than the one he'd engaged in with Charity. She excused herself, leaving them to it.

She walked right by Scarlett, shouting over her shoulder. "I was expecting worse. I thought you were stronger." She then blew a kiss at her, or maybe Anton, and walked off towards the bar, leaving Scarlett to stew in Anton's arms.

Scarlett twisted round and tried to go after Charity, but Anton prevented her. I got the impression that the only reason he held on was to prevent any more harm coming to Charity.

I left Forrest and Julian for the next few songs. They had to get home soon, or find somewhere here. Combining drinks, heat on the dance floor, and Julian's hard torso against mine had Forrest wanting to act on every urge, and it was my body too that was responding.

Spyder knocked into me as he stumbled, despite being carried by the same man and woman from earlier. "Afterparty at mine!"

He didn't make the best decisions while drunk. His adopted parents would be furious. They wanted him to set an example, especially coming from his Apex background, but he was still in mourning in his own way. I looked at Julian, not needing to spell out what I was asking, and he nodded. We would all return to Abduco Manor where we could monitor him. Spyder was great fun, until he drank to keep the memories of his parents, his actual parents, away. He needed a friend. He'd had no choice but to take over the Hydras after losing them. Having never had a chance to mourn their loss, he'd turned to partying instead. But if this made him happy, and I could keep him safe, who was I to deny him some reprieve from his sadness over losing his entire family?

"Okay, mate," I said to him. "It's time to go home, but let's do the afterparty in Abduco."

"Your wish is my command." He saluted me and gestured to the Shifters beside him, accidentally hitting the man in the face. "These good people have agreed to help me back to mi–you–wherever we are going." Surprisingly, the man didn't look bothered. Spyder was pretty unique, but with his alternative style, off-the-wall personality and toned physique, he had no shortage of admirers.

"It's fine, I can fly the helicopter," I turned to whisper to Charity who'd joined us and was looking at the drink in my hand frowning. "He forgets it has autopilot."

She looked relieved. The idea of a drunk Spyder being in charge of anything, let alone a helicopter, was a scary thought indeed.

We loaded Spyder into the helicopter as easily as you would expect for a Shifter who was over six feet tall and all arms and legs, along with his shouts of, "Don't hurt her!" *Her* being his helicopter. It was amazing he would still get laid after this. Likely several times.

I helped him up. "Do you think you're a better candidate to keep *her* safe, Spy?"

He considered this as he slumped into a seat between his new friends. "You make a fair point, Vik, and that is why I love you. And I love you, and I love you." He tapped the noses of the Shifters on either side of him as he spoke. Crazy bastard.

Despite the sadness behind his reasons for drinking, I laughed. He needed the laughs.

Bronx had climbed into the pilot's seat undetected with his stuffed cows in the co-pilot seat. The group cut quite an image. Once the three of them were safely in the helicopter, I turned to the rest of our group, running through the numbers again.

"We'll need a Shuber home. Too many of us have been drinking."

I was counting the heads when I realised I didn't know where my date had gone. The cons of being the sensible one in the group, making sure everyone got home alright.

Right on cue, my Shiftsung buzzed with a message. She'd sent a picture of what I was coming back to in my bedroom. *Fuck*. Forrest and I were going to have to split the night between us. It's just as well I cared little about sleeping.

Julian was watching over my shoulder, understanding. "Fine, but you owe me for taking the first shift." We both grinned. I always did. He was a good guy, Julian.

We made our way down to the taxi rank underneath the casino. I saw Charity shrink back as we approached the lifts.

"I can't go in there."

Scarlett gave her a cruel look. "What's the worst that can happen? It won't break down and leave you in the dark. Or maybe it will. *You* don't mind the dark, do you, Charity?" She gave a cruel laugh as the rest of us looked at each other uncomfortably.

I was surprised to see Allium's light eyes, given he'd kept himself away from Charity at all costs, given their hatred of each other.

"Scarlett, we're leaving. I'll drive," he gritted out, his teeth clenched.

Scarlett turned towards him and recognised the change. Charity looked confused as she turned from the lift. "You've been drinking all night."

To all our surprise, Allium took a long breath and answered. "Anton has, I haven't. Come on, we'll take your car. Julian, here's the key to mine. Get everyone else back."

Julian didn't drink. He raised a brow as he caught the keys. Neither Anton nor Allium let anyone drive their car. Ever.

Allium and Scarlett left without another word. Charity stared after them. But for once, I didn't see the hatred on her face I expected. She just looked confused. I felt sorry for her. She couldn't understand the nature of their relationship. Unless she understood more than I thought after all.

I made it my mission to improve her night as our cars drove off under the starry sky, alight with a thousand images reflected from the billboards, as we headed back to continue the afterparty at mine.

17

ALLIUM

Shifter 101: Humans entering Domain are under the protection of the prophecy and cannot be seriously harmed.

All I could think about, all I could ever think about, was: I fucking kissed her.

I thought she'd been under the influence of Mindchill that first night at her arrival party. She might not have even known someone had arranged for her to take that one glass off the tray. By the time I pieced it together, I was already too late. She would have been sharper, more focused. She would have known it was me and not Anton. But I'd seen the detachment in her soul, her senses dulled. But I couldn't stop thinking about that megawatt smile, visible even in the darkness.

Charity never gave Anton a name for who had done it to her. I found it bizarre, but assumed she hadn't known. After all, she'd been so new here. How could she have made such an enemy? She barely knew anyone else. I assumed it was someone who didn't know her. Some nobody that I wouldn't have even known. I figured someone had been jealous of her prophecy status. As much as I despised her, her arrival here was a big deal for every Shifter in Domain. I cursed myself for letting my confusion get in the way. I'd been too blind and distracted to figure it out. Sure, I'd been suspicious, but I had no proof. I had to be careful before I did anything stupid. And then I did it, anyway. Because of a drunken throwaway comment which revealed it had been Scarlett she'd met that night.

I'd made no secret of the fact I wanted Charity gone. I had a family to protect, people I cared about, and I didn't need another person to add to that list. Especially not someone who was the current centre of attention in Domain. Friends became targets, and it was my mantra to keep as little people as close to me as possible. If she was in relation to the prophecy and had anything to do with the impending war it spoke of… fuck. It didn't bear thinking about.

But I pushed that to the back of my mind. It wasn't possible. Draven made it clear it wouldn't be the worst thing if she went back to her own world after her Actuation and, frankly, I needed the biggest distraction I'd ever faced gone.

Her smell of sweet destruction, like charred petals.

Fuck.

Without even meaning to, she roamed the corridors of my mind. Not literally, I'd never fucking allow that, no matter how much she tried. She was ballsy, but that wasn't what drew me to her. She was shy too, and had a kindness that I hadn't encountered before. And though she could be cutting, she didn't regard me with disgust like most Shifters did around here. She reacted only to the hate I sent her way. Maybe I was delusional after all. I blamed her for that. The only place I could get any peace here was my bedroom. I kept the door to my sanctuary closed at all times so it wouldn't begin to smell like her–I was worried I'd enjoy it too much.

Why had Scarlett had to use Mindchill? I didn't tolerate Mindchill anywhere in Abduco. And it was all my fucking fault. I'd messaged

Scarlett the day I'd met Charity. I'd been furious the time we'd met. Her audacity to question me. Yet there was a vulnerability concealed beneath the layers built by a lifetime of keeping people out. I knew it well.

I'd panicked. This wasn't how I was. I didn't notice these things about people. Anton had joked before that I wasn't capable of caring for anyone beyond my immediate family and I'd taken it as a compliment. It's how I'd intended to be. I'd asked Scarlett to intimidate Charity, and I assumed their meeting that day she arrived had been successful. I didn't realise they'd even met again. Let alone the night of her arrival party. The night I kissed her. Stupid. Idiot. Mindchill was a parasitic drug, sucking the life out of someone so much they might as well be off to Langison. Charity was lucky the dose had been so low. That Scarlett even had the drug confirmed my suspicions about it leaking from Caedes. These missing persons were already a growing issue; and if they linked to the disappearances like I thought they were, then this was a big fucking problem.

This was why I needed my focus back. It was why I'd kissed her, pretending to be Anton. I knew she would never trust him again after it and she'd avoid us both. That's the only reason. Fuck, *I kissed her.*

I'd been thinking the same thing for weeks now.

Now that I knew what Scarlett had done, I couldn't find it in me to be in her company for a minute longer without breaking her. Scarlett had taken Charity's worst fear and exploited it. It was something I'd done to others a million times, which I didn't give a fuck about, but hearing she was the target snapped something inside of me. I was even more furious, I'd wanted her to be scared after all, so I couldn't explain why I was feeling so angry about it.

I was pretty fucking broken to say the least.

It had been smart getting away before I exploded in front of everyone. Scarlett's comment had been the final nail in the coffin, figuratively speaking of course. *You don't mind the dark, do you, Charity?*

It had taken me all of about three seconds to decide what I was going to do. The second we'd arrived back outside hers in Caedes, she'd raised a brow at me. We never went to hers. It had always been my family's home.

The warm air around us chilled. The anger must have been rolling off me in waves, because Scarlett was silent for once. She was always more vocal around Anton. I was sure that she feared me, not that she'd voice it. I preferred it that way, anyway.

"It's over." I didn't want to drag this out any longer than I needed to.

"What do you mean, *over*?" she looked at me indignantly. "You know what my father—"

"I don't give a shit what Draven said." I'd called him Draven instead of her father. Strictly speaking, he wasn't, but she didn't need that reminder. The hurt in her eyes almost caught me off guard. Almost. Until I remembered why I was doing this. "That's between him and my father."

"So, after everything, just like that?" Her bottom lip was wobbling.

"I don't know what you mean by *everything*. But yes, just like that. See you around." I decided being cruel was the best. I wouldn't give her even a glimpse of hope. It would be easier for her to move on. Not that I thought she was ever infatuated with me, but more with the idea of an Apex lifestyle and the safety it could provide.

She lingered on the doorstep, crestfallen with a dash of fury. It was no surprise she was Caedes through and through. I'm sure she'd hoped I was going to come in when I'd brought us here.

I did it for myself. Not for Charity. *Not* for Charity. I repeated it to ground myself. I needed to keep my focus, and this was just another thing distracting me. Anton had been in the back of my mind telling me not to, telling me we had to keep playing the game, to keep everyone safe.

That's what I was doing, though. Playing the game. And no one fucking tells me what to do.

No one.

Fucking.

Tells.

Me.

What.

To.

Do.

I Shifted back to mine and climbed the steps towards the flat, about to call Anton back forward so he could deal with Charity, given they were getting on like a house on fire and we were not. I wondered if she'd be back from the afterparty already, likely not.

My Shiftsung vibrated in my pocket. I opened it, expecting a torrent of abuse from Scarlett, but instead found it was from my father.

Verde: Your presence is required at the headquarters. Urgently.

The last word prickled my anger. Anger I now had to relieve first, otherwise I might end up snapping at him too. He'd made no secret about the fact that Anton was the favourite son. He'd suggested frequently that Anton remove me permanently, so I guess that summed up how he felt about me.

If only he knew how much Anton relied on me to carry out the dirtier work, that ironically came from our father himself. Fucking hypocrite. I pushed Anton back as we stepped inside. My father could wait.

I delivered punches in time with the music. I was never happy. Anton was always the more cheerful out of the two of us, and that was saying something. It wasn't in our nature as an Abducos. But I would have to admit I reached a superior level of satisfaction as the heavy bass thumped through my soul. Who was I kidding? I didn't have a soul. Hymev, I didn't even know who I was hitting, or why.

I had asked Bronx to find me someone deserving of punishment. There was no shortage of assholes trying to distribute Mindchill throughout Domain, usually to underagers. That wasn't all that was happening; there had been reports that Shifters were going missing, and I was sure there was a connection between the two. Once again, I had no concrete proof, but *The Notion* was becoming more overrun with faces and pleas for their safe return. If we could find anyone who had information, I didn't care how we got it out of them.

Bronx had delivered no questions asked. It was one perk of having a bodyguard who rarely spoke. He followed orders, just as I expected him to.

It felt good to get this out of my system.

The man strapped to the chair appeared to have accepted his fate. He was here to receive pain in order for me to feel better. He hadn't even tried to talk me out of it before the punches started landing. How weak.

A crunch against my knuckles told me his nose had just shattered. Not broken. Shattered. My hand didn't feel all too great from the impact, either. I should find a healthier way to relax. I used to design things in order to calm my chaotic mind, but, recently, I found violence more helpful.

"Who is he anyway?" I directed at Bronx rather than the bloody face in front of me.

Bronx looked up from his phone and I pretended to ignore the video I could see on his screen: *Cows grazing 10-hour playlist.* Wow, the man thought I was in it for the long haul tonight.

It wasn't uncommon for me to spend the night torturing someone. But I wanted it to be scum who deserved it. Someone worse than petty Mesos or Demis. They were weak, but I didn't want to punish them just for that. Tonight, I just wanted to land a few punches on someone deserving to relieve my stress. Then I'd send him to Nexus to heal up afterwards for all I cared. Or I wouldn't. Anton would have told me to focus on the bigger goals we had with the gang, to extract information. But I'd pushed him back. Sometimes I just had to hurt. That's just the way things were here. No one said being an Apex was easy. He was just lucky I wanted to feel the pain with each hit and wouldn't use weapons tonight. I wanted the pain to spread across my knuckles just like the damage it was inflicting. Yeah. I was pretty fucked up. It wasn't a secret.

Bronx answered my question. "Local rival. A Meso connected to Draven, but no one he miss, boss."

I licked my lips. That sounded ideal. I landed another punch, the wet slap against the blood now pouring from his nose only fuelling the adrenaline in me.

I wasn't evil. Though I was far from good. No one likes to think of themselves as pure evil. Though by most people's standards, I suppose that's what I was.

After another hour, the man teetered on the edge of consciousness and I was getting bored. I'd even untied him to see if he would fight back. I enjoyed the fight as much as the aggression, but he hadn't been willing to strike me because of my status, despite the pain I was inflicting on him.

Now *that* was fucked up.

I finally returned to my parents' manor. I loved that even my father couldn't refer to it as my home and the habit had stuck. It would always be Abduco Manor to me, never home. It's why I had built the flat and designed the glamour technology around it. I had to admit, I loved our fortress where everyone had to leave Anton and me the fuck alone.

I gave Bronx the rest of the night off. He'd been following Anton and I twenty-four seven, apart from the time I spent in my apartment. He left, muttering something about a herd as he went. He was a good man and deserved a break from my corrupt self.

I flew tonight. The fighting had been good, but I hadn't had quite the physical release I was craving. There was something else I could do, but given I'd just ended my relationship, that was off the cards. There was something, or rather someone, that would help more than anything, but the chances of that were about as likely as Spyder becoming a librarian.

She is not an option; I reminded myself. I *hated* her for making me like her. Not that she was trying to. That was the even more infuriating part.

It's the way of an Abduco life. Don't get attached, unless you're told to. Don't get unattached, unless you're told to.

I'd made myself quite unpopular over the years by doing what I wanted. Anton attributed his success to me and made no secret of the fact, people just didn't want to listen to him. It was the single thing of his that everyone seemed to ignore. Other than Viktor, he was the only person I trusted.

I landed in front of the imposing doors to Abduco Manor and folded my wings in on themselves. My wings were one of my favourite things about being a Shifter and all the shit that came with it. I had to admit these were pretty special. Anton hadn't told Charity about his wings, or what else we could do. I don't think she'd even grasped at the fact we were fucking *Shifters* for Hymev's sake, i.e. we could Shift to another form. Apparently, he didn't want her to be interested in him just because of his Apex abilities. I guess I could understand that. My wings were huge, bigger than anyone else in my family's, much to my father's fury. I loved the way the air whipped through their leathery exterior as I flew through the sky. It was a good thing Bronx had to stay on the ground in his bear's form whenever I Shifted. He would have skinned them off me in a heartbeat. That man always smelt of leather. I'd stopped questioning it.

Scoffing at the doors that were meant to be intimidating, I made my way up the steps. I just saw them for what they were. Attempts to make us appear to be a bunch of things that we weren't.

My family were slaves to the rules, set in place by generations before them. Every Shifter wanted to be an Apex, but little did they know the restriction on freedom that came with it. I'm glad Anton took such an active interest in bringing me forward and letting me live. I'd hate to see him restrained by such a bullshit regime.

But a necessary bullshit regime, Anton added. I had my walls down now, the flying relieving some of the tension that had been rolling off my body. Anton kept his doors open to me, allowing me to see everything. We were in the same body after all. What was privacy, anyway? It was testament to his decency that he allowed me to keep so many closed. It's not that I didn't trust him, it's just that if he knew as many of his images of Charity matched mine, he would find more reasons to make her stay. And I couldn't have that. So, as far as he knew, my mind was a closed book concerning her. He'd written it off as me not wanting to offend him. I knew fine well how he felt, despite being with Scarlett. In all honesty, I'd done him a favour.

Get inside, you're keeping him waiting. Anton urged me on.

I pushed the heavy doors open and tensed my shoulders when I saw my father waiting for me. He wasn't alone, however; he had company.

Draven stood to greet me, his eyes menacing. I didn't fear anyone, but he was someone to watch out for. He was as unpredictable as they came, and I'd just ended things with his daughter.

Fuck it, I'd take the hit. I wasn't going back on my decision, so I stared him down. "Can I help you?" I could feel the curl of my lip as the disgust I held for this man threatened to show itself.

"I see you've been busy tonight," Draven said, pointing out the blood staining my face and clothes. "But I think you know why I called you here. I know you ended things with Scarlett, like it was even your decision. You're going to regret that."

And that's just the thing. Once someone has lost everything, there's nothing left. He'd never hurt Anton. He's the prize boy, one of the future rulers of Domain provided the Cerebral Council bless his succession, which they will. Me, I'm nothing, I've got nothing. Which means I've got nothing to lose.

And no one EVER.

Fucking.

Tells.

Me.

What.

To.

Do.

18

CHARITY

Shifter 101: Abduco Shifters exist to lead humans away from poor decisions.

A haze of white, dense fog covered the forest ahead, limiting my visibility to a few metres in front of me. Had I not been standing on higher ground, I would have barely seen anything. From my vantage point, I looked out over the woods, then turned towards the village behind me. As I gazed out over the semi-urban horizon, I saw it was not a village at all, but an entire city made up of houses, or rather, mansions, that were very village-like in their appearance.

The only sound I could hear was the crash of the rain hitting the leaves and ground around me. I inhaled, the earthy aroma that could only occur during a sudden downpour filling my nose.

A dampness hung about the air that suggested the rain never stopped. Instead of being gloomy, the greenery flourished and took over whole stretches of ground and buildings alike, giving the area an overgrown look. I had never seen such dense areas enveloped by moss. I walked past a stone angel with tendrils of ivy spiralling round it, encasing it in a green blanket. Nearby, a bench was encumbered by the thick vines, rendered useless.

The whole place looked abandoned, yet if I looked, I could see signs of life. Perhaps the of this place were choosing to hide themselves. Ivy clung to the windows of most of the buildings here. The atmosphere pulsated with the antiquity of wealthy families, past and present.

It was a city in the forest. Or forests situated among the city. Both were so immense and appeared to be so longstanding; it was impossible to tell which had been there first.

My skin prickled from being woken before I should. It was five a.m., and I had heard no sign of Anton arriving home. I rubbed my forehead to soothe the pain away that accompanied my vivid dreams. I must've fallen asleep out here of Abduco. The last thing I remembered was coming out to the balcony to reminisce about the night's events. It had been some night. I'd won more money than I had ever seen in my life. But that was nothing compared to the fact Allium and I had managed a civil encounter. And I hadn't even processed what had happened on the drive there.

Was that the wind? The sound pulled me from my thoughts. No, it wasn't the wind, but it was coming closer. Rhythmic. Like . . .

Flapping?

It was my last thought before a massive weight swung into me, knocking me off my feet. My head smacked off the wall behind me and pain whipped through my skull. The blow would have knocked me unconscious had something not softened the impact.

I opened my eyes, disorientated. It was Anton who seemed to have fallen from the sky. But for once, my attention wasn't on him.

It was the long wings that were spread from his back.

Holy fucking shit. Of course, I knew things didn't function in Domain the same as my world. But I'd not considered the fact he would have fucking *wings* like this.

Broad, leathery wings protruded from his muscular frame, blocking out the light from the low fairy lights above us on the balcony. They spread out around two metres on either side of him. His stance caused him to take up most of the small outdoor space. Black cartilage stretched across the bones, and I didn't have to know much about Shifter anatomy to tell they held a mass of strength. I lay there frozen, wondering how hard I'd hit my head. In a strange way, they were quite beautiful.

I was stuck. Pinned down by Anton. Something was wrong. He'd normally have made some remark and been a gentleman about wondering if I was alright.

"Are you hurt?" I wondered if he'd cushioned my blow and injured himself. He didn't answer me. I tried to lift his weight, but he sagged into me–the pressure of him bearing down in an intense but not comforting way.

All the grace I'd known him to have had vanished. I was being crushed under his weight. Something was wrong. I tried again, giving him a small shove. "I need you to get off me so I can help you."

Anton rolled off me onto his back with a roar of pain and I saw it. Blood. Coming from him. All down his torso. Now down mine.

His wings folded in on themselves as he balled his fists from the pain. His chest and torso were laced with giant lashes like something razor-sharp had whipped him. But that wasn't the worst of it. His ribs were so shattered that the entire left side of his torso just looked broken. It jutted out at awkward angles, and I gasped in horror as I realised that there were areas where the snapped bone was in danger of breaking through the skin. I shuddered just looking at him in pain like that. I wasn't squeamish, but something inside of me broke seeing him this way. So hurt. So helpless.

He needed help. Serious help.

The front door nearly swung off of its hinges as Bronx came barrelling into the flat. I knew very little about Anton's bodyguard, but I could see from the panic in his eyes that he was just as scared as I was.

"He say leave him. I had no idea!" he panted. He must have followed Anton here on foot.

"What happened?"

"No time. I get help. Stay with him!" He took off. Reaching for my phone, I sent simultaneous messages to Perrine and Viktor, telling them to come to the flat immediately. I'd used the thought mode, so I didn't have to bother with typing and could focus on stopping the flow of blood from the worst of the lashes.

He winced in pain as I removed my thin dressing gown and used it to staunch the worst of the cuts on his chest, holding the fabric in place over the wound. I barely noticed the cold air nipping at my skin through my nightdress as I worked. I was careful to avoid applying any pressure on his ribs. Those would have to wait.

"Jesus, Anton." My voice was shaky as I took in the full extent of the damage. "What the fuck happened to you?"

"Not Anton." His breath came out in rattles. His eyes were still closed.

"Allium?"

His eyes snapped open. They were bloodshot, but the unmistakable lightning green flashed across them, and I knew who I was speaking to.

"What have you done to him?" The truce evaporated in my rage. "Is it so difficult for you to stay out of trouble?"

His reaction wasn't what I was expecting. Not at all. "Do what you need to do, Serrk," he said through gritted teeth.

"What?" He wasn't making any sense. He tried to sit up, and I pushed him back down as gently as I could, shivering as I watched the out-of-place ribs move with him.

"My mind is too hurt. If I go, Anton will stay. You'll get him and you can both be together."

"I don't know what you mean by that." I was confused over Allium's riddles. We'd kept our encounters short and even then, he'd been repugnant. The only exception was when I'd kissed him, but that was under his false pretense. So that spoke volumes. He'd made no secret that he despised me and wanted me gone, so why was he suggesting I be with Anton now?

He didn't want you harmed. Just back in your own world, said a voice in my head.

"I know you and Anton would be happier if I was gone. Here's your opportunity. I've got nothing left. Everyone would be better off without me," he gritted out.

His words sent shockwaves through me. Enemy or not, he didn't deserve that. No one should ever feel that alone. And he wouldn't die, or whatever it was that Shifters did, just because I'd allowed it.

"Why are you being–" I struggled for the words, "like this?"

"Surprised I've got some depth to me?" He grimaced from the pain as he spoke.

"Oh, I don't think that for a second. You're as shallow as they come," I responded, trying to keep him conscious. "But you're shit out of luck. I don't fancy your death on my conscience tonight."

He cracked a weak smile, then clutched his ribs in pain. I hissed in frustration at not being able to do anything while I waited for help to arrive. "Help is coming. Tell me what I can do in the meantime." I couldn't let him go. It wasn't just my conscience that came into play: Anton's words echoed in my mind from earlier. I knew how much he needed Allium.

He groaned in pain. "The physical stuff isn't as bad as it looks. I can heal. The actual damage is in my mind. Keep me talking until someone comes. It's the only way I'll keep my memory."

"Keep you talking?"

"Yes, Serrk, use your mouth to make sounds."

Well, I was glad he seemed to still have some of his sour demeanour, something I thought I'd never say.

I braced myself. Talking to Allium. That was something I didn't know how to do. Before I could overthink it, I launched straight in with something that had been on my mind for weeks.

"Why did you kiss me?"

He grinned. "Now, *that* is a long story. But the short version is I wanted you gone. Wanted you away from Anton and I. I knew you wouldn't trust him as long as I was around."

I staunched a bad lash with the hem of my nightdress. "You're evil, aren't you?"

"The very same." His eyes flickered to my leg, then met mine. I could tell he was being honest.

"Then how can I trust you?" My dressing gown was becoming saturated from the blood, but I didn't have a better option and didn't want to risk leaving him even for a few seconds.

"You can't." His face was grave. "Ever. And now is your chance to finish the job and run off into the sunset with Anton. You don't want me around. Girls like you should be afraid of guys like me. I'm the monster that people fear waking up to in the night."

"You think I'm scared of you?" My forefinger wiped a trail of blood from his mouth before I realised what I was doing. "Maybe you don't know enough about where I'm from. Some people worry about the monsters under their bed. Me? I used to sleep with my arm out, hoping one would take it. Because even that would offer me more than the life I had." I took a long breath, realising how raw a statement that was.

"Wow, Serrk, that's deep. Who hurt you?" He winced.

"Who didn't?" I figured I might as well be honest. I applied some gentle pressure to the fabric on his ribs, careful to avoid any of the broken ones.

"Oh, you're dark. I kind of like it." His hand found my arm. I didn't move from his touch.

"Keep talking." I could only hope the thrill I got out of his words wasn't visible. "You won't be going on my watch. I know how much Anton needs you."

"I bet you wish he didn't. You probably wish he'd just remove me like everyone else does."

"That's not what I want."

"Oh?" His face was pale, but alight with something else. It looked just like *hope*?

"He needs you," I gritted out, all too aware of the tightness in my chest. *I need him, I need them.* I thought. But I kept that to myself. Now wasn't the time for big gestures and revelations. Not from me, anyway.

His voice became more strained. "He wants you gone, and I want you to stay."

That sounded like a strange thing to say about Anton. Allium's eyes were closing. I was losing him. Maybe Anton was coming back? I had to keep him talking. "Who wants me gone? Are you talking about Allium? Am I speaking to Anton?"

"I'm still Allium," he said through gritted teeth. "Forget I said it." He looked panicked at his words, as if he'd revealed something by mistake, so I quickly changed the subject.

"What the hell happened to you, Allium?" I couldn't believe even an Apex like him had enemies that would cause him so much damage.

"Another question. I'm not ready to–FUCK!" A sickening crunch came from his abdomen as he tried to sit himself up. He clutched his side in pain, his eyes squeezed shut.

"Don't move! Okay, okay, never mind my question." My heart hammered like a hummingbird against my ribs. He looked like he was going to pass out from the pain. I had to keep him talking. "Explain your wings. Why did I not know you had these?"

His eyes opened again. "Ah, Anton didn't tell you."

"No, he didn't. I'll be taking that up with him later."

Allium seemed to regain some of his colour. "Help me sit up."

"Are you sure you can–"

"I won't ask again, Serrk."

I did as he said, and, with great difficulty, propped him against the wall, keeping the pressure applied to his chest. He looked like he'd been flayed by a sharp object then beaten by something capable of causing bruising damage and broken bones. I wished he would tell me what had happened.

"What have you learned about Shifter forms?" He leaned back against the wall in relief.

I kept him talking. "Next to nothing. I haven't been ready to study it yet as I haven't Shifted location."

"Because of your fear?"

I remembered his presence outside the lift at the casino. He'd seen my reservation to enter. Heard Scarlett's comment. He knew. I'd assumed after my conversation with Anton, it wouldn't be long before he found out, anyway.

"Because of my fear," I confirmed. There was no point in denying it. "Tell me about your wings."

"I'd rather show you." His wings unfurled behind his back.

"No! Don't!" My heart pounded again as I watched. The pain must have been unbelievable. Despite my protests, he continued.

"I have to do this. Have to check if they work." Clenching his teeth from the effort, he leaned forward and stretched his wings out to full length. Each tip met the edges of the balcony, and the sheer size of them overwhelmed me. His smirk showed his satisfaction with what they could still do.

And damn if he didn't look *hot* with them.

A wave of lust ripped through me. I'm glad my thoughts were my own, as it was totally inappropriate given the situation. *It's just because he looks like Anton*, I told myself. *I'm getting caught up in what Anton and I said to each other earlier tonight. That's all it is.*

"Are they injured?" I took them in, struggling to keep my awe from showing.

"They're fine. Like I said, the major damage is in my head. Keep me talking. This is good."

"Tell me everything about Shifters and the forms they can take."

Allium leaned back and folded his wings again with some difficulty. "Well, it's in the name. We wouldn't be Shifters if we didn't have another form we could take."

"Go on." I was eager to keep him distracted.

"Well, Apex Abducos are famous for being dragons. Every single one of us is, except for Viktor who Shifts to a manticore. Apex Shifters can Shift to what you would know as fantasy creatures: dragons, kraken, phoenixes, kelpies, unicorns, and so on, whereas Mesos are limited to the animals you'd find in your world."

I was so overwhelmed by the names he'd just thrown at me; I failed to take in what he'd just said. He could Shift to a dragon. *And I was just finding this out now?!*

It was tempting to ask more, but something told me this wasn't the time for pressing him. I had a flashback to strong paws on my chest when Scarlett had overpowered me. I'd been too reeling in shock at the time to understand what was happening. Though now I knew. "What form does Scarlett take?"

"Ah, Scarlett. A hyena."

That was kind of hilarious. "Fitting."

Allium cracked a smile, then inhaled as he held his ribs. *Okay, no more jokes for now.* Help couldn't be far. I just had to get him to hold on.

"Anton says you like technology."

"Everyone likes technology." His voice was getting fainter.

He was fading. I had to keep him awake. "Tell me about it."

"Too tired." This time, it was barely a whisper.

I had to do something. Frustration swirled among the panic inside of me and I reacted in a split second without thinking.

I slapped him across the face, hard.

His eyes snapped back open and flashed. *Good.* It was risky. But I'd never played safe, anyway. Whatever kept him awake and talking.

"Don't you dare think you're going anywhere, Allium; that's an order." My harsh tone surprised me, but I had no time to dwell on that.

"What the fuck, Serrk? It's taking too long. Just let me go. They'll be better off without me."

"I already told you, there's not a chance." I kept the pressure on his chest. It was becoming more and more difficult as he slumped down. I squeezed myself under his arm and used everything I had to keep him upright.

"As if anyone would miss me. There's too much damage done." He looked down at his arm curled round me and met my eye. "I'm the Other, Charity. I'm the afterthought. The one no one wants."

He sounded so hurt. Anger channelled itself into my veins. "Who did this to you?"

His eyes closed again. "It's just the way life as a Drago is, sweetheart. We understand the risks. People like me don't need saving."

I was going to end up slapping him again. "I'm saving you because Anton needs you. And I need him. And I'm not ready to let you go either. So stop swithering between whether you want to live or die and just stay with me."

This caught his attention, and he pulled himself up and stared down at me. "You think he should keep me around?"

His gaze was intense, but I held it. "Of course I do. Even if I'm going to go to hell for this."

He used what little energy he had to muster a chuckle. "I think you'll find at the end of days, hell is already coming to me, so you'll have good company when you arrive."

I chuckled. "Shut up and save your energy, you idiot. Help is on the way."

He fell back again. "For this, I owe you everything, Serrk."

"Then will you tell me one thing in exchange?"

"Name it."

"Why do you keep your thoughts about me secret from Anton?"

He paused, either to consider or because I was losing him again. I wasn't sure which. "Because of the destruction it would cause."

I frowned. "Because he likes me and you hate me, you mean?"

He barked a harsh laugh. "If only it were that simple. It would be so easy to hate you, Charity. But I don't. I wish I could."

"Then why?" What was this feeling in my stomach? Why did I feel drawn to him on hearing those words?

"Maybe I should show you. I have nothing to lose. But you'll have to trust me. Can you do that?"

"Yes. It doesn't mean you're both forgiven. But I need Anton, and he needs you. So I need you too."

"You've never said that to me before." He leaned forward and stroked my cheek, taking me by surprise. His touch set parts of me alight I didn't know I had. "Perhaps there's something I can do to help you trust me again. See behind some of my doors."

"You'd let me in? To the locked rooms?" I stared at him, incredulous.

"They're yours to enter." His tone was final.

This was huge. I'd expected nothing like this from Allium. I'd barely even seen inside Anton's mind. It had to be done. For Anton. For myself. I braced myself and dived right in.

I left the balcony and stood in Allium's mind. It was hard to believe I'd come here by his choice. I had to admit, he was right; there was serious damage to his mind. The ivy-covered fortified steel doors were burned away. As I looked closer, I saw some more damaged doors. The flickering memories left behind exposed many violent scenes, acts he'd carried out in the name of the Dragos. I left them, those weren't what he had wanted me to see.

I found the door he'd intended for me to find. It had the most locks. Though this time, instead of being destroyed, it was immaculate. The sound of locks unbolting echoed down the hall and I stepped inside, feeling his voice in my head as I saw myself through his eyes, a memory from a mere few minutes ago.

She's sitting in front of me. Fucking beautiful. I know she doesn't think so. She's crazy for not thinking so. How could she not see it? How could I not see it at first?

She's sitting too close. Analysing me. Her grip tightens on her thigh to show she's trying. I'm trying too. I'm letting her in. Giving her an actual glimpse of me. Not everything, but a start. More than anyone has seen.

The parts of her touching me are so soft. Her nightdress leaving so much exposed. Why did she have to choose green to wear to bed? I want to rip everything off her using only my teeth. The effort might kill me, but I'd do it, anyway. But I can't. I need to show her. Show her I care. Show her I can change.

The worst thing is, she looks at me like I'm something. Like I'm not hiding behind the mask of an Apex. Like I'm not walking in the shadow of my father. The shadow that he hates and longs to separate from. Like I'm not being used as a puppet in this supposed utopia that we live in. Sometimes, I wonder if there really is truth in the idea that ignorance is bliss. Because to me, being conscious means being fucked up. Being aware of the fact that I'll always be the Other. I'll always be the one people question over why Anton keeps me. I don't need more reminders of who I am.

She looks breathtaking sitting there as she studies me. She's still angry. Hymev, I'd fuck her there and then to have her scream my name. She's chewing on her lip. I can tell she feels something even though she's trying to make her expression unreadable right now. It's driving me crazy. I would sell my soul for the opportunity to see the images playing in her mind.

But I've fucked up too many times to have someone like her. To have anyone at all. I wish I could help her understand who she is and why she is perfect. She just never can be mine. I can never be hers.

She narrows her eyes like she knows what I'm thinking. I'm terrified of losing her, but I expect to. Why would she want someone like me? Full of self-loathing behind the bravado. If I allowed my whole broken mind to be on display around her, she would run. Yet, I also hope that she wouldn't, as I see similarities in her. She's lost and wants to belong. I belong, but want to be lost. It's like a fucked up kind of yin and yang.

Hands were pulling me back. Perrine was here. Allium had passed out and was now unconscious against the wall.

"Thank you, Charity. I'll need to take it from here."

Anxiousness clawed at me. "Is he going to be okay?"

She skated her hands over him, taking in the damage. "He's in terrible shape. Physically, he'll be fine with some work. But mentally, his mind is in tatters. Whatever he's been saying, it's probably the fever kicking in, so best to ignore it."

I didn't have the energy to absorb what that meant right now. I just had to sit back, let her heal him, and pray that he'd be alright.

Only time would tell.

19

Charity

Shifter 101: Persen Shifters exist to inspire humans and facilitate creative thinking.

Three days passed, and I didn't see Anton or Allium. He stayed locked in his bedroom under Perrine's orders. She stayed around the flat and assured me that leaving him to rest was the best thing for him. I passed the time reading, desperate to keep my mind occupied and avoid my encounter with Allium replaying in my head. I'd never had the time for it back in my old life, but here, it was almost becoming a hobby. Along with running of course.

I'd thanked Perrine countless times for what she'd done. I'd been able to stall things, but I didn't possess the healing attributes she did in order to mend him. She'd assured me that while painful, the wounds were superficial and while he'd have some scarring, there wasn't likely to be any lasting physical effects.

As far as mentally, we would have to wait and see.

By the end of the third day, I gave up on books and paced in my room, debating whether to knock on his door. Being afraid of what I'd find, I finally made myself some dinner to distract myself.

My feet cooled on the kitchen tiles and a breeze from the open balcony door showed someone was out there. I knew Perrine had gone out to get supplies, so it could only mean one thing.

He was awake.

I darted outside, slowing when I saw Anton smoking on the outdoor sofa, as if his body had not just undergone a significant trauma. The t-shirt he wore highlighted every ripple of muscle, and it was snug enough to expose the bandages underneath. Angry red lines snaked down his neck and disappeared under the fabric. Another ran up his arm. Given the state he'd been in mere days ago, it was a miracle it looked the way it did.

I had so many questions. *What happened to him? Did Allium mean the things he said?* The things I'd heard in his mind. I'd been turning them over for days. But I wasn't sure how fragile he was, so instead started with something easier.

"Should you be doing that?" I sat down next to him, pointing at the cigarette. "I thought you were supposed to rest."

Anton took a long drag. "I've recovered for three days. I was lucky to have a talented healer present, thanks to you, so my body is fine. Allium, however, needs to rest, so he won't be coming forward for a while."

"Will he be alright?"

Anton took another drag, exhaling slowly. "The major damage was to his mind. I'm only grateful that you were there to prevent even more from happening. Thank you."

"How did it happen? Who was responsible?" The questions poured from me, unable to contain myself.

"It's complicated. I'll tell you in time, but now is not the time."

Well, that was cryptic. But I carried on asking, anyway.

"What state is his mind in?" I pressed, aware it must seem odd, me suddenly showing concern for Allium, but when it was life and death, things changed.

"I'm not sure. Believe me, I've tried looking, but most of it is closed off, even to me. He blocked me out for most of it, and has since. But he's in there. He just needs time."

"I thought you were going to lose him."

He locked eyes with me as he put out his cigarette and straightened in his seat. "Without you, I would have. Thank you, Charity. I owe you everything."

"That's what he said."

He gestured to the seat next to him for me to join him. "What happened on the balcony? He shut me out more than he ever has before, so I have no clue of what happened. I think it was his mind shutting down."

I described how I'd come outside and had woken up when Allium had fallen on top of me. Then said I'd messaged for help and kept him going until it had arrived.

What I didn't say was that I'd felt something and from Allium's words. Perrine had warned me he might not be making sense, and something told me it wouldn't be fair to Anton either. Just nights ago he'd taken me on the best drive of my life to help me conquer a fear. And I'd repaid him by getting all confused over his Other.

And saved him, a voice told me. I tried not to think about how I was feeling drawn towards Anton again, despite feeling the same way about Allium almost exactly where we were sitting now. Maybe I was the monster after all. I pressed for more answers. "Was it to do with your part in the Dragos?"

Anton's jaw ticked, a sign that what came next would either mean he was closing up again or that he was lying. "Gang life isn't always pretty, Serrk, that's all. I'll be forever grateful that you were there. Without you, Langison would have claimed him.

"You've mentioned that place before. What is it?"

Anton finished his cigarette and extinguished it into a tray. The smoke evaporated and his scorched earth scent crept through again. "When a Shifter dies before they are ready, their soul goes to Langison. Their body continues to exist, but it's like watching a car on autopilot. I suppose the easiest way to imagine it is like your hell. It's our middle ground to the beyond. The souls there have no way back, so they float throughout the rivers of Domain endlessly, unable to speak or move. It's a fate I'd wish on no one. It's different when someone removes an Other, as the body still has a soul in Domain, but the fate for the Other is the same."

I stood stunned. Allium couldn't have been talking sense if he was willing to undergo that. I also couldn't believe Shifters could rid themselves of an Other and subject a part of them to such a fate. "Well, I'm glad I was here to stop that then."

Anton's voice dropped, and he moved a fraction closer. "Why *did* you save him, Serrk?"

"I–" I couldn't admit how much Allium had let me know without revealing everything and confusing everything Anton and I had between us. I couldn't even pretend that I'd acted to keep Allium out of Langison, having just asked what it was. Instead, I said, "I know how much he means to you. I understand you need him as much as he needs you."

"In doing so, you saved both of us." Anton reached out and stroked my cheek once, just like Allium had, before removing his hand. The blaze of his touch lingered and set every nerve ending in me alight. This had to explain my reaction to Allium the other night. I felt a physical attraction to Anton as well as an emotional one. How could I not confuse the two when they were in the same body?

"Maybe he'll be good enough to grant us another night like our visit to the mountains?" A girl could dream.

Anton stared ahead.

"Are we ever going to discuss that trip?" I studied the veins in his arms that only became more prominent as he clenched his fists.

"What about it?" He kept his eyes away from mine.

"What it meant. It was nice." That was an understatement to say the least.

He relaxed his posture in defeat and tipped that exquisite jaw back. "It was perfect, Serrk. But it came with conditions. I need to stay away from you, I really do."

I looked around us. "You're not doing a very good job of that with me living here."

"I know. Things are more complicated than I'd thought. I wish I could tell you more, but I can't. Or tell you to trust me, but you shouldn't do that either. I'd rather endure wanting you while you're here, than knowing you're somewhere like Abduco Manor."

What the fuck did he mean by that? He was winning all the cryptic awards tonight.

"Where's Scarlett?" She would be eager to see how he was doing, and I wanted to avoid another encounter if I could help it.

Anton was now staring into the vast forest below. "He broke up with her, you know. Allium."

My traitorous heart leapt for joy, but I fought to keep my features straight. "Is that why he ended up hurt?"

Anton didn't confirm or deny. He was closing in on himself again, the way he always did when I asked too many questions. Rage like I'd never felt exploded inside of me. I'd find Scarlett, and her piece of shit father, and I'd destroy them. I'd ensure they could do nothing like this again.

"And you broke up with her, too?" I asked, already knowing the response.

"Yes, me too. After we learned that she'd drugged you, there was no way we could stay with her." He stared at the floor.

My eye twitched. I felt white hot. If she was out here now, I would consider throwing her off the balcony. The dizziness, the reaction to the alcohol, it all made sense now. The second I had control over my Shifter abilities, I was taking her down.

"I know what you're thinking, Serrk," he said.

Well, I bloody hope you don't.

"You're wondering what's stopping us, right here, right now?"

Wow. I forced the fire inside of me to a small flicker. *There was that too.* But I knew what was stopping us. Allium.

"Allium doesn't bother me, you know. Not anymore. But you're right. Now isn't the time." That was about as truthful as I could be right now. I wasn't lying, just not sharing everything.

Anton raised his eyebrows but gave a small smile of surprise. "I didn't expect that. What happened between the two of you that night?"

"I'm sorry. I need to speak to him first," I admitted. A big part of me longed for Anton, for this moment right now. But after that moment between us on the balcony, I would be lying if I said a part of me didn't want Allium, too. As much as I hated myself for it.

Could there be a future for us all?

"We make a right pair, don't we?" Anton smirked. "Wanting to confide, but limited by our secrets. You know, you'd make a great Abduco when your Actuation comes and you pass with flying colours."

I gave him a nervous laugh. "At this rate, I'll just be happy to pass. I don't mind where I go. I still need to manage my Shifting."

He had moved closer. Although we kept saying we shouldn't, we both gravitated towards each other.

His velvety timbre reached the depths of my soul. "Remember what I told you the other night? I'll come to some of your sessions to remind you of what you can achieve."

"Thanks. I'll bear that in mind." I focused on staring straight ahead so I didn't get lost in his beautiful face.

The gentlest of touches swept my hair over my shoulder and I inhaled at his breath at the shell of my ear. "I know I'm trying to stay away, but I realised something. The only place that I'm happy is when I'm with you; and right now, there's nowhere else I'd rather be."

"Me neither." If I turned around to him, our faces would be almost touching. I wondered why my voice had changed so much.

I felt his smile inches away. "Even if you are a vicious poker player."

I risked meeting his eye. We were only about an inch apart. "Is that why you let me win?"

Surprise crossed his face. "How did you know that?"

I grinned wickedly. "You have tells too, Anton."

The surrounding air crackled with tension. *Fuck it.* I took his hand in mine and laced our fingers. "You both do."

I leaned into him, just to *feel* more of him. He wrapped an arm around me and I cuddled into his chest. We weren't doing anything wrong. But then he took my hand, and without warning, his lips were on my wrist. In one swift movement, he sucked it between his teeth and bit on it gently, but also like he couldn't help himself.

I couldn't hide my groan. "Anton–"

"I'm sorry," he said into my skin. "You make me lose my mind around you. Shit, why do you have to smell so good?"

His head moved to my neck, and he made a noise not unlike a growl. Hunger was swirling in my stomach, but it wasn't for food. He muttered in my ear, "You're going to need to move away from me before I do something we all regret."

I became aware I'd tipped my head back to allow him more access. "Don't make promises you can't keep."

His lips grazed my neck, sending divine shivers running over my body. "You'll be the death of me, Serrk."

He was right. Getting caught up in the moment could have huge ramifications. I'd already seen what happened to Shifters who stepped out of line here, Apex or not. Allium was proof of that. If anything was going to happen, it should be when we were both thinking clearly and not keeping a thousand different secrets from each other.

It took every ounce of self-restraint, but I untangled myself from him and moved to the furthest away chair. It was almost physically painful. "Happy?" I pouted.

"Not in the slightest," was his reply, grinning but looking equally disappointed.

I leaned back in my chair and looked up at the stars illuminated in the sky above. With the space separating us, we could discuss things like two normal adults again and before long, the tension had evaporated. That said, I was grateful for the cool air on my face. It was always temperate in Abduco, despite the constant rain.

We stayed there all evening, just talking for a change. It wasn't until we were discussing the politics of Domain even later into the night that the front door slammed and we jumped, remembering where we were.

I tensed and met Anton's eye as footsteps headed towards the balcony, but before either of us could react, Viktor's broad frame stepped through the door followed by Spyder. "I thought you two might be out here. Where's our hero?" He put a hand up as if to block out Anton. "No, not you. We're here for Charity."

Viktor lifted me off my feet in one of his hugs, and Spyder tipped me a salute, before giving me a bow of approval.

These two knew how to make everyone feel better. We stayed out there all night discussing the events of the last few days, the versions Anton and I were prepared to share, anyway. His dark eyes didn't leave my arm, and he tortured me several times by dragging his lip through his teeth. Once a bastard, always a bastard.

But, despite everything, I couldn't help but wonder if, against all odds, there was a place for that bastard in my future.

20

CHARITY

Shifter 101: Nexus Shifters exist to heal human minds and allow them to move on from negative events.

The first thing Allium said when he came round a week later was that he had remembered nothing since breaking up with Scarlett. Apparently, Shifter bodies worked differently when there was an Other present. As long as one of them was around to take physical care of themselves, the other could stay hidden for as long as they liked.

He wasn't as condescending when I spoke to him however, so at least the knowledge of who had saved him seemed to count for something. He still needed to rest, and I saw little of him. I was too terrified to go into detail about what he'd said that night, mostly because I didn't want to hear that he'd meant none of it. Perhaps he'd been right, maybe ignorance was bliss.

The last weeks leading up to my Actuation were flying by and before long, I'd been in Domain for nearly two months. As the December nights turned a fraction colder, Abduco revealed its festive side: the ivy tendrils wrapping the streetlamps became adorned with fairy lights, and a giant Christmas tree stood outside the Bureau, filled with shimmering baubles of swirling mist. Everything was green here, of course. Personally, I felt it missed the traditional reds, but given I'd never had much opportunity to celebrate Christmas, I wasn't about to complain about the limited colour scheme.

Anton had stayed true to his word and had shown up at various sessions to see how I'd been getting on. It was always at the moment my mind got distracted, and I would muck up just in time for him to arrive.

We'd worked on my mental training together and had continued to make good progress in breaking through and creating mental shields. Anton's mind had doors that were deep mahogany as opposed to Allium's steel, just like the ones found in Abduco. Like Allium's, he'd locked most of it off, I was disappointed to find. Not that I could admit that I'd seen into Allium's mind in the way I had yet. I would have loved to have looked around Anton's mind, but it seemed he wasn't ready for that. I'd also made progress in personalising my mind, where the doors were a lighter cherry rosewood, giving my hallway a much brighter feel.

The week before Christmas arrived and other than a small drop in the temperature, Abduco mornings were still misty and wet. It wasn't my kind of weather unless I was curled up with a good book and a hot chocolate. Though I had to admit as I stepped into the ring, hearing the rain on the skylights was therapeutic. It was a juxtaposition against the intense training that only seemed to get more difficult each week.

Unable to leave it any later, we were tackling Shifter movement after our usual session today. The thought sent a shiver of panic down my spine.

I'd just dodged one of Viktor's predictable punches, earning a whistle from him, when the back of my neck prickled like there were eyes on me. I looked around but only saw Viktor. We continued for a few more moves: jabbing, ducking, and dodging. when something flashed in the corner of my eye.

This time I knew I wasn't imagining it, and sure enough, Viktor was grinning.

I should have known. Anton stepped out from behind a pillar. He'd been watching all along.

"I'll take it from here, Vik," he said, pulling on a pair of gloves.

I stiffened. He'd been showing up for my training, but had mentioned nothing about training me *himself*. We still hadn't discussed how close we'd come to doing something stupid on the balcony, and I hadn't even discussed my time on the balcony with *Allium*, either. *I should just avoid the balcony for the foreseeable future.*

"Hands up, Serrk. Defensive stance. Don't expect me to go easy on you." The corner of his mouth flicked up in a smirk as he jolted me back to the present. He wasted no time and struck out with his hand. By some miracle, I moved just in time. His eyes widened, and I wondered if he would have in fact landed the punch if I hadn't been so quick.

"Why can't you call me by my proper name instead of my surname?" I ducked another blow. "I can't just call you Abduco. It would be like addressing half the people here."

"Sucks to be you, Serrk." He grinned, and I landed a punch on his shoulder. "Your strength is impressive for your size. Your reflexes are astonishing. But–" In one clean move he knocked the balance from my feet and I found myself pinned down.

Heat rushed to my cheeks from the intimacy of the position. I'd never ended up like this with Viktor during any of our sessions. I should have felt compromised: no one pinned me down like this, not with my claustrophobia. But, despite everything, I trusted him.

Anton leaned in, causing my breath to hitch.

"Viktor tells me you fight using your emotions," he stated, the words dripping from his all too lovely mouth.

I was feeling many emotions, that was for sure, but I wasn't giving in. "What would you know about emotions? You're too busy closing yours off."

He leaned in just an inch further so that he was close to my ear. "Maybe if you weren't too busy thinking about how much you're enjoying being pinned down by me."

I couldn't see any sign of Viktor. I was relieved he'd left us to it and we didn't have anyone to observe whatever this was.

"Maybe I enjoy it a little," I started, then, using the weight of his body as leverage, I flipped him onto his back. "Though anyone who knows me knows I'd be much more comfortable here."

A flush rose to his cheeks that warmed my insides in the most delightful way.

Then, a flash of lightning green. Allium was taking over. "Not bad, Serrk, but I wonder how you'd fare against me?"

I hesitated. It didn't feel wrong sitting where I was, even though it should. "Can you, in your condition?"

"It's up to me to determine that." He straightened up with so much force that if I hadn't moved, I would have lost my balance.

We separated and returned to opposite sides of the ring. I was about to ask Allium about that night when I noticed he was taking the boxing gloves off.

Was he changing his mind?

He then took an offensive stance, and I realised he hadn't changed his mind at all. He just wanted to hit me with his hands if he landed a punch.

It seemed he'd answered my question about what he remembered from that night just fine. He must have blocked Anton out so he wouldn't be able to share anything, just to infuriate me further. Well, two could play that game. I shook off my own gloves, and we circled each other.

I avoided his eyes. Knowing I'd get lost in their depths and become distracted. I also didn't want him to see the hurt in mine.

He struck first, landing a blow near my ribs that showed me Anton had been holding back. He didn't look pleased; if anything, it just enraged him more.

"Stop thinking about him, and I won't hit you," he growled, sending another painful kick my way that was sure to bruise.

"We're boxing. You don't use your feet!" I jumped back to avoid another hit.

His reply was a snarl. "Do you think in actual combat, people follow any sort of rules? You use whatever advantage you have."

I'd known that before I came here and cursed myself for having lost sight of that. He came for me again. And again. If it weren't for my reflexes and my training, he would have overpowered me straight away. My speed was the only thing keeping me going. That and my endurance, thanks to my running.

"Why are you so angry at me all the time?" I gritted out, dodging his attacks.

"That's for me to know, and you to wonder," came his infuriating reply.

He was strong; there was no doubt of the power behind his enormous frame. But I was a small target, and with my size, came speed. Time to show him what I could do. I moved to the left, dropping my stance a fraction and readying myself for his attack. When his arm reached out, I swerved to the side and tripped him, using the full weight of my body to power my forearm into the side of his elbow.

Had the situation been reversed, he would have broken my arm. I didn't do much damage, but he swore in shock and staggered back.

"Fuck, Serrk, I like it." He raised both brows as he brought himself to his feet, grinning. "Now I've got an actual opponent."

We lasted several more rounds of getting minor hits on each other. I was happy knowing that for every one he'd landed on me; I had managed two on him, much to his annoyance. Eventually, he roared in frustration and stalked off to the corner of the ring.

"Why are you so angry at me?" I called after him.

This time, he ignored me and jumped back into a range of frenzied attacks. Though this time, I could sense his agitation, dodging and returning with more effective counter-attacks of my own.

When we called it quits, he handed me a bottle of lotion. "Use it in the shower. It's from Nexus. It'll heal you so those injuries don't amount to anything. Consider it a thank you for saving my life."

"Thanks," I said, taking the bottle from him and examining it. A light purple liquid swirled among iridescent gold dust.

I met his eye and tried one last time. "Why are you so angry at me, Allium?"

He stalked forward like a hunter eyeing up his prey and leaned his forehead into mine. The act wasn't one of affection; it was in defeat.

"You want to know why I'm upset?"

"That's what I'm asking," I answered back, running my mouth as usual despite the importance of the moment.

He dropped his voice so that it was a growl, though so quiet it was for my ears only. "I'm angry because even breathing the goddamn air around you is painful."

My chest compressed in on itself with the glare that followed. His words rattled through me, unsure if he meant them as a strange form of compliment or an insult. I questioned my reaction. *Why did this hurt so much?* Of course, it could never be him. I knew how I felt about Anton, and I was coming to realise how Anton might feel about me. But it didn't mean that there wasn't a part of me that wanted Allium too. *How is this possible?* I'd never been interested in two people at the same time. And both Anton and Allium were much more worthy of my sole attention than anyone before coming here.

I angled my nose up towards him. "What do you remember of that night? On the balcony?" I was pushing it now. "You remember, don't you?"

"Remember what, Serrk? Your little saving act? Talking rubbish to me until the real help came? Wandering the halls of my fractured mind?"

Shit. He remembered. That had to count for something.

"How can you keep up this act of going between? Pretending you're just cruel when I see more?"

He broke away from me, retreating to the other side of the room as he grabbed his gloves. "It's not an act, Serrk. It's who I am. Take it or leave it. And seeing as taking it isn't an option, we might as well leave it."

A voice interrupted us. "Okay, you two. We've got company." Viktor walked back into the room with Scarlett in tow. I swallowed the lump in my throat. This day just got better and better.

"Trying to sleep with the people training you, Charity case? We both know that's the only way you'll pass your Actuation." It was Scarlett.

Allium's face was impassive as his eyes passed over her with a disdainful look, but he said nothing.

I was sick of her. Anger bubbled beneath the surface of my skin as I eyed her with venom. It was one hundred times worse since I'd learned from Anton that she'd drugged me that night she'd broken into my mind. She was lucky I didn't know the extent of what I could do and would settle for physical damage. I picked up my gloves. "You think you're that much better than me? Let's see what you can do when I'm expecting you."

"Charity, don't." I knew it was now Anton's voice warning me, but I wasn't listening. I was tired of being picked on my whole life, by my mother's boyfriends, by people at school for not fitting in, and now by Scarlett. It was time to let my rage out and after weeks of training, I might just stand a chance.

A cruel smile played along Scarlett's mouth, showing off her white teeth. She ducked into the ring. "My pleasure."

She didn't pick up the gloves, though. Instead, claws snapped out from her nails, the long talons ready to do some serious damage. *Fuck. I haven't thought this through.*

"No weapons!" said Anton, about to step into the ring.

I backed into a corner as I threw my gloves to the side. "Leave us, I've got this." Even though I didn't. But I wouldn't go down without a fight.

Scarlett rushed forward, slashing with her talons. I put my arm up to block her, sending a searing pain burning across my forearm. Adrenaline surged through me, the same way that it had in the alley with the men. Though this time she didn't crumple and start screaming about shadows. Instead, I gave in to the instincts channelling through my veins.

I forgot everything I knew about Shifters and punched her right in the face. My hand connected with her nose, and there was a satisfying crunch. She drew back, eyes streaming, and blood already running through her fingers.

Shocked that I didn't feel as guilty as I should have, I cracked a grin. It felt damn good. *What kind of person does that make me?*

"My nose! You psychopath!" She clutched at her face.

I stalked towards her, watching her flinch. I had no intention of harming her further, but I wanted to get the message across. "Your games end here."

Scarlett regained some of her composure and spat at my feet. "You think you're so brilliant, but your type will *never* belong here."

It took a long breath to steady myself before I went back on my mental promise and lashed out again. I couldn't hold it in any longer and spat, "Save it. I learned a long time ago to shut out people like you. Not that you'd know what it's like to have to silence the voices that constantly say you're not good enough."

That last part was unnecessary. I didn't know where she'd come from, other than some fancy family connected to Anton. At least she'd grown up in comfort.

Her eyes filled with fresh tears and she ran off, confirming my suspicions that it had been the wrong thing to say. Viktor whooped at her exit, though he hadn't seen her cry. Something about her reaction meant my victory didn't feel as sweet as it should have.

Anton ducked through the ropes and was at my side in an instant. He held my arm up, inspecting it. "Are you alright?"

"It's fine. Nothing that Perrine can't sort. I'm more worried about her," I said, indicating the door Scarlett had left through.

Viktor joined us. "That's a strange reaction for someone that just took her out badass-style! I don't think she'll be bothering you anymore for sure."

"We'll see." Anton frowned, still holding my arm. "May I?"

I'd forgotten he could heal, too. The cooling sensation tingled up my arm, and I watched with fascination as the wounds knitted themselves over and faded to red scars. "They'll disappear in a few days. Why was she here, anyway?"

Viktor looked embarrassed. "That was my fault. I left to give you two–*three*, some privacy, and she was waiting outside. I think she was looking for you, Anton, but when I said you weren't available, she started trying to flirt with me, so I brought her inside so she might see you'd moved on."

"Charming," Anton said, my arm still in his hand. He didn't deny that he'd *moved on* however, and the thought alone sent butterflies dancing across my stomach.

"Anyway, if you're up to it, there's one more thing we need to practise today: travel." Viktor gave me a nervous glance as he spoke.

This was the hurdle I kept coming to. I was sure I'd felt tingling one day when I focused, but other than that, my attempts were still unsuccessful. There were now a mere few days until my Actuation and I was yet to complete some of the key elements. Viktor kept assuring me it was normal for someone in my position, but doubt crept into my head at every opportunity, making me question if I could succeed here.

Today was different, though. Despite the outcome of the fight with Scarlett leaving me confused, adrenaline was buzzing through my veins. Now was as good a time as any.

I planted my feet into the ground and focused on Anton who stood several feet away.

"Remember, Serrk, it's just a tunnel."

I can do this.

I closed my eyes and visualised myself travelling the distance between us to close the gap. An idol wasn't necessary–humans didn't receive them until after their Actuation as they only practised small distances. I'd learned that all Shifters could travel a few feet without them, though no one ever did.

Anton was studying me, surveying me. His expression was part possessive, part concerned. He was silent in my mind, giving away as little of his thoughts as possible. I could tell he didn't want to distract me.

Then it all became simple. I just had to let go of everything and focus on where I wanted to be. I knew where that was. Right next to him. I closed my eyes and willed myself to just *go*.

In the blink of an eye, his features enlarged. He was closer. I was closer. I'd done it. Pride swelled inside of me, unfamiliar, yet not unwelcome. It was only a metre or so, but *I'd done it*. I'd still need to travel using side-along Shifting if I wanted to go longer distances, until I had my idol, but for now, knowing that I could do this was enough.

Anton's eyes were alight. His mouth curved up in a genuine smile. "I knew you could."

If Viktor hadn't been in the room, I might have done something stupid like run up and kiss him. Instead, I settled for the look he gave me, which was powerful enough to set my core alight. Once again, I was thankful that Viktor was so open and didn't get embarrassed about these kinds of situations.

Anton walked over to stand next to me and trailed his hand down my arm. "Now that you have shown you can travel, there's just one more aspect of Actuation that we need to cover–Shifting."

Holy shit. Full-blown Shifting. If I wasn't still on a high from my travel Shifting, I would have outright laughed in Anton's face at the suggestion. I'd been wondering about this for a while, but every time I'd asked, I'd been told not to worry about it, and that we'd cover it only when I was ready. It seemed like that time might just be today.

"Can you show me?" The question had been on my mind for weeks now about Anton in dragon form.

"There's not enough room in here for me. Viktor, you can do the honours."

"With pleasure," came Viktor's reply.

There was a flash and my brain shook as a flaming lion replaced Viktor. Wait, not a lion, a whole *host* of different creatures. He had the head and body of a lion, leathery bat-like wings, and I couldn't hide my gasp as a scorpion's tail snapped out behind him. If I hadn't known and trusted Viktor, I would have turned and fled from the room.

They couldn't expect me to turn into something like this, could they? Though I remembered Allium telling me that most Shifters took the form of animals from my world. The idea was barely any more conceivable.

My hairs stood on end as Viktor the giant killing machine approached me and nuzzled my hand. I was relieved the flames were not hot to touch, though I imagined not everyone on the receiving end would be so lucky.

"Seems like you're doing a lot of thinking there, Cee." Anton's velvety words broke me out of my thoughts.

"It's just rather a lot," I said to Anton, still taking in the creature in front of me. There was another flash and Viktor's broad form returned, clothed.

He winked at me, causing Anton's arm to twitch where it hung next to mine. "Gutted I'm not naked, girl? It's okay, it happens to the best of us."

It was much easier to relax with him in his human form. "Don't Shifters lose their clothes when they transform though?"

"That's the Shifters in books in your world. Here, everything we have on ourselves at the beginning is there when we return."

I'd seen manticores in my fancy fairy-tale book, the one I'd cherished until I'd left it in my world. I'd enjoyed looking at it so much, thumbing the pages over and over. Whoever had gifted it to me had gone to the trouble to write *For Charity. Your only limit is your imag-*

ination. D., on the inside front cover. I asked Mother about it once and she said it was "Dylan, or something," so I'd built my own fairy tale where I pretended it was from my real dad and I had a normal life. Over time, I'd realised that kind of thought process would get me nowhere, and I'd hardened into the person I was today.

I turned to Anton. "Is there really any way I'll be able to do all this?"

He nodded. "I'm certain of it."

At that moment, Bronx came running in with the paper. I still found the concept amusing that a dragon Shifter would need a body-guard.

He held *The Notion* under Anton's nose and I did my best to scan the words as they flashed across the page like a frantic live feed on social media.

I only made out one headline: *Mindchill Deaths Triple Overnight: Missing Persons Linked to Drug*, before Anton swore and turned to me, apologising and insisting he would be back as soon as he could.

I spent the rest of the evening practising Shifting with Viktor, though we could have been playing Scrabble for all the difference it made to my progress. It was impossible to channel my energy into something I didn't know existed yet. Viktor had the patience of a saint. reminding me that no humans had Shifted like that before, and had still had a successful Actuation. It didn't help remove the pit of dread from my stomach, though. I'd come so far and felt like this was the last barrier I had to cross.

That night, I showered and used the lotion Allium had given me. It was divine, and I already felt the benefits by the time I fell into bed, exhausted. It had been kind of him to give it to me. *Shit.* I was in big trouble and none of it was to do with my upcoming Actuation.

21

CHARITY

Shifter 101: Caedes Shifters exist to destroy human minds where no other Houses of Domain can perform their function for the better.

A rare ray of sunlight was climbing through the chink in my curtains, signalling I'd slept later than I should.

I reached for my phone. Eight a.m.–*shit*. I was sure I'd set an alarm, but this phone still confused the hell out of me. I used it as little as possible, terrified I'd turn on the function that spoke my thoughts aloud and sent them to the relevant people. Now *that* would be a disaster.

I still had time. I'd just be more rushed than I would have liked. A quick scan of my messages revealed most of them were from numbers I didn't recognise, either wishing me luck or a few wanting me to fail–the latter likely Scarlett's friends.

Perrine's message materialised in front of me in her signature swirly handwriting.

Perrine: Remember everything you've achieved so far in our training and everything you offer. I can't wait to celebrate later! P x

I waved the beautiful letters away with my hand, smiling. Despite my reservations about using it, it was a genius piece of technology that Allium had invented. Plus, it was nice to have a friend.

Yesterday, Perrine had given me a full reminder of what to expect today. I'd barely seen her since her help in healing Allium. She'd said her work had been keeping her busy, yet she still found time to help me. She'd informed me the mental tests would be first, followed by the physical ones, before the one that would determine my House. If I was successful, there would be celebrations that very night, though I didn't want to think that far ahead and get my hopes up. Whether or not I admitted it to myself, I was getting attached to being here, and perhaps some Shifters here, too. I wasn't ready to leave. Everything hinged on today.

I snapped out of my thoughts and rushed to get myself ready, choosing a pair of fitted Lycra trousers and a black cropped top with combat boots. I left my phone; it was already buzzing with more notifications from names I didn't recognise and it wouldn't help me today.

A soft knock at the door signalled Anton was outside my room. His eyes roved over my outfit, but he stayed silent. He looked immaculate, as always in suit trousers and a shirt.

"Just dressing up for later, when we celebrate you." He winked.

"Everyone seems to think that's how things will go today," I said, a fresh round of butterflies fluttering across my stomach.

He held the door open for me as I gathered the last of my things and we stepped out into the hall. He raised a brow at me. "Don't you?"

"I don't know." It seemed selfish to worry about such things when there were people going missing. And it was on the rise. I'd questioned

Anton on his return about the headline I'd seen in *The Notion* that had caused him to leave my training, but he'd brushed it off, telling me it was exaggerated and that I should focus on my Actuation. His dark expression implied there was more to it, but there wasn't anything I could do about that now.

I blinked as I walked into the shared kitchen and living room. With everything going on, I'd almost forgotten it was Christmas Eve. It seemed even Anton had a festive side, and had added a Christmas tree with a green dragon at the top. I chuckled when I saw it, forgetting my nerves.

"Amused, Serrk?"

"Of course *you* would have a dragon at the top of your tree."

"What else would you have? That's traditional in Domain."

"In our world, we put angels at the top of a Christmas tree." Not that I ever had one. But if I did, that's what I would have put.

"Well, we'd better sort that then." Anton smirked as we headed for the door.

I didn't even see him do it, but as I glanced back at the tree, I saw an angel sitting at the top, side by side with the dragon, looking down at us.

We reached the grounds where my Actuation would take place.

I followed him round a high wall that spanned into the distance, housing some kind of large outdoor area, *perhaps a courtyard?* As we entered through the doors, I saw that the ground dipped and the area inside was in fact laid out like a stadium, with a large grassy clearing in the middle and rows upon rows of seats where bystanders could watch. There were *thousands* of people here. I swallowed, my heart in my mouth. I hadn't expected this kind of audience.

"Anton, I–"

"–Hadn't expected this?" he finished for me. "I know. I didn't want you to overthink it. You've got this. Everyone here is waiting to see what you can do." That didn't help. If anything, it only encouraged the nerves writhing in my stomach. He must have sensed me stiffening as he then leaned closer so I could feel his breath on my ear. "Show them, just like you've shown me. And remember, I've got you." He then squeezed my hand, slipping something into it, and glided away, leaving me to take in his words as I approached the judges' table.

I couldn't prepare any more than I already had. At least by the end of this, I'd know one way or another what my future held.

The judges comprised ten Shifters from all the different Houses. Three were from Abduco, their hair colour and green cloaks made that obvious. Three were from Caedes, with flaming red hair, and dressed in a deep crimson. One woman gave me a small wave, and I recognised her resemblance to Perrine. I wondered if she was a relation of hers. The man next to her also gave me a warm smile. They must have been from Nexus. That left the woman dressed in white and the man with rainbow hair belonging to Persen. I noticed a man and a woman both around my age standing next to them. The girl looked just as nervous as I did. The boy stood with his shoulders back. He'd likely spent his life training for this moment having grown up in Domain. After all, I hadn't heard about anyone else from my world arriving in the time I'd been here.

The woman from Persen stood first. "Follow me to the centre of the court where your first challenge will take place."

I did as she instructed and tried to block out the crowd who had now fallen silent. I focused on her turquoise hair and keeping one foot in front of the other as I followed her to the middle of the arena. She led me to a spot in the centre where she held a hand to her mouth and her next words amplified for the audience. "Your first test will be endurance and speed." She then turned to me and gestured above her where the sky had darkened. "To pass, you need to avoid the rain until the timer reaches zero."

A large timer emerged on a board on the far side, which read ten minutes. There was a picture of my face along with seven blank boxes to keep score of my progress in the challenges.

Ten minutes wasn't long at all, though for outrunning rain, I hadn't managed for that long yet. I uncurled my fist and realised Anton had given me my headphones for the first task. As I opened the box, I realised they weren't mine at all, but a much newer version, one that didn't need to be connected to a phone to play music. A message materialised in front of me despite the absence of my phone:

Just think what you want to hear, and it'll play. Merry Christmas - AA.

As I put them in my ears, they cancelled the cacophony of the surrounding crowd. *That bastard. That brilliant bastard.* I found his face in the crowd, and he gave me a smirk. He knew he'd done well.

A clock struck, signalling my countdown. Wasting no time in building up my speed, I ran to the edge of the arena. The larger the ground I had, the less time I had to waste on turns, and could focus on putting one foot in front of the other. I remembered the technique Anton had shown me where I could part the rain. I'd been practising ever since. It was easy when standing still, but required speed in order to keep it going while moving. I caught his eyes up in the crowd and it gave me courage. I would not fuck this up.

Within seconds, I'd found a comfortable pace that I could maintain that was still fast. My music kicked in and I forgot about everything around me. Forgot the other candidates. I wasn't competing with them, anyway. There was only me, the rhythm of my feet, my breathing, and the music. It was like time had slowed right down. I could see the raindrops above me, but I knew they wouldn't make contact. They meant for this test to push me, but what they didn't know was that this was my comfort zone. This was where I was free.

Before I knew it, a muffled strike told me I'd completed the first challenge. The man who had stood confidently at the first challenge was now arguing with the judges, as they informed him he would have to resit his Actuation at the next opportunity because of disqualification, despite his protests of innocence.

Shame.

Cheers erupted from the stadium, which spread a warmth through my chest. People wanted me to do well today. And they were cheering. *For me.* I skidded to a halt and summoned an umbrella into my hand, *because I fucking could*. Once you had the hang of them, Shifter abilities were very useful.

The Shifter judge from Persen smiled coyly. "Not bad at all, consider your first test passed."

She took her seat at the table and the one of the men with short red hair came to meet me back in the centre of the arena. He amplified his voice in the same way as the woman before him. "The next challenge will test your mental shields. I'm now going to break into Charity's innermost revealing thoughts. If I'm successful, they'll play out on the score screen to the entire stadium."

Like hell you are. If I wasn't motivated already, I sure was now.

The examiner smiled at me wickedly. He was enjoying this. This time there was no countdown, and he was in my mind in an instant. His words were only for me. "I'm going to enjoy embarrassing you. You *Nihils* don't deserve to compete among our ways."

I ignored him and concentrated my efforts on securing every door with a single key. I locked the final one and kicked the key away into oblivion. It was too fucking easy. He never stood a chance. But that didn't mean he didn't try. He threw his weight against the door, again and again. It was exhausting keeping him out, but I knew I wouldn't be able to find the key. And it was that thought that kept me going as he pounded the doors in my mind.

Just as my muscles were about to give in, I heard the cheers. They were louder this time when the examiner admitted defeat after being unable to breach a single door. My smile only widened when it became apparent the third challenge would involve me trying to break down his shields.

His mistake was assuming I had used up all my energy keeping him out. Yes, I'd struggled, but I'd had a lifetime of shutting people out and my mind learned fast. His walls shuddered as I pushed harder, taunting him with the idea that someone half his age could break down his doors. One of his thoughts danced in front of me. *She's only a girl. She won't be strong enough.*

I sent back my response. *Fucking watch me.* I forced myself to keep going, and eventually the shadows gave way, the doors behind them crumbling into oblivion.

I browsed his thoughts and memories for something that would humiliate him beyond belief, selecting his fondness for being tickled during sex. An embarrassing scene appeared on the giant screen above my score, causing the audience to roar with laughter.

The man turned as red as his hair, and started shouting for my disqualification, but the other judges were too busy joining in the laughter to take any notice of him.

The fourth challenge was hand-to-hand combat where I lasted three rounds with the man from Abduco with no punches landed. It turned out when I didn't have an emotional attachment to whoever I was fighting; it was much easier to focus and use my advantage of speed. When I'd landed over ten hits, the man stood back and took a bow, informing me I'd completed the round.

Fifth was Shifting to another location. This was where it got tough. The nerves pushed down by the previous rounds bubbled back to the surface and threatened to suffocate me.

I looked up into the stands to steady myself. Viktor was cheering and waving, Perrine and Spyder next to him, their faces just as enthusiastic. Anton wasn't smiling, however. Instead, he was mouthing something, his eyes ablaze with a mix of him and Allium. *What was he saying?*

Then I realised what he was getting at.

Tunnel.

I thought back to that night when we'd entered the tunnel, his hand in mine. The beat of the music. I hadn't given a single thought to my fear of spaces, and this was no different. If I could get through this, he'd be waiting for me. And right now, that was all I needed.

I narrowed my gaze on a space in front of me. One split second and I could be there. I focused on the tunnel and visualised where I wanted to be.

There. I'd done it. It wasn't far. Less far than most Demis who completed this round did, but it didn't matter. I'd managed. Euphoria erupted within me, reaching from fingertips right the way to my toes. *I belong here.* The pressure lifted from my shoulders and I dared to dream about the life I might have, before locking that thought away and focusing on the task at hand.

As the man from Nexus replaced the judge, I looked at the scoreboard and couldn't believe how far I'd made it. There were only two challenges left.

The sixth challenge, however, was Shifting to another form. The test I'd yet to complete. I'd tried and tried, but to no avail. But if today was anything to go by, I was learning sometimes I just had to be in the moment to utilise my abilities here. And it didn't get much more in the moment than this.

Silence fell across the stadium, and every stare from the crowd scorched my skin. A crow called, echoing across the hushed arena. I closed my eyes and reached out, looking for something I could put my form into. Something I could connect to.

I searched and searched.

But there wasn't anything. I put all my effort into it.

Nothing.

Not a single fucking thing.

Humiliation washed over me, heating my cheeks and causing my arm to twitch, looking for something to throw in frustration.

There was one thing. But it wouldn't help me here.

Because all I could feel was–him. All I could connect to was–*him*.

The seconds dragged on, and it became more and more apparent that I wouldn't manage. The judge from Nexus put a hand on my arm and spoke in a soft voice. "It's okay, dear, this one gets everyone. As long as you complete the next one, you'll be fine."

He held up a hand to signal that the challenge had passed, and a red flag appeared next to my name on the scoreboard, spoiling my line of green.

The crowd became split in their opinions. There were a few cheers at my downfall, but much more of "Oh!" and a few comments like, "You didn't need that anyway, it's okay!"

Anton was looking at me from the crowd. I clenched my fists when I saw his mouth in a hard line. It couldn't be pity on his face, *could it?*

Another of the judges from Caedes stood and glided to meet me. He was a good deal older and taller than the others. His long auburn hair fell to his shoulders, and his voice prickled my ears with its power. "The ultimate challenge determines the core of a Shifter. In this challenge, we will present you with the mind of a human. What you do with it will determine your House. If you cannot wield the mind, you will return to your world."

He didn't meet my eye as he said, "Meet your human and choose."

I was too busy watching the other contestant to notice who was in front of me. Despite her nerves, she'd aced every challenge.

Then a flat voice I hadn't heard in years turned my world on its head. "Charity?"

I spun to meet a face I never thought I'd see again. "Greg?"

I would have recognised his sandy hair anywhere. He was the reason I still got the creeps anytime I met anyone light-haired with a beard. I'd always have the reminder of him. Of what he'd done. His watery blue eyes were round like saucers as he eyed me up and down, as if unable to believe I was standing right in front of him.

There were shouts from the stands.

"She recognises him!"

"Shifters cannot work with minds they know!"

"Call off the Actuation!"

I ignored them. I was facing the man who had created my fear. Somehow, the human mind they'd brought into this world was Greg, one of Mother's old boyfriends.

The one who'd locked me underground.

Whether it was my anger from the previous test, a knee-jerk reaction to meeting Greg, or something else, I was ready to destroy. Hatred whipped through me as I entered his mind with ease. There were no shields.

Shadows weaved in and out of his twisted thoughts. I shattered entire rooms with my rage, intent on destroying every dark memory I came across. I slashed at the shadows that roamed his limited corridors. Their wispy forms writhed as if in pain until there was nothing left. When I opened a door to a much older memory, I saw a small boy cowering in terror from a figure older and bigger than him. It was his own father, just like his father had done before that. The chain went back generations. It didn't have to continue.

I could end this. End him. Ensure no one had to experience what I did again.

Or I could help him move on. Could I do that and still ensure no one else suffered at his hands?

I could.

I wrenched every remaining shadow from his hallways, twisting them off doors and walls, shattering a few in my process. They vaporised at my command. It took some time, and when I was done, I slumped against the wall, exhausted with the effort, before willing myself back to the stadium.

I fell back onto the grass, landing several feet away from Greg. There was a weight lifted from his shoulders and his eyes were brighter, even if more fearful. "Please help me," he said, crawling towards me. "I don't know where I am."

Somehow, I knew he was telling the truth, but said nothing. I was still reeling from what I'd done.

The judges entered his mind one by one in front of me to determine what had happened. They declared the other candidate a member of the House of Persen and led her off without so much as applause for her incredible efforts.

By the time the last judge with the turquoise hair returned, I was shaking in anticipation. "Charity destroyed most of his mind. Though enough remains for him to live. He will return to the human world now."

They led him off; and I cringed as I heard him utter something that sounded chillingly like, "Who am I?" Once he'd gone, the deadly silence throughout the stadium spoke volumes about what had just happened.

I'd passed, and I'd chosen to destroy his mind. I belonged to the House of Caedes.

22

CHARITY

Shifter 101: Shiftsungs use Shiftstant technology in order to deliver messages using thought.

"**S**o you could destroy the darkness, but not the mind?" Perrine said as we sat in front of my mirror getting ready for the celebration party.

I hadn't seen Anton in the chaos that erupted in the stadium when it became clear about my House. According to Viktor, Anton had gone to see the judges. I wondered why he'd done that. I dismissed the idea that he was annoyed. He couldn't be. Belonging to Caedes changed nothing. *Or did it?*

There had been a huge debate over whether I healed the mind or destroyed it. After all, there wasn't a lot left of humans once Caedes Shifters had finished with their minds, but Greg would live a normal life.

For a terrifying moment, I thought I'd done something wrong that meant I was going to leave after all. Then the judges had revealed my actions spoke the clearest of the House of Caedes. I breathed a sigh of relief; the memory of Greg had haunted me for the best part of my adult life, but I didn't want his death on my conscience. This felt right. I felt a sense of closure, knowing that he would live but wouldn't be able to harm anyone else like he had with me. It filled the void in my heart that I had left underground all those years ago.

After the drama of my Actuation, being a Shifter felt very ordinary. I don't know what I'd expected, for there to be a great clap of thunder and suddenly I'd have another personality jump out of me, but there was nothing. None of that had happened. Everything was incredibly normal. Had I not done some of the things I had during the trials, I would have assumed the whole thing had been a failure.

Perrine sensed my worry. "I know what you're thinking," she stated. I raised a brow at her and she continued, "You're feeling like you let us down because you didn't Shift to another form."

Well, there was that too. "I guess that's partly it."

Her kind eyes searched my face. "Remember, you've grown up in the human world. You can't expect every ability to manifest itself in the same way as someone who has spent their whole life here. All Demi-Shifters are different. You may never Shift, or you might Shift tomorrow. We're in uncharted territory here. Not to mention, you're another step closer to fulfilling the prophecy. We're looking for some-one from your world who could be exceptional, and your Actuation was nothing short of that."

For once, her words didn't help me feel much better, but I told myself to give myself a break. I had just completed a near impossible feat and here I was moping because I didn't get an A-plus on the exam, like I'd ever had one of those before.

I reached into my bag for my phone to see if I'd heard from An-ton, but there was nothing. My hand brushed against the envelope containing my prize money. I was still wrapping my head around the fact that I now owned such a sum. Since the currency was all mentally processed, the piece of paper was worthless. It was a formality so that they could show me how much I'd received, like a cheque I could never cash. It seemed unfair that Demi-Shifters received almost fifty times the amount that Meso Shifters did on completing their Actuation. Apexes too, though Apexes never had to worry about money, anyway.

"It is a competition, after all," one of the Nexus judges had said as he beamed at me. "Congratulations on your acceptance into Domain. While your journey has not been the most common, you have reached the same destination. Your celebration will begin tonight."

And here we were.

I outlined my eyes until they looked positively feline. There was something magical about the makeup here. Everything was much easier to apply, and the finish was perfection. I had to admit; it was useful. Perrine herself looked stunning with her brown hair in loose curls and subtle makeup framing her bright features. My dark hair fell down my back in waves, so I kept it like that. I'd never had access to styling products, so I wouldn't know where to start with them.

I studied my reflection, searching for any change from the events of the day, but found none.

Perrine traced her lips with the lightest of pinks, her glazed eyes revealing her deep thoughts.

"Everything okay?" I knew that look well.

She sighed. "It's just my mum and I. We had a row this evening, and we never fight."

I sat myself next to her. "Do you want to talk about it?" Perrine had been there for me over the last few weeks. This was the least I could offer.

Perrine took a deep breath. "My mum is amazing, and she only wants the best for me. But recently, she's interfered in my life and while I can understand where she's coming from, I want to decide for myself. Today she even mentioned removing Ordette because of how outspoken she is for a Nexus Shifter."

Wow, no wonder she looked upset. "Have you spoken to her about how you feel?"

She gazed sadly at her reflection. "That was what happened tonight. I told her I wanted to pursue writing. After all, I'm a Meso Shifter. I'm never going to work with minds full-time. My mum wants me to follow in the footsteps of my sister Nora who's one of the top doctors in Domain. She was one of your judges today. She's amazing at everything she does. Being a doctor is a natural profession for Nexus Shifters. I can heal, but I'm not passionate about it. My passion is telling stories, but Mum says she doesn't want me wasting money that we don't have in a profession that isn't guaranteed to make me successful."

"I'm sorry to hear that," I said, putting an arm around her. "I suppose her interpretation of the word successful differs from yours."

"Exactly. Although I know it's only because she doesn't want me worrying about money forever."

"I see the way your face lights up when you tell us the greatest moments of Shiftstory. You are a natural storyteller. I wouldn't give up your dream, but I can see where your mum is coming from," I said. "Perhaps if I can help fund–"

"I'm not looking for money, Charity," she cut me off with determination. I understood and dropped it. Her face then softened. "But enough about me. I want to hear more about today. What does darkness in the mind look like to you?"

I took her hint at a subject change and thought back to the minds I'd entered. "I suppose it's like shadows. They wrapped around things, but they weren't part of it, so I could remove them. I'm guessing others can do that too, though."

Perrine had turned to face me, her lip brush hovering in mid-air. "Quite the opposite. No one has ever done anything like that. We're quite clear about our capabilities here. You either lead the mind away from bad choices, heal it, inspire it, or destroy it."

Self-doubt washed over me again. A lifetime of being told I'm not good enough had that effect. "So, I did something wrong after all."

Perrine's eyes flashed in excitement, Shifting between her and Ordette. "On the contrary. I think you did something exceptional, and they know it."

Well, when she put it like that, it didn't sound so bad. "I know my decision put me in Caedes, but I never wanted to destroy Greg, just the evil parts of him. There wasn't anything obvious to heal, or inspire, and he was too far gone to lead away from any poor decisions, so it was my logical choice to remove the bad and leave the good."

Perrine turned back to the mirror. "You are going to be one interesting Shifter, Serrk. But, for now, we have a party to get ready for. What are you wearing, by the way?"

I hadn't even thought about that. I would just have to pick something from my wardrobe. Anton's taste was impeccable, and everything in there seemed to fit well, so I was sure I would find something. I pulled open the door and couldn't help the intake of breath when I saw what was hanging up inside.

I had underestimated how big a deal tonight was, which was stupid, as everything in Domain seemed important, and anything that involved a party even more so. Hanging up was one of the most beautiful dresses I'd ever seen. Green sequins adorned the full length of the ballgown, catching the light in a way that made them appear as if they were moving. Wait, they *were* moving. It was a dress made from one of those fabrics that Perrine and I had seen on our first shopping trip. I gulped when I thought about how much it had cost. I had my money now, and even if I didn't, I didn't need things like this, however exquisite. Running my hand down it, I watched the moving fabric. Despite the sequins, the material felt like silk.

Perrine's eyes widened when she saw it. "That was in the window of *Venelles and Vêtements;* it only arrived yesterday."

And somehow, in that time, Anton had purchased it, tailored it, and got it here. My nerves settled as for a wonderful split second, I realised everything was fine, and the fact I was in Caedes changed nothing between Anton and I. Then just as quickly; they resumed as I realised he put this dress here before my trial. It was green, after all. He'd been expecting me to belong to the House of Abduco.

My Shiftsung buzzed in my pocket with a message from Anton. The knot in my stomach tightened as I read his words.

Anton: Thought the colour might suit, see you soon - AA.

Shit. He had been expecting me to be in Abduco. That explained why he'd gone straight to the judges.

Viktor burst into the room, bottle in hand, cutting my thoughts short. I could tell he'd had a few drinks already, as he was speaking twice as loud as Perrine and I.

"It's all very sombre and serious in here," he said. "I thought we were getting ready for the party of a lifetime!"

"We are." I forced a smile and tried to inject some enthusiasm into my voice.

"Oh dear, what's that look for?" Viktor was never fooled. We'd trained together so often, he recognised every emotion my face betrayed. There was no hiding anything from him.

I sat back down in front of the mirror and continued applying my makeup. "I just wonder if I got put in the right place, if I'm where people expected me to be."

"You mean where Anton expected you to be?" he said, taking a swig from the bottle. He didn't miss a thing.

"Well, yes," I admitted, figuring it was easier to be honest with them both. I had a feeling they knew anyway.

Viktor flopped down on the edge of the bed so I could see his reflection in the mirror as I continued getting ready. "We all have parts of our partners we'd love to change. Anton and Allium are no different. Allium is trying to find a place for you among the values he was raised with. That alone should suggest how he feels. Plus, Shifters argue with their Other all the time, yet we manage. Take Forrest and me, for example. We just threaten to bring each other out during the middle of sex, and that's enough to keep us on good terms."

This pulled me out of my slump. I had to put my brush down to stop myself smearing mascara everywhere as Perrine and I laughed hysterically at the image. "I'll never get over how open you are, Vik."

He leaned forward to rest a hand on the back of my chair and gestured dramatically with the bottle. "We all have our demons, Charity. I am who I am. I like sex. Making people happy is what I do. Yes, I'm a disgrace to the Abduco sour demeanour, but what can I say? People like having me around."

"I can see why." I took the bottle from his outstretched hand and tasted the bubbly liquid. The taste of roses evaporated on my tongue as I swallowed.

There was a low rumble overhead that had to be Spyder landing on the roof in the helicopter. We could have Shifted there, but given I still hadn't been able to go beyond a few metres and didn't have an idol yet, Viktor had decided a helicopter would allow us to travel together. Travel Shifting was still something I'd need to work on in the future, but for now, I had to keep reminding myself that I'd done enough.

"The party has arrived, chaps," said Spyder as he swung into the room, grinning. "Congratulations on your Actuation, prophecy girl. Now get ready for a night you won't forget."

This was it. We were at Abduco Manor once again. I had voiced my confusion why Caedes wasn't throwing the party, not that I minded. Abduco had started to feel like home, and I was putting off asking whether I'd have to leave, too afraid of the response. Viktor muttered something about preparations being made here given I'd completed my training in Abduco, so I could only hope I'd be able to stay for a while longer.

Despite the grandness of the building, I suppressed a shudder as I remembered how my encounter with Scarlett had ended the last time I was here. I shook it off. That fear wouldn't paralyse me anymore. I hadn't forgotten about my revenge, and wondered how she felt about me being placed in the same House as her. I hoped she was furious.

Gaining control over my mental shields had allowed me to come to terms with what had happened to me, not to mention meeting Greg. It didn't forgive what he had done in the slightest, but knowing he couldn't inflict it on others meant I was ready to live without it weighing me down.

As Viktor led us through the giant doors, I pushed the negative thoughts from my mind, and instead found my mind wandering to whether Anton still had a room here.

I stepped into the main room, and the rhythmic beat of the music soothed my soul. The Abduco family home bustled with people. I marvelled once again at the Gothic style, with ornate carvings, arched windows, and climbing tendrils of ivy in every direction. I could see why it was a popular place for parties. The dramatic location was perfect.

A variety of sounds danced around the room: a merge of chatter, clinking glasses, and laughter. Fancy suits and vibrant, yet elegant, dresses of all colours surrounded me as the party guests glided by. However, I didn't feel intimidated this time. I had passed my Actuation, and hell, I was the one responsible for this party happening right now. I had as much right to be here as anyone else. The thought gave me confidence.

We moved around the room, taking the time to mingle with different guests. We seemed to bump into everyone except for Anton. Despite my best efforts, I failed to remember the multitude of people I met as I searched the room for him. The faces I saw were striking: a variety of skin tones, shapes, and sizes, many resembling the same Abduco features of green eyes and the mix of jet black and platinum blonde hair. Though there were countless Shifters from the other Houses, too.

Viktor kept his hand on the small of my back as he guided me through the rounds of congratulations, while Perrine and Spyder headed towards the bar to get us drinks.

Viktor's touch was warm, like he'd been standing in front of a fire. Then I remembered his Shifter form, and wondered if Shifters kept certain characteristics of their animal. I noticed a woman raise her eyebrows at us and hesitated, before piecing her reaction together. I turned to him. "Will people assume we're together if I'm here with you? I don't want to upset any of your partners."

Viktor moved his arm and draped it around my shoulders. "I date a lot of girls, Charity. They know what I'm like and what to expect.

They know they'll see me with someone different next week. I hurt no feelings. I make it very clear beforehand. Forrest is loyal to Julian, and they trust each other."

I grinned at him. "You've got it all worked out, haven't you?"

He removed his arm, took my hand, and kissed it in a polite gesture as he winked at me. "Like you wouldn't believe. Now we just need to do the same for you. Speak of the devil, I think the speeches are starting."

Sure enough, the crowd was parting at the foot of the stairs to allow Anton's family through so that they stood elevated above everyone. I inhaled when I saw him, just as I had done when I'd seen what I'd be wearing.

Because he wore a dark green suit that was identical to the shade of my dress.

They were a perfect pair.

He had worn a matching tie and a crisp white shirt. They offset the different colours of his hair, and I couldn't break my gaze from him, even as a glass clinked somewhere. The sound chimed through the room as his father started speaking, thanking everyone for attending.

"I'll leave you to listen in. I'm sure he'll come and find you after the speeches. In the meantime, I need to find my date for tonight." Viktor excused himself and disappeared into the crowd.

I nodded and turned my attention back to the Abduco family. They were all stunning in their own way. Sage looked immaculate, as always, in a dress that was somewhere between midnight and dark green. Real ivy wound through her hair, moulded into a tiara for effect. She looked every part the queen. She kissed her husband lightly on the cheek, stepped down from the stage, and disappeared into the crowd.

Verde was working through the list of people to thank for the party. He was handsome, yet carried himself with even more wariness at his surroundings than Anton did, and I couldn't help but notice he looked more tired than the last time I'd seen him. His eyes were cold, and he surveyed the room with the same aloofness I'd seen in Allium.

Anton's eyes found me through the crowd like sunlight between trees. For a split second, everything around us evaporated, and it was just us. His mouth curved into a smile as he saw my dress and tried to hide it by drinking his champagne.

My head swam. Could there be a place in both Anton and Allium's life for me?

Because I have a place for them both, a voice in my head admitted. For Anton's determination, his dare to dream, and his charm. For Allium's loyalty, and the fact he would make himself the villain in order to keep everyone around him safe.

Anton's father, Verde, was still speaking. "*Of course,* we need to acknowledge the reason for tonight, Charity Serrk's success in her Actuation. Caedes will be fortunate to have her. My son, Anton, would like to say some words on behalf of Abduco Apexes."

For a moment, Anton looked thrown, but he recovered as he stepped forward and addressed the room. The suit complemented his dark eyes and both hair colours perfectly. Though I could see less of his blond side, I knew Allium would look just as handsome.

Anton's words rang around the large space; of course, he was a natural at speeches. "I want to thank everyone for attending today. It is a busy season for Apexes, Mesos, and Demis alike, and I am confident the upcoming year will be a good one. But back to tonight, which wouldn't have been possible without my mother and her obsession with decadent parties." Applause and laughter echoed around the room. Anton paused tastefully until it had finished. "Now, for the person you're all interested in. Today's Actuation left a lasting impression on every Shifter in this room. Abduco would have been lucky to have you, Charity, but your actions have shown you to be not only a powerful but a unique Shifter. I think we can all expect great things from you."

Time seemed to have stopped. *Were these really his words for me?* I had forgotten there was anyone else in the room as I drank in his words instead of from my glass. After all, he hadn't had time to prepare a speech. He was speaking from the heart.

Verde's jaw was twitching. I could tell this was not the way he thought this speech would go. I imaged he expected something more reserved. But he should have known that Anton and Allium did what they wanted.

It was one of the many things I loved about them.

Anton finally rounded off his speech. "I won't keep you any longer. Enjoy your night, all of you. Some of you have travelled a long way to be here–make the most of it. Finally, a toast in honour of our celebrated guest, Charity." His eyes never left mine, and my stomach flipped as "Cheers!" echoed around the room. There was another giant round of applause.

I have to be close to him. The thought was loud in my head.

We had only been across the room from each other, but it took me several minutes to navigate in the direction that Anton had been standing as I shook yet more hands and muttered thanks over the success of my Actuation. Not that I wasn't grateful for the attention, there was just a pressing need to be near Anton, near Allium. Everyone else would have to wait. I knew he had a greater chance of finding me with his height and hoped he was seeking me out, too. But before I could finish that thought, the sleeve of a tailored green suit snaked around my waist, and a voice purred in my ear, "Follow me."

23

CHARITY

Shifter 101: The four principal Houses of Domain are: Abduco, Caedes, Nexus, and Persen. Literature often cites that the terrains of each House reflect the personality of the Shifters within.

There you are, I thought.

As always, came Anton's voice.

I wasn't sure if Anton had spoken, or if I'd imagined it, as I couldn't see his face, but I slipped my hand into his anyway and enjoyed the warmth of his grip. He steered me through the crowd with ease, acknowledging Shifters as he passed, but never stopping to speak until we reached someone that it seemed he could not ignore.

We came to an abrupt halt, and I was surprised to see one of the Caedes judges from my Actuation was here. Given the reason for the party, I suppose it made sense that they were here.

"I've been looking for you," Anton directed at the man now facing us.

The man's face broke into a cruel sneer. He stood towering above me, nothing short of terrifying. "Manners, Anton, we have a guest."

He gestured to me. His wavy hair sat just below his shoulders and his eyes looked full of malice as they flashed with a subtle red tinge. Given that he was from Caedes and all, I should have felt some kind of kinship, but instead I shivered as if I'd plunged into icy water.

Anton seemed to have forgotten I was standing there. He removed his hand from mine and wound it round my waist instead. As he did, he leaned forward in the man's ear. The little of his face that I could see was awash with venom. "Why did you give her a mind that she knew? You hoped she would destroy it because of the history there. You knew she'd be in Caedes. Why would you want her in Caedes?"

His words didn't match the placement of his warm hand still burning at my side. I scrambled to keep the crushing effect of his words from reaching my face. He had an issue with me being in Caedes. If it was where Shifters like the man in front of me went, I suppose I could hardly blame him.

I had wondered at the time why I could work with a mind I knew when that wasn't standard procedure, especially following the shouts I'd heard from the audience uttering the same thing. Obviously, I hadn't questioned it. The last thing I'd wanted was for the whole thing to be cancelled or worse, told to return to my world.

The man with red hair ignored Anton and held out a rough hand to me. "Allow me to introduce myself. Draven Caedes, House of Caedes and member of the Cerebral Council," he said in a gravelly voice.

Ah, that's why nobody asked questions during my Actuation. He'd been a judge, and I guess if you were on the Council, you could get away with just about anything. I should have refused his hand. But the tension between him and Anton and the manic glare in his eyes told me that would be a terrible move. I allowed my fingers to be crushed in the handshake, suppressing any visible discomfort, before drawing my hand back.

Draven turned to Anton. "I asked for a mind known to Charity to be permitted to see what would happen. The Council granted my request because I asked them to." He then fixed me with a smile that almost seemed proud. "Welcome to Caedes, Charity. You'll do well here."

I didn't know what he meant by that, but I didn't get to voice it, as he immediately turned back to Anton. "Have you seen Scarlett?"

"Why would I have seen her? I have nothing to do with her now."

"You know why," Draven said, his voice loaded with meaning. If I hadn't spent so much time around Anton, I might have been jealous about what Draven's words implied. But I knew Anton was being truthful about any involvement, or lack of, with Scarlett. There was something going on between these two here however, and it wasn't pretty.

"This isn't a conversation for right now." Anton jerked his head at the ongoing party.

The man's eyes narrowed. "Remember your place, Anton. I decide when it is appropriate. I'll find you later."

Anton took my hand without another word, and we disappeared into the crowd.

"What was that about?" I said when we were out of earshot. No one had spoken to Anton like that before.

"He has business with my father." His mouth was a thin line which said this wasn't the time to press it further.

He led us up a staircase that I hadn't noticed, and we emerged into a deserted hallway.

"Free at last. I'm sorry about that. I will explain another time." He bit his lip as he ran his eyes over my dress. "But right now, I don't want to ruin the image in front of me by thinking about him."

Something inside of me melted, along with all my doubts, at the feral look he gave me, and I forgot all about the conversation I'd just heard. I tried not to make too much of the fact he hadn't let go of my hand.

"It's good to see you, I mean, properly." *Good is an understatement.* But a mix of Viktor's bravado and the early champagne had given me confidence, and I gazed up at him through my lashes before I could change my mind.

"I'm surprised to see you still in the green. Though, I love it." His hand was back at my waist again.

I gave him a quizzical look. "How couldn't I wear this dress tonight? It's beautiful."

His eyes searched mine. "I'm pleased to hear it. But I meant the colour. It's almost perfect for you."

My heart sank. His speech had been for show. He was talking about the green. He hoped I'd been in Abduco.

Anton watched my face drop and to my surprise he smirked. *Why was he smirking?* We were on different pages here.

"Shiftcoin for your thoughts, Cee," he said, still grinning.

"Well, I'm wondering what's funny?" I pouted at him.

He pulled me closer. "I got you a green dress because it is one of my favourite colours."

"Like Abduco. I gathered that." I sighed.

"But that's what's funny. Didn't you see what it does?" He pulled me in further so I was now resting my hands on his chest.

I looked up into that face that was carved by gods. "What do you mean?"

His voice was a growl in my ear. "Charity, you look beautiful in green, but you look devastating in red."

I saw stars as the weight of Anton's other hand brushed up my thigh, moving against the sequins. As he did, they shimmered and changed colour to a vivid red. It started a chain reaction with the material, and before I knew it, I was standing in a brand new dress. My favourite colour. And the colour of Caedes.

He turned me to the full-length mirror I hadn't realised was there, the hand on my hip burning through the fabric. I took in the full effect of my dress, hair, and makeup. I'd never had a problem with the way I looked, but I'd never felt quite like this either.

Anton met my eyes in the mirror. "What's the point of seeing if you don't open your eyes, Cee? Oh, and Merry Christmas."

I made every area of him I was touching count. "Thank you. I didn't get you anything. I'm not used to celebrating Christmas with presents."

Anton kept his hand on my hip and wrapped the other even tighter around my waist, pulling me fully into his embrace. "Seeing you in this is enough of a present for me. I'm sure even Allium would agree."

My heart skipped a beat at the sound of his name. "He was never my biggest fan."

But . . .

Had I just heard his voice in my mind?

Anton kept talking out loud. "Despite what he keeps hidden, I know his thoughts towards you have changed. Which, for us, our upbringing, and especially for Allium and his viewpoints, is unheard of. You did that, Charity. *You* changed us for the better. Shifter or not, you have a place among us."

We both do. This time, the voice in my head was mine. *What the fuck is happening?*

I wasn't sure who was speaking anymore. I could hear words coming from Anton without his mouth moving. But I could hear my voice in my mind too.

Anton pulled me closer so that our faces were almost touching, then, his hand wrapped in my hair as he pulled it back. The anticipation had heat pooling low in my stomach, driving me insane. I followed his movement and tilted my head back for him, exposing my neck. He planted his mouth there and grazed his teeth against a sensitive spot right in the middle. It sent something deep inside my core crazy, and I pressed myself into him, enjoying every sensation. I drew back at the last minute, heady with the rush and my mind racing. It was all too good to be true.

"Tell me what's wrong," instructed Anton, understanding my body language perfectly.

"Do you have an issue with the fact that I'm in Caedes?" I said, needing to know for sure before things went further and we lost ourselves.

Anton's smirk was back. "I guess you weren't listening to my speech that well. You didn't destroy a mind for the sake of it. You removed only the evil and used your power for good. Something Caedes Shifters rarely do. But what could ever make you think I wouldn't want you?"

Warmth was spreading through my chest. "Well, you didn't say it quite like that during your speech."

He chuckled as he leaned in closer again, his husky voice hitting all the right parts of me. "I knew you were a threat from the moment I met you. What you did and where you ended up is a perfect fit for you. You wrote your own story. Your actions determine you. You could be an Abduco Shifter on that alone, but wherever you ended up, I assumed you'd be nowhere other than next to me."

"You assumed that right away, did you?" My words found a way through the grin that was spreading across my face.

"Well, it was maybe more of a hope."

His words were giving *me* hope that this could work out. Too much hope. "But I'm not perfect like you," I admitted. I needed to be honest, even if it changed how he felt about me. Pushing the tension in my chest to one side, I took a deep breath. "I like Allium too, and you both deserve more than someone who can't choose between you."

My shoulders sagged in relief. I couldn't quite believe I'd blurted it out. I froze, savouring any moment of contact in case he pushed me away.

But Anton spoke into my hair. "Allium *is* all of me. And I am all of him. It complicates things, I'll admit that, but I've never chosen the straightforward path, anyway."

"I suppose I haven't either." I grinned at him, feeling giddy with disbelief that this was happening.

The smell of mint and smoke was causing me to lose my mind as his cool breath caressed me. "I think I've known for some time."

This I didn't expect. His words steadied me as I met his eyes. "How?"

He smirked again. "Since he started shutting out everything to do with you."

I had to smile at that, then frowned as one last doubt reared to the surface. "But are you sure there isn't someone out there more suitable for your status as an Apex Shifter?"

"Given the rules we have, yes. I'm sure there is. But I'm not interested in that. There's always going to be more than one person out there who is a brilliant match for you, but you need to find someone that makes you feel like there isn't. And with you here, Cee, why would I even want to look?"

"So you don't care about the consequences?" It felt irresponsible, even by my standards.

"Oh, I do, and we'll need to be careful. But let's just say I care about losing you more." He curled a finger under my chin and tilted my gaze up to meet his.

Hope was threatening to suffocate me. I kept expecting everything to come crashing down. "I know enough about Shifters to know that one person can't have both a Shifter and their Other."

"But you're not most people." He was so close now.

"It could tear you apart." Our faces were almost touching.

"That's for him and I to decide. We wanted to throw you something you deserved, so we insisted on having your celebrations here tonight instead of Caedes. See, we can work together, after all."

I wrapped my free arm around his neck, my resolve evaporating as I looked into his eyes. "But why go to all this trouble? Surely you know I'm already yours."

"Why the party?" He ran a finger down the side of my face. "Because you deserve it. And because I can give it to you. We both can."

His teeth then resumed their grazing of my neck before sucking on it, causing a moan to escape my mouth.

Merry Christmas, we're both yours too. I don't know if I spoke aloud, but something caused Anton to spring into action as he wrenched himself from my neck. For a split second, our eyes blazed into each other before our lips crashed together. Euphoria coursed throughout my entire being, and my world ceased to exist beyond him.

Our kiss built momentum, and I parted my lips, allowing Anton's tongue to explore my mouth. He groaned from the back of his throat, and I deepened the kiss, unable to help myself as our tongues sought each other out. This was better than anything I had experienced, even any sex. I had never felt so connected to anyone. It was like he could tell what I was thinking.

We pulled apart and our eyes met, burning. His pupils dilated and his irises flashed between light and dark green.

Anton and Allium were both here.

Wait. *Why wasn't Allium stopping this? Was he as on board with this as Anton?* I knew he had hinted at feelings, but neither of them seemed like the type of person who could share. I knew they both felt something. Their thoughts were in my mind: They both wanted this.

Without breaking contact from our kiss, Anton moved my legs apart using a knee, nudging me until my back was against the wall. I lost my mind as he bit down on my tongue and sucked on it. Fuck, I wanted Anton; I wanted Allium. I wanted all of him: the kind, the cruel, and the parts of him trying to be better. But I also wanted him. Right now.

More crucially, I could tell he wanted me. All of me. I could hear him. He was telling me. But I hadn't stopped kissing him. He was in my mind; I could hear his voice.

You're so fucking perfect. I didn't know you were in there.

I gasped into Anton's mouth as I heard that voice identical to my own from within me.

You came. I just needed the right person to find me, Allium.

Anton sprang away from me, his hands on my shoulders. He stared at me with wide eyes. I knew he had heard too. He choked out, "You have an Oth– who is that?"

I didn't know where the name came from. It was like another presence was floating near the surface of my mind, ready to speak for herself. I knew what to answer. "She's Una."

Una, what a beautiful name for a beautiful person, inside and out. It was Allium's voice, but inside my head.

Then came Una's. *Allium, we are opposites, yet we are a perfect match.*

Anton's arms wound around me, crushing me with his intensity as I gave myself to him. The ecstasy between Allium and Una danced back and forth as they shared all the same sensations felt by Anton and

I. I could hear him in my thoughts celebrating the match between the two pairs, coupled with Anton's growls as he lifted me and I dragged both hands through his hair, running my nails across his scalp.

Everything made sense. Why my personality seemed so split. Why I was fiery but had moments where I melted around Anton. It answered why I craved the adrenaline of running but recently enjoyed reading much more. Why I was bold and outspoken but also reserved. It wasn't just me; it was Una and I. There would be time to work out which traits belonged to who.

I could read everything going on in Anton's mind, as well as Allium's and Una's. They dashed across like quick fire messages, exposing what he was thinking. Images that gave me too many ideas flickered in front of us and between my legs pulsed in need.

"Covalents." Anton broke the kiss long enough to say the word before pulling me back in again. After another kiss, he said, "When two Shifters match, and their Others are also a match."

I drew back to check this wasn't some kind of joke, hardly daring to believe it. "That's impossible."

He grinned into my ear before biting on it hard, sending me moaning into his neck. His words were like music as he said, "I don't know why I'm surprised. One person would never be enough for you. Now both of me are yours."

I pulled myself back from Anton, the action painful. I could have remained there for the rest of my life and been happy. Running my hands over the muscles in his shoulders, I enjoyed Una's reactions, as well as my own. It wasn't like having another person in my mind. She was me, an extension of my personality. If I had felt giddy before, I was near delirious now. Weeks of pent up frustration left me as I kissed him again. I didn't dare think of what else that tongue was capable of. I'd likely pass out. Surely this man couldn't be ours, both Anton and

Allium a match with Una and me?

After what felt like an eternity lost in our embrace, I found the strength to unwrap my arms from his neck and put my legs down. Giving me one last kiss, he dragged my lip out between his teeth and sent my eyes rolling back into my head.

"I can read your mind when we're touching, by the way, so your thoughts aren't safe around me anymore." He grinned. "It's a Covalents thing. Look at your arm. When Covalents match, they're marked to warn off other Shifters."

I looked at my left arm. Sure enough, near the top, two silver bands had appeared there, winding round the full circumference of my arm. Anton unbuttoned his shirt and pulled it off the shoulder to reveal he had ones in the same place though his were thicker. They looked a bit like wedding rings; just bigger, and more permanent. Tattoos danced across Anton's chest. I'd forgotten he had so many. I lost myself in their movement for several seconds before dragging my eyes away as he did his shirt back up.

"How long do you think before people notice?" I was still entranced by the new mark.

"I imagine about five minutes. Covalents are a pretty big deal, even in Domain. But right now, I just want to enjoy every second with you."

"Is it a good idea to go out there together? Won't there be consequences?"

"That's the beauty of it." Anton smirked. "Apex Shifters and Demi-Shifters can't be together until their parents or guardians approve." My breath hitched until he said, "*Unless* Covalents are concerned. Even the Cerebral Council won't be able to do anything about it. That's not all. You're also free to choose the Domain you live in, regardless of the House you belong to."

My heart swelled with elation and we kissed again, my dress riding up and giving both of us more ideas. *Shit, is he going to see everything inside my head?*

You'd better fucking believe it.

By the time Anton pulled away, I was sure I'd have makeup everywhere. Then I remembered how much more resilient Shifter makeup was. It really was great stuff.

I adjusted my dress. Had Anton explored further up my thighs, he would have seen just how much he had excited me. I watched his eyes follow the hem as it fell to the ground again. They were feral. Perhaps he already knew.

We pulled apart and regained a sense of clarity as he wrapped an arm around my shoulders. "They say the nights in Abduco are longer for a reason, and while I'd love to show you why right now, it'll sadly need to wait."

I pouted and crossed my arms in mock annoyance. Though my thoughts betrayed me, and revealed to Anton that was exactly how I felt. He laughed. "I haven't been able to hear anything before tonight, if you were wondering, but I'm enjoying this insight into you now. Anyway, this hallway is empty at the moment, but I don't like the idea of this being the first place we take this further. Someone could walk in and while they'd get a good show, I'm too selfish. I want you all to myself." His eyes were glittering again. I knew he was speaking about both him and Allium.

"Well, I've waited until now. I'm sure I can manage a little longer." I smoothed my hair back into a tamer version of what it had been.

I could feel them both grinning at my words. *Did being Covalents mean we could sense each other's emotions as well?*

"It does." Anton wrapped an arm around my waist as he read my thought. I could feel Allium behind the touch as well. "I know we are going to need answers about what happens now, but in the meantime,

I think we owe it to ourselves to celebrate and enjoy the rest of the party."

"Lead the way," I said, as we made our way back towards the murmur of the party next door.

Just as we were about to leave, he hesitated. "Wait. Do you want to turn your dress back? It looks like you got changed, and given we disappeared, people might draw their own conclusions about what we were up to."

"Do you mind?" I stared up at him, still hazy with everything that had just happened. "Because I don't one bit. In fact, being Covalents means no one can say a fucking thing about us being together."

"Like I'd even let them try." He grinned as he opened the door and we stepped back out into the party.

24

CHARITY

Shifter 101: Prophecies serve to give an indication about the future of Domain. They have been around for centuries but have become rarer, owing to the main prophecy in circulation.

Electricity buzzed between us as we took the same route to Persen as we had last time. Anton sat with one hand on the steering wheel, the other in my lap. It wasn't the safest way to drive, but given his and now my Shifter reactions, I let it slide.

I wasn't sure what *we* were yet. We'd kissed, we'd enjoyed the party, we'd got drunk, and we'd all come back to Anton's flat. Spyder had been in Anton's bed with at least three other Shifters. At least, that's how many I'd counted before Anton had slammed the door shut in horror. Viktor and Forrest had taken my bed, which left Anton and me on the sofa. Even then, Perrine had come crashing through the door hours later, wrapped in the embrace of a Persen Shifter. Good for her. And as much as his flat seemed to be hosting some kind of orgy, Anton was right. I didn't want to share this moment with anyone else. Instead, I'd fallen asleep wrapped in his arms, enjoying the scent of smoke and spearmint.

With all our company in the morning, we hadn't discussed the events of last night. Anton was right, someone noticed our marks within a few minutes after we arrived back at the room and there was uproar with the celebrations continuing until sunrise.

As news of our status as Covalents spread throughout Domain, I realised that this was very much a big deal. Almost as big as the prophecy. I glanced at the coffee table and saw we had even made the front page of *The Notion*. The photo accompanying the article showed Anton and I–me in the red dress–clasping hands and revealing our marks. I was pleased that my hair didn't look as dishevelled as I had first thought. But how did it get printed and arrive so quickly?

Things travel fast when it's digital, Allium answered for me.

I noticed there were still mentions of the disappearances through-out Domain, and I hadn't asked Anton about it again. It appeared I was the only one that even noticed, as Spyder scanned the page with-out a second thought. "So, Una is from Caedes too? This is amazing news. We've got a spy in the camp. Welcome to the team!"

"That's how it works." I knew Allium enjoyed speaking for Una. I could read his thoughts through our clasped hands and understood Una allowed him to carry on, despite my instinct to speak up for myself. He'd had no one to do this for before, so who was I to stop him?

"Hey, I've just realised–Charity and Una, we could call you Unity!" Viktor slapped the table at this revelation.

And now, after a few days of celebrations, here we were. Away off on a date. An actual date. If we were Covalents, bonded together in a perfect match and all that, that meant we were some kind of item, right? We hadn't discussed it yet, as was customary in my world, leaving me confused about where we stood.

Anton looked as handsome as ever in a new suit, once again in the darkest of green. This time, he had paired it with a black shirt. His sleeve of the arm in my lap had ridden up, and I studied his watch as his thumb traced the back of my hand.

"What does this do?" The dials were much more complex than anything I'd seen before.

"It tells the time, Serrk," said Anton, full of that smugness I loved. Hearing this, he added, "The fact you love my smugness isn't so much of a secret when we're touching, remember?"

Damn him. "You're lucky I don't have a full grasp on my abilities yet, otherwise I'd have no problem at all with putting you in your place."

Anton squeezed my thigh, sending a wave of anticipation through me. "I'd be lying if I said I wouldn't enjoy that. But since you asked so nicely, it tells me not only the time, but when to act in relation to the minds I am dealing with." He brought his wrist to the wheel so he could point to a small separate dial filled with small moons and stars before returning it to my leg. "I use this when I'm working to know when to intervene and when to stay back because I'm not a mind reader, not all the time anyway. I was called away from most of my duties to focus on your Actuation, so it's been a welcome reprieve, though I expect they'll want me to start back soon."

It wasn't clear whether he was talking about his work with minds or his gang life with the Dragos. The more I learned about Domain, the more fascinating it became. I tugged my dress down. I'd chosen a black one tonight to mix my colour palette up. It hugged my figure and had a plunging neck, made more modest by a mesh panel that covered some of my cleavage.

That dress is many things, but it's not modest. And I'm absolutely fine with that.

Una laughed at Allium's comment. I was becoming used to them having their own conversations in our heads without us.

Anton and I sat back and allowed them. He turned up the music, and I focused on his rings on the steering wheel, his Abduco crest along with the others. I could only see the blonde side of his hair, but everything was pristine as always. The rain battered off the windscreen; the droplets forced backwards as we sped along the road.

One of my new favourites came on and I turned up the volume until I could feel the beat between my lungs. I tipped my head back and closed my eyes, unable to remember a time when I'd been so happy.

When I opened them, I realised Anton was looking at me rather than the road. He sucked the air between his teeth, his eyes positively feral. "If it weren't for my upbringing to never be late for dinner reservations, I would pull this car over right now."

I wonder if he had a thing for necks. Maybe in another life he'd been a vampire.

Anton chuckled at my thought. "I know what I'll be dressing up as for Halloween. But no, it's not that. You look at something long enough, sweetheart, it's easy to become obsessed."

I huffed out a breath at his hand still on my leg. I'd never get used to this mind reading thing.

The view over Persen was just as spectacular this time around. If anything, it was even better, as I didn't even feel a trickle of terror as the darkness of the tunnel washed over us. Between my thoughts, Anton's, Allium's, and Una's, there wasn't much room for any of my fears or self-doubts, and that suited me just fine.

Anton parked in a busy street across the road from a huge restaurant named *Abruzzi's*. He opened the car door for me and I stepped out, greeted by the unmistakable smell of Italian food.

The restaurant staff ushered us to our table, apparently there was no need to stand in the queue outside. One look at Anton and no one objected.

We sat down at a small booth at the side of the busy room. Mirrors adorned the space, making it hard to see where the actual restaurant ended and the illusion began. There was a large brass bar in the centre where waiting staff dressed in white tossed drinks and balanced more plates than I could fathom.

I opened the menu and shivered with delight at the options. I had never eaten out at a restaurant back in my old life, let alone one like this. "Mmmm, I love Italian," I said as I scanned the options.

Anton laughed. "It's Shiftalian. Another cuisine we introduced into the human world through dreams so that Shifters can enjoy it while they spend time there."

"Why am I not surprised? I knew it was too good." I closed my menu as I saw the waiter approaching. Anton removed his jacket and ran a hand through his hair. I never missed the way his shirt tightened around the muscles in his arms and shoulders.

He ordered a bottle of champagne from a menu I hadn't even seen on the table and gave the waiter our orders, reading my mind to find out what I wanted. Sneaky bastard.

The waiter noted everything down, clarifying, "That's two arancini starters, one pizza prosciutto e rucola, and one Brasato al Barolo." He then turned to Anton. "And do you want bread with that, sir?"

"No thanks." He looking me dead in the eye as he answered. "I'm not in the mood for a sandwich tonight."

The waiter raised a brow and left us giggling like children at the table. I made a promise to get him to laugh more. The way his face relaxed when he smiled and his eyes crinkled was nothing short of perfection.

Our starters were excellent, the main course even better, though I think I still preferred Anton's cooking. Once again, the chatter and bustle around us faded into the background, allowing us to become lost in our own world. The champagne sparkled on my tongue, leaving me tipsy, but not drunk.

"I noticed the tunnel didn't bother you this time," he observed as the waiting staff cleared the plates.

Stroking the stem of my glass, I said, "I suppose you taught me well." I wanted to say more, allow him to understand that side of me, but Anton lifted his hand off my arm, breaking our mental connection. "You don't have to show me. If you want to close that off, you can."

I moved my hand from my glass and took his. "No, it's okay. This is behind me now; I want you to know."

It was true. If someone like Scarlett knew, Anton should, too. I let him in through my mental shields and allowed him to stand in my hallway. He nodded in approval at the few tendrils of ivy I'd allowed to decorate the columns and doors. My prolonged stay in Abduco meant I was getting used to their decor. Maybe even liking it.

I led us up towards the darker end of my hallway. The one I'd never ventured into willingly. We kept walking until we reached a heavily fortified door.

"Are you sure?"

"Never been more sure." I swung open the door and stepped in. We found ourselves transported back to the memory that Scarlett had seen that night. I watched my younger self dragged across the kitchen floor and forced into that small space. But I didn't cringe this time. Instead, I watched it through fresh eyes. Understood that Greg behaved like that because he had experienced it himself and didn't know any different. Not that it made it okay. But it had confirmed it wasn't my fault that it had happened.

"How long were you under there, the floor?" Anton gritted out, his fists clenched.

I swallowed, thinking back. *Long enough for me to accept I might die there.* I had no way to keep track of time other than the light fading to night. By the time the light faded for the second time, I was too tired to notice and was succumbing to dehydration.

Anton was eerily still as he listened to my thoughts.

Perhaps a part of that sixteen-year-old girl would stay with me forever, but one thing was for sure. I would never find myself in that position again. I'd never be that weak again.

"You were never weak, Cee, you were a child." Anton wound an arm round me and steered us away from the door. "Thank you for sharing this with me. I understand now. You're stronger than most for what you've been through and overcome."

I was glad he knew, and couldn't help but agree with his words; a lot had changed since then. Without my past, I wouldn't be who I was.

We returned to the dinner table and continued on lighter topics for some time. We were making our way through our second bottle of champagne when I noticed Anton staring.

"What is it?" I was distracted as I drank him in. I wanted to run my hands through that two-tone hair, have him do things to me that would make me dig my nails into his scalp. If we weren't in such a public place, I might have started already.

He put his hand on my leg under the table, causing me to slide further towards him. "Do you not see how men notice you? And some women too, I might add," he said, amused.

I hadn't. "No. I'm only concerned if one person notices me. Well, two."

Anton's hand remained just above my knee, unable to move any further because of my dress being so form-fitting. He chuckled, and I cursed at the fact before remembering Anton could hear everything. I wanted his hand up further, despite being in the middle of a busy room.

"You're something else, Serrk." But his hand remained there as we received dessert menus, while we ate pudding, and even during our cups of tea that followed. Then, just when the heat in my core was becoming unbearable, he gripped my thigh tighter and said, "How about we have a proper dessert now?"

I couldn't agree quickly enough.

Anton tapped his temple towards one of the waiting staff to pay, and we left.

We stepped into the cool night breeze, but I didn't see Anton's car. "It's parked elsewhere. I've arranged for something different." He pointed with our clasped hands to a much taller building further up the street.

Curious to see what he meant, I asked no questions. It was amazing how a couple of months of training, an eternal bond, and a few life-changing experiences could build your trust in someone.

We walked into the smart glass building and he guided me to the lifts, Allium mentally checking that I was now comfortable with these. A doorman greeted us across the deserted room by tipping his hat.

As the lift doors closed behind us, his eyes flashed and I could tell both he and Allium were present. Before I knew it, he crashed his mouth into mine, the force of it knocking me back into the wall.

It wasn't a moment too soon.

I kissed him back with the same enthusiasm, angling myself into him as his hands curved round my thighs, moving my dress up so that I could wrap my legs round him as he lifted me.

Yes. This was good. This was fucking great.

Without warning, the doors opened to one very stern Abduco Shifter who gave us both a harsh look. "I'll just wait," she pouted.

"Great idea." Anton grinned into my neck, not bothering to raise his head as he slammed a hand on the buttons to close the doors. I was too turned on to care about our rudeness.

We were moving upward again. I wrapped my legs around him tighter, bringing him closer. It was impossible to miss the hardness as he pressed between my legs. I ground into him, searching for friction, sending him growling into my neck. I closed my eyes and rolled my head back in response.

Wait, where is that icy breeze coming from?

I opened my eyes and noted that all too soon, we'd reached the roof. The cool air rushed in to greet us, the sky now clear of rain.

I'd never enjoyed lifts for obvious reasons, but I'd accept a surprise like that any day.

"That wasn't the surprise, Cee. Though I'm glad you enjoyed it as much as I did." Anton composed himself as we stepped out. I huddled into him as the late night chill sank past my clothes.

"Did you know each Domain has a season?" he asked as we stepped into the centre of the roof overlooking the city. "Nexus is spring, Caedes summer, Abduco is autumn, and Persen is winter."

"So it just stays that season all year round?" I looked around, wondering where he was going with this.

"Pretty much, there are some slight differences, but that's why each House has the terrains that it does."

"Well, I wouldn't mind a nice cosy car heater during our drive home." I shivered. The snow on the mountains in the distance reminded me it was very much winter here.

"We're not driving back."

Damn. I enjoyed our drives. Why did Anton have to be such a sexy driver? If we weren't driving, it meant side-along Shifting, which to be honest, I hated as it was over with too quickly. Plus, there was always the risk of another panic attack if I didn't concent–

We're not side-along Shifting either, Allium interrupted my thoughts.

"Then what?" I answered him out loud.

He grinned down at me. Even in my heels, he was still so much taller. "What about flying?"

The stars shimmered above us, as if someone had taken a handful of glitter and tossed it into the night sky.

I made my decision before I could overthink it, butterflies unfurling in my stomach. "What are we waiting for?"

There was a crack, and the roof seemed much smaller. That's because Anton now covered most of it. But it wasn't Anton anymore. Instead, an enormous black and white dragon had replaced him. The two halves were perfectly even, one black, one white, just like his hair. Ivy green scales wrapped themselves around the legs of the creature, making him unmistakably Abduco. The only part I recognised was his eyes. They were the darkest green, flecked with lighter flashes.

Anton extended his head down for me to swing my leg over the bottom of his neck. It was a bit like climbing on a horse, or so I thought. I'd never tried. But I'd climbed a lot of trees, so I did a decent job of clambering up, even in my heels.

"I'd have thought you'd have been bigger." I adjusted myself between his wings.

Anton snorted, puffs of smoke coming from his nostrils. We both knew I was joking. He took up the entire roof. He was enormous. And after our encounter in the lift, he'd given me an idea of just how sizable other parts of him were, too.

He didn't give me a moment to second guess what we were doing as he spread his giant wings and took off over the city. There was nothing to hold on to, so I wrapped my arms around his neck as best as I could and held on for dear life. The adrenaline rush was extreme. Better than running. Running was good, driving was great, but flying, that was true freedom.

We soared among the bright lights, ducking and winding our way through the roads that hung suspended in mid-air. Cars, taxis, and vehicles I didn't even recognise were no match for our speed. Soon, we'd left everything behind so that the entire city was nothing more than a postcard nestled among the mountains.

"This is incredible." I stayed close to Anton's neck, the wind whipping at my hair. He turned his head, and I saw the satisfaction in his expression.

It was hard to tell how fast we were going, but we continued like that for about an hour. Fortunately, Anton's colossal form blocked out most of the chill, most likely from the heat that radiated from him. I made a note to ask if he could breathe fire once he could speak again.

Before long, I recognised the leafy terrain of Abduco, and Anton's building appeared on the horizon. We drew closer, and just as we reached the balcony, he ducked his head and I dropped the last three or four feet, landing neatly.

A second later, Anton landed back in his human form. He read my expression and closed the space between us, kissing me again. "Let's finish what we started."

25

CHARITY

Shifter 101: Covalents occur when two Shifters and their Others both match. This allows two separate relationships to exist and both Shifters to keep their Other fully realised.

There was a giant clap of thunder when the storm broke above us as we stood entwined on the balcony. He nipped at my ear and his hand explored dangerously close to my aching core.

"I think the storm is getting closer," I said, even though there could be a tornado storm for all I cared. I wasn't moving from his embrace.

Anton pulled back to glance at the sky. "I'm okay with it if you are. Thunderstorms are pretty much the soundtrack for Abduco life. I'm used to it." He removed his jacket and shirt in two quick movements. Then he laid them down on the ground.

Oh, we're doing this here? Well, fine by me, at least we have that view. I filed away his comment about working out for another time.

"Is this okay?" He sensed my thoughts. "We can go inside if you want somewhere more comfortable. I just haven't sorted my room since Spyder."

My head tilted back. I looked over his shoulder at the dramatic scenery around us, thunder rumbling in the background. We knew how to part the rain. Neither of us was going to get wet, not like that anyway. "Here is perfect. Stop being so honourable."

Anton drew back and his eyes flashed as I unzipped my dress slowly. "Oh, Cee, there's nothing honourable about what I'm about to do–"

"*Was* about to do I'm afraid, mate," Viktor's voice startled us both.

"For the love of Hymev," Anton growled, positioning himself in front of me, even though I was still dressed. "What is it?"

"Easy scales," laughed Viktor, unfazed. "If either of you had checked any of your messages tonight, you'd already know. Draven is looking for you. He said he'll be round soon. I came to warn you." With that, Viktor grinned and gestured to the pair of us. "Anyway, enjoy, and thanks for the image."

Anton lit a cigarette in frustration and motioned for me to sit beside him. "He did us a favour." His eyes glinted at my crumpled dress. "I was about to get carried away. You don't know how much I want to tear that off you. But I can't let us go any further without admitting something about Draven."

A lump formed in my throat. "What is it?"

"One second." He picked up a blanket from under the seat and handed it to me, along with drinks for us both. He then fired a message off from his Shiftsung. I watched the letters glide off into the night.

Don't bother coming. I will see you tomorrow - AA.

"Is that for him?" I asked.

"Yes." He stared into his drink.

This wasn't where I thought this was going to go, but it had to be important, so I threw water on the fire that was building in my core and zipped my dress back up. "What about him?"

Anton pulled his shirt back on, but didn't button it. "It was him. He sent me into your world to monitor you."

"What? Scarlett's dad?" Numbness coursed through me, replaced by an uncomfortable hotness. I didn't like the coincidence. I felt on the back foot, like I was missing something. "You didn't think that was worth telling me?"

"No. He made the operation sound routine and, until his interference in your Actuation, it was. It didn't differ from any of my other jobs on paper. Remember when I mentioned all of my other mind clients had to stop until I had fed back about you? Didn't you wonder why I wasn't working while I was here?"

"I'd assumed it was to do with being an Apex." I'd supposed he could work when he chose to.

"No, usually we have to work with around seven minds at a time. But Draven wanted me to focus on you."

I frowned at this. "And you didn't find that strange?"

Anton's voice dropped, his mouth turned down in a sneer. "I had no choice. If he asks me to do something, I have to."

"Why?" I didn't understand. I knew there were family ties between his father and Draven, but this seemed extreme.

His face was slipping back into the mask I'd met. "It's complicated."

It seemed simple enough to me. "You always have a choice."

"Not when it concerns the safety of your family."

I didn't know what to say to that. But it still didn't excuse him for keeping this from me. Anton nodded, noticing my conflicted expression. "I know. I came to your world to oversee your arrival and give feedback to him. The last thing I expected was for you to walk straight into me and show me what you were capable of, all on day one."

"You have the quick reactions–you could have moved out the way,"

I said, still angry.

"That's the thing. I didn't want to. I didn't understand it. Allium was in my head, screaming at me to get away, but part of me just wanted to stay and speak to you. I wanted to have an excuse to stay. To look after you."

I was getting sucked into his side of things. I drew back. "Whether or not they forced you into it, you should have told me."

"I know," said Anton for the second time. His face twitched as I made it clear that I felt betrayed. If he'd known someone had been looking into me, I should have, too. Not to mention the fact that it was the same person who'd tampered with my Actuation. I was missing something here, but I was too angry to fit the puzzle pieces together. His sharp features pulled into a grimace. "For what it's worth, I'm sorry. I couldn't let anything else happen before you knew everything."

I could feel him in my mind, trying to get in. For once, I shut him out. "Why couldn't you have told me this before?"

Anton lit another cigarette in frustration. After taking a long drag, he continued. "I was terrified you would think I feel the way I do about you because of the prophecy. But on top of that, I needed proof that he was associated with the missing persons across Domain. I've been working on intelligence that would suggest he is. I'm sorry, Cee, but like I said before, Draven is dangerous."

His words still gave me chills that were nothing to do with the storm above us. I wrapped the blanket around my shoulders. "Keep nothing like that from me again."

"Of course. You can hold it against me forever. Just don't go anywhere." His eyes widened a fraction, and he tightened his grip on my legs that rested in his lap as if he believed I might leave.

I weighed up his words and already knew I was staying. "Why do you think he asked you to look into me?"

"Other than the prophecy, I don't know, sweetheart. When there's a war at stake, people do many things." He was being truthful. I didn't need to see his mind to understand that. I could sense his emotions through our bond.

"But he didn't seem that interested in me the last time we met. In fact, the two of you were speaking like I didn't even exist."

"That's the part I don't understand. There's more to this, Cee, and we need to figure it out, but not after this many drinks. I'm sorry I spoke over you that night. I just wanted him to pay you as little attention as possible. He's dangerous." He followed my gaze as he took another draw. "Still don't care to join?" he said, with the ghost of a smirk. I could tell he was trying to lighten the mood.

I narrowed my eyes and followed his drift. "All the mind power in the world and you still use those to relax you?"

"Like I said before, Cee, we all have our vices. I don't like to deprive myself."

I looked out across the familiar view of Abduco. Despite seeing it many times, it still took my breath away.

Meanwhile, Anton contented himself by taking his own breath away with his cigarette. His eyes rolled back, and his shoulders relaxed. He exhaled, the smoke lost to the dark clouds above us. Personally, I wasn't a smoker, but why did he have to make everything look so good?

"I'm not perfect, you know," he answered my thought out loud.

I looked him up and down, tutting at him reclining in his chair like he was advertising cigarettes. But I'd seen his vulnerable side too, and something told me this was the time to ask a question that had been on my mind for some time. "Tell me about your father."

Anton's posture changed. He picked up his glass and gripped it; the veins standing out on the back of his hand. Even though I wasn't in his mind fully, I heard several doors slam and lock.

Maybe I'd asked too much of him. "You only need to tell me what you want. But I want to understand."

He looked out across the hidden mansions under the stars. He sat like that for almost a full minute before he said anything, the seconds punctuated by my heartbeats. "It's okay. You shared your past. I want you to know me. To understand me. Understand why I'm like this."

I considered his words. "Everything I know so far, I understand, Anton."

"You shouldn't. What if I'm not the good guy, Cee?" For the first time, he looked scared. His face was paler than usual, and his colossal form sat hunched over instead of with his usual poise.

"What makes you think I'm the good girl?" My heart cracked at seeing him like that. Why should he doubt himself so much? I wasn't perfect, either. Hell, I now belonged to the House of Caedes. He tutted at my comment and disappeared to refill our drinks. By the time he returned, he was ready to talk.

He pulled my feet back into his lap. "It all started for me twelve years ago. The political situation in Domain was tense because of the upcoming elections for members of the Cerebral Council, and people were wondering if it was time for a power change." I did the maths. That would have made Anton only fifteen. He continued. "Draven and his followers began gaining traction throughout the different Houses. He wasn't always bad, Draven. There were many here who wanted change, a more reliable system, myself included. They found Shifters who were tired of the emerging ways and agreed over how to deal with the prophecy. As a result, Caedes formed a joint alliance with Abduco, even though the two Houses had never worked in tandem before. But my father, being an Apex, wanted the best for us, and led the group that joined Draven's side." Anton swallowed. He looked like he was going to be sick.

I traced the swirls of smoke coming from Anton's dragon tattoo as I waited for him to compose himself. The head was out of sight, but must have been somewhere around his shoulder. The body wrapped round his back, reaching the other side where the tail curled round the opposite arm. He kept talking. "The problem was, there were many that took the hunt for power further than we ever thought possible. By then, my father had lost track of the fact we already had the best. He wanted more. He wanted to protect us. We always had protection, but he kept chasing a dream that didn't exist. Eventually, Abduco couldn't offer him enough. Draven was looking for recruits for the Cerebral Council and before we knew it, my father had signed up to join."

"But I thought the Cerebral Council were the ones in charge here?" I said.

"They are. But Draven has infiltrated them with his followers. They refer to themselves as the Reapers."

A shiver ran down my back. I recognised the name of the Caedes gang. "But couldn't you go to the rest of the Council and explain what was happening?"

Anton gave a bitter chuckle. "Charity, I've never explained what the Reapers do. Draven started with followers, but the Reapers were his inner circle of the most depraved Shifters imaginable. They carried out his work in the most violent ways possible. He was smart. He made sure that anyone who was associated with them had collateral. Mine was my family, and most recently, you. They manipulated minds and destroyed any that wouldn't yield to them."

I took a breath. It was unimaginable. "I'm sorry. I didn't know you all had this burden."

"Why do you think we live in this world walking on eggshells? A world where people talk down to Mesos and Demi-Shifters, treating them like lesser people and no one does anything about it? It's because they are making it that way." Nexus doesn't interfere. They are too busy with healing, which is their primary concern. Most of Persen turns a blind eye, too. It's why Spyder had mentioned such low numbers recruited for the Hydras.

Guilt gnawed at me. I'd spent my time in Domain obsessing over Anton and Allium, but I'd not even scratched the surface in what I knew about the world as a whole. "I wish I could have known sooner."

"You couldn't have. I've kept this door closed to you. It's in my nature to keep secrets from everyone, from myself. I'm so ashamed of what my family was part of. What we are part of. We'll carry that with us forever."

"Your mother was involved too?"

"No, she wasn't. Though she knew we were and would do what it takes to keep her family safe. She still will."

"That's not your fault." I shifted in my seat, aware I'd grown numb, and pulled the blanket tighter around me. Perhaps it was the Caedes side of me talking, but I wanted to say that anyone in his position would have done the same. After all, what wouldn't people do for those they love? I shivered away the nausea at what I'd just contemplated.

"There's more."

The darkness of the guilt that consumed him weighed on our bond. If I squinted, I could see a few tiny shadows woven amongst the ivy.

Anton continued to speak. "For a while, I joined my father. Not because I wanted to. They knew who to threaten to make me do what they wanted."

I had to know. "Did you kill other Shifters?"

I could see the tension in his jaw as he admitted, "Yes. I spared as many as I could, giving people the heads up, telling them to run or pointing them towards those who would help. Where I could, I killed Shifters who deserved it from our side and glamoured their body to look like someone who didn't. But I couldn't save everyone. Sometimes I was too late. Sometimes there were too many people watching, and I just had to enter my victims' minds to calm them so they wouldn't feel anything. They wouldn't have been aware of what happened to them, but that doesn't make it any better, knowing there are souls floating through Langison because of me."

"Anton–" My heart was breaking for him.

"Don't, Cee. I don't need your pity. There are a lot of things I want from you, but not that."

"What about Viktor? Was he involved?"

"No, I didn't want him to have anything to do with this life. I ditched him on the way to every meeting, pushed him off buildings, tied him up, damaged him just enough so that he couldn't Shift when he was required to. He thought it was brotherly rough play, but really I did everything I could to make him not a suitable candidate to be enlisted in Draven's Reapers."

All this time, Viktor must have thought it was just Anton's moody persona, but there was much more to him. I wondered how much Viktor knew now.

I shuffled next to him and extended the blanket to wrap around his shoulders, sliding my hand under his shirt to meet the exposed skin. But I flinched when I brushed against roughness that I hadn't expected. Anton's eyes closed; he hadn't expected me to touch him. I hadn't meant to, at least, not in that way.

"You'll see at some point anyway," said Anton. "Just another perk of being an Apex Abduco. I deserved it."

He dropped the blanket along with his shirt, and I gasped. Giant lashes marked his back, shredding the bottom of his dragon tattoo.

There were so many, too many to count. The skin had long healed and faded to white, leaving angry scars behind. The sound of my shock crackled through the night air, amplified by the surrounding silence.

"Who did this to you?" White hot anger radiated from me.

"My father."

"When?" My tongue felt like acid. I wanted to throw something. I was struggling between anger and hurt for him, wanting nothing more than to march over to Abduco Manor and wrap my hands around his father's throat. With Una's help, I steadied myself. If Anton hadn't been able to take him on, it was unlikely I could. But it didn't stop me from seething. "You didn't deserve that."

"You're maybe right. Based on why I got them, I didn't deserve them. But I'm glad I did."

"Why?" I slipped my hand underneath the blanket and stroked the skin to show I had flinched from surprise and not from their touch.

His words were bitter. "It allowed me to see my father for what he was. It happened when he found out I was helping people to escape. He said I had put our family and Domain at risk. He was furious."

"Couldn't someone from Nexus have healed you?" I kept myself talking before I started throwing things.

"My father used tools immune to Nexus healers, so I had to heal in the same way humans do. It's why I asked Nexus to train me in healing, so that I wouldn't end up in such a state again. It's also why Allium blocked me out that night. He knew he was going to get hurt. He didn't want me to intervene."

Draven was barbaric. My stomach churned, and I wished I hadn't taken that last sip. I didn't know how to react. "Anton, I'm so sorry."

"It was a long time ago, Cee. Like I said, I deserved them. I had put my family at risk and was looking for punishment. "

"They put you in an impossible situation," I said.

Anton put his head in his hands. "I *had* a choice. You told me we always have a choice."

I didn't know what to do with that. "So, how did it all stop? The Council are still in charge, with Caedes and Abduco answering to it."

"When the Cerebral Council got wind of the coup, they sent everyone involved to Langison as punishment. There was initially outrage about it in Caedes, but even they accepted some of their Shifters had overstepped the mark."

An uneasy tingle ran down my back as I remembered what Anton had told me about Langison. "So why were your father and Draven spared?"

Anton grimaced. "Well, Draven turned on all his associates in return for immunity, but spared my father. To this day, he holds it over him. If he does not do as he asks, he will reveal his involvement and send him to Langison."

The horror of the situation shook me. For a split second, darkness ebbed at the sides of my peripheral vision. I blinked it away. Anton was looking at me with the weight of the world behind his eyes. Now I understood why.

For the first time in Anton's company, I wasn't thinking about sex. I just wanted him to feel better. To offer whatever comfort I could. I slid my hand out from under the blanket and wound my arms around his neck. I rested my head in the space in between his jaw and his shoulder, hugging him tightly. He returned the embrace, and we stood like that for minutes. Perhaps even hours.

He opened the door in his mind that he had locked for so long and out poured the guilt, the self-doubt, everything that he hid behind the bravado. His reliance on Allium. Allium's role was in helping him to play the persona they needed to keep his family safe. Between them, they could exude confidence without believing they were good or deserving.

After a long time, I released my grip on him and felt him reluctantly do the same. I looked into his dark eyes, flecked with light green. Both Anton and Allium were here. Una found the words to speak for us both. "You, of all people, have helped me to understand myself. I wouldn't be a suitable partner if I didn't help you do the same."

"I'm complicated, Cee. You wanted deep, I'm the Mariana Trench." He sighed.

"Then it sounds like there's room for at least two more down there."

He smiled at that. "Touché. Anyway, here I am going on like you don't have problems of your own. I just needed you to understand."

I clenched my fists, thinking about his father and Draven. "Someone needs to stop him, you know, Draven. Maybe this is what the prophecy is talking about, ending what he's doing, along with the Reapers."

"Of course it's crossed my mind," said Anton. "Though I'd never expect you to have to help me with that. I know the risks. I've already tried."

Nudging him in the ribs, I shot back, "You've never had someone who can destroy the shadows before. Just because I'm Caedes doesn't mean I don't care about those close to me." I stumbled over my words. "In fact, it makes me more likely to protect them."

"Well, in that case, we'll try the library tomorrow and see what we can find, and we'll take it from there." He yawned, causing me to do the same.

I rested my head back on his shoulder as we looked out at the city, remaining like that for a long time. It wasn't until the warmth of the rising sun hit my face, that I realised we'd both fallen asleep under the stars.

26

CHARITY

Shifter 101: The four recognised gangs within Domain are the Caedes Reapers; the Persen Hydras; the Abduco Dragos; and the Nexus Archangels (now disbanded).

"**S**houldn't you meet Draven? To keep up appearances, I mean," I said, as we made our way to the library. We'd stayed out on the balcony all night, so if Draven had come round to Anton's flat, he wouldn't have made it through the glamour. Either way, we hadn't heard from him.

"Fuck him." Anton scowled at the mention of his name as he tightened his hand in mine. "I already know what he wants, *you*. And that's not happening."

It seemed irresponsible, but I knew better than to tell him outright what to do. It's not like I was bouncing off my seat in anticipation of visiting Caedes. The more I learned about it, the more I wondered why they had placed me there.

"You think he's linked to the missing people, don't you?" My heart skipped a beat as I realised just how dangerous this man was.

"The more I learn, the more it seems likely."

"What about your family? Won't they be in danger?" I was thinking about his mother and Viktor. I couldn't bring myself to be concerned over his father after what I'd learned last night.

"They'll manage. We're keeping in touch."

The thunder and rain last night had cleared most of the clouds, and we had walked together in the crisp, clear air. A rare sunrise shone across Abduco, highlighting every blade of grass and spider web in the morning dew.

Anton had offered to fly me again, but we'd decided against it, not wanting to draw any attention to ourselves. Shifters only chose their animal form during combat in Domain, I'd learned, or when they wanted to transport large objects. Otherwise, people viewed it as showing off. Shifter customs were strange.

I wasn't touching him, but I got the feeling last night was playing on his mind. The bond worked that way, offering tiny glimpses of what the other was feeling even without contact.

"You know, I'm sorry for all this." I said. "Do you ever wish the prophecy didn't exist?"

He stopped and pulled me into an embrace. "All the time, Cee," he said in a soft voice that still surprised me. "But then I wouldn't have met you, so you should never be sorry. And it's about time things changed. You're one of us now. You need to know what you're in for."

"I'm ready." It hit me how little time I'd spent thinking about my old world. The realisation that I belonged here washed over me, like sinking into a warm bath. I didn't miss my world, not one bit. I'd struggled to build a connection to anything there, maybe except from running. But here it was different. I could tell that this was where I belonged.

"We're going to need to look into every inch of this prophecy. And we're going to need to train harder, help you Shift further. It'll be hard work, but I want you to be as safe as possible here, especially when we don't know who we can trust. You're sure you want to do this?"

Last night was definitely playing on his mind, but I had to agree with him. "If the prophecy relates to me, I don't think we have a choice." Even if it didn't, Draven didn't seem like a Shifter anyone should have on their wrong side, and if he had taken some kind of interest in me, that couldn't be good news.

We arrived at the library.

It was everything I expected for a library in the middle of the forest. Built in a clearing, the building soared above even the tallest of the trees. It looked more like a cathedral than anything else and matched the aesthetic of Abduco. Anton led us in through the tall narrow doors into an enormous entry room that was floor to ceiling marble. Several doors spread across two levels, the largest of them reachable by a giant staircase that cascaded into the middle of the room, like a cloak trailing along the ground.

Despite the height of the ceiling, Anton's steps made no noise as he crossed the room. It was almost empty, save for one or two Shifters who were entering or exiting, books tucked under their arm.

The door led us to a network of staircases stretching to various floors of the library. I jogged up them, pleased to have continued my running as part of my training and able to keep up with Anton's large strides without catching my breath. We said nothing; I was too busy examining the artwork and the carvings on the marble columns.

We reached the floor we needed and Anton led us away from the stairs. Until recently, I'd never been much of a book person, I hadn't had the time or money, and sitting still was my idea of hell. As a kid, I had enough peace to enjoy fairy tales, but once I outgrew them and understood the real dangers around me, I had to find more effective ways to escape. However, as I looked around the dimly lit room with shelves piled high, Una swelled with happiness inside me. This felt like home for her. I felt a pang of guilt. Had I known she was in there, I would have tried to indulge more often.

It's okay, you didn't know, Una's voice sounded in my head.

We found a couple of squashy armchairs in the corner that were obscured by bookcases. I sat and let Anton pick out the titles, not having a clue where to start.

A frown crossed his face. "*The Book of Prophecies* is missing, likely everyone wants to read it because of you. I'll check at the desk. I won't be long. In the meantime, look at these."

He placed two books in front of me and strode off. One on Shifter creatures and the other on Covalents. I opened *Creatures: A Chronology* first.

All Apex and most Meso Shifters can take the form of an animal, should their power be of a certain standard. Apex Shifter forms vary across a wide range mythical creatures including but not limited to: dragons, kelpies, chimeras, unicorns, sirens, hydras, werewolves, archangels, fairies, mermaids, sphinxes, gryphons, basilisks, and manticores.

"Enjoying yourself?" Anton's deep voice broke my concentration. That hadn't taken him long at all.

I pointed at the page in front of me. "I'm reading about Shifter forms, seeing if there's anything more badass than a dragon out there."

Anton grinned as he sank down in the chair next to me. "Careful, Cee, I'll show you just how dangerous I can be."

His voice made it sound more exciting than a threat. I ignored the flush that crept up my face at his words and kept my eyes on the book in front of me. "What does it feel like to Shift into something else?" I said.

He folded one leg over his knee. "They are just *there*; I can't describe it any better than that. Similar to the way you feel Una there, it's just another form you can unlock."

Well, I didn't feel that. We hadn't come across any instances of humans in history who had Shifted to another form, so I knew I shouldn't feel disappointed. I'd already gained so much since being here, I'd just have to let this one go.

The trouble was, I'd never been good at that.

We pored over the books for hours. Anton stacked more titles on our table and together we searched for any signs of prophecies and general human involvement in Domain. Any cases we could find were non-starters. Any humans who had entered had either failed their Actuation, or passed and lived under the radar. There was nothing about unique abilities or anything out of the ordinary during their Actuation.

"That means you'll have stood out. And everyone here will know it." The protective edge to Anton's voice split the silence that hung around us.

Despite everything, we couldn't find a link between the prophecy and me, or anything at all that Draven would be interested in, other than my performance in my Actuation. But there had to be something, as his interest had peaked before then.

We had even tracked down the Shiftagram social media profiles of any people from my world who had undertaken their Actuations in the past year—there were only four—but only one of them had even heard of Draven, and even then had still had no contact with him. I had to admit; it was nice to hear about other people's experiences here, though their journeys had differed from mine.

The library was cooler after the sun went down. My eyes prickled after a full day of reading, likely more than I'd done in my lifetime. Despite my pains, Una was still happy and showed no signs of fatigue.

I stood up and stretched, my muscles tense from being hunched over those pages. Anton's eyes followed my every move. I had the urge to touch him, feel his embrace. Was this an Anton thing or a covalent thing?

I didn't care. The relief at knowing why I'd felt the attraction for Allium caused me to hold his stare. I wasn't betraying Anton. I wasn't betraying Allium. There was a reason I wanted them both. Because both of me wanted them.

I walked over as boldly as I dared and sat in his lap.

Hello sweetheart, I thought you'd never ask.

I saw Allium flash in Anton's eyes as he leaned forward and moved his whole body towards mine, meeting my lips with a crushing kiss.

I could stay like this forever. Una's voice sounded in my head.

The things I would do to make that happen.

Anton bit my lip, sending my head spinning as I moved myself further into his grasp and wound my arms around his neck. Despite sharing many kisses since that first night, each felt as intense as the last. If anything, the thrill was only building.

I tilted my head back as Anton explored my neck once again. It was becoming one of my favourite things for him to do. He was an expert, sucking and biting, causing me to moan into his ear as he responded with a throaty growl. He wrapped a muscular arm around my lower back and pulled me closer, his other hand on my thigh. As our kiss grew, he slid his hand in between my thighs, and when nudged my legs wider open, I obliged. He leaned into me, and I couldn't ignore his hard length that once again was pressing into me.

Anton pulled back, pausing. "Do you want to–"

Yes! "Yes!" I wasn't sure what he was asking, but both Una and I cut him off. Whatever he was offering, we were interested.

Allium's words inside my head caused my stomach to flip. ***Now let's have some fun.***

His eyes darkened as he moved his hand up my thigh. His other hand remained wrapped around me like an iron vice, holding me in place. I had thought about this for too long. He was so close I could see the pulse on the side of his neck. I should have been concerned about someone catching sight of us, but I was too engrossed in the moment to care. We weren't doing anything terrible–*yet*.

The back of his fingers brushed the top of my thighs just as a door closed in the distance. I snapped my legs together on instinct, trapping his hand there. I hadn't worn tights, and his hand was dangerously close now.

"No secrets now, Cee; I can hear everything going on in your head. I know just how much of a thrill you get out of the possibility that someone might find us."

Well, fuck. If he wasn't right.

He brushed his hand up my centre, over the top of my flimsy underwear, sending a fresh wave of heat coursing through me. I lost all sense of how I looked. All that mattered was that his hand stayed there.

I sat in his lap facing him, grinding my hips as I searched for the friction I so desperately wanted. His voice was a growl as he responded, "Good girl. I see you know what you want."

I moved my hips again in response. My heart jumped as he slid his hand under the fabric of my knickers and moaned as I heard him hiss at how wet I already was. He moved close to my entrance, then as he moved up, the pad of his finger connected with just the right spot. I saw stars from the immediate intensity. The pressure was exquisite, and I didn't know how long I'd be able to last if he continued like this.

It really was a miracle that it was late and no one walked in, as I wouldn't have let him stop.

I lost all sense of awareness as his hand drew down, and I gasped as he plunged a finger inside me, drawing it out before adding another as he sucked on the lobe of my ear. In my mind, Una kept nagging me to go somewhere less sacred than a library, but even she became lost to the warmth building low in my stomach. I made to move my hand under his t-shirt, but he stopped me, instead grabbing both wrists and pinning them behind my back with one hand.

He leaned in. His tongue was in my ear now. "No, Cee, tonight is all about you." What I could see of his eyes was feral.

He moved his hand back and forth, and in that moment, I knew I was his. My thoughts spelled everything out for him, making my needs clear. He paid attention, and the effect was staggering. He listened to me begging him to say my name and came undone as he said, "Oh, Cee, you'll be the death of me."

I was already wet, and something else was building inside of me too, the feeling of needing to release.

Anton continued moving his fingers in and out, building speed. I was losing control–all I needed was more pressure on my centre. On cue, Anton's hand was there, massaging and sending me into a state of ecstasy. I felt myself going over the edge. I had no idea what I screamed as Anton's fingers slid inside me again as I enjoyed the ride of my orgasm. But I shook from the intensity of it as it stretched right down my legs. As it passed, I could feel my muscles in the backs of my thighs, arms, and back aching, despite not having moved much.

I twitched at Anton's fingers still inside me. I was so sensitive, even the slightest brush of skin would set me off. Anton's teeth clamped down on my ear as he enjoyed this thought before removing his hand slowly. The friction was enough, and I wrapped my legs together to continue to enjoy the muted sensations. The act of clenching my legs sent me right back into the ecstasy that I hadn't quite left yet as I orgasmed again, the room around me lost to a sea of stars.

I came to and straightened as I met Anton's stare. He was mesmerised. He then looked down at his hand, and the corner of his mouth quirked. Without hesitating, he put his fingers in his mouth and sucked on them, maintaining eye contact the whole time. The image nearly sent me over the edge again.

I stood up as I adjusted my underwear, still breathless. "Was that you or Allium?"

He grinned. "A bit of both."

I raised an eyebrow. "You work well as a team."

You sure do, added Una.

Anton bit his lip and raised both eyebrows. "It's been known."

I finished adjusting my clothes as we climbed back into our separate chairs. Anton's face was still flushed, something I hadn't seen before. I must have looked a sight, but I was too excited to care. We sat there for several minutes in silence, processing what had just happened.

A thought occurred to me as I returned to reality. "Anton?"

"Yes?"

"How will this work here with us being Covalents? If it hasn't happened for hundreds of years, why us?"

Anton leaned across and twirled a strand of my hair. "Honestly, Cee? I don't know. I thought there might be answers here. Though, admittedly, we aren't doing a very good job of finding anything, are we?"

"We have tomorrow—perhaps you'll just need to be a better Apex and use the power of concentration." I grinned at him, knowing he wasn't used to being spoken to this way. Una gasped inside my head, and we knew Anton and Allium would have heard too.

In one swift movement, Anton picked me up and slammed my back against a bookcase, his hand breaking my impact. A couple of dusty books fell to the floor. "You're lucky we're in a place that I respect enough to not take this any further. Otherwise, I don't think we'd stop before people saw us."

A door opened and closed again in the distance, though no one could see us. I looked back at him with a newfound confidence as I kissed along the sharp line of his jaw, then brought my mouth to his ear. "Maybe one day I'll see for myself."

He looked at me with savage eyes, then smiled, showing perfect teeth. "You can bet on it, Serrk."

27

CHARITY

Shifter 101: A hierarchy exists within Domain. Apex Shifters rule over their respective Houses because of their relation to the original rulers of Domain. Meso Shifters are Shifters who have always existed in Domain but do not have Apex status. Demi-Shifters are Shifters who arrive in Domain from the human world. It is not appropriate to use the derogatory term Nihils in everyday conversation when talking about Demi-Shifters.

I snaked through the roots and into the Hideout. It really was an amazing place. The main room where we trained was in the biggest clearing and meant there was space to fight in the middle and hiding places to evade enemies, like I was currently doing.

"Think of it as your Actuation times ten." Anton emerged from behind a giant root that cascaded down from the ceiling. It felt nostalgic being back at the Hideout, though this time it was all real, not just for some competition or to prove my status. Although I was scared, I was more motivated than ever to learn, provided what I'd heard from him a few nights ago.

Anton had eventually been to see Draven. Unsurprisingly, the Caedes Shifter had wanted to see me, to discuss my place there. Though what he wanted after that, we still didn't know. Draven had agreed to wait a few weeks, to allow me to round up any business I had in Abduco. Then, he expected me to return to Caedes with him. Of course, I was intending no such thing. But the longer he kept thinking I was going to follow him like an obedient little puppy, the less time he'd have to prepare for what we were planning.

In several weeks' time, we would meet in neutral territory. I couldn't help the unease that swirled within my stomach at the thought of seeing those cruel red eyes again. Something still didn't feel right, and I knew Anton felt it too. It meant we had to be as prepared as possible.

I dodged Anton and found a suitable hiding place in the shadows caused by the dense roots at the side of the room.

"There are no exceptions here. Even with training, we'll need to make sure you're protected," he said as he attempted to stalk me. Fortunately, hiding was something I had a lifetime of experience in. I knew how to wrap the shadows around me and disappear.

I said nothing, not wanting to give away my position. I inhaled the telltale burning wood that meant he was too close and shrank back further. It was a fun game; mid-fight, I'd run off into the darkness and he'd try to find me. I shouldn't have found the chase so exhilarating when we were training for so much at stake, but I knew he felt it, too.

He was on the other side of me, but if he knew how close I was, he didn't show it. "Mentally, you should be fine as long as you can keep your shields strong. But you'll have to work on your hand-to-hand combat to include weapons, as we can't rule out the need for them when we meet Draven."

He stepped round the root and faced me. Of course, he'd known

I was there all along. If I could sense him, he could sense me. It had something to do with the Covalents bond; if we hadn't already been hyper aware of each other, we were now.

"I guess you got me," I breathed.

As he leaned in until our noses were almost touching, I realised how easy it would be to get lost in the shadows with him, despite Viktor and Perrine lingering nearby.

"I'll always find you, Cee." Anton cupped my face for a second, then in a flash, he was gone. It was my turn to find him now.

This was our warm up. After a few rounds of this, we'd get down to actual combat.

By the time we finished, Viktor was tapping his foot and texting. He was frowning, which was unusual for him.

"Everything okay?" Anton asked. It wasn't like Viktor to be anything other than ecstatic after all.

Viktor smiled, though it didn't quite reach his eyes. "I can't reach Julian. I'm sure he'll make it up to Forrest later. It's no matter."

Whatever was bothering him, he didn't seem to want to share. Anton seemed to respect this and didn't press him further.

We engaged in several rounds of hand-to-hand combat, only stopping when everyone's bodies were glistening with sweat. It had been an intense couple of hours, though I was proud of the fact I had outsmarted Anton and Viktor as many times as they had me.

"You've done well," summarised Anton, as he leaned against the wall and drained a bottle of water. "Combat, along with travel Shifting, will be your principal lines of defence if things go pear-shaped at the meeting, given you can't Shift into another form."

Something about his statement unravelled something in me. It was innate. Covalent or not, I didn't like being told what I could and couldn't do.

"Don't say I can't." My voice came out more aggressively than I intended. Red clouded my vision.

"Interesting," said Anton. "I said it to provoke a reaction. When channelled, anger is good for you. It helps Caedes Shifters focus their power, just like indifference does for Abduco, kindness for Nexus and excitement for Persen."

I raised a brow at him as the mist behind my eyes cleared. "And you didn't think you should tell me that."

Anton held my gaze, surprised. "I assumed you knew." Then smirked. "What with that attitude and all."

Viktor chimed in, "What he means by that, is he was terrified of what you might do once you unlock your full power."

I tensed when Viktor's comment earned him a crossbow bolt to the head that Anton had lifted in one swoop. The thing looked both powerful and high tech, like a modern version built for military combat. Fortunately, Viktor seemed well used to this and deflected the bolt with his own sword that had appeared from nowhere.

"Don't worry, we've been practising together for so long, we know each other's tricks," Anton said, smirking.

I wouldn't lie. It was pretty hot seeing him with a weapon in his hand. *Jeez, I need help if this is what I'm attracted to now.*

"You're pretty freaky aren't you?" I enjoyed seeing the darker side of him as much as the gentleman.

His smirk deepened, Allium flashing at the forefront. "What can I say, sweetheart? Don't get a dog, then be surprised when it barks."

I wondered when it had got so hot in here. Anton pulled a lever at the side of the room and a target lowered from the ceiling. I stood transfixed as he fired bolt after bolt, each splintering the one embedded in the bullseye until there was nothing left apart from a series of shavings. His aim was impeccable. How Viktor had avoided it I didn't know, unless of course Anton hadn't intended to hit him.

Meanwhile, Viktor was performing a series of fancy jabs and swirls using his sword. Within seconds, he reduced the target dummy in front of him to a stack of hay. He turned around, looking pleased with himself. "Not bad, huh?"

I gave them an over-exaggerated round of applause, undeniably impressed. It was clear they were both competent in using weapons. Though I hoped they weren't expecting me to produce similar results; I didn't have a lifetime of experience behind me.

Anton fired his last bolt and strode over to me. "Something on your mind, Cee? Remember, weapons are a last resort when we meet Draven. The purpose of this is to teach you to defend yourself. Hopefully, you'll never need to do even that."

That was our plan, after all. We were going to meet him and tell him he couldn't have me, Cerebral Council status or not. No one was going to force Anton and me apart and we'd fight our case if we had to. After some persuasion, Anton's parents, Verde and Sage, had agreed to come, though they hadn't realised that we were training with weapons, just in case.

Part of me hoped he was right and we wouldn't need weapons. Another part of me was eager to learn more. I didn't have to be a genius to work out which was Una's influence and which was mine. It was making more sense why I'd reacted to Greg's mind the way I did. I was grateful to have Una by my side and shuddered to think what I would have done had she not been there.

You would have handed it just as appropriately. I believe in you, affirmed Una. I wasn't so sure.

He led me over to an extensive arsenal stacked at the side. "Is there a reason you don't use guns?" I said, as I reviewed the weapons in front of us. After all the technology I'd seen in Persen, I'd practically been expecting lasers.

Anton's mouth quirked in response. "I suppose we evolved, and sometimes to do that, we look back. We sometimes use them, but swords don't malfunction, don't run out of battery, or require updates, like the guns do here." His face darkened as he considered his next words. "Also, killing stays with you. Guns allow you to act in a split second; Nexus used to be full of healers having to treat gunshot wounds from trigger-happy Shifters. Over time, some of our gangs realised that the old ways were superior, although not everyone shared that sentiment.

I couldn't argue. I was much more comfortable with the idea of a melee weapon than a gun.

Taking in my options, I walked up the line of swords, bows, axes, and spears.

"Take your time," said Anton over my shoulder, giving me goose-bumps in the most delicious way. "The right weapon is here for you; it just may take a few tries to find what suits best."

I didn't know what he meant by that, but I figured I'd commit myself and picked up one of the larger swords. It was heavier than I expected, and I held in both hands, feeling self-conscious.

"What are you waiting for?" Anton was baiting me to get my power going again. "Try it."

"Where?"

He stepped back against the wall. "Well, not me. Try at the ground to begin with."

I brought the sword above my shoulder and swung it at an invisible enemy below me.

"Good," he said. "Now try with one hand. It's not a two-handed sword."

"Easier said than done." I tried again, holding it up. A stab of pain shot through me as I overstretched a muscle trying to prevent it from falling over my shoulder. "Can't I use both hands?" It felt much easier that way.

Anton stepped behind me and wrapped his arms around me snugly, his biceps pressing against the tops of my arms. He cradled my wrists in front of us, supporting the weight of the sword still in my grasp. "No, you can't. See the hilt here, it's too small for both hands. It could slip out and injure you, but we can try a two-handed sword next."

He selected one from the pile. The blade was long and curved, and I liked the look of it straight away. I took another swing. It was still heavier than I thought, but much more manageable than the straight sword. Well, it was until I hit my target and the shock that rattled through me along with the weight of the sword caused me to drop it.

"Not to worry." Concentration was written on Anton's face. "Two-handed, but not a Katana. Let's try a bow and arrow, one of my favourites."

He handed me a black and shiny shortbow, the string taut enough to cut skin if I pressed hard enough. I couldn't lie. I felt pretty fierce holding it, clunky as it was. Despite my speed and improved strength from all my training, I struggled to pull the string back, which was surprising.

Anton read my expression. "Can you manage?"

I gritting my teeth. "I can try." I shot the arrow, but it missed the target. Frustrated, I aimed with another and hit the very edge of the target, but it was a complete fluke.

I heard Anton over my shoulder as he sensed my frustration. "No, it should feel natural. If you're having to try, it won't work."

Power flared within me, looking for shadows to stamp out. Looking for something to destroy.

Fuck this.

I stalked over to the weapons stacked against the wall and traced the edges of handles, tips of arrows, and bowstrings with my hand. Nothing felt natural, but why would it? Coming from where I'd come from.

Then, I saw it.

I picked up a sword from the weapons stacked at the side of the armoury. It was smaller than the rest and felt weightless in my hand. This, I could work with. I turned and slashed it at the nearest root, my frustration putting weight behind my swing. It disintegrated at the sharpness of the blade.

It was perfect. Almost perfect. It was so light; I felt like I could manage with two.

Anton wasn't touching me, but it was like he had read my mind anyway, as he walked to the far end of the pile and picked up an identical one. His perfect teeth were on full display as he handed it to me. "Well, you passed the test."

"What test?" I took the matching sword from him with my free hand and examined it.

"They're a pair. I had them made for you, but wanted to see if you'd choose them for yourself." He grinned at my startled reaction. "I knew if I just gave them to you, you'd use them regardless of whether you liked them, but this way is much better."

"Thank you." I ran my thumb along the cool handle of one blade. Now that I looked closer. The hilt flashed the most subtle shade of crimson.

"It's a pair of Wakizashi. They're shaped like the Katana, but are smaller and designed for one-handed use."

"They're perfect," I breathed. I understood what he meant now. These blades called to me, to Una, to other things deep in my mind. To the darkest shadows, but not in an unpleasant way. I knew these were what I should use.

"Do your worst, Cee." He stepped back as several more dummy targets lowered.

My vision narrowed, and it was just me and a handful of targets. I lost myself in the slashes and jabs of the blades, the two of them working together in harmony.

"How did I do?" I realised Anton and Viktor had stopped what they were doing to watch me.

"I'd not want to get on the wrong side of you, girl," remarked Viktor, showing the shavings I'd left behind.

Anton stalked over and lowered his mouth so only I could hear. "I said you were devastating in red; and it seems you are just as breath-taking with a weapon in your hand. Any enemies should be terrified of you indeed."

The adrenaline was singing to me, and his words had heat pooling in my core. "Let them," I said, dizzy from the power I felt holding my new weapons.

"Not wise." Anton allowed me to continue my assault on the targets. "Letting them think they have the advantage over you is one of the best ways to disarm an enemy."

"But who cares what they think?" I was still distracted by the beauty of my new swords.

"You should. Because if they believe they've won, then you know they've already lost."

That got my attention. I shook myself when I remembered our real reason for being here, for needing weapons, for what had happened to Anton. The arrogance that I could only assume came from belonging to Caedes evaporated. None of that mattered. This was about him.

"Got it," I said.

"That's not all." He was still smirking.

"Oh?" I turned the swords over in my hand, still admiring them.

"They're your idols as well, seeing as you never received one at Actuation. You'll be able to use them to travel large distances once you're ready."

"Thank you." I was taken aback. "I guess that's one way to ensure I'm always carrying a weapon around Domain."

"It's what they do in the House of Caedes," replied Anton.

My anger flared for him. I could feel it channelling into the swords. I shut up and put my effort into absorbing every word for the rest of the session.

28

CHARITY

Shifter 101: Object Shifting: Shifters can summon an object within close range into existence.

It turned out a few weeks of sword practice were sufficient when you trained for every waking hour. New Year came and went, the event lost on all of us, as our group remained at Anton's flat and focused on keeping under the radar. I wasn't a master swordswoman by any stretch, but I knew how to defend myself from a range of attacks and that in itself was some comfort whenever I ventured out on my runs. That said, I couldn't shake the feeling that the more I found out about Domain, the more unlikely the fact we wouldn't need weapons was.

"You're the one that woke me up at what-the-fuck-o'clock in the morning with your 'afterparty'!" Viktor spilled his drink everywhere as he gestured wildly. Anton wouldn't be happy about the stains on his carpet. He must have known a trick for getting things out though, as the place was always immaculate.

"I'm sorry, it's not my fault I've got stamina! I guess you're not familiar with the concept," Spyder joked back at him.

"Hey, I've got plenty of stamina!"

I choked on my wine as I listened to their conversation, which was very much for the entire room to hear. Viktor wasn't lying. We'd all heard what Spyder had been up to the night before.

Between brushing up on my Shiftstory, training to use weapons, and learning the finer details of being a Shifter, it had been a very intense few weeks. That, and the company we had, was the only reason that had stopped me jumping on Anton at every opportunity. As much as I could feel he was as drawn to me as I him through our bond, I could tell how much was weighing on his mind and I didn't want to take advantage of that.

It had been Spyder's idea to have a night of drinking and games to make us all feel better about our meeting with Draven tomorrow. According to Draven, this was my last night in Abduco. Fat fucking chance of that.

My eyes lit up when Perrine revealed she had successfully obtained a classic edition of Monopoly and pulled it from her bag. If I had to be honest, board games were the one thing I missed from my world. And now I finally had people to play with.

We'd settled into the game as I rolled the dice and moved my piece round to landing on Mayfair. "I already own that!" I said, causing Spyder to put his head between his hands in defeat. I had to admit; it felt good to do something normal. Though as the game went on, it became apparent I was the only one who found this *normal*.

Despite being highly intelligent, Anton could not grasp the concept of Monopoly. He kept saying he already owned everything in life, or had the monopoly, so to speak. So he couldn't understand why he would have to go round the board and collect things.

Viktor didn't understand why he couldn't talk dirty in exchange for deals on the properties, and Spyder just kept rolling the dice over and over to compare with his own one, cheering when they rolled the same number. Perrine was the only one who played the game in a way that resembled something that I knew. By the time Julian joined us, everyone had given up and various properties and hotels were scattered about the room, much to Anton's annoyance.

"I'll help you clean it later," I assured him, knowing how much of a neat freak he was. I sat leaning against his chest as we drank by the fire. He wrapped his warm arms around me, and the heat spread to my chest. Knowing what faced us tomorrow, we stole that moment for our own. The nerves had set in for everyone, and it was nice to have even the smallest of reprieves.

I had seen very little of Julian during my time in Domain. He worked hard visiting the various minds he worked with. I now realised what Anton had meant about the time Shifters were expecting to spend dealing with minds. I found it interesting that no one had summoned me yet. Anton had said it was likely to do with my human origins and because of the way I'd reacted during my Actuation. Perhaps they thought I was a bit of a loose cannon.

Maybe they were right.

Any free time Julian had, he spent with Forrest. The pair made a perfect couple. Julian echoed more of Viktor's loud energy, whereas Forrest was more reserved, preferring to sit on the sidelines.

Julian was mid-speech, his deep voice slurred from their drinks. "–And then Anton punched him in the face. The Wings and Ivy has banned him since."

"The Wings and Ivy?" I hadn't heard of that place before.

Anton smirked into the glass. "Our local bar. That prick had it coming."

He was insufferable.

I heard that, Allium interjected. I let go of his hand as I sat down, his stare causing me to blush. It was amazing that despite being Covalents and a perfect match for each other in every way, he still had that effect on me.

But I could still wind him up, too. "Let me guess. Someone had enough of you being a spoiled little Apex?"

Even Forrest spat out his drink at my accusation. I never could have spoken this way in previous relationships. Most of the guys I'd been with didn't get my humour, but Anton understood every little thing.

Oh, the things I would love to do to you to remind you there's nothing little about me. It was Allium's voice in my head again. I gripped my glass. It was like having him right in my ear.

The drinks were having the desired effect and had dulled my fears of what tomorrow would bring. For now, I had a crowd where I felt like I belonged. I'd never had real friends in my world, but I realised now what I'd been missing out on.

Julian was now slapping the table as a scowling Anton watched. "Hymev, Anton, I didn't think you'd find someone to meet your savage nature, but you've met your match."

Anton's face softened at the word *match* as he met my eye. "For once, I can't argue with you there."

By the time the fire died down, Spyder had crashed out propped up against the kitchen island, and Forrest's head was drooping with tiredness. He hadn't spoken for a while now. As the conversation continued, I watched him fall asleep on Julian's shoulder. Julian curled an arm around him, and before long, the pair were fast asleep, leaving Anton and me alone.

"Should we go through to yours?" I was all too aware of the fact that I'd yet to see Anton's room properly. He hadn't stopped me from going in, but it felt like an invasion of privacy.

"I need to fumigate it after Spyder's antics in there." Anton grimaced. "There is no way I'm letting you in that bed until I've had everything changed. That kid is crazy. When I get you to myself, I want to make sure it's exactly that. Just us."

It made me laugh that Anton referred to Spyder as a kid. The guy was only a year younger than me. But I couldn't argue with him about the room. As we'd needed to lie low after my Actuation, everyone had been staying here. It was the one place where we could come and go undetected by Draven. The downside was Anton and I had been sleeping in the living room as Spyder had taken over Anton's room. My room was also out of action as Viktor and Forrest had been alternating turns depending on whether Julian was staying. As much as I had enjoyed the thrill of someone barging in on us in the library, taking things further in front of an audience of our friends was not an option, especially with Bronx camped out on the balcony day and night. I'd offered him a place indoors, but he'd told me in a heavy accent the fresh air was good for his soul.

Between scouring *The Notion* and Shiftagram, we could keep tabs on what was happening across Domain. My Actuation had thrown everything across the four Houses into chaos, with the Cerebral Council claiming I was to take my place in Caedes where I be-longed–undoubtedly the work of Draven behind the scenes. These days, it was a very different Domain than the one I'd entered. Out of the six of us, Julian was the only one still going to work, as his relationship with us was less known across Domain.

There were times I didn't mind the wait for Anton's company alone. It was nice by the fire, and Anton's comfortable sofa meant that we always curled up together at night. That said, I'd be lying if I said I couldn't wait for him to get his room back.

Anton stroked my hair and pulled me closer. "Oh, me too, Cee, you can count on that. It'll be worth the wait, I can assure you."

I kept forgetting that he could read my damn mind whenever we were touching, but the fire was so cosy, and his touch was so comforting, I couldn't bring myself to care as I drifted off to sleep.

The city in the mountains differed from the first few times I'd seen it. This time, I was viewing everything from the water instead of from the mountains. It was amazing how perception could change everything.

Boats bobbed on the harbour. How such a volume of water was accessible to such high terrain, I did not know. It was still like glass, the only movement from the lights painted in the reflections.

The city spread before me like a digital canvas, the buildings secondary to the screaming colours of the many adverts playing on loop. I imagined the skyline looked similar to Shanghai, but this was even more impressive. It was so other-worldly. Numerous structures towered above the smaller buildings, each individual in their design. Everything here was modern in style. The tops of the buildings were only identifiable by the neon lights drawing my eye upwards, bringing my attention to where the structures stopped, stark against the bright sky.

Glass façades stretched across buildings that stood fifty floors high. Buildings connected by walkways that bustled with people.

The place was vibrant with a positive energy. It hummed with electricity. A digital era. Vehicles travelled at an impossible speed. It was like watching a time lapse as I scanned the horizon. It was uncertain how many lived here. Easily millions.

Something occurred to me. I'd seen the city before. It was even more vast. It was almost like time had passed since it looked like this.

A thought struck me. Perhaps these weren't dreams at all. Perhaps they were memories.

29

CHARITY

Shifter 101: Form Shifting: Shifters can take the form of another animal. Apex Shifters can take the form of a mythical being.

The air was heavy with tension as we got ready in Anton's flat. I couldn't believe today was the day, although I'd been thinking of little else for weeks. We moved around each other wordlessly; no one knew what to say. Even Spyder fell into an unusual silence. It was even more surreal watching everyone assemble their weapons and strap them in.

Not knowing what to expect, I chose something from my wardrobe suited for combat. The thick black leggings I selected still hugged my hips and my top looked like it would offer some protection should things turn ugly. I would have stuck out if I'd walked around my world wearing something like this. But given that this was my home now, and the very real dangers we faced today, it all made sense.

"Ready?" Anton nodded at me. He was also dressed in black; some form of military fighting gear. Allium checked in on Una at the same time.

"Ready," I said. Even though my breakfast was sloshing around in my stomach, and I wished I hadn't eaten at all.

I picked up my swords and headed for the door that everyone was filing out of, all armed to the teeth.

A hand gripped my arm as I made my way to follow. "Where are you going to put those?" Anton pointed at my new weapons.

I hadn't given it any thought. "I figured I'd just hold them."

He smirked, which made my heart flutter and eased my nerves. "And walk in looking like the biggest threat in Domain?"

I snorted in response. "I'm not the biggest threat in Domain, not even close."

The others had already left to Shift to our destination, while Anton and I were flying. I knew he'd suggested it because he understood I still wasn't the biggest fan of side-along Shifting, but he'd passed it off as a layer of extra security. With everyone gone, it was just us now.

Anton's hand swept down the side of my arm. "To them, that's what you are, and if you go in with weapons drawn, you're guaranteed to need to use them."

Anger pulsed at my wrists. Perhaps that wouldn't be the worst thing.

No, Charity. There's got to be another way. Una chimed in my head. It wasn't always easy having one fiery personality and one pacifist in the same mind, but we made it work.

Anton interrupted my inner conflict. "Hopefully they won't be necessary, but either way, you'll need somewhere to store them." He stood back and handed me a pair of sheaths, which I took, lost for words. I slipped the straps round each thigh and sheathed my swords. It was like they weren't even there.

I tested them by sliding my blades out and swirled them round in my hands like I'd practised. I felt like a threat, even though I could feel

Una shaking her head at me.

"You're terrifying in your own brilliant way, you know that don't you?"

"You think of everything. Thank you," I said as I kissed him. It was the best I could come up for now. Despite everything we faced, I left the flat smiling at his words, feeling as ready as I'd ever be.

Flying wasn't something I would get used to anytime soon. I sat nestled on Anton's back, more secure and focused than the last time I'd flown. With my swords out of the way, I had both hands free to hold on. I kept my hand to his neck, his slow pulse steadying me as we grew nearer to our destination.

We'd chosen to land at a vantage point near the edge of the neutral territory between Abduco and Caedes. It was a small section of land, surrounded by water on one side, and mountains on the other, the Abduco forest, and the Caedes desert extending out on either side.

As our destination neared, Verde and Sage came into view, waiting with Viktor, Julian, Bronx, Spyder, and Perrine. Anger fizzed inside of me at the sight of Verde as I remembered Anton's scars. I wanted nothing more than to draw my swords, but Anton had already warned me this morning that it was his battle, and I had to respect that. I reminded myself that he was not the enemy I had come to confront today.

We landed, and Anton returned to his human form. There was a crack and Perrine Shifted to a larger than normal bobcat which patrolled back and forth, her eyes fixed on the scene below her.

"Nice one, Perrine." I couldn't help but admire her sleek coat and sharp claws. I would not want to get on the wrong side of her. One look at her amber-flecked eyes told me it was Ordette that I was speaking to.

I guess we meant business after all.

"They came armed. This could turn ugly." Viktor's face was grim as he nodded in greeting.

I turned my attention to the scene below me. Around thirty Shifters stood by Draven and–surprise, surprise–Scarlett, all armed with a variety of bows, swords, axes, and daggers.

"I guess neither side trusts each other," said Anton, retrieving his crossbow from his brother.

The enemy had a significant advantage in numbers: they had at least five Shifters for every one of us. I studied the surrounding faces. Verde met my eye, his expression giving nothing away. I glared at him, hoping he would read the hate in my expression. Sage looked determined, and I wondered how much she understood of her family's situation.

Ordette looked tense even in her giant bobcat form, her tail standing upright. Meanwhile, Spyder was too busy rolling his dice and miming shooting the Shifters, though I imagine everyone expected this sort of unhinged behaviour from him, anyway.

The gravity of the situation appeared to hit everyone at the same time as Verde and Sage spread giant dragon wings behind them and shot into the air, still in their human form. Another crack signalled Spyder had taken the form of a giant serpent, and Viktor into his manticore. They took off down the side of the hill towards our targets, leaving Anton and me alone. There was so much I wanted to say to him, but now didn't feel like the time, instead I took his hand, the gesture saying everything I couldn't in that moment.

Make sure she holds her temper, Una warned him.

"I will." Anton spoke aloud.

Without warning, he scooped me up, and we were airborne again. This time, Anton kept his human form, Shifting only his wings just as Verde and Sage had. It felt more natural than I'd expected, being carried in his arms. It was all too easy to enjoy the comfort in those few seconds, before the cool air rushed back in as he set me down and increased the distance between us.

I took in the surrounding scene. Draven stood in the centre, the flashes of red that tore through his gaze unnerving. I wrenched my eyes away from his and my stomach flipped as I met Scarlett's stare instead. I hadn't seen her since our time on the mat, and I'd be lying if I said I wasn't itching for any excuse to fight her again. Maybe I belonged in Caedes after all.

You're more than that, Una reminded me.

"I see you came," Draven said curtly. He was also dressed in heavy combat gear, his the colour of rust which matched his hair. I noted he was the only one among his followers that didn't carry a weapon. Perhaps he had something more dangerous up his sleeve.

Anton stepped forward. "As you requested. Though if you think you're taking Charity, you've got another thing coming."

Draven laughed. It was a loud, ugly noise. "Her mind chose where she belongs. It's not your decision to make." He then surveyed me the way a lion would a fresh carcass, making my skin tingle in discomfort. I rested my fingertips on my swords, ready to unsheathe them at a moment's notice. "And she has an Other present, too. I'm not surprised. What's her name?"

"Una," I gritted out. Of course, he could see from my eyes that we were both here.

His eyes widened a fraction. "A delightful addition, I'm sure. Anton won't have a choice. Caedes has to have you now."

Anton stepped in between us. "Try telling me what to do one more time and I promise you we'll settle this much quicker."

I moved to hold him back but didn't get the chance, as several things happened at once.

A crossbow bolt flew. Anton moved. Draven Shifted.

I heard it let loose before I saw it. Had Anton not favoured the same weapon during our training, I would have never become so accustomed to the sound.

But the bolt hadn't come from Anton. It hadn't come from our side at all.

One of the Caedes Shifters at the back of Draven's stood still poised, his crossbow pointing at us.

Time slowed down as I registered the split seconds I had left before the bolt hit me.

At the same time, Draven Shifted into a creature so enormous, I couldn't tell what it was. It looked like a dragon that had no wings, but at least five heads. Fortunately, he was so large, one head took the force of the bolt. It barely injured his giant form.

Shouts broke out as both sides sprung into action, the bolt the catalyst for chaos. A Shifter from Draven's side stepped forward as if to challenge me. Anton blocked his path, crossbow drawn. "I'll only warn you once. You don't go near her."

"And why's that?" leered the Shifter, trying to edge round Anton towards me.

"Because she's *mine,*" confirmed Anton with a growl.

"And *mine.*" I recognised the slight change in register that meant Allium had taken over.

"Watch me," the man said in his slimy voice, making a grab for me.

Allium shot the man straight through the chest at close range without a second thought, snapping his lightning green eyes round to me.

"Keep your mental shields up and your reactions strong. I won't let them hurt you."

The reality of the situation hit me like a bus. Anyone could die here today. Whatever Draven wanted, it was clear the time for reasoning had passed. There was no way I was allowing myself to end up somewhere like Caedes.

I won't let that happen, Allium gritted out in my head, letting Anton take back over.

Neither will I, added Una.

And I certainly wouldn't either.

We sprang apart and into action. My swords were out in one smooth motion, and I blocked an attack from a larger-than-life panther that had been about to cut into one of Anton's folded wings.

I just had time to catch his nod of thanks before he materialised behind me in time to block a blow about to land on my shoulder. I couldn't afford to watch him. Today, I needed my reactions more than ever.

Before long, he was out of my peripheral vision and I was too busy to scan the area for him. The shadows that danced in the background, obstructing the light, told me more and more Shifters were using their animal forms. I fought off several more attacks before the aches in my muscles crept through. I wouldn't be able to keep blocking forever–it was kill or be killed. And I didn't want to die.

I slashed wildly with my swords as I struggled to keep two male Shifters from landing any blows. Had my weapons not been so light in my arms, there was no way I would have been able to fend off two at once. Then I stepped backwards and my foot connected with an unknown object, causing me to topple over.

I knew I was done for when the larger Shifter dived forward. The only thing that had saved me so far was the fact they hadn't Shifted to creatures.

This is it. I told myself as I hacked again, aiming at his torso, expecting everything to end any minute.

I didn't realise I was screaming until I drew breath, having exhausted my air supply. The pain in my side was blistering. I forced myself not to inhale as I lay there still. Let him think I was dead. He bent down and rolled me onto my back, chuckling to his friend, thinking he'd won. It wasn't until I brought one of my swords out from behind my back and his warm blood splashed across my face that he would have realised his error, the shock on his face the last reminder of his mistake.

I didn't have time to think about what I had just done. I ran a hand down my side to see if there was anything embedded, but it was just a deep cut. If I wanted to stay alive, I had to keep fighting. I rolled to dodge another attack from the other Shifter, stopping only when I saw his face drain of colour as he looked over my shoulder.

I heard Spyder before I saw him. He sprinted towards us, his axe pointed at the Shifter. "I'd run if I were you, because if she doesn't kill you, you can bet I will. Slowly."

I was working to keep my body from convulsing in shock from what I'd done, but it was clear not everyone had the same reservations over killing. For some, it was second nature. In fact, Spyder looked happier than I'd ever seen him, his face coated in blood, the whites of his teeth shining through like a gruesome mask. He was one of the few who remained in his human form to fight, which was interesting given he could Shift to a deadly creature.

"Oh, I love this one," he cheered as he ran at the second Shifter I'd been fighting and cut him down with one swoop of his axe, all the while singing.

"Are you listening to music, mate?" I heard Viktor's voice shout across at us.

Spyder retrieved his weapon from the Shifter on the ground with a sharp tug and then helped me up, grinning. "Drowns out the screaming nicely, doesn't it?"

I gulped. I'd never met a true psychopath before, but I was pretty sure he fitted the bill. For all that, he was someone you wanted on your side in combat. He tipped me a salute before delving back into the throng of bodies all locked in battle.

I scanned the field, searching for Anton. There was so much going on around us, I couldn't tell who was winning and who was losing. They had numbers, but we had the actual players. Half of them were merely following orders and were unskilled with strategy.

Then I saw him, in his dragon form. Half black, half white. Beautiful, but deadly, and very much breathing fire, as he roasted a group of Draven's henchmen in one go. I guess that answered whether he could then.

Another scan of the field showed me Draven's form changed once again. He now had over ten heads. I remembered a line from my fairy-tale book as I realised with a shudder what he was.

Removing the head never killed the hydra. In fact, every one cut off only caused it to grow two more in its place.

Maybe it was because of his colossal form, but Draven seemed to take out more of his own Shifters than anyone else. The tightly packed bodies around us made it difficult to distinguish who was who, even at ground level. Aside from Anton, I only recognised Verde's black dragon and Sage's white one. They were both fighting a harpy and, perhaps, a gryphon in the air.

Without warning, a hyena knocked me to the floor as it ran ahead into the packed bodies. Anger fueled my abilities. I knew who'd just passed me. I had been helpless to her once before, but there was no chance of that happening again. Without thinking, I charged after her. The scenes around me were brutal, the creatures beautiful but terrifying.

I wanted to find her. I wanted to destroy her.

As if she sensed my thought, she turned, her amber eyes giving her away.

"You're mine, mutt," I snarled, in a voice I didn't recognise as my own. I could have sworn she smiled at me before vanishing on the spot. I only realised what she'd done as I felt her hot breath just inches from my neck.

Then she was gone. Thrown across the ground away from me.

Anton stood where Scarlett had been, fury written into every inch of his face. He was covered in blood, but as I scanned him in a panic, he said, "It's not mine."

The pain in my side was back. His eyes widened as he cast them over the wound, and he opened his mouth to say something.

BANG. The sound of the shot alone threw me off balance as I whipped my head round on instinct to see where it had come from.

I could only see darkness.

For a terrifying second, I thought my life was over.

As I opened my eyes, enough light crept through the thinner membrane of Anton's wings to allow me to realise he'd cocooned us in their embrace.

The world stood still. For a second it was just him and I. His wings encased me, their enormous form shrouding us from view. His eyes were wide with panic and passion as he pulled me in and kissed me hard. Tears stung my eyes as I returned the kiss with this as much fervour, shuddering with relief into him, accepting how fleeting life was here and how nothing could be taken for granted.

It was only when he pulled away; I saw the gaps in his wings where the light could filter in.

About the size of three bullet holes.

But that wasn't my main concern. The bullets weren't in his wings. They'd torn straight through and found another target.

Red was spreading across his torso.

Too close to his heart.

I screamed for help. Bronx was the closest, already locked in a vicious fight with three other Shifters. I couldn't see anyone else close by.

I let out a noise I didn't know I was capable of. Somewhere between a roar and a scream. All I cared about was getting him out of there to make sure he was okay. My back prickled. I had to find Perrine. She could help him.

I screamed for him. For her. For anyone to come and fix this. It wasn't until I gave a final a sob of frustration as he collapsed to the ground that I let the pressure inside of me explode.

Something burst from my back. I could see giant white feathers stretching out on either side of me. They cocooned us just like he had, shielding us from the attacks that hammered into them. I barely even registered they belonged to me. All I hoped was that they'd keep any more bullets out.

Nothing will get through, they will keep you safe. Una was here, more present that I'd ever felt her, but I needed every ounce of my concentration on keeping Anton alive. If I could just stay here until help arrived . . .

"STOP!" I recognised Draven's voice laced with panic. His words amplified across the battlefield, and his allies quickly followed suit. A quick scan of the area showed me, by some miracle, everyone I'd arrived with was all still intact.

Except Anton.

My heart broke. His skin was too pale, his hair slicked against his forehead. His eyes were barely open. They were so dark. I could only see the faintest hint of jet green shimmering in the background. I was too busy examining Anton, only vaguely aware of the broad figure running towards us at breakneck speed.

Before I could draw either of my swords, the three of us plunged into darkness for a split second, only to emerge in the forest's thickness. The rich earthy smell marred with the scent of blood on all three of us, revealing we were back in Abduco.

Without allowing myself time to overthink why Draven had brought us here, I drew my swords and charged at him. It was surprising he didn't stop me, as it only took mere seconds before I was holding one of them against his neck. He didn't show any fear, even though he didn't have his lackeys tensed around him. It was just the three of us now.

Anger bubbled to the surface of my skin until it felt like every nerve was alive with rage. If he wanted a Caedes Shifter, I was ready to destroy him right in front of my eyes. "This is all your fault. You'll pay for everything you've done." The venom fell off my tongue as I forced myself to follow my words through.

Draven held out an arm to still me and something flickered in his expression. "I'm sure of that, Charity. After all, *your only limit is your imagination.*" He looked me dead in the eye as he said those final words.

I dropped one of my swords in shock and scrambled down to retrieve it. But it was too late. He'd taken my hesitation and used it to back away from me, his hand on his own sword, though he hadn't drawn it. He now eyed me as if assessing my reaction.

I was stunned. "Why would you say that?"

His hand loosened on the hilt of his sword. "It's what you always tell yourself isn't it? From when you were younger."

Of course. "You've been watching me." It didn't take a genius to work out that he'd found out all sorts about my life after looking into me. He was a complete psychopath. The second he was dead, I'd get Anton back to safety and come up with a plan from there. Anton tried to unfurl his wings in agreement but tensed, sucking the air in through his teeth from the effort. I held a hand out to stop him.

Draven ignored Anton's struggle. His grin now focused on me. "I have been watching you, but that's not why I know. I know because *I* wrote it. It's something I often tell myself, and I wanted to share that with my family. Especially with my only child. My only *proper* daughter."

Daughter.

The world collapsed around me.

30

CHARITY

Shifter 101: Travel Shifting: Shifters can travel short or long distances by using an idol. Abduco Shifters use rings, Caedes Shifters use weapons, Persen Shifters use a range of small objects, and Nexus use bees.

"You're lying." I was instantly on the defensive, ignoring the goosebumps that rose as things fell into place. D for Draven. His strange reactions towards me. His reason for sending Anton into my world.

No, it couldn't be. I turned and looked at Anton for support, but his pallor told me he was just as shocked as I was.

"I don't think he's lying, girl." This time it was Viktor's voice who spoke, causing us to all jump. "We've been tracking Draven. This is what Julian, Forrest, and I were working on. We've been watching him travel to this part of Abduco, so we assumed he'd come here when he Shifted with you."

"And you didn't think to share that with us?" Anton said, then grimaced at the still healing wounds in his chest. Sensing Draven wasn't about to attack, I ran back to Anton, which was harder than I'd expected with heavy wings weighing me down. I regained my balance and helped him add more pressure to the bandages, stopping the blood flow.

"Sorry, mate." Viktor's voice came from behind my shoulder. "You're not the only one with secrets."

Draven made a grab for my arm. "Charity, regardless of what I said, that book, it's everything–"

"I have nothing to say to you." I blocked him, not wanting to reveal how much I relied on that book throughout my childhood to escape.

"Let me explain." Draven's red tinged eyes flashed wildly.

"I've seen everything I need." I was numb of all emotions. I wanted to be cold. It was better than letting the hurt escape through the cracks that were already forming in my composure. This man couldn't be my father. That would mean he'd been there all along. Watching my pathetic excuse for a life. Frustration mingled with disappointment, but I forced it all behind a door and turned the key.

I focused my attention back to Anton who needed help. He needed healers in Nexus. Viktor helped him up, leaving Draven and me facing each other. I eyed my so-called father with disdain. He was the reason I had never felt like I belonged my whole life. It wasn't even just about me. He had caused suffering to so many.

The change in his tone surprised me as he spoke. It was softer than I had ever heard, and the tinge of red in his eyes disappeared. "Charity, we don't have long, and I need you to listen. I've not been honest with you. I never have. You need to understand, I didn't want to reveal our connection because of the danger it puts you in, but you have to believe me when I say I didn't want to harm any of you. The Reapers' aim was to bring you back to Caedes, kidnap you if we had to. But I wasn't going to allow that."

Kidnap? I shuddered at the thought.

"I won't allow it either." Anton struggled to stand as he held his chest, but refused any help. "How can we even trust you? You've been holding Langison over my father for years now. Plus, you had no problem almost destroying Allium."

I remembered that night on the balcony all too well. Draven had nearly killed him.

Draven's face was ashen. "I'm sorry about your father. He got caught up in the cause. I hold that over him in order to help the Reapers understand that he'll do anything I say, that he's not a threat. I'm doing it to help him." He indicated Anton. "As for Allium, they wanted to destroy him for breaking off things with Scarlett. They rely on our connection to Abduco. The only way I prevented it was by making an example out of him. But I ensured he lived."

"A likely story," Verde cut in as he appeared and rested a hand on my shoulder. "You've had your time. Now you need to accept your consequences."

Draven's tone was a vicious snarl directed at Verde. "Don't talk to me about consequences. You think I didn't know Anton attacked his own instead of killing innocents? Didn't you wonder how he got away with it for so long? A fifteen-year-old-boy never caught by a group of the most talented Shifters? I helped him of course. Where I could, I directed them to the worst of our kind on our side that he could despatch of."

It rang true based on what Anton said that night. I shook Verde off, conscious of the fact we needed to be getting Anton help. Anton must have sensed my turmoil as he held out a broad arm to Verde and said, "I can wait. I want to hear what he has to say."

Draven narrowed his eyes at Verde one last time, before addressing me. "Charity, I want to be very clear when I say this is much bigger than you or I."

Verde was back at my arm again. "Okay, that's enough."

Once again, I shrugged him off, snapping, "No! Wait. I need to hear this." Things were falling into place. I thought about his diminished numbers. He'd killed enough of his own men today to prove the point he was making. Horror washed over me as I thought about the number of people who had died today. I couldn't help but feel a traitorous stab of pride that he'd killed for us, to help us. I realised bitterly that we weren't as different as I'd first thought.

"Sometimes you have to be cruel to protect the ones you love. From the moment you were born, I could tell no one had ever existed like you. The prophecy later that year confirmed my worst fears, and I knew I had to protect you at all costs." Draven kept speaking, but I hardly heard him. I was numb, unable to process what he was saying. "I didn't want to send you away. I thought you could avoid it in your world if you grew up without knowing what you could do."

I was confused. "Where I come from, people don't turn their backs on the ones they care about."

He waved a hand at me. "I never said I did. You are blind with love. Would you not do the same for Anton? Send him away to save him?"

I would, and he knew it. As much as I hated to admit it, we were both driven by passion and by love.

"So why have me watched? Why bring me back?" I still gripped my swords. I felt safer with them in my hands.

Draven glanced up at the darkening clouds. "I'd hoped that by keeping you in the human world, your abilities wouldn't materialise, or you would be so unremarkable that you'd be able to stay there. When I realised you would always stand your ground, not to mention the mind you almost destroyed before you even got here, I knew I couldn't keep you away any longer." I shivered at the memory of that alleyway. "But you have to realise I never intended to have you here.

To put you in danger."

It reminded me of something Allium said once: *He wants you gone, and I want you to stay.* At the time, I had been convinced that I was talking to Anton, who had been referring to Allium, but he had meant Draven. Not that Allium knew about our connection then. Draven must have told him he'd wanted me out of Domain.

As the pieces connected around me, I still couldn't bring myself to forgive him. "So you figured me being miserable for years was preferable to a life here?"

"You being alive was preferable," he replied. "Even if it meant me being unhappy and doing whatever I could to create the image of a monster so that no one would suspect what I'd done."

"You were happy with us both being miserable, then? That was your big solution?" Tears stung my eyes. I was sick of things being unfair with family. I wasn't sure what was worse, knowing my dad had taken off at the first opportunity, or knowing that he'd wanted to stay and had still found it in himself to leave.

Draven looked at the sky again as thunder rumbled in the distance. "Don't you see? The second that prophecy came into existence, it placed a target on your head. There will always be people in Domain who resist the way things are run, and the Reapers were, and are, exactly that. They will destroy anything, or anyone who threatens their way of living. I had to infiltrate them in order to keep them close. By joining them, I ensured I knew their every move, and it worked, until your abilities manifested, which put the attention back on you. Leaving you was the hardest thing I've ever had to do, but it was worth it to keep you safe."

My anger rivalled the growing storm around us. "Do you consider what I was raised with *safe*? Did you not see who my mother brought home to replace you? I should have known you'd fit the bill for her terrible taste in violent men." I embodied venom as I drew my sword again and stabbed it into the nearest tree. It was probably breaking a cosmic rule in Abduco, but I didn't care. Better ending up there than embedded in someone. It wasn't until I saw Anton eyeing me that I composed myself. The quicker I got answers, the quicker I could get him home.

There was the sound of breaking twigs as the rest of our gang appeared. The fact there was no one following them said enough about how loyal Draven's allies were in that moment. Anton gestured for them to hold their fire as Draven began speaking again, his voice becoming more frantic. "Didn't you ever wonder why none of them stuck around? Greg was the last of them. They won't hurt anyone anymore. They can't."

I stood stunned at that. It didn't make what he'd done right. He was far from forgiven, but things were piecing together.

"As for Anton," he continued, "I didn't know that you two would ever . . ." he let the thunder settle. "That you would end up tied to here. Do you know what the Reapers, the Council, would have done to you if I'd kept you here in the circles I operate? They wouldn't have allowed you to live. The relationship I had with your mother was forbidden, as was the result—you. It would have endangered you both."

"And you thought deciding for us was a better option?" My voice rose over the thunder.

"A disappointing life there was better than a dangerous life here." Sadness filled Draven's eyes as he spoke.

"You made your choices about who you associated with," I said coldly.

Draven dropped his voice, which was unnecessary given the loud clap of thunder. "Listen to me, Charity, there are dark things on the horizon. It didn't start with me, and it won't end there, either. I wasn't as much a part of it as the stories would have you believe. I have done terrible things, yes, but I have prevented a lot more. Mindchill, the prophecy, you, it's all connected. It's not just that, they have other things planned, the Reapers, the Council. Your parents' death too. It was no accident." He indicated Spyder who'd been silent since he'd arrived. Spyder's eyes widened, and he stiffened in response. According to Viktor, he'd always thought that his parents' deaths were suspicious, and now it seemed like he wasn't the only one who thought so. But we didn't have time to dwell on that right now. Draven's tone became more urgent, as if his time was racing to an end. I gave a quick scan of our surroundings but couldn't see any immediate threat, even though the hairs on the back of my neck stood on end. Something was coming.

I didn't want to believe him. But I thought back to my dreams, and the last piece of the puzzle clicked into place.

If only he could have her, but he couldn't. It was not his place to decide who belonged, only to remove who didn't. There was too much of a risk. If they discovered him, he would lose everything.

He knew what he had to do.

My Caedes dream. It was Draven's memory mixed with mine. My dreams–they were memories from the places I'd visited with him as a baby, kept all this time.

"My dreams," I started.

He cut me off. His eyes widened, as if he had noticed something. "Something is coming, Charity. You need to use the b–" The thunder had reached a crescendo. It was deafening.

Then, a massive *CRACK* of lightning lit up the entire sky.

A single bolt struck down from the darkest section of clouds above us.

Right where Draven was standing.

I jumped back in response, but it hadn't touched me. All I could focus on was the horror etched on Draven's face in that split second.

And then he was gone. Reduced to nothing but ash quicker than I could blink. In the confusion, I barely registered one more body that had joined us, now in her human form as she dropped to her knees and sobbed where her father had been standing. I remembered what Allium had told me about him adopting Scarlett as his daughter and recognised what she was feeling. Pain very different to the one at my side filled my chest.

Loss was the mental equivalent of getting stabbed. And right now, despite everything I'd just found out, I was bleeding. My wings snapped in as if they'd never existed.

"What the fuck was that?" said Spyder, looking up at the sky as it cleared above us.

"That," said Verde, "was Hymev."

31

CHARITY

Shifter 101: Mind Shifting: This is the predominant form of Shifting which allows Shifters to travel into human minds in order to perform their function. They can also access unguarded Shifter minds if they can overcome their mental shields.

Perrine's words echoed through me the entire journey back to Abduco. *Anton will live, but he's going to need to rest. His wings will be fine, but the exertion on his chest would be too much. He won't be able to fly for some time.*

I couldn't mourn now. Anton needed me to be strong. My chest tightened. A few hours ago, I'd been ready to hurt, even kill Draven. Now I was mourning the loss of a family member I didn't know I had. Not to mention the fact I'd killed someone today. Someone had started their day, and it was my fault they wouldn't end it. Although I knew I'd done it to save my life, it didn't stop the guilt that spread through my chest as I replayed the light disappearing from the man's eyes as he fell to the ground.

I'd let myself fall apart once I knew Anton was in safe hands, refusing to think about what I'd do if I lost him too. Since he couldn't Shift in his current condition, we strapped him to Verde, who carried him on his back in his dragon form. My wings had still disappeared, and I had no clue how to get them back out again. I allowed myself to be carried by Sage—her bright green eyes sought mine out in the now inky sky, looking for my reaction as we flew under the pinprick stars to the House of Healing in Nexus.

Scarlett had stayed behind for a few moments, though accepted my invitation that I'd passed to her just as we were leaving. She knew it was fruitless going back to Caedes now, given her father would be seen as a traitor. I still didn't understand the full extent of what he'd been involved in, but I knew his true allegiance had been elsewhere. Everyone would know that now, his followers included.

No one spoke during the journey back, everyone still reeling from the shock of what had happened. By the time we arrived, Bronx, Perrine, Viktor, Spyder, and Scarlett were all waiting for us, having Shifted instantly.

We raced into the House of Healing, too fixated on Anton to notice much about where we were. It appeared to be a hospital, though clinical was the last word to describe it. There were long corridors punctuated with doors that led into small cosy rooms with a single bed. If anything, it looked more like a hotel, were it not for the staff bustling around in medical coats and scrubs.

Bronx set Anton to his feet and helped him into a bed further up the hall. Perrine ran after them, her brown hair flowing behind her. I recognised Nora, Perrine's sister, leading the team of healers that saw to Anton. I wanted to go with them, but I knew it was better to let them work in silence. Bronx had a way of blending in with the surroundings that I hadn't mastered with people I cared about. I couldn't keep my heart steady at how pale his face had become and knew it would show on my expression.

I tried to piece together what had happened as we made our way to another available room, and Spyder opened up a bag of medicines to tend to my side. He wasn't as careful as Perrine or Anton had been, but I didn't mind. If anything, I wanted the pain to block out everything else in my head. A Healer Shifter with round glasses and freckles raised her eyebrows at us and offered to help, but I turned her away, wanting as many Shifters as possible available for Anton.

"Is anyone going to explain why Hymev appeared and what happened?" said Spyder, a needle in one hand and ointment in the other.

Verde stepped forward. "I think that Draven was in deeper than any of us knew. Hymev doesn't interfere unless he has to. If he saw a reason to intervene, there must have been one."

"I don't understand." I winced as Spyder started stitching my side, giving me an apologetic smile in return. "Why Draven?"

"They were working together." Verde's face was ashen. I wondered if he feared Hymev.

"And you believed working with someone like that was the best thing for your family." I couldn't keep the disgust out my voice. I knew this was Anton's business and I should keep my mouth shut. But I couldn't get those scars out of my mind.

"After today, I don't know what to believe anymore," said Verde. It was the most honest thing he'd ever said. "I'm going to check on Anton."

"I need a distraction." I spoke through gritted teeth as I faced Spyder instead. "No offence, but these are brutal."

"On it." Without breaking his focus, he reached into the bag and pulled out a copy of *The Notion*. "Tell me what they're saying about today."

I scanned the page that was already dancing with information. They'd chosen a picture of everyone at the initial standoff. The picture had been taken so none of the faces were visible, as if someone had deliberately positioned themselves in order to keep the identities of those involved a secret.

Despite the front page positioning, the article glossed over the details of the actual fight, citing the deaths as a terrible tragedy. Draven's name was absent. That in itself was interesting. Perhaps whoever wrote the article didn't know. After all, there wasn't anything left . . .

I stopped reading as my mind went into overdrive, and the pain at my side paled compared to the hurt that cracked my heart in two.

"They do that, you know," said a voice from behind us. I turned, careful not to pull at Spyder working on my stitches, and met Scarlett's tear-stained face. I hadn't seen her come in. "They tell everyone that things were accidents when they weren't. It's been happening for decades. They won't want the rest of Domain knowing there's someone out there like Hymev with the power to cut us down whenever they choose, but that's the world we live in."

"Then it's a pretty shitty world to live in." I was unable to come up with anything more articulate at the moment.

Scarlett continued to speak. "I've heard from my sources still loyal in Caedes that the Reapers are using their influence with the Cerebral Council to fuel their ascent to power. The standoff you saw earlier was nothing. Their numbers are vast and the lengths that they will go to rule Domain even more so."

My stomach dropped as I realised how bad things had got. "We need to stop this. Because of what they're doing. For what they did to yo—our father. I'm sorry for what happened to him."

"Me too," she said after a pause. "I collected the ashes, you know. Just for the future. I can't think about it now, but maybe one day, we could go together."

"Yes, we could." The thought was almost too painful to bear. I couldn't explain it. I'd been so ready to kill this man, so eager to hate him because of the position he'd put me in. And that's what he'd wanted. He'd wanted me to loathe him so that it put as much distance between us as possible. It really was the ultimate sacrifice to have your family hate you in order to protect them. And now it had ended with his death. I couldn't imagine how Scarlett must be feeling; I forced myself to smile as I could see she was trying, even when she was hurting, too.

She answered with a small nod. "I'll leave you to it. One more thing. He kept mentioning your book. When things are calmer, I think you should take another look at it."

"I will, thank you." He had seemed fascinated with it. Not that I could face reading those words I'd poured over as a child just yet, now knowing who they'd belonged to. She nodded again and turned to go. I called after her, "Scarlett?"

"Yes?"

"Why are you being so nice?"

She rolled her eyes, then her face became serious. "Let's say I've had a few things put into perspective today, and it's not worth holding silly grudges anymore." She eyed my puzzled look. "I've been in your mind. It's only fair you see mine. Look for the red door with the gold lock."

I entered her mind, grateful for the distraction from the pain in my side, which was much sorer now the adrenaline from the fight was wearing off. Finding the door, I stepped through and saw a round-faced younger version of Scarlett playing in the sand with a carefree Draven. They shouted and laughed together, until someone came and whispered something in his ear, and the look on his face changed as he muttered something about having to go.

The memories flashed forward a few years. Scarlett looked

four-to-five years older, whereas Draven looked like he'd aged decades. Lines marked his face, and he looked exhausted.

"Hold your shields," he snapped. "You're never going to last in this world if you can't look after yourself."

The memories changed and changed as they played similar scenes, all showing Scarlett's efforts not quite living up to Draven's standards. One stood out. Being forced to remove Carmine, her Other, just like Draven had removed his. "They're a liability. Just extra collateral," he said, as if that justified such an act. I knew it was common practise in Domain to remove Others, but to decide for Scarlett was inhumane.

I saw my arrival in Domain as she had. Seeing the obsession in her father's eyes. Ordering her to get into my head and find out as much as she could about me. The hurt when he'd spoken about my performance during my Actuation. Not to mention Anton and Allium, who had always been polite but aloof, growing even more distant.

I stepped out of her mind. I understood her point. If the roles were reversed, I would have hated me too.

"I'm sorry things turned out that way." I shuddered at what she'd been subjected to.

Scarlett shrugged. "As am I; at least you now know. But I'm ready to leave that behind. There are more important things that need to be dealt with."

I gave her a small smile. "You should stay with us while we figure out what we're going to do. And if you ever want to talk about Carmine, I'm here."

She smiled in return, a tinge of sadness lingering in her expression. "Thanks, Charity, maybe one day." She then brightened. "I might take you up on your offer of a place to stay, though."

We'd forgotten Spyder was in the room until he spoke. "Does someone want to check if I hit my head harder than I thought earlier, or are you two friends now?"

This time, Scarlett rolled her eyes as she reached the door.

"I wouldn't say friends," I said, grinning back at her.

I was just able to hear her response before she disappeared. "Maybe allies."

"Yup, definite concussion," Spyder said under his breath.

Several long stitches later, Perrine entered the room just as Spyder was finishing up. With a combination of antidotes and his handiwork, my mouth fell open as I saw the wound knitting together. I nodded in thanks and jumped up. "How is he?"

"He's fine, or rather, that's what he wants me to tell you. He's hurt, but he will be okay as long as he rests. His sense of humour has remained intact." She then paused as she studied me and remarked. "Charity, your eyes."

I turned to the nearest mirror. Sure enough, they had lightened. While still brown, I could see thousands of gold flecks dancing across them. I could feel Una at the forefront of my consciousness, more present than ever. They'd now be recognisable to anyone, not just those who knew me.

Fully realised. Your forgiveness has allowed me to materialise. You've shown how well you can heal yourself as well as different people.

I knew Una was just trying to help, after all, she *was* me. But I didn't feel good, or healed, or forgiving. Without her, what did I bring? What was I without her?

You're everything I'm not. And I'm everything you're not. There are many ways a pair can match Charity. You can find your equal like Anton, or you can be two parts that make up a whole through their contrast, like Allium and I do. I like to think you and I are also like the latter.

But if you're the good in me, does that just make me evil? I asked her.

No, because I am you. We both come together to form you. You are unique.

The thing was, I didn't feel unique. Despite all I had, I could only think of what I'd lost.

The room stood still as Anton walked in. Relief flooded me as I noted the colour had returned to his face. They had cleaned off all the blood from earlier, and although I could still see the tension from the day in his posture, all I wanted to do was to feel him for myself to know that he wasn't a hallucination.

I ran up and hugged him, using as little pressure as possible.

"I'm not made of glass, you know," he said into my hair as he wrapped his arms around me.

"Thank fuck for that." I took in his smoky, woody scent, not wanting to let him go again.

I knew enough about my reactive side to know it was my way of unpacking everything that had gone on that day. My body craved an outlet for grief. I wanted to run, but not to escape anymore. In fact, I wanted the opposite.

I wanted to belong. Somewhere. To someone.

I didn't need to be touching him for Anton to understand. He gave me a look which told me everything I needed to know.

He pulled back and ran the back of his hand down the side of my face.

What can I do? Allium sounded in my head.

Una voiced the words I couldn't. *We need to forget. Just for a while. Until we work out what to do.*

Anton nodded before gesturing to the door as he addressed the room. "I'll be *resting* at mine. We're leaving."

Surprisingly, no one questioned us.

I felt guilty for even noticing the way his white t-shirt showed off the muscles in his shoulders, back, and arms as we arrived at Anton's flat. Anticipation danced inside of me, unsure what was going to happen. What I even wanted to happen.

"I'd like to shower first," I blurted out, aware that I still had blood on me and was in my combat gear. I wanted to rid myself of all traces of what had happened today.

He hesitated for just a fraction of a second, which told me he was just as unsure as I was. "Want company?"

"Not–" I hesitated. I wanted to separate my feelings. I didn't want to let my grief spoil the miracle that he was okay. "Not this time, but another day."

"You've got it."

Scenes from the onslaught flashed before my eyes as I showered, but better that than looking at the pool of red at my feet that danced at the edge of my peripheral vision. I locked the memories away and tried to allow the warm water to cleanse me of the horrors from that battlefield, though when I stepped out, I found myself clean but still mentally tarnished.

Anton's eyes widened a fraction as I walked back into the living room, taking in my silk dressing gown that left little to the imagination. I would have worn something more practical, but other than my fighting clothes, everything was very fitted and all of my nightwear was much more on the sexy side than cute.

Without allowing myself time to think about what I was doing, I sat in his lap, facing him. Anger, sadness, betrayal, lust, and love were running through me in one big confusion mix of emotions. I just wanted Anton's touch. He would make everything feel better.

What I didn't expect was to burst into tears the minute I met his eye. He pulled me into his chest, my head resting on his shoulder as I sobbed into him, the woody, smoky scent giving me some comfort.

I choked out, "I didn't even know him. I don't know why I'm so upset."

"I know, Cee. I know."

"I was so ready to kill him." My voice broke on the word kill.

"I know."

"This is so fucked up. Everything is so fucked up."

"I know."

It didn't bother me he kept repeating the same words. It was what I needed. Something to ground me. An outlet where I could try to work through everything that had happened. He stayed there as I poured out my grief, taking in my words like scorched earth in a storm. Eventually, I'd cried my heart out and my sobs reduced to sniffs, so we sat there in silence. Not needing to speak, just grateful for each other. I felt an odd sense of peace as I lay on his chest with him stroking my hair. It didn't change what had happened, but it had lessened the immediate shock and had dampened some of the emotions running through me. Though as they left, different emotions heightened and flitted between us.

"Are you healed enough?" I bit my lip as he rested his hand on my leg.

"Yes," he said. *No*, his thoughts told me. I debated what to do with that.

But when his other hand moved to my leg, I didn't stop him.

And when he made its way up my thigh, I didn't stop him.

I didn't stop him either when he was brushing the side of my lacy thong, and I became all too aware of his hardness underneath me. I ground into him, even though my brain screamed that this wasn't the time.

"Fuck. We aren't making this easy, are we?" Anton said, sensing my conflict. "But you're right, I'm selfish after all, and when I get to claim you, I want to be the only person you're thinking about. Give me that and I'll wait as long as you need me to."

It was the right thing to do, even if the throbbing between my legs protested. But it was true. I wanted things to be perfect. Not because I was romantic and soppy, but because I expected things to be earth-shatteringly orgasmic when I finally climbed him like a tree.

"I'm still listening, sweetheart." He gripped my leg tighter. His eyes had turned feral and his voice had dropped an octave.

"Sorry." I burned the image of him like that into my mind and gave him a small smile. It would be a long time before I got used to the fact my thoughts were always visible when we were touching. We'd been through a lot today. We deserved time. Allium and Una deserved time. After all, we were four halves–

"HOLY SHIT!"

"What?! Are you okay?" Anton shot up, holding me at arms length to analyse me, the distance painful in the moment.

"I've just realised. Four halves make a whole. In the prophecy, it's us. You, me, Una, and Allium." Anton's eyes widened at me. "I think I've got it figured out. The answer is in Nexus. We need to go back there now."

Anton adjusted his trousers. "Right now? We just left."

"It could wait a couple of hours." I considered his still hard length. Although I felt lighter, I was so caught up in a wave of lust, loss, grief, pain, and ecstasy, I wasn't ready to face my future yet. That said, I also wasn't ready to take things further with Anton either, as much as I wanted to. Though, perhaps we could still steal this time for each other differently.

If I said we agreed the prophecy was more important and travelled straight to Nexus, I'd be lying. Anton needed some time to process everything, too. After all, Draven had also been a large part of his life. I gave him privacy and stayed out of his mind as he pulled me into him and we both lost ourselves in our thoughts, the weight of his arms anchoring me in place.

32

CHARITY

Shifter 101: The Notion, est. 1474, is the primary source of news across Domain. As of 1963, The Notion has existed in an entirely digital format.

"Out of all the ways I thought our first night would play out, Serrk, it wasn't that." Anton's voice was husky in my ear.

"Me neither," I admitted, reading from his emotions that he wasn't in the slightest bit disappointed. "This was better."

I mentally messaged Perrine that we weren't far away, and we walked through the warm breeze that permeated the skies. I'd forgotten how stunning the architecture was in Nexus; like Paris, but with more greenery, more warm tones.

As hard as it was to admit, last night wouldn't have been the right time to take things further. I didn't want my first time with him to be caught up in emotions over what had happened with Draven.

Being in Nexus was like walking inside a painting. Despite everything that had happened yesterday, I felt at ease here. Like there was light at the end of everything. That I would gain closure over my father. That I could find it in my heart to forgive my mother for wanting to fill the void he'd left in her life, just like I wanted to fill the one he'd left in mine. I wondered how they'd even met. After all, humans and Apex Shifters couldn't be together. And they certainly weren't Covalents. There were still so many unanswered questions.

My mother's actions didn't excuse the life we'd ended up with, or who she'd allowed into it. But I now understood her in a way I had never had before. Perhaps being in Nexus was rubbing off on me.

Something about this place called to me, though, like home. Never had I taken the time to appreciate the beauty of nature on a balmy day: the blossoms in the breeze, the buzz of the insects at the honeysuckle, and the echo of the birds up high. It was both mesmerising and calming.

"Where are we going?" Anton was at my side as I led us up a narrow street.

"To Perrine's house. I think I'll find answers there," I said, guided by pure instinct.

Shifters were much kinder here. Everyone we passed said *good morning* like they really meant it, before bustling by on their way. I noted their clothes here were much plainer than the rest of the Houses I'd seen in Domain. As we continued up the narrowing street, I noted the buildings grew much more unremarkable than their Parisian counterparts. Again, they were simple in design, dirtier, and mostly hidden in the shade.

We came to a tall narrow door and buzzed for *Rivers*. A second later, the door swung open to a winding staircase, and we climbed towards the top floor. With every step, the pain in my side twinged, causing my breath to hitch.

The staircase was dark and cramped, appearing to narrow the higher we climbed. I took a deep breath, *Your only limit* . . .

I couldn't finish the thought; it was still too raw. As we climbed,

I channelled my hurt into determination until we reached a small landing with two doors, indicating that the floor was divided between the two apartments. I rang the bell for Perrine's door and she answered almost immediately. Her face brightened, then momentarily frowned, as if she could tell something was on my mind. "You made it. This way." She invited us in.

She led us through the small space, which was simple in style, yet had a warmth that I'd never felt before when stepping into someone's home. The place echoed of laughter and happy memories, despite the sparse surroundings.

We made our way to a patio on the roof that overlooked the city. Instantly, any leftover discomfort from my side evaporated as the warm summer breeze caressed my face and I gazed out over the Parisian-style rooftops that stretched into the distance.

Anton and Perrine were clearly used to the view and paid it little attention. They sat on benches that appeared from thin air. I supposed Perrine must have summoned them. In the same fashion, a tray appeared with tea and several dainty snacks that looked like wafers. I tore my eyes away from the beautiful city and sat down to join them. I took a wafer and turned to Perrine, who was studying me carefully.

She spoke first, taking a sip of her tea, then setting down her cup. "How are you feeling? How is your side?"

"Spyder did a good job of stitching me up. Thank you for the antidote. It's almost healed already." I addressed the straightforward part of her question only. *If I'm being honest, it's surprising how quickly I've healed.* Perrine narrowed her eyes and silently pressed me for an answer to the rest of her question. Anton squeezed my hand in support. I swallowed the lump in my throat. "I haven't thought about how I'm going to deal with it yet. If I think about it too much, I worry that I'll never get over it. Scarlett collected his ashes, and I'd like to honour his memory, but I'm not ready yet. It feels too final. I only just found out about his relationship with me."

Perrine contemplated this. "That's certainly understandable."

Anton nodded. "Whatever you decide to do, you're not alone. We'll be here for you."

"Thank you," I said to them both. "But that's not why I'm here. I came here today because I think there's a connection to Nexus that will help with the prophecy. I can't explain it yet. I just *know* there is."

Anton was looking at me proudly. "I always knew you were extra-ordinary, Cee."

His statement faded into nothing as my self-doubt crept in. Caedes or not, I couldn't undo what I'd been told for all my life. Allium sensed my thoughts immediately.

Don't even consider that. You are successful, and you won Anton over. You even won me over—now that is extraordinary.

I had to allow myself a laugh. I went to lock the door in my mind, but found Allium's foot wedged in it. Apparently, he hadn't left.

But if you still don't believe me, then we will deal with it together.

Both Una and I smiled. We would.

Perrine said, "I'll help you in any way I can." She then turned to Anton. "Any word on how the Reapers have taken the loss of Draven?"

I watched a muscle in Anton's jaw twitch as he spoke. "They are slowly seeping into other Houses from Caedes and are infecting the way people think. We believe their principal weapon is Mindchill, but we can't rule out other measures. We are going to have to be extremely careful if they have the influence of Hymev on their side."

There had to be a way to stop all of this. I stood up and walked over to the flower boxes at the edge of the terrace, noting the bees deep in the honeysuckle spread across. The bees were as large as my hand, but they didn't intimidate me. The rose gold instead of yellow really was quite beautiful. I felt an overwhelming urge to stroke one that was close to my hand and discovered that it didn't resist when I gently ran a finger down the fuzz of its back. The answers were here–I just had to find them.

Perrine watched me out of the corner of her eye quietly. "I want you to try something. Forget everything we have been discussing, and explore deeper into your own mind instead."

"My mind? But I already know my mind." Her request seemed odd.

My answer didn't deter Perrine. "I think you might surprise yourself. Keep looking, try some new doors."

I took a deep breath and entered my exhausted mind. I hurried past the doors that contained my grief, threatening to spill out. Then I heard Perrine speaking, even though it sounded muffled.

Her voice sounded in my head. *I want you to get through one of your own locked doors. One near the bottom of your corridor.*

I didn't remember my mind being so extensive. I took a deep breath as I glanced around me in awe of what I'd created. Perhaps it was from my training. I saw doors I'd never laid eyes on before. Walking deeper into my mind than I had ever been, I knew which door to approach without consciously being aware of it. It stood before me, a sleek rosewood with a gold handle.

I visualised the lock on the other side. It was the same as the one I had practised with. A mortice lock, held with a surprisingly robust dainty gold key. I tried to imagine it turning, but there was no effect. I could faintly smell Anton's signature scorched earth scent. He must have moved closer. He smelled so damn good.

Focus.

It was Allium's voice. He must have been in my mind, too. I followed his instruction.

I focused every ounce of my mental energy on visualising the key turning in the lock. Slowly, the door vibrated. I crouched at the keyhole. Sure enough, it turned.

I grasped the handle and exhaled as the door swung open.

As I took in the scene before me, something strange happened. Una rose from the back of my mind and brought herself forward. Something about this room called to her.

The room was from Nexus in every sense. The same spring breeze fluttered across my skin. Cherry blossom petals floated from the trees and danced across the open space. The room appeared to speak directly to Una and in doing so; I recognised just how distinct a being she was inside of me. She had her own qualities, ones I didn't recognise in myself. She belonged somewhere else, to Nexus. Finally, I understood the different sides of my personality. These were two elements to me: Nexus and Caedes.

"Amazing." It was Perrine who spoke. I realised I'd left my mind and returned to the rooftop.

It was like wearing glasses for the first time. I could view everything with a new clarity. Everything I heard sounded as if channelled through headphones. My senses were sharper than ever. It was Una and I working in harmony for the first time, rather than as individuals. Something was driving me forward, like listening to a favourite song during exercise. My senses had amplified to match the two beings inside of me.

"Una belongs to Nexus," I stated.

"I wondered the second I met you." Perrine's eyes were twinkling.

I hardly dared to believe it. "But Draven is from Caedes. So, I have to be Caedes."

Perrine shook her head. "You can be whatever you like. There is a passion and fierceness in you as well as a kindness. You, my dear, are as much Nexus as you are Caedes."

Anton was frowning. "You forget, Perrine, Shifters and their Other cannot belong to more than one House."

Perrine straightened out the creases in her skirt. "Indeed, they couldn't. Until today. Her mind has chosen a dual allegiance, and perhaps with your mixed heritage, that's why."

Anton sounded confused. "So, you're saying she belongs to two Houses?"

"If she wants to."

"That's never happened before."

Perrine carried on speaking. "We've also never had a Shifter manifest their House during their Actuation in the way that she did. There had never been a debate about which House a Shifter belongs to following their actions. Perhaps the Nexus element comes from her mother's side. Perhaps it is her own choosing."

"I'm right here, you know." A wave of anger overcame me, then, as quickly as it had arrived, it faded, and I muttered an apology. "Sorry. I'm realising why I can suddenly lose my temper and feel bad about it seconds later. I'm still learning how to control two different sides of me."

Anton grinned. "No matter. What is important now is that you never need to feel you don't fit in. You are your own creation."

I looked back into my mind once more. My corridor had extended even further. I now noted the cherry blossom from the room had positioned itself at the end of the hallway. I belonged.

"Thank you." I meant it for them both.

"For what?" they said in unison.

"For helping me to understand who I am." I felt lighter than I had in weeks, despite everything I still faced.

"It's you that helped me." Anton wrapped his arm around me and kissed the top of my head.

Perrine watched our display with affection. "While we're on that subject, I've actually got another theory about what you are."

I raised a brow at her, my stomach twisting in anticipation.

"I'll be right back." She disappeared into her apartment and returned with a large, heavy book. "Look." She pointed. "It's your wings".

She had the same book I'd been reading in the library: *Creatures: A Chronology*. She flipped through the pages until I faced a picture of myself with wings. Or rather, at first glance, it looked like me, though on closer inspection, I saw she was much taller and had lighter hair. I read the inscription below.

Andromeda was the first being in Shiftstory to take the form of an archangel. She founded and headed the Nexus Archangels until the gang disbanded in 1894 because of their diminishing numbers.

I looked up at Perrine in disbelief. "You think this is my form?"

"I'm sure of it." Her tone was certain.

Somehow, a part of me knew too.

"Well," Anton paused. "You were looking for a way forward on how to deal with the Reapers and I think you just found it. It looks like the fourth gang in Domain, the Archangels, is up and running again."

"Holy shit." I'd come to Nexus expecting answers, but I hadn't predicted this. But if it would help Domain, it was a path I was happy to take.

"What are you going to do now?" asked Perrine. "The Cerebral Council will await our next move. Perhaps an announcement about your dual Domainship so you can have the protection of both Houses.

What do you propose?"

I grinned wickedly. "I'm not sure yet, but I've got the perfect start."

Anton and I left Perrine's with the promise of meeting again soon, after I'd completed one last thing. I hadn't forgotten our conversation about her hopes to launch her writing career and had thought of something that could help, even if indirectly.

It was a risk leaving the slip of paper on their kitchen table, well aware she'd refused money from me once before. But if it weren't for her, I wouldn't have got this far in the first place.

Before you ask, it's not charity. I mean it is me, Charity, but what I'm doing isn't that. It's an investment. You told me once that the dresses in the designer stores in Nexus are worth a fortune. Venelles and Vêtements sent me their spring collection in pastel green in the hope I'd wear it, but it's not my colour. They won't accept my returns, so would you be able to sell them on ShiftIt.com? Keep any profits to fund your writing. In return, I'll happily take the first read. - C x

Perrine's family hadn't seemed like they'd needed money to be happy, from what I'd observed from her home. But I also knew what it was like to grow up with not enough, and now that I had more than I knew what to do with, I was happy to share.

I sent a quick message to Spyder asking where I could get a tattoo done without drawing too much attention to myself. Anton raised a brow when the letters came back promptly through the air and arranged themselves in front of us.

Spyder: I know just the place. I'll warn you, the tattoos in our world are much more complex than in yours. Are you ready?

"You like his ink more than mine, Serrk?" Anton teased.

"I asked him because I didn't expect you'd be as forthcoming when you saw where we were going." I smirked right back at him as the rest of the message materialised.

Anton frowned when he saw the address Spyder had given us. "This is in Caedes," he said flatly.

"Exactly. I want them to see that we can get in and out undetected."

We slipped between the streets; me searching for shadows in the minds we encountered and avoiding any clouded in darkness. A war might be on the horizon, but that wasn't what we were here for. Today, we were just here to make a point.

We made our way up the sandy alleyway towards a building with a blank sign hanging from it. Caedes called to me just like Nexus had, but it was harder to be drawn in when I knew what many of the Shifters here were capable of. Plus, the thought of being separated from Anton didn't even warrant consideration.

Anton sensed my thoughts. "I thought you would have learned, Cee, that wherever you go, I'll follow. Whether it's Nexus, Caedes, or somewhere else."

I smiled at him. "I think I'll stay in Abduco for now. I don't know exactly how Shifter responsibilities work, and I'm aware I'll have ties within both Houses, but I want to learn as much as I can in order to be an effective leader of the Archangels, and who better to learn from than the leaders of the Dragos and Hydras."

"Well said, Serrk. You're going to make an interesting leader for sure. Caedes and Nexus are lucky to have you belong to them."

"I might belong to them, but I belong to Abduco, too. Belong to you. So, I figured I would make my own rules."

"Spoken like a true Caedes." He chuckled.

Several hours later, my skin was on fire. I was sitting in the tattoo parlour having told them what I wanted. I'd seen enough of Spyder's tattoos to know that this woman knew what she was doing, even with the complexity of my idea. Presumably she knew who we were, but she didn't ask questions.

I'd asked if Anton would wait outside for the last stretch, wanting to see his reaction at the end.

He walked in just as my tattoo was being finished, all the pain leaving me at the sight of him. Perhaps it was a combination of everything, but seeing his eyes light up at the sight of me gave me an adrenaline rush that was so strong, I didn't even notice the artist was still working away. I knew straight away that my idea had worked. Until that moment, no one had looked at me that way before, even him.

"Fuck, Cee." He sat down next to me, eyeing my back.

"All finished." The artist set down her needle and held up a mirror so I could see what she'd done.

"Whoa." I didn't have the words to show how impressed I was. Sat between my shoulder blades, it was perfect. The artist had captured the charred edges of the rose, the embers of the fire, and the flame perfectly. It almost looked real. The thing was, Shifter tattoos were like that. The flames weren't stationary like they would be on a tattoo in my old world. They danced up my back, blackening the rose to ash until the whole thing started again. It played in a loop, repeating the process again and again, the scene dancing across my skin. It really was a work of art.

"It's stunning. Thank you, it's perfect. How much?" I asked the artist.

She waved her hand and ran it through her crimson pixie cut. "It's already taken care of."

I raised a brow at Anton who grinned at me sheepishly. "What's mine is yours, isn't that how Covalents work?"

"You tell me." I grinned as I thanked him.

As we walked out of the parlour and into the night, I pondered my decision to belong to Caedes *and* Nexus. "Will I have to change my name?"

Anton wound his fingers through mine. "Charity Caedes Nexus or Charity Nexus Caedes both have a ring to it, but you can call yourself whatever you'd like."

"You know, I think I'll stick with Serrk. It feels more me." I gathered my hair and brought it round to the front, leaving my back exposed.

"Well, here you are, a true bridge between our worlds, Charity Serrk." He grinned, stroking either side of the rose and setting my skin alight in a very different way.

I couldn't help but smile at his words. It was what I had always wanted, belonging to something, even when that meant not fitting in with the groups I was told to.

Anton wrapped his arms around me as he brushed his lips against mine, breathing, "I understand why you went to Nexus for answers. It's you. It was always you. When fire burns a rose, the two combine to create something new. You too are now your own person, helping to create a new world for us. You are, and always will be, my burning rose."

33

CHARITY

Shifter 101: The Cerebral Council handles the creation and upholding of all rules in Domain. Their word is final, even to Apex Shifters.

We behaved until we arrived at the flat. I was just taking my coat off as Anton pressed me up to the wall, his hands on either side of me. I was already dizzy from wanting him so much.

"You're sure this is what you want?" His voice was a growl as he buried himself into the space between my neck and shoulder.

"Yes." *Yes, yes, yes!* I was unsure if this was a normal reaction to trauma. I just wanted to feel something other than hurt, and my body and mind were more than ready to take things to the next stage with Anton anyway, now that we had the place to ourselves for the first time since realising we were Covalents.

Ever the gentleman, he pulled away. He must have seen what I was thinking. "Care for a drink?" Every word was like velvet, leaving me wanting to drink *him.*

I watched him make his way into the kitchen and prepare the drinks. I caught up to him and traced the veins on his arm. Anton's thoughts betrayed that his mind was elsewhere, because he was thinking about bending me over the kitchen island rather than what had happened today, and I was okay with that. For now, I wanted to forget everything but him.

So rude, Anton, said Una.

"I don't recall you and Allium complaining," Anton said out loud. "Actually, I've got a better idea. There's one place we haven't explored here yet."

"I can think of more than one." I fluttered my eyelashes at him in what I hoped was an attractive way.

He gave me a dark look full of promise, but his words spoke of another meaning. "This is my most sacred place in the flat. I don't share it with anyone. Viktor almost found the key once, and I might have considered moving if he had ever worked out what it was for."

Now he had me intrigued. Anton walked over to the bookcase against the wall in the living room and took out a tiny key from a box that rested on the shelf. It was an emerald green. Then he moved a stack of books to the side to reveal a tiny keyhole. Locks ground as they turned in the wall. Far more than the small key would have led me to believe were present.

There was a grinding as the bookcase became a fully fledged door and swung open to reveal another glass one. Behind it was a wine cellar. Bottles covered two of the walls, the remaining one housing a large desk that held many devices that I'd never seen before, both electrical and mechanical. A mix of shimmering artefacts and tinkering devices. A table and a chair sat in the middle of the room. It was cold, but not freezing. The perfect temperature for wine. I couldn't believe I'd been here for months and had not known this place existed.

"What is this place?" I looked around, taking everything in.

"This is my workroom. It's where we created everything using a blend of our technology and yours. Allium developed some of the systems for our currency and social media here, as well as the messages Shiftsungs use to communicate. I like to come here when I just need to get away from everyone. Until now, no one knew it existed. I must admit, it's been fun hearing you singing from time to time in the mornings."

I looked at him in mock horror. "So you were spying on me? I could have been naked."

"You mistake me for a good person, Cee." There was a glint in his eye. "If you'd been naked, it would have been my treat."

I grinned at him as I ran my fingers along the mahogany desk, taking care not to touch anything else. "It's brilliant." I caught the flicker of a smile at my words as Anton turned towards the drinks cabinet.

"What's your poison tonight?"

"I'll have champagne, if you have it," I said, aware of the cool air on my exposed skin.

"Of course I have it. I'm not an animal, Cee. Though give me a few hours and you might think differently."

A few hours?!

I did my best to remain calm as my heart hammered in my chest. Both of us were acting, enjoying the moment as if we hadn't just had our lives shattered. But we had each other. And if I had to act like everything else was fine for a night in order to enjoy this, then so be it.

Anton poured glasses for us as if he had been a waiter his whole life. I rolled my eyes. He just had to be good at everything.

"Now you couldn't possibly know that I'm good at everything yet, Serrk." Anton's eyes glittered as he brushed my waist. I wondered if he should drink in his condition, but I knew better than to ask.

Good girl, you don't ask. That damn mind reader. I laughed as I tipped the glass to my lips and looked back and forth around the room.

"Where will we sit? There's only one chair."

Anton raised a brow. "An astute observation; how you passed so long without being identified as a Shifter is beyond me."

"Careful, or you'll be the one who's left standing." I gave him a very gentle, playful shove, which amounted to only a tap, terrified of hurting him.

He bit his lip before taking a gulp of his drink. His throat bobbed as he swallowed. "I've never brought anyone in here before, but I don't think either of us will need that chair tonight."

"Oh?"

"Sit on the edge of the table, Serrk," he said with enough force to set my pulse skittering.

"Are you sure you can do this? That you're not too hurt?"

His eyes flashed. "Try telling me what I can do again. Table. Now."

His command took me off guard. I was so used to him asking. I obliged and perched myself on the table like he had instructed, nervous and excited in equal parts. *What did he have in mind?*

He answered me out loud as he stroked his hand up the outside of my thigh. "Oh, many things. But I'm more interested in what *you* want right now."

My mind flashed to the kitchen island before I could stop it, to being restrained, or being with him until the small hours of the morning.

His eyes were dark as a grin stretched across his face. "Aren't you a dirty girl? Your ideas rival my own. Can I try something?"

For him, *anything.* "Of course, but aren't you meant to be resting?"

"Believe me when I say if anything is going to make me feel better, it's this. But if it's too much for either of us, I want you to think of a safe word."

"Tinsel." It sounded absurd. But hey, it was a word I wasn't likely to use by accident.

"How festive. Tinsel, it is. Now, put your hands behind your back."

I did as he asked. As soon as they met, they bound themselves tightly. I checked behind me to see what he had used, but saw nothing.

"It's a glamour. It really is very handy mind magic. I'll show you one day. Maybe."

Vulnerability cloyed at my pride, but for him, I was happy to be whatever he needed. I trusted him. Plus, the idea of being at his mercy had arousal building inside of me.

He walked up to me, grinning at my attempts to move my arms, and brought his mouth to mine. The spike of mint hit my nose as I took in his scent.

My mouth opened to accept him, and the rest of the world fell away from us as we kissed. We just moved in perfect synchronicity, Anton balancing biting, massaging, and sucking until desire had well and truly unfurled in my core. He tasted even better than he smelled, like fresh rain. I could see right into his mind where he wanted me to be. I wanted it just as much as he did. My abdomen was almost painful with desire once more.

His hands reached the tie of my robe. They were gentle but eager as they skimmed my shoulders and then my legs. As my clothing pooled on the floor, he broke the kiss and moved down to plant his mouth on my knee, then onto the inside of my thigh. I could only moan in response.

"Do you know how many times I've thought about being here, Serrk?" His eyes darkened.

I did. I could see it in his mind. Seventeen thousand, three hundred, and sixteen times. A staggering number.

He read my understanding. "So, you'll know I've had plenty of opportunities to play this scenario through in my head."

My mouth felt dry compared to other parts. My chest was tingling with need, the desire in my stomach ready to do anything as long as it meant him. I wanted to wrap my arms around him, but found myself unable to move them from the glamour–it was arousing and frustrating at the same time.

"I've wanted to kneel before you for a long time now," he growled. This was too much. I had never had so much attention on myself, not in this way. My breath hitched as he hooked a long finger into the lace of my knickers and dragged them down my leg. He then drew his warm tongue up my thigh, licking a stripe that caused another rush to my abdomen as I became even more wet just from watching him.

I normally would have been self-conscious, sitting, restrained in such a compromising position, but something was so unfamiliar about all of this–it consumed me.

Then, just as my breathing became harsh in anticipation, he pulled away.

"Anton, please." My voice came in jagged breaths, surprised by the broken contact.

His voice was soft, yet filthy, in my ear. If I could have seen his eyes, I would have seen Allium there, too. "Tell me what you want."

"I want all of you."

"All in good time, Cee." He nipped the lobe of my ear, causing me to tip my head back and cross my legs. "Oh, no you don't." He slid a hand between us to open them again. His eyes widened at what he found there. "Fuck, are you this wet for me?"

I nodded.

His lips crushed mine with more intensity than before, determined to explore everywhere as he removed my excuse for a bra. I sat back as he moved down my neck and finally to my breasts, licking and biting the tender skin there. I gasped as he sucked at them hard, using a free hand to slide a finger inside me. Unable to control myself any longer,

I moaned, "I need you to fuck me."

He moved his mouth down again, kissing my ribs, stomach, and hips. He stopped just above my apex and stared up at me, well aware of the power he held. "How do you want me to fuck you?"

I was so lost in the moment, I couldn't think of anything better to say than, "Hard."

"You can count on it. But first, be a good girl and wait a little longer." He laid me back and kept his hand to my stomach, pinning me to the table as he ran his tongue up my centre. My world imploded in itself–he knew where to go. Curling and flicking his tongue and sending me into a growing state of ecstasy. He swirled around the spot where I felt it the most and I whimpered again, this time louder.

I ground into the table, wanting him everywhere, wanting him to touch as much of me as he could. Then I lost it when he put his tongue inside me and drew it out, smiling as he added, "You taste fucking perfect."

He spread my legs wider as he drew his tongue up me once again and increased the pressure, stopping only to ask, "Are you going to come for me, Cee?"

"Yes," I replied breathlessly.

"Then tell me what you need. I want to hear it from your mouth."

I didn't hesitate. Knowing I could have come in time from the arc of his tongue as it hit all the right spots, I still craved the release that was building inside me and wanted it now. I said, "Your fingers too."

I could see how excited my words were making him as the bulge in his trousers grew. If only I could free myself and grab him. I wanted more. Wanted him deep inside me. Trying to read his thoughts was impossible, as I couldn't even think coherently to understand my own.

"So greedy, but I'm happy to oblige." He slid two fingers into me, in and out. Slowly at first, but building momentum. Then he sucked on the bundle of nerves near my opening and I saw stars, needing to release.

I was speaking some nonsense like, "Yes, just there, that's amazing, that's perfect," but I didn't care. All I knew was that this was the best sensation ever and I would fuck him all night.

I exploded, and for several seconds forgot where and who I was. Anton slowed his fingers, groaning through his teeth at the added wetness. The bastard kept his mouth there, sucking on the same part that sent shock waves right through me until he released both me and the bonds on my arms as I slid into his lap.

I sat, still giddy with the aftermath of what I'd just experienced. "I'd better clear myself up," I said, trying to stand.

Anton pulled me back down, his eyes black. "You're not done. We're only just getting started."

34

CHARITY

Shifter 101: Shifter stamina is comparatively higher than human beings.

I had seconds to compose myself and partially dress before Anton led me into the kitchen.

My thighs clenched together in anticipation. It wasn't normal to feel this way about someone. Every sense seemed to be emphasised around him. The sharpness of his cologne was intoxicating, the clink of the ice sang across the room, the brush of his thumb stayed with me as he handed me a glass of water and stared into my eyes.

I knew it would irk him, but sat myself up on the kitchen island in my underwear anyway, sipping away. Anton pretended to huff and came to stand between my legs, his head the same height as mine, although I was sitting on the high unit.

He set his drink down and turned around to survey me with the same look I'd had seen in the wine room. "I meant what I said. We're far from done. But first, I've got somewhere else to show you."

I thought he'd been joking–I didn't know if I could manage again already, but I was up for the challenge. "This isn't real."

"You're right there. This is Domain." He grinned back.

The desire was there again, sending waves through me as if nothing had just happened moments ago to cure it. In a flash, our mouths met again.

"You're sure?" I said between kisses.

"Serrk, if you ask me one more time–"

Somewhere, to the side of me, my glass knocked over as I cut him off with a kiss, but I didn't care. I wound my legs around his waist as he lifted me. Then he God damn carried me through to his room–*our* room now–as if I weighed nothing.

I inhaled as we stepped over the threshold. I didn't know what it had looked like before, having only seen odd glimpses, but it hadn't been this. It was like unlocking another piece of him.

I'd seen nothing like it. Half of the room had dark walls, somewhere between a dark grey and black. However, the other half of the room resembled a greenhouse. It jutted out and offered a perfect view of the misty forest below us. Plants lined the wall and ivy tendrils hung down from the ceiling. The room was empty save for a bedside table and a low bed that was made up with dark green silky sheets and a generous number of pillows. One side of the room had a wardrobe built into the wall, but otherwise it was empty, making the bed and the view very much the focus. Rain pattered against the glass, adding to the moody atmosphere.

"I thought you said you'd only made a few changes," I said, my mouth hanging open.

"Well, Cee, I don't do things by half."

I laughed at his choice of words, realising the glass side of his room represented Anton and the dark walls Allium. It split down the middle, just like him.

We made our way across the room and laid me down on the bed. He paused above the lace of my knickers, as if waiting for my approval as I looked around the room and took everything in.

"Tell me what you want, out loud, and it is yours." His eyes bore into mine, sending goosebumps down my spine. His words were my undoing.

I sat up and kissed him. "I want everything." I allowed myself to run my hands through his hair, tugging it and causing him to make a guttural noise into my mouth. Then I raised my hips to allow him to once again pull my underwear from me.

Anton went to move his mouth back to my core that was already craving him, but I gathered just enough resolve to murmur, "All in good time, darling."

Because I could be a tease too.

In the split second Anton took to consider what I meant, I put my full weight into him and flipped him onto his back. Unlike our time in training, I caught him off guard, but despite his surprise, he allowed it. I knelt before him and curled my fingers around his belt.

Anton's breathing was harsh. "Fuck, Cee."

I smirked. "Let me know if anything is uncomfortable or hurts. This wasn't what they had in mind when they said 'rest up'."

He smirked. "I think you can see that my body has other ideas about what it wants."

Even through the material, I could see the sheer size of him. I undid his belt and pulled his trousers down over his legs. I bit my lip as I saw the muscles in his thighs and calves, imagining the power behind them.

But first, this was about him. He had proved himself capable of rendering me insane with pleasure, but I had cards I could play too. I guided him to sit up and lifted his top over his head, taking the time to enjoy every muscle. I admired the dragon tattoo that spanned his back, the tail curling round his broad forearm. Unable to help myself, I ran my finger along his scars, tracing each one and pressed a kiss to it.

He tensed as he sat on the edge of the bed, and I realised he wasn't used to other people taking control. I ran my hand along his collarbone as I said in his ear, "This time, it's all about you."

It was the words he needed to hear as he relaxed and allowed me to push him backwards onto the bed so that he was lying on his back.

I swung a leg over him and brought my mouth to his. Our kiss deepened, and he grabbed my hips, pulling me closer to him and allowing me to grind back and forth.

"You're driving me insane," he growled.

"That's the plan." I grinned back as I unhooked my bra once more and allowed him to feel me as I threw my lips back against him. Our tongues danced together as they lost themselves in the kiss, and the intensity of the moment grew. Anton's hands dug deeper into my hips. I dared to reach behind me and pressed my hand to the length of him as I held his gaze. He was rock solid.

I swung my leg off him and in one fluid movement that any Shifter would be proud of, and slid off the bed so that I was kneeling in front of him. "My turn."

I locked eyes with him and pressed my hand to him again. He was fucking enormous and exquisite in my hand. The fact he hardened even more with my touch only encouraged me further. He needed no encouragement as I grasped him and pulled him free of his boxers, then removed them. I licked the tip, savouring the taste of him that had already collected there.

He sucked in the air around him as I did so, breathing, "Fuck, yes."

I dragged my tongue up his length, watching him fall backwards and closing his eyes in appreciation. Then, I took him between my lips and sucked down the smoothness of him. Anton watched every second. His eyes were wide, showing me every shade of green.

"Tell me how you want it," I asked with a newfound confidence.

He was struggling to form sentences, so I offered him an explanation. "Like this?" I ran my hand up and down in feather-light strokes.

He nodded, leaning back. "That's nice."

"Or, how about this?" An odd sense of power had filled me. I wanted to show him everything I could do. I brought my mouth down, taking as much of him as I could between my lips and adding my hands into the mix.

Anton sat bolt upright, his breathing heavy as he grew harder still in my hand. "Fuck. Yes, like that."

I held him with more force, and he groaned, sending another rush through me. I was growing wetter just watching him. Of course he had to have girth as well length. I continued to work him, using my mouth and hands, his moans guiding my pace. I was thinking more rationally than earlier now I was in control. I could now hear him in my head, was seeing myself through his eyes. Saw things I had never noticed before as Anton and Allium appeared to be lost in thought:

The curve of her hips.

Need her now.

Never needed to come so hard.

I sent my mouth straight down and back up again, sucking the tip each time I reached the top. Exploring every part of him. Forcing myself as far as I could go, he grazed the back of my throat as I mewled into him.

It was his undoing. He wound his hand into my hair, gripping me hard, and he thrust his hips into my mouth.

Fucking perfect.

Would do anything for her.

Warmth hit the back of my mouth as he fell apart around me. He pulled me closer into him and I moaned, enjoying every drop as he emptied himself down my throat. After there was no more of him left to come, he loosened his grip. With a great effort, I drew my head back. Just the sight of him like that had me ready for more, but I removed myself, dragging my tongue up his hardness once more for good measure. Anton tensed at the contact, but allowed me, still lost in his own wave of ecstasy.

His eyes cleared, and I saw the recognition as he processed what had just happened. He fixed me with a look of pure lust as he stroked himself, his cock rigid in his hand.

"You know, I'm glad I didn't opt for a higher bed," he said, leaning back against the pillows.

I slid up towards him. "And why's that?"

"I've waited a long time to fuck you, Cee. The least I can do is make sure you don't have far to fall when we break it."

I was molten inside at this point. "That better be a promise."

"Come here," he instructed. It wasn't a question.

After taking my time to enjoy the image, I brought my legs either side of his sculpted body and lowered my now aching core onto him. I allowed him to fill me, gasping at the sheer size as I had to stretch to accommodate him.

"Wet again for me. You drive me crazy, Cee. Your body, it's–"

Fucking artwork.

I moved, taking in Allium's words. They were both very much here. Anton looked at me with fervid desire, his eyes following my hips as they met his.

Allium's thoughts shot into my mind:

Fuck her right through the night. Hard.

I wanted more of him. Even if it hurt. I fucked him harder, and his eyes widened, as if he couldn't believe what was happening. He was still holding back, terrified he would hurt me with his size.

I shut my eyes tight as I relaxed into the waves of euphoria that were consuming me.

No, you don't get away that easily. I heard Allium in my mind before he spoke. "Look at me."

Though it was an effort to keep my eyes open, I did, and his face was a picture. A faint blush was creeping into his cheeks, his wide eyes flecked with light and dark green, his breath far from steady as I continued to ride him.

You're everything.

I made sure he entered me all the way each time. The sensation building inside me only caused me to become wilder as I ground my hips into him.

I was shouting now, a string of nonsense coming from my mouth. But it didn't matter. I wanted fucked deeper still. Knew that's what he wanted, too.

Anton read my thoughts, and in a second, I was on my front, propped up on my elbows. In one long stroke, he filled me, the extra length painful, but not unpleasant. It was the only thing that could cure the ache that pooled inside of me.

I was hoarse, but I said what we both needed: "Don't hold back."

It was the permission he had been looking for. He plunged back inside me again and again, filling every inch of me and giving me every inch of him. I would give him anything as long as he fucked me the way he was and didn't stop.

"Charity . . ."

My name on his lips sent me shattering around him, releasing all the tension within me, forgetting everything that had happened in the past twenty-four hours, my scream filling every corner of the room. He threw me onto my back and repeatedly sank into me as he reached his release, never taking his eyes off mine, only glancing to the sides. I was too consumed by my pleasure to pay attention to what he was looking at. My fear of being trapped had never allowed me to enjoy this kind of sex with anyone, yet it barely crossed my mind with Anton.

I dug my nails into him as he shook through his own aftermath. We stayed like that for a while with him still inside me, too drained to move, yet not finished.

"Well, that's some impressive party trick you've got there." He said, stroking my back.

Wait. I wasn't lying that far over in the bed. Turning my head, I saw my wings stretched across the bed.

"I've seen nothing like them. They're beautiful." He continued to stroke the feathers. It felt incredible.

"I don't know how to get them in and out," I admitted, realising how little I knew about how this aspect of Shifting worked.

"They usually appear and disappear during periods of intense emotion to begin with. But it gets easier to control them the more you get used to it."

"They're huge." I noticed just how far out on either side of us they spread. The remaining length that couldn't fit on the bed draped onto the floor.

"I've seen bigger." Anton winked, then grimaced as his own wings shot out, reaching each side of the room. The black, leathery wings were a sharp contrast against my white feathery ones. I could see where the bullets had torn through, but was pleased to see they were healing. The bullet holes in his chest were still angry red marks, though he seemed to manage like an unwounded man tonight.

Before I knew it, I'd navigated myself upright and had lowered myself onto him again. The more we did, the more my need grew. It was addictive. Two personalities, perfectly suited. With every orgasm, I felt Una's, Anton's, and Allium's, making everything a thousand times more intense. Not to mention the connection we had, meaning

I could see everything he saw through his eyes, and him mine.

He curled an arm around me. "I won't get the memory of tonight out of my mind for a while, Serrk." His tongue shot out and caressed my ear so quickly that I could have almost missed it.

"Let's make it a night worth remembering then," I grinned.

Between us, we tested the glamour of the building as we shook the walls of the flat several more times that night. He was right: by the time the bed did collapse, at least there wasn't far to fall.

35

CHARITY

**Shifter 101: The Book of Prophecies
includes all created prophecies. In order
to preserve these physical originals, it is
common for prophecies to be passed down
through word of mouth instead of in written
form. Two original copies of The Book of
Prophecies exist, but one has been lost for
some time.**

"So, you're the burning rose," Spyder said as we sat around the table. Three weeks had passed since we'd visited the tattoo parlour and we were out for coffee at The Wings and Ivy along with Perrine, Scarlett, Viktor, and Julian, with Bronx lurking in the shadows. Anton had assured me that his absence at lunch was to do with his busy schedule and nothing to do with his ongoing ban.

I'd needed those weeks to clear my head, to accept that I'd had a father, and attempt to come to terms with what had happened to him, as well as the things I'd done. The life I'd taken. I was still working on those last parts, and perhaps those horrors never would leave me, but I'd been running again, which allowed my mind to slow down, even when my body wouldn't.

Apart from our small group, Anton and I had sealed ourselves off from the world of Domain. Our closest friends were the only ones who knew where to find us while we took the time we needed to heal–him physically and me mentally. I wanted to be ready when I took down the Reapers and whoever was at the head of them, Hymev or otherwise.

Your only limit is your imagination.

I kept those words with me, their meaning now even more close to my heart.

Viktor spoke, jerking me from my thoughts. "Yeah, the burning rose is a metaphor, it's when–"

"I know what a metaphor is!" Spyder nearly snapped the puzzle piece around his neck in frustration.

I laughed at their ongoing quips at each other, pushing my darker thoughts to the side. Julian shook his head at them, well used to it.

"Can I hear the prophecy again?" I'd memorised all the parts, but wanted to ensure I had missed nothing.

They all recited it in unison, like some sort of cult:

Woman of both worlds,
A revolution on the horizon,
Four halves can be whole.
Unlikely allies hold answers to the past;
Only the burning rose connects it all.

"Yup, that's still scary," I said, as they all ended at the same time.

"Sorry." Perrine grinned. "We had years of chanting it at school assemblies together."

Wow. I hadn't realised things went that far back for them all. "And you've been expecting a war for the last twenty-three years because of it?"

"We have," confirmed Anton. "For most of us, it's all we've known. So sometimes we didn't appreciate the significance as much as we should have."

Viktor chimed in, "But I think we've covered everything now. Woman of both worlds, that's obvious. It was never our world and yours. It was Caedes and Nexus. Undoubtedly Charity."

"Four halves can make a whole. That refers to us as Covalents." I gestured to Anton and I.

"A revolution on the horizon is the impending war we're always warned about." Perrine twirled a lock of her brown hair.

"The unlikely allies are Scarlett and Draven," said Julian.

"Which leaves our very own burning rose right here, Charity, symbolised by your now-healed ink," finished Spyder.

We'd been inseparable the last few weeks: Anton, Perrine, Viktor, Spyder, Julian, Scarlett, and I, the seven of us spending most of our days together as we planned our next move. Bronx had requested some time off: he took Anton's injuries to heart, and although Anton assured him he was not to blame, everyone agreed that shadowing twenty-four seven was not sustainable, and that everyone needed occasional breaks. He'd given Anton a rare smile and muttered something about a herd, promising to be back and more focused than ever.

Perrine had sold the dresses and promised to return the profits once she'd written a bestseller. I'd grinned and told her I'd hold her to that, delighted she was following her dream. Now wherever we went, she always took a notepad with her, ready to jot down ideas.

Despite our best efforts, we were no closer to finding out what Draven had got himself mixed up in; but I would keep trying until we did. It wasn't just him and I that were concerned now: Spyder had reopened the case of his parent's deaths with the Nebulari–Domain's police force–following Draven's words. We didn't expect them to come up with much; after all, who knew how many of them were working alongside the Reapers. But it was a start.

Scarlett and I had spent a surprising amount of time together, with me learning about Draven in order to honour his memory.

"I wonder what he'd think about the two of us working together." She asked as she sipped on her iced coffee.

"I think he'd be surprised, but happy." I took a drink of my own, smiling.

"Like us all then," chirped Viktor.

We all laughed, with Spyder slapping the table so hard my book fell to the floor. I'd always struggled to channel my academic side until Una had awoken inside of me. I'd all but devoured the books Perrine had recommended to bring my Shiftstory knowledge up to date and a few popular fictions.

The rattle of the coffee machine drowned out the conversations from any of the surrounding tables. "That guy is staring at you," remarked Julian, pointing at a brown-haired Shifter across the room.

Spyder made no secret of looking the man up and down. "He's cute."

"Hmm." I was focused on picking up my book from the floor. The brown-haired Shifter was indeed looking at me, and while pleasant to look at, he didn't turn my stomach the way Anton did.

Spyder scoffed. "You're allowed to admit if other people are attractive, you know. Relationships can be even more fun when you're both open to other people."

"I'm worried there's an offer in there." I pulled a face.

"After what I did to Anton's room the last time, I think I'm on a permanent ban from your flat."

I was so busy laughing I barely noticed the Shifter approach our table and leave a thick green envelope in front of me.

"So, you're not interested in him?" Spyder indicated the Shifter who was making his way out of The Wings and Ivy. "Or me?"

I smirked to myself, Anton's words echoing in my mind. *There's more than one person out there for you, but you need someone who makes you feel like there isn't.* "Afraid not, buddy."

"Buddy, Christ. Oh well, I'll catch you all later, waste not, want not." Spyder got up and ran after the brown-haired Shifter.

I opened the envelope in my hand to reveal an invitation on thick green paper, gold letters embossed on to the page.

"What do we want to do now, then?" Viktor was reading over my shoulder.

I glanced at the invitation in my hand. "I suppose we get ready for another party."

It's time to make a statement. To show the Reapers and all those that stand with them that they cannot break us, no matter how hard they try.

That's what Anton's party invitation has said. One last party at Abduco manor before everything changed, this time a masked ball. Shifters from all over Persen, Abduco, and Nexus received invitations, along with a few trusted individuals from Caedes, based on Scarlett's recommendation.

Even though it was a masked ball tonight, I still took the time to apply my makeup, opting for outlined eyes to shine through and a brighter than usual lip.

I'd surprised myself by visiting *Venelles and Vêtements* for my outfit. They'd still had the mirrored dress I'd seen the first time I'd visited. After a few trials with my mask, I realised it was perfect. I had asked the dress shop to make a few small additions to prepare for the night ahead and was astonished at the striking effect it had. Anton had said tonight was about making a statement, and that's exactly what I intended to do.

I got ready myself tonight. I'd be making an entrance with what I was wearing, as much of a political statement as one could make in Domain. I wanted to make sure the party was in full swing when I entered, so I'd let the others go ahead without me. Hopefully Perrine had enjoyed picking out her dress and that her mother hadn't given her too hard a time about her writing.

Anton had been curious what I was wearing tonight, but I'd told him with a wink to trust me. It was testament to him he hadn't read my mind to find out, even when he had given me a hard kiss before he left, promising the proper party when we arrived home later tonight.

I finished curling my hair into loose waves and removed the dress from the hanger. It glided up my hips like silk and hugged every inch of my frame. Once I was ready, I picked up the mask and headed for the door. I was going to fly there tonight, having gained control of my wings. Channelling my determination to protect the friends I'd made here was all they needed to respond to my command, and I now found that I could produce or retract them every time.

I studied myself once more in the mirror. Domain had always been a certain way, four houses, four distinct types of Shifters and four purposes. If this didn't say a massive *fuck you* to the order and traditions that existed here for centuries, I didn't know what would.

The flight to Abduco manor was smooth. Only light rain fell from the sky and even then I avoided it, using Anton's trick to ensure I stayed dry and my hair tame.

I landed on the balcony on one of the upper floors so I could enter on the stairs for effect. I let myself in the open doors and headed towards the bustle of conversation below.

As I turned the corner, jubilant conversation, clinking glasses, and busy footsteps revealed I'd chosen the right moment. The party was indeed in full swing. That was until I entered. There were over a thousand Shifters here, all in masks aligned with their respective houses. A glass or two smashed as people took in what I was wearing in shock.

My mask, half rose gold and half red, showcased my decision to belong to both houses. The mirrored fabric of my dress reflected my mask, sending the material into a frenzy of red and rose gold that danced across my figure, making my statement hard to ignore. On top of everything, I kept my wings folded behind me, making it clear just what I was.

Despite wearing a mask, Anton's face, always so cool and composed, was a picture of shock as he mouthed *holy fuck*, at me from across the room.

I made my way towards him, as if this was all completely normal, and kissed him for the room to see. I could feel the eyes around the room taking everything in: the mask, the dress, the burning rose tattoo flickering between my shoulder blades.

It said everything it needed to. *Things are changing, and I don't give a fuck about the rules.*

For a second, we lost ourselves, forgetting about political statements, and loss, and grief, and for a wonderful moment, it was just us, locked in each other's embrace.

Anton broke away to caress my ear with his words. "You know how to make a point. I'm lost for words."

"So I did okay, then?" I leaned into him again, unable to help myself.

Anton's mouth was about an inch from mine. "You are always nothing short of phenomenal, and yet you still take my breath away." He pulled me closer, belting an arm round my waist. "You know my thoughts on audiences, Serrk, or are we breaking all the rules tonight?"

The cruelness of reality beckoned me back. Murmurs started back up around the room as the party resumed, my spectacle the main topic of conversation. "I think tonight is about making our own rules, but that one can stay. You'd better keep this, though." I indicated his black mask.

Anton bit his own lip. I wished it were mine. "Want me to climb through your window at night wearing this? Because I'll do it."

"Tonight?" I said, excitement building inside of me at the thought.

Anton opened his mouth to reply, but closed it as he glanced over my shoulder. I felt a light tap and turned to find Scarlett, in a dress matching her name, who pulled me into a warm embrace.

"Charity, you look divine. The colours of that dress are just so–you. It's truly stunning." Her eyes lit up as she scanned the moving material. I felt a pang of guilt as I realised she must have watched Sage closely during her time with Anton and adopted some of her mannerisms.

My cheeks warmed. I hoped it would not be too obvious against the colours of my dress. I stammered a thanks as we turned our attention to Verde who was speaking to a large group of Shifters. He was saying something about the turbulent times going forward, but how Abduco would rally with those who stood with them. I didn't trust Verde yet, and told myself until I was more sure, I'd have to monitor him.

I always do, Allium reminded me.

"Do you have a minute?" Scarlett asked, unaware of Allium and I's mental conversation.

"Sure." I already knew what she wanted. Verde, and now Anton, were working the crowd, so now was as good a time as any. She led me out the room and towards one of the smaller staircases. I hesitated, remembering what had happened the last time I'd left to meet her on my own.

Scarlett seemed to notice my reservation as she paused and pulled out a small box from her bag to confirm her intentions. "I thought now was a good time to scatter his ashes, if you're ready."

I nodded, fighting the lump in my throat. It was true. I'd been ready for a while but had pushed away the opportunity, knowing it was easier to put it off. But Draven deserved more than that. I knew it, and Scarlett did too.

We took the stairs that led into a deserted hallway and out onto a small balcony similar to the one I'd landed on.

Scarlett toyed with the box at the edge of the railing. "Dad always used to say Abduco was the House he should have been in. He was much more serious than most people in Caedes. He was always trying to lead other people away from their decisions as opposed to destroying them."

I wrapped an arm around her. "You knew him more than anyone. If you think it's the perfect place for him, then I stand by that."

"Plus, this way you'll always be close by."

"But what about you?"

"I've had a lifetime with him. It's time you had a turn," she said.

I squeezed her shoulder as she tipped the box upside down and we watched the contents scatter into in the evening breeze. My eyes watered and tears spilled down my cheeks; but I said, "Thank you, Scarlett. I couldn't have done this without you."

"I think he'd approve of this, you know, of us working together," she said, even though her sorrow mirrored mine.

Pulling a face, I tried to lighten the mood. "Well, it was in a prophecy. We couldn't avoid teaming up."

Scarlett failed to grasp my humour as she looked hurt. "Either way, I'm glad."

"Me too," I said, to show her I'd been joking. "I mean that."

"We were wondering where you got to, what an entrance, Cee!" said Viktor, as the rest of our crowd followed us out. Anton came and put his arm around me, noting Scarlett's box and nodding in understanding at what we'd been doing.

"So you two are really friends now?" Spyder was dressed in a vibrant pink suit that matched the tips of his hair. He'd already discarded his mask and had lipstick down one side of his face.

"Looks that way." I said. Then I had another thought. "Oh, Scarlett, did you bring my bag with the fairy-tale book? I think I'm ready to look at it again."

"I did." Scarlett summoned the bag onto the balcony. After she'd started hanging out with us, I'd learned that Draven had returned to my world and brought my things to Domain where he'd kept it hidden.

I unzipped it, studying the meagre contents that I'd deemed worth packing when I'd been told to leave home what seemed like a lifetime ago. For all that, I knew I'd always keep this. I wanted a reminder of where I'd come from.

Ready to look at the book from my father, I drew it out of the bag and sat down on a stone bench to read the inscription that I'd pondered over so many times.

"Charity, someone has cast a glamour on that book."

I looked up at Anton. "What? You're sure?"

Anton stepped closer to the book, running his finger along the spine. "I'd recognise my mind magic anywhere. Draven used to ask me about it. He must have wanted to use it himself."

Viktor's head poured over my shoulder. "I can't believe I didn't notice. It's so subtle, but he's right."

"Can you lift it?" I was too eager to see what he might have hidden.

"Of course."

I watched as Anton lifted the glamour from my prized book. I turned it over, my heart in my mouth, to reveal the new title:

The Book of Prophecies.

"I wonder why he left you this," said Spyder, puzzled, as I leafed through the pages. The fairy tales were now replaced with various prophecies.

"Maybe there's a new message." My heart was in my mouth as I searched for his inscription. But the handwriting at the beginning stayed the same.

Your only limit is your imagination. D.

I continued flicking through the book, turning page after page as I hunted for the message he had intended to leave. I ignored the crossed out sections, assuming they were not significant. Draven had gone to some lengths to deface the book in order to make sure we didn't miss what he had wanted to say.

Anton tapped his foot. "It is a strange choice. He must have known we all knew the prophecy that relates to you."

A chill settled into my bones when I found it. One page where the letters continued untouched down the thick parchment.

My prophecy.

"I thought you said you knew the prophecy about me." My eyes widened as they scanned down the page.

"We do," replied a few voices in unison.

"Everyone knows the prophecy of our future. We had it drilled into us at every opportunity. That's why we can all recite it," elaborated Anton.

"But did any of you ever see it written?" The last piece of the puzzle fell into place.

A resounding *no* sounded from the group. I showed them the page before me and watched their eyes widen as they scanned the writing, just like mine had.

Anton's voice was rough with shock. "We never thought they weren't telling us the full story. How could Draven have kept this from Domain for so long?"

My hand was shaking. "He didn't keep it from everyone. Someone else knew." Anton's eyes narrowed as I carried on speaking. "Remember that book we tried to check out from the library on prophecies?"

He nodded once, his mouth a flat line. He already understood. The full prophecy existed in two books in Domain. I had kept one copy in my world for the last twenty-three years, while someone had checked out the other from the library before Anton and I had tried to access it. The missing copy in the library meant someone else knew what we did, too. *But who?*

I looked down at the page once again and took in every word laid out before me, my heart clenching at Draven's annotation.

I made a deal with Hymev for the rest of the prophecy the year you were born. We can only hope it pays off. Your only limit is your imagination. D.

Woman of both worlds,
A revolution on the horizon,
Four halves can be whole.
Unlikely allies hold answers to the past;
Only the burning rose connects it all.
An army builds like no Other.

There is strength in bonds as well as numbers.
When the land of no thoughts takes too much,
Face the heartbroken mother.
The fallen angel is the key to the war,
Only then can she rule.

I met Anton's eyes and found Allium at the forefront too.

"Well, shit."

Acknowledgements

The idea for Burning Rose started years ago during lockdown, when my head was firmly in the world of fan fiction and innocent of ACO-TAR and fantasy romance. I gave writing a go, intending to publish my work on a site just for fun. I never imagined how the World of Domain would grow, and that it would actually become a physical book. It wouldn't have been possible without the following people who shaped Burning Rose into what it is today.

Daniela Mera and Elayna Gallea, for reading my earliest chapters. Your feedback was invaluable during a time when I was learning to write, and it's amazing to see you both do so well with your many published books.

My beta readers, ARC team, and proofreader, for the feedback that took this from a rough draft into something much more readable.

Joanna, for recommending I read the Crescent City series and Zodiac Academy. Without them, certain elements of Domain would never have been inspired–such as Spyder, who I think we can all agree is a fun addition.

My SSS girls, for always being at the end of the phone during our daily conversations about all things fantasy, dark romance, and filth. Alice, Alice (Alan), Ashley, Cathy, Chelsea, Chloe, Courtney,

Elle, Emma, G (Gary), Jess, Joanne, Lilla, Louise, Megan, Canadian Megan, and Sarah, I'm so grateful to have found friends like you.

Katie and Nádia, for cheering me on during my early BookTok days and ever since.

My Ceres girls, for being incredible friends and a constant in my life since nursery. You keep me sane even when my taste in reading questions that.

Mum, Dad, and my sister, Elle, for always championing my love of reading and encouraging my over-active imagination. Thank you for everything you've done, and everything you continue to do. This might not be the genre you envisioned for me, but I know you'll love elements of it all the same. It's probably too late to tell you to skip Chapter 33 and 34.

Andriy and Alexandra, you are both my world. Beyond any I could ever create on a page. Thank you for supporting the late nights, endless to-do lists, and my constant pitching of ideas.

Finally, I said it at the beginning and I'll repeat it now. To you, for taking a chance on a new author and starting this journey with me. Burning Rose kept my brain active during some very sleep-deprived months, and I hope you enjoyed reading as much as I loved creating it.

About the Author

Kirsty spends her life living between the real world and the ones found in pages. From a young age, she has imagined what the *About the Author* section in a novel might say about her at different stages in her life. A graduate of English Literature and also Primary Teaching, she lives in Scotland with her husband and a small dragon. When she is not reading or writing, she enjoys watching The Office on repeat, playing Tomb Raider–especially the old ones–and eating Italian food, preferably with a Gin and Tonic.

You can find her across your favourite platforms below, or see more at https://linktr.ee/authorkirstyarcher.

instagram.com/authorkirstyarcher/

tiktok.com/@authorkirstyarcher

facebook.com/authorkirstyarcher

Surprise Announcement

Seeing as you're still reading, you deserve a little something. Perhaps a title reveal to soften the blow of that cliffhanger?

Charity and Anton's story will continue in book two: Fallen Angel, which will release during autumn of 2024. For now, enjoy this short teaser, the content of which is subject to change.

The stadium roared around me as a small, blonde player crossed the opposing line down on the pitch below. The Frontfeather for *The Winged Ryders* had made it, signalling the end of the game and their victory.

Viktor was among those jumping up in excitement while Spyder sat with his head in his heads. Chasm meant a great deal to Shifters across Domain. With a new year, came a new season. It was about a month since we'd realised the full extent of the prophecy, and a lot had happened in that time.

I put it to the back of my mind as I met Anton's eye. "Let's get out of here," I said, indicating the emptying stands.

Has hand was already at his ring as he sucked the air in through his teeth. "What did you have in mind?"

You can preorder Fallen Angel at https://books2read.com/fallena ngelsequel or scan the QR code below. If you're reading from the UK, or anywhere else outside of the US, you may need to search on your own version of Amazon if it doesn't automatically redirect to your country.

Want to stay in the know? You're amazing. Subscribe to my newsletter to hear from me about future book updates, character art, bonus content, and more at https://kirstyarcher.com/subscribe or scan the QR code below for my Linktree.